PRAISE FOR *THE MOONGLOW SISTERS*

"Page-turning and passionate, Lori Wilde's novels are always a delight!"

—Jill Shalvis, *New York Times* bestselling author

"*The Moonglow Sisters* is everything I love in a book. It's emotional, funny, tender, and unforgettable. I couldn't stop reading until the last wonderful page. Lori Wilde writes characters who always speak to my heart."

—RaeAnne Thayne, *New York Times* bestselling author

"The resilience of the bond between sisters is tested on a rocky path toward healing in this engrossing tale of secrets and betrayals. Lori Wilde's infinitely relatable characters make *The Moonglow Sisters* a must-read."

—Julia London, *New York Times* bestselling author

"Every now and then a book comes along that touches every emotion, from heart-rending tears to belly laughs. *The Moonglow Sisters* is a one of those rare books. From the first line to the last sigh, it was amazing."

—Carolyn Brown, *New York Times* bestselling author

"Wilde reunites three estranged sisters in this powerful tale. . . . Wilde's fine characterizations and pulsating plot will please readers who enjoy family sagas."

—*Publishers Weekly*

The Keepsake Sisters

Also by Lori Wilde

The Christmas Key

Cowboy, It's Cold Outside

A Wedding for Christmas

I'll Be Home for Christmas

Christmas at Twilight

The Valentine's Day Disaster (novella)

The Christmas Cookie Collection

The Christmas Cookie Chronicles: Carrie; Raylene; Christine; Grace

The Welcome Home Garden Club

The First Love Cookie Club

The True Love Quilting Club

The Sweethearts' Knitting Club

AVAILABLE FROM HARLEQUIN

THE STOP THE WEDDING SERIES

Crash Landing

Smooth Sailing

Night Driving

THE UNIFORMLY HOT SERIES

Born Ready

High Stakes Seduction

The Right Stuff

Intoxicating

Sweet Surrender

His Final Seduction

Zero Control

WILLIAM MORROW

An Imprint of HarperCollins*Publishers*

The
Keepsake
Sisters

A Novel

LORI WILDE

THE KEEPSAKE SISTERS. Copyright © 2021 by Laurie Vanzura. All rights reserved. Printed in the United States of America. No part of this book may be used or reproduced in any manner whatsoever without written permission except in the case of brief quotations embodied in critical articles and reviews. For information, address HarperCollins Publishers, 195 Broadway, New York, NY 10007.

HarperCollins books may be purchased for educational, business, or sales promotional use. For information, please email the Special Markets Department at SPsales@harpercollins.com.

FIRST EDITION

Designed by Diahann Sturge

Title page image © Lifestyle Travel Photo / Shutterstock, Inc.

Library of Congress Cataloging-in-Publication Data has been applied for.

ISBN 978-0-06-295318-6

21 22 23 24 25   LSC   10 9 8 7 6 5 4 3 2 1

For Suzanne Spicer. Your kind and loving heart means more to people than you can possibly know. Keep shining your love light!

CHAPTER ONE

Before

In her nightmares, the elderly midwife can't escape her sins. Alzheimer's has eroded her ability to read and recall details, but her dreams are as lucid and real as the night it happened. She's a faded shell of who she used to be . . .

. . . until she sleeps. . . .

Slumber sends her sliding back to Moonglow Cove Memorial Hospital. Back to 1986. Back to the grave mistake that changed everything.

Gale force winds howl and lash the steel-reinforced brick building that was completely reconstructed after Hurricane Allen devastated the coastal town six years earlier.

As with most small towns, the hospital is the community nexus. It's here where people are born and die, suffer and recover, linger and languish in a never-ending life-cycle drama.

The lights flicker and the windowpanes rattle. The staff hold their collective breath and recall that other hurricane. A full moon lurks beneath the layers of storm clouds, invisible but substantial. Scientists pooh-pooh the effects of lunar influences on the human psyche but ask anyone who works in health care or law enforcement and they'll tell you that during a full moon, things get wild and weird and whatever can go wrong, will.

In the obstetrical department, nine women actively labor. Four of them are fully dilated and begging to push.

A dearth of nurses.

One called in sick, one got pulled to ICU, one had a car accident on the way to work and fights for her life in the emergency department. Leaving only the RN midwife and the shift supervisor to tend the toiling mothers.

The on-call doctor hasn't yet arrived.

Relatives pop in and out of the ward. Expectant fathers, gowned and gloved, await the delivery of their offspring. Anxious grandmothers worry their purse straps and grandpas pace the floor with hands jammed into pockets. Siblings squabble. In-laws ask nosy questions.

Too many people.

Too much stress.

In a wide-open, ten-bay ward the groaning mothers labor with only drawn curtains separating each bed. This is a county hospital, not a state-of-the-art birthing center with private rooms.

One woman in the far corner is quieter than the rest. She pursues her sacred business with focus and intent, bringing her first child into the world. She is, at thirty-five, what medicine dubs a "geriatric" mother.

Her husband sits on a wheeled stool at her bedside, smoothing her hair with a damp washcloth, feeding her ice chips, and coaching her breathing. His name is Heathcliff Straus. He and his wife, Robin, have tried for over a decade to get pregnant. He's thrilled and can't wait to be a father.

Amid the hustle-bustle, the ward's double doors fly open.

An orderly wheels in yet another screaming pregnant woman. Her eyes are wide, her hair electric, her face furious. She spews curse words.

Startled, Straus says a prayer of gratitude that he isn't the man with the large black umbrella—still opened in his hand—trailing after the woman.

Bad luck, Straus muses, even though he's not superstitious. *Bad luck.*

Umbrella man is not from Moonglow Cove, where everyone knows everyone else. Water drips off his expensive suit tailored to fit a hard, trim body. He wears a fedora, wing tips, and a pocket square as if he's stepped from a 1930s mobster musical.

Straus thinks, *Please close the umbrella.*

As if reading his mind, Fedora snaps the umbrella closed, splattering water across the linoleum. A few errant drops hit Straus's face.

"Get these brats out of me!" the woman screeches. "Now!"

Straus shakes his head. He knows the mother must be in great pain, but he can't imagine his wife calling their precious child a brat under any circumstances. Robin loves children, and until she got pregnant with this baby, taught kindergarten at the elementary school near their home.

The midwife rushes to the newcomers.

Straus knows the midwife well. Her name is Winnie Newton

and she's a compassionate soul. He played football with her son, Paul. He and Paul were best friends until Paul died in a hunting accident their senior year of high school. Paul was Winnie's only child and losing him devastated her. Since then she's thrown her whole identity into her job of welcoming infants into the world.

Winnie gives Straus a tight smile and a half wave as she brushes past him to help the laboring woman from the wheelchair into the bed.

The new patient glances around and exclaims, "Good God, what a shithole! Thanks a million, Frank."

"Sorry, honey, sorry," Frank mumbles and bows his head.

Straus rolls as far from the couple as he can get while still clinging to Robin's hand. Sweat beads her brow, and he leans over the bed rail to dab it away with the edge of the bedsheet.

"I'm here, sweetheart," he whispers to his wife. "Always."

She squeezes his hand as another pain hits. Straus grimaces right along with her.

Frank turns to Winnie; the umbrella tucked under his arm is soaking his fine suit, but he doesn't seem to notice. "My wife's expecting twins, but she's four weeks early. We were traveling across country and the hurricane forced us off the road. She went into labor." He speaks in a robotic tone with a mild midwestern accent.

Straus wants to ask why they were traveling across country with the wife in such a delicate condition, but he doesn't. It's none of his business.

"Do you have them?" the woman snaps. "Do you have the bracelets?"

From his pocket, Frank pulls out two delicate silver bracelets embedded with tiny pearls linked by diamonds. They are the kind of baby bracelet meant as forever keepsakes.

From where he's sitting, Straus can see that each bracelet has a silver charm engraved with a name, but he can't read them.

"Right here, honey, right here." Frank lays the keepsake bracelets on the table between the two beds. "Both of them. One for Amelia, and one for Anna."

At Robin's sonogram appointment, she and Heathcliff asked their doctor not to tell them their baby's gender. They want it to be a surprise. Soon, Straus will know if he is having a son or a daughter and his pulse quickens. Either gender is fine. They just want a healthy baby.

The lights flicker once more, and a fierce rain batters the windowpanes.

"Keep an eye on those bracelets," Frank's wife warns. "They cost a fortune. Those diamonds are real. No cheapy zirconia for *my* girls."

Winnie frowns. "You must put those in the hospital safe."

Across the room, another mother cries out. "It's coming! It's coming! My baby is coming!"

Winnie spins on her heels and darts for the mother.

"Wait," Frank says, his voice suddenly commanding and animated. He grabs Winnie by her scrub jacket and stops her in her tracks.

"What is it?" Winnie's tone is barely polite.

"I demand the best care for my wife." He pulls a wad of cash from his pocket and starts peeling off hundred-dollar bills. "*She comes first.*"

Winnie's spine stiffens and she stabs the sharp-dressed man with an angry glare, shoves away the hand fisted with money, yanks free from his grasp, and flies to the side of the woman ready to deliver.

Lightning crackles, thunder crashes, and that's when the lights go out. Bedlam. Pandemonium. Chaos. People gasp and shout.

Outside the wind roars, freight train loud.

Straus can't even hear his own thoughts, and terror grips him. He lived through Hurricane Allen, just barely, and for the first time he fears none of them will survive this night.

His wife squeezes his hand. "Tell me it'll be okay, Heathcliff."

"It's going to be okay," he whispers, pressing his lips close to her ear.

"Promise me."

Straus clings to her. He loves this woman with every fiber of his being. "I promise."

The emergency generator kicks on, but it's only got enough power to fuel the lights in the hallway and delivery room that lies just beyond the main ward. He can make out shadows of beds and patients, but that's it.

Winnie and the shift supervisor switch on pocket flashlights. In the crook of her elbow, Winnie holds a baby out to the shift supervisor. The woman whisks the newborn away to another area where Straus assumes is an awaiting incubator.

"The baby," Robin whispers. "The baby is here."

"Yes." Straus nods. His gaze follows the retreating shift supervisor. "The lady had her baby."

"No," she whispers so softly he can barely hear her. "*Our* baby."

Stunned, Straus moves to investigate.

Blood is everywhere. So much blood. Too much blood. Warm and sticky. The taste of fear fills his mouth, hot and slick and coppery.

"The baby isn't crying. Heathcliff, why isn't our baby crying?" Robin's voice is weak, almost inaudible.

Alarmed, he knows the truth before he ever sees his child.

A girl.

She is still and pale, with blue lips and the umbilical cord wrapped around her neck. He removes the cord as if doing so will save her and scoops the child into his arms. She's covered in her mother's blood.

Still she does not move. Her eyes are forever closed.

No, no, no!

Tears wet his cheeks. It cannot be. His heart is beating out of his chest. How will he ever tell Robin? They've waited years for this baby. She can't be dead. He shifts his attention to his wife, but she has fainted.

Winnie and the shift supervisor tend patients on the far side of the room.

Straus opens his mouth to scream, but no sound emerges.

From the bed next to him, Fedora yells, "The twins! The twins!"

Winnie comes running, the gleam of her flashlight bathing their dark little corner in a thin beam of illumination.

Pop, pop.

Two babies.

Screaming and wriggling, fully robust and vocal, they are alive. Winnie catches one, the shift supervisor the other, and they exchange triumphant glances.

The twins' mother doesn't ask after her infants. She flops back on the mattress, an arm draped dramatically over her eyes, and exclaims, "I'm exhausted. Knock me out. Knock me out. I want drugs. Knock me out now!"

"I'll put this one in the incubator," the shift supervisor says to Winnie. "You stay with the mom until I return for the other baby."

"I'll come with you." The new father's tone brooks no argument. "I want to see my daughter."

The shift supervisor nods, and they disappear.

Straus stands there, holding *his* daughter. Someone makes a keening noise and he realizes it's him.

Winnie turns to see what is happening.

Their gazes meet.

Her eyes widen, and when she sees his infant, her expression collapses.

He reads the truth in Winnie's eyes. She knows a stillborn when she sees one and her gentle face fills with unnamable sorrow. Heathcliff and Winnie have shared a great sorrow before. It bonds them.

Their mutual grief.

The baby in Winnie's arms wiggles and squalls. Their eyes lock in the dim glow of her flashlight and Straus understands that the same insane thought bulleting through his brain has just entered Winnie's mind.

His baby is dead while the other mother has two healthy infants. Two babies, while he and his wife have none. These out-of-towners. These interlopers. These strangers.

It's not fair.

Straus trembles. Tears spill down his chin and drip onto his shirt. He tries to imagine life without his beloved daughter— knowing how devastated Robin will be when she wakes up to find that their girl has died—and pain slices his heart wide open.

Winnie nods at him, yes.

Heathcliff stops breathing. Does he understand correctly?

There is an unprecedented opportunity. The storm has circumvented protocol. No one is paying close attention. Not in a hurricane. Not in the dark. These other parents live far away. They will soon leave town. No one in Moonglow Cove need ever know. Not Robin. Not anyone. Just his secret and the midwife's.

Winnie Newton extends the lively twin toward him.

His pulse gallops and he feels dizzy.

Could he? Should he?

Winnie pulls the curtain so no one in the dim room can witness their dirty deed. For one second, Straus hesitates.

Their fates not yet sealed. There is still time to turn back.

And then without a word ever passing between them, they do the unthinkable and switch babies.

Holding the live child in his arms, Heathcliff melts. He is instantly in love. As much in love as if the baby was biologically his.

"Wait," Winnie whispers.

He stops. Yes, she's right. They can't do this. Resigned, he prepares to switch the babies again.

"Here." Winnie grabs one of the keepsake bracelets from the nightstand and presses it into his palm. "Take this."

Grateful to the bottom of his soul, Straus vows to take this secret to the grave.

As he turns to rouse his wife and show her their healthy newborn daughter, he sees that Winnie has handed him *Anna*.

CHAPTER TWO

Amelia

The Long-lost Twin

*I*rony.
   Such a contradictory word.

The first four letters straight as the flatiron Amelia once used to control her unruly salmon-colored locks before she'd whacked off the mop with pinking shears three days ago. She did the chop job in distress after she'd discovered her identical twin sister, Anna, had not died at birth as she'd always believed.

Reaching up, she fingered the jagged edges of her spiky pixie, her mind still toying with the concept.

Iron. Hard, humorless, functional. All that cold strength followed up by the saucy curlicue *Y*. Playful, mocking, ornate. That one letter morphed something staid and serious into an astonishing, the-joke-is-on-you truth.

How ironic, irony.

Irony had brought her to Moonglow Cove, Texas. She, the woman who'd set up her life so that she'd never need anyone for anything, had come begging for a favor of epic proportions from a complete stranger.

Rolling down Moonglow Boulevard that bright first Tuesday of June in a crazily inappropriate stretch Hummer limousine the shiny bright color of Meyer lemons, droplets of sweat sliding between her breasts, Amelia felt a surge of panic.

She was in the town where she'd been born during a hurricane. The town she hadn't set foot in since she'd come squalling into the world one August night, thirty-five years earlier.

"Just call me Jumping Jack Flash," she muttered.

No, not just me.

Her, too.

Us.

"Miss?" The driver eyed her in the rearview mirror. "Did you say something?"

"It's nothing." She waved a hand.

Gulping, she switched on her cell phone, opened the social media app, and stared at the page, as she had solidly for the past three days. The home site of her doppelgänger.

Anna Straus Drury.

A hard shiver, half excitement, half fear, ran through her every time she saw that face that looked exactly like her own. Yes, Anna's cheeks and jaw were fuller, and her hair was long, plus she had numerous ear piercings, but in every other way they looked identical.

From her social media posts and abundant pictures, her twin led quite the charmed life, filled with adoring family and friends. Anna had been raised by doting parents who'd showered her with love. Check.

She'd married her high school sweetheart, the love of her life. Check.

She had two fantastic children, a boy and a girl. Check.

There was a Barbie dream house, white picket fence included. Check.

And she ran her own thriving business, the Moonglow Bakery. Check.

Amelia pressed a hand to her mouth, jealousy a sharp jab in her chest. My, my, my, life sure had turned out splendidly for a dead girl.

Running a finger over her cell-phone screen, she traced Anna's cheerful smile. How had they gotten separated? What hinky things had gone down at Moonglow Cove Memorial Hospital thirty-five years ago? What dark secrets lurked in this sunny beach town?

Those questions and more had plagued her nonstop for three days. But at the heart of it was an even bigger question.

Did Anna know anything about her?

Somehow, Amelia doubted it. *Oh, sister mine, that nice little world of yours? I'm about to rock it like a magnitude nine earthquake.*

Just as Amelia's own world had suffered a bone-shaking hit when she'd gotten that genetic report from 23andMe and learned that Anna was alive and well in Moonglow Cove.

The ludicrous limo pulled to a stop.

From the road, she couldn't see the cute farmhouse featured so prominently on Anna's social media accounts. Stone archways flanked by twin large bay laurels immaculately manicured into spiral topiary blocked her view.

Sudden fear swamped her.

Reluctant to leave the safety of the vehicle, Amelia stalled. She took her time leafing through her oversized handbag, searching for the stack of twenties she'd taken from the ATM at George Bush Intercontinental Airport. The limo rental went on her American Express black card, but she liked to tip cash.

One by one, she removed the individual, color-coded, zippered compartments and set them beside her on the seat.

There was a vivid scarlet Elizabeth Arden cosmetic bag stuffed with expensive makeup that smelled of ylang-ylang and roses. A lavender silk tote held toiletries and extra underwear, just in case the airline lost her luggage. There was a clear plastic case with a virtual pharmacy of medications, Dr. Ellard's emergency contact information, plus instructions from her specialist on when and where to seek immediate treatment if her condition worsened. And an Eiffel Tower souvenir coin purse containing the birth-to-wedding pearl-and-diamond baby bracelet that her mother had given her the day Amelia had gotten engaged to Robert.

Pausing, Amelia moistened her lips. She opened the coin purse, took out the delicate keepsake bracelet, designed with an extra link to go from birth to wedding, and cinched the fragile chain around her wrist.

The small silver medallion, engraved with her name, fell against the pulse point underneath her thumb and she watched it move with each hard tick of her heart.

She located her wallet and replaced the zipper compartments just as the back door opened, letting in the harsh glare of humid coastal sun.

"Ma'am?"

"Yes?"

With an exaggerated flourish, the driver bowed. "We have arrived at your destination, Ms. Brandt."

The man, tall and gaunt, skin the texture of tanned leather. His voice hinted of the tropics. Trinidad, perhaps? But years ago. The accent faded like a long-forgotten song.

Forcing a smile that belied her anxiety, she slid across the seat. He extended his hand to help her out.

She passed him five crisp twenty-dollar bills and slipped her wallet back into her handbag. The driver turned to fetch her luggage from the rear of the vehicle, and she stood blinking at the wrought-iron trellis covered with climbing yellow roses.

Did yellow roses represent jealousy?

Quickly, she googled it because she was the type who took refuge in knowledge and she came across a reference that said while yellow roses once signified jealousy in a romantic relationship, in modern times, yellow roses had come to represent friendship and were a favorite gift for Galentine's Day.

But that was from a florist's website, so perhaps the story was just a way to sell more yellow roses.

Amelia hitched her bag up on her shoulder, wishing now that she'd gone straightaway to her accommodations at a local bed-and-breakfast where she'd made reservations, checked in, and dropped off her luggage.

What had she been thinking?

Thinking?

She wasn't thinking. She'd been running on adrenaline for

three days. Yes, and that was unlike her. She was a planner, cautious and controlled. She'd learned a long time ago that giving reins to her emotions never worked out in her favor, and yet, she'd done just that.

Amelia clamped her jaw, fighting for control, trying to find inner strength amid the wreckage of her life.

A canopy of trumpet and Mandevilla vines twined up and over the long arbor, creating a lush, green tunnel dotted with the flame of scarlet-, ginger-, and saffron-colored flowers, offering a beguiling respite from the relentless sun and perfuming the air heavy with a scent that reminded her of Bit-O-Honey taffy and Juicy Fruit gum. Around her, the hummingbirds whizzed and squabbled. Other than the quarrelsome creatures, the grounds were eerily quiet.

Amelia canted her head, listening. As a musician, sounds drew her attention before other sensory input. She was an auditory learner and noticed the soft *snick-snick* of water sprinklers, the lazy drone of a faraway lawn mower, and the slap of the driver's footfall against the asphalt.

She shaded her eyes with a hand and glanced back over her shoulder. They were parked at the end of the long cul-de-sac. Stately Victorians, complete with whimsical gingerbread trim, framed both sides of the road. The houses sat on generous two- and three-acre lots, plenty of elbow room to keep the neighbors at bay.

So homey here. Peaceful. Dull, even. A far cry from her penthouse lifestyle in downtown Chicago.

Standing there, she experienced the same fugue she'd experienced following her visit to the specialist's office two months ago, where he'd confirmed her diagnosis. She'd spent an entire day stumbling around Chicago, not knowing where she was going, or even who she was. She felt disassociated, as if viewing her life from a long distance.

How had she landed in this surreal environment? Why had she come here?

The driver set the luggage at her feet. "You got sumbody to carry this inside for ya?"

Amelia drew herself up. "I can manage."

He eyed her skeptically. She knew what he saw. Skinny white woman. Arms like pencils. Legs like straws. Hacked hair. Designer slacks, pricey white silk blouse, gauzy cover-up jacket, and modestly high-heeled pumps. Weak. Helpless. Northerner. Out of her element in coastal, slow-talking Texas.

"Ya sure?" His brow furrowed in mild concern.

She gave him a short, tight rubber-band smile along with a terse nod.

"Okay." He shrugged and ambled around the limo.

A minute later, he was gone, leaving Amelia alone in a strange place. She missed him already and fought the urge to call the limo service and ask them to send him back. There were wheels on the luggage. She could and would handle this.

Beneath the arbor a cobblestone path stretched out in front of her, and when she stepped to the other side of the archway, each hand towing a suitcase behind her, her oversized handbag hiked up on her shoulder, the temperature seemed to plummet at least fifteen degrees.

From this vantage point, she couldn't see the end of the path as it turned slightly some distance ahead and disappeared from view down a steep slope.

She sucked in a deep breath. "Here we go."

The suitcase wheels made ragged clacking noises as they hung and tugged against the uneven pavers. Moss grew up through cracks in the bricks, and she had images of Goldilocks and three disagreeable bears. Of Red Riding Hood and a ravenous wolf. Of Hansel and Gretel and a cannibalistic witch waving a stick of butter.

"Your fierce imagination is your worst enemy," Dr. Ellard told her often. "You build farfetched stories around your emotions. Try not to think too much."

What lovely, useless advice, Doctor. Don't think. What kind of thing was that to say to an introvert who lived inside her head?

The arbor seemed to lengthen endlessly as Amelia walked, giving her the sensation that she was moving in place. *The longest journey begins with a single step.*

Was that how it went?

She'd gotten that quote once in a fortune cookie. Robert had taken her to a celebratory dinner at their favorite Chinese restaurant after he'd crushed an opponent in court and won an award in the high seven figures.

Amelia ordered her old standby, egg foo yung. Robert had Peking duck. His fortune cookie said, *Eat, drink and be merry at your peril.* He'd laughed, and said she'd gotten his fortune, and he'd gotten hers. He'd switched their scraps of paper, grinned, and kissed her.

Robert.

The pain hit her then, a blow to the forehead. Sharp as ever. She had to stop walking, close her eyes, and hitch in a labored breath. The gutted sensation cleaved her body, from her head to her feet. She closed her hands into fists, huddled trembling beneath the sheltering canopy.

She'd had no answers. Nowhere to turn.

Her parents were dead, killed in a car accident two years ago, along with her fiancé.

Robert had been driving her folks in his Bugatti on their way to see Amelia at her first cello solo with the Chicago Symphony Orchestra, where she'd performed Tchaikovsky's Variations on a Rococo Theme.

Anxious to get to the concert, Robert had run a red light.

And her life, as she knew it, had changed forever. She fisted her hands, engulfed by the memory.

This is your one chance to save yourself.

Yes, but at what cost? Was saving her own life worth wrecking the lives of others? Amelia bit her bottom lip and thought of what she must do to survive.

Cowered.

"Fresh start. This is your fresh start. Keep moving." Amelia raised her head, squared her shoulders, and sallied forth.

Abruptly, the path bifurcated.

Amelia paused at the fork, uncertain which way to go. To the left, the arbor continued. To the right lay a valley of sunshine and the cheery bird sounds. She recognized some of the calls—the harsh jeering of blue jays, a dove's throaty coo, the thready lisp of a warbler, a covetous mockingbird appropriating everyone's song and blending it smoothly into nature's underlying soundtrack.

Left?

Or right?

Cool shadows or hot light?

Amelia hesitated, her knees unexpectedly knocking together. The shadows called her, darkness snaking out like the twining vines. *Stay safe. Come. This way. Hide. I'll keep your secrets.*

The sun encroached upon the cobblestone, slanting rays over her shoes, giving her another message. *Prove you're brave enough to face the truth. Dare to step here.*

She ran a hand through her chopped hair. In the sun she would sweat, her pale freckled skin would grow sticky and damp. Or she could stay privileged in the shade where she'd lurked her entire life.

Well, except for . . .

No! She shoved that thought aside. Not thinking that.

Which way to go?

Fast decisions at a crossroads had never been her strong suit. She left her luggage behind, took one cautious step to the right and then another.

Just for a peek. She could always retreat.

The light dazzled. Sparkling white. Starbursts exploded behind her eyelids. Her pulse thumped, and a strange prickling raised the hairs on her arms. The path broadened into a promenade with a stroll of flowers enlivening the borders. There was a Zen garden and cement benches for resting. Numerous waterfalls splashing over lavish stone.

And a mesmerizing circular labyrinth made of pink crushed gravel.

She knew the difference between a labyrinth and a maze. Many people thought they were the same. She had, too, once. Until Robert taught her the difference on their first trip to Paris where he'd pulled her into an alcove in Versailles and planted a kiss on her neck.

"Don't, Robert." She'd laughed and squirmed in his embrace. "The guide will leave us behind, and I want to see the garden maze."

"Labyrinth," he corrected. "A labyrinth has only one entrance and exit point. It's a circular path to the middle. A maze, on the other hand, has multiple paths. In a maze you have choices to make. With a labyrinth you simply enjoy the walk. While a labyrinth sounds more mysterious, true mystery lies within the heart of the maze."

Then he'd gently bitten down on the hot pulse point of her throat, shifting her attention to the heady mystery of his mouth.

She shook her head. Shook off the memory. Gone. All that was long gone.

Straight ahead, down the hill, beyond a wooden pergola shrouded by lavender wisteria, sat a small white two-story farmhouse, elegant in its simplicity.

The limestone walls and tin roof glimmering in sunbath. The jalousie windows as provocative as a 1920s flapper. In her imagination Amelia envisioned the house as it must have looked newly built a hundred years ago. The owners hosting parties rife with slick-haired young men in tuxedos and sophisticated suffragettes wearing scarlet lipstick, giddy with the novel right to vote. She could hear the rumble of Model-T engines and the jaunty tinkling of a ragtime piano. Smell the gin and cigarette smoke. Taste the Parker House rolls, Jell-O molds, and Waldorf salad.

She yearned to fold her arms around the beautiful visage, pull it into her or herself into it.

This storybook cottage was well cared for and magical. What sort of people lived here? Were they whimsical and fun? Did they cherish gardens and serenity? Did they respect history and a sense of order? Did they value home and family?

All signs pointed to yes.

Hope filled her. Too much hope, really. So much could go wrong and that significance wasn't lost on her.

This house was where Anna lived. The identical twin she'd mourned every day of her life. The sister, her mother had told her often enough when she got angry at Amelia, that should have lived instead of her.

But Anna *had* lived. They'd just not known it.

Amelia's chest tightened, and her hands trembled. She rushed the rest of the way, anxious to get past this ambush meeting. She was in such a mad dash that she almost didn't see the dog.

The Doberman looked calm enough, peeping at her from behind a dog run of chain-link fence, quiet and alert, and standing at attention. Not barking, just watchful, ears pricked.

Amelia froze, but her heart beat wildly, adrenaline carrying terror to every nerve cell in her body. She breathed only from the top part of her lungs, inadequate air chuffing in and out.

When she was seven, sent off by her parents to enjoy the park on her own, she'd gotten mauled by a dog and ended up with nineteen stitches on the back of her legs.

The medical staff at the emergency room made a fuss about calling Child Protective Services, but a fistful of cash later, her parents' lawyer mounted a defense in what later became known as "free-range parenting." The lawyer not only got them off the hook, but he'd turned the case to their advantage by prosecuting the dog owner and winning a tidy sum. After that, though, her parents paid a nanny to take her to the park.

They really were great parents; the best parents ever, she reminded herself. They simply held strong beliefs that children should be neither coddled nor overindulged with too much attention. They believed that soft snuggles and tender cuddles caused dependency and that unwarranted praise turned kids into wimps who couldn't handle adversity.

Sure, she would have enjoyed more praise, but her stoic upbringing had forged resilience, independence, and the ability to regulate her emotions. It taught her how to be self-contained, self-reliant, and self-sufficient.

Amelia was *glad* for it.

Yes, some people thought her a cold fish, but they didn't understand how deeply she really did feel things. So deeply, in fact, she never dared give her emotions free rein for fear of falling apart completely if she did.

The dog growled, a low, dark, threatening sound.

Eyes rounding, she saw the gate's latch was unlocked. If he charged, the gate would fly right open and the Doberman would be at her throat.

Terror clubbed her and she was seven all over again.

Amelia slunk back.

The dog growled again and the hairs on Amelia's arm lifted. The air, which earlier felt heavy and heated, now seemed frigid and frail.

Immobilized by fear, she was afraid to go forward. Or back up for that matter.

The dog was behind a fence; even if the gate was unlatched, he probably didn't know it. *Just tiptoe on by.*

Logical, yes. But emotion trumped logic every time. The old scars on her calves throbbed with each skip of her heart.

Giving the Doberman the side-eye—she'd heard never make direct eye contact with a dangerous animal—she took a tentative step toward the house.

Instantly, the Doberman jerked his head.

Or rather tried.

His head did not move, but the rest of his body flinched, his tensed muscles visibly spasming down his neck and across his broad chest. Something was wrong with the animal.

She stopped again, this time out of concern instead of self-preservation. She might not be a fan of dogs, but she hated seeing anything or anyone in pain.

The Doberman whimpered softly, and his pupils widened.

Stretching her neck, she leaned farther over to see what'd happened.

The dog's thick leather collar had somehow gotten looped around the top of the T-post, holding him immobile. If he moved, he'd choke himself. The poor thing was in desperate straits. No telling how long he'd been hung up like this.

Then, she spied the sign so bold, she couldn't believe she hadn't seen it right away. Posted on the fence in neon orange letters: BEWARE OF DOG.

And on the blue plastic water bowl, a name.

CUJO.

Clenching her hands, she sucked in oxygen. It took everything she had to force her feet in the direction of that fence.

Briefly, she thought of just going to the front door, and telling whoever answered that their dog was in trouble, but she knew once that door opened and whoever was behind it got a good look at her, things would quickly spiral out of control.

Besides, the dog was up on the tips of his paws. If he even so much as sat, he'd cut off his air supply and strangle to death. He needed help and he needed it now.

The dog's eyes pleaded with her.

Save me.

All right. Maybe she was anthropomorphizing him, but there *was* desperation in his gaze.

"Hey boy," she cooed in a shaky voice.

He tried to lunge, but his collar slipped, sliding farther down the T-post, tightening the noose. The dog made a strangled, gargling noise.

If she didn't do something now, the dog would choke to death in front of her. Galvanized, Amelia raced toward the fence and the BEWARE OF DOG sign.

The Doberman's head was so close to hers, his long sharp teeth bared. His upper lip curled back in a snarl, spittle foamed from his mouth, and his eyes bugged from his head. The collar twisted so tightly his neck veins engorged.

She hesitated, panic ripping through her. *Compartmentalize, compartmentalize, compartmentalize.*

Yes, it sounded good, but she couldn't quite bring herself to touch the dog. *Don't think*—dear God, did she overthink things—*do. Act. Go, go, go.*

Gritting her teeth, and quivering from head to toe, Amelia faced her long-held phobia, experienced the dog's hot breath against her skin in a moment that stretched out like millennia as she reached to unfasten the collar.

Her fingers hesitated at the buckle. Once she freed him what if the Doberman turned on her? What if he attacked?

Her heart pole-vaulted into the middle of her throat and anchored there. Maybe that's how her life would end. Not a slow withering away from renal failure but mauled to death by the dog she'd tried to save.

Amelia let out a short, jolting chortle. There it was again, that fat, juicy slice of irony.

But death by dog might not be all bad. At least she wouldn't have to knock on that door, stare into the face of the identical twin sister she'd never set eyes on, and say, "Um, you don't know me, but could you spare a kidney?"

CHAPTER THREE

Anna

The Housewife

Inside the house, Anna stood at the ironing board, spray-starching her husband's crisp white dress shirt.

Laundry surrounded her. It was piled on the floor and waiting to go into the washing machine, stacked on the folding table ready for dresser drawers, and wrinkled in baskets next in line for the iron.

Items of summer were scattered about the mudroom: Logan's water wings and flip-flops on the floor by the back door, sun hats and caps hung from the hooks mounted above the sink, a dark yellow tube of sunscreen, float toys, and a pair of cymbals that Allie had brought home from band the last day of school.

And then Anna spied a stubborn dark orange-red stain embedded near the second button of the shirt's cotton fabric.

Her stomach dropped. Not again!

"Kev!" she yelled so that he could hear her in the master bedroom where he was packing to go out on the road again. A late-season tornado had wiped out a big swatch of a small Oklahoma town. He would be processing insurance claims for weeks.

"Yeah?" he yelled back.

She ran a finger over the stain. "Have you been eating Toad's chili again?"

Kevin mumbled something she couldn't hear.

Scowling, she shook her head. She understood that her husband was a red-blooded, chest-thumping carnivorous male, and naturally resistant to the plant-based meal plan she struggled to keep him on.

Dammit, they'd talked about this after his last physical when his cholesterol count came back over two fifty. Toad's Diner, the place that served triple-meat chili and chicken-fried everything, was off his diet permanently. Anna wanted to keep Kevin around for a long, long time. She loved her sexy, noncompliant beast.

Kevin wandered into the mudroom looking slightly shamefaced, holding a black leather loafer in one hand and shoe polish in the other. Tall, blond, broad shouldered, with Nordic heritage, he dominated any room he entered.

Anna's heart gave a romantic lurch. Even after twelve years of marriage and two kids, he could still quicken her pulse. At the same time, she felt a twinge of loneliness, missing him already. God, she wished he had a job where he didn't have to travel so much, but alas, it was the nature of his business. He followed the catastrophes.

Her husband believed in looking his best at disaster scenes. The other adjusters ribbed him for being a clothes horse, but Kevin felt that in times of crisis, people craved security and certainty. Wearing dress clothes and polished shoes was a small price to pay to instill confidence in his clients.

Happily, Anna ironed his shirts when she could simply have sent them to the dry cleaner. She enjoyed doing little things for him to show her love, plus it saved money when their budget was beyond tight.

"The stain is forever." She sighed and tossed the shirt to the floor. "I'll turn it into a cleaning rag. But could you do me a favor, big guy, and go easy on Toad's? If you want chili, I can make some with tofu and kidney beans."

He rolled his eyes, stuck out his tongue, made a "yuck" face, and held up three fingers in a Boy Scout salute. "No more Toad's. I promise."

"You were never a Boy Scout and I don't trust you to stay away from chili." She shook her head. "So I'm willing to compromise."

He made happy grunting caveman noises and wriggled his eyebrows comically.

"Stay out of Toad's and I'll make turkey chili with extra chili powder and siracha to pump up the flavor. Deal?"

Kevin brightened. "Deal."

Laughing, Anna shook a finger at him. "Don't think this means regular meat munching."

"Unless by 'meat' you mean—"

"Behave." She blushed.

"Crack that whip. It's part of my fantasies."

"I'm serious, Kevin."

Grinning, he leaned in for a kiss. She caught the scent of

starch, shoe polish, and his basil shaving soap. The smell of her man getting ready for work.

"You know I love it when you get bossy." He winked. "Hey, you wanna quickie?"

"Not bossy," she corrected, sidestepping the hand he tried to slide around her waist and tapping his chest with her index finger. "Assertive. Your health is important to me, Viking."

He dropped his hand and looked mildly disappointed. "Says the woman who never takes a spare second for herself. Seriously, ask your mom or mine to sit for the kids while you get a massage."

Anna shrugged. "Who has the time?"

"Make the time." He picked his shirt up off the floor. "Don't worry about the stain. My tie will cover it. One less chore off your plate."

She was about to protest, but her cell phone dinged with a text message.

Anna switched off the iron, wishing Kevin wouldn't wear the shirt, stain and all, but she was too pressed for time to iron another one. Sometimes, she had to let things go. Not that she was happy about it.

Tugging the phone from the back pocket of her denim shorts, she read the text.

Mom: Don't forget our hair appointment at 10.

As if she'd ever forgotten an appointment with her mother. One punch on the screen with her thumb: K.

Another text came through.

This one was a group text from Gia, her sister-in-law. Gia was heading up the church bake sale and Anna had promised to make specialty cupcakes for the vacation bible school fundraiser, but she hadn't even started them yet.

Gia: Reminder. All baked goods should be at the rectory no later than 5 p.m. tonight. Our volunteers need time to arrange and price the items. Sale starts promptly at 8 tomorrow morning. Let me know ASAP if you can't meet the deadline.

Cringing, Anna checked the time.

It was almost nine now. She had to get Kevin out the door, usher the kids to the car and drop them off at her mother-in-law Veronica's house, pick up her mom, hit the salon at ten to spend three hours in the chair for highlights and a cut, grab a late lunch with her mother. Pick up the kids.

Hmm, that put her getting home around two thirty. Cutting it close, but she'd have just enough time to whip up some cupcakes, let them cool, and frost them by five. Easy peasy, lemon squeezy.

Or you could just swing by your bakery and pick up three dozen. As tempting as that was, she'd promised specialty cupcakes and that was what she'd deliver.

"I'm gonna finish packing." Kev kissed the top of her head, picked up his shoe and the polish, and sauntered down the hall.

She craned her neck, watching him walk away. Heavens, but

the man still had a gorgeous ass, even eighteen years after he'd played running back for the Moonglow Dragons. Anna hugged herself. She was lucky, and she knew it. So damn lucky. Even if Kevin was on the road more than he was home, they had a strong marriage and she'd do everything in her power to keep it that way.

Family first. Always.

Another text came through.

Sighing, Anna checked her phone again.

Moonglow Hospital Robo-text: As someone in our database with a rare blood type, we urge you to donate to our semiannual blood drive. You are needed! The mobile van will set up at Moonglow Community College from 8 a.m. to 5 p.m. Saturday June 12. Text STOP to unsubscribe.

Needed.

The magical word that galvanized Anna. She was two pints away from being Moonglow Cove's top donor. Yes, yes. Give blood. She was on it and saved the date into her calendar. Okay now, where was she? Oh yes, get the kids loaded up and . . .

Ding.

A fourth text. Really? The morning was starting off with a bang.

This text from her bank telling her they had exactly $213.87 in their joint checking account. How had it gotten that low?

She bit her bottom lip, recalled a few extra expenses: the clogged bathroom drain requiring a plumber, the run to the minor emergency clinic with Logan that insurance hadn't yet re-imbursed, and the night out at Chez Jacques to celebrate Kevin's thirty-sixth birthday. It was pricey, and they shouldn't have done it, but as Kevin said, "Sometimes you just have to live large."

Shit. She would have to juggle some things. Maybe get a cash advance on her credit card. *Not bright, Anna, not bright.*

Maybe not, but Kevin didn't get a check for another week and she'd invested last month's bakery profits in new signage. Tem-porary cash flow problems. That's all this was. True enough, but juggling bills to rob Peter to pay Paul was happening more and more often. Time for a serious budget adjustment.

You could skip the hair appointment.

She fingered her overgrown mop of unruly red hair, looped a strand around her finger, and stared at the split ends. Mom was looking forward to their salon time together. Maybe she could barter with her stylist. Haircut in exchange for a month's worth of free baked goods? Her stylist did love her Italian bread with olives and sun-dried tomatoes.

Another text. *Heavens, did someone mix up my phone number with Grand Central Station?*

Another group text, this one from the Harmonious House-wives: Music practice canceled tonight. Jeannie's son broke his arm falling off the jungle gym and Amber's sister went into labor.

Anna sent a sad face emoji but thanked heaven that something on her schedule had gotten postponed. She adored her weekly amateur musical group and they were playing in the Moonglow Music Festival in the park on Friday evening, so they really needed the rehearsal, but honestly who cared if they sucked buckets? It was a free show and they just wanted to have fun.

For the fifth time, she put her phone down and as she did, it played the ringtone of her favorite song, "Let It Go" from the *Frozen* soundtrack. Right now, she didn't really want to hear it. Especially when she saw the call was from Moonglow Cove Memory Care Center.

Don't answer, she told herself. *They could leave voice mail.* Yeah, that sounded good, but then the guilt-inducing angel on her shoulder whispered, *What if it's important?*

"Babe," Kevin called from their bedroom. "Have you seen my . . ." The rest came out as a garbled *mufflestuffisit*.

"Hello?" she answered.

"Anna?"

She recognized the voice of the director of the memory care facility, Myra Marts, and tried not to sound put-upon. "Good morning, Myra."

"I wish it was."

Uh-oh. "What's up?" she asked, her voice coming out chirpy as a bluebird on Adderall. *Dial it down.*

"I'm afraid Winnie's gone missing again."

Anna rubbed her temple with her free hand. Winnie Newton was the midwife who'd delivered her, and the elderly woman had been exceptionally close to Anna's dad, Heathcliff.

Because her parents had had her so late in life, Anna had never known her grandparents and Winnie had filled their shoes, stepping in as a surrogate grandmother. When she was young, Winnie had had a substantial presence in her life.

Out of a sense of loyalty and sheer kindness, her father had been the one to look after Winnie when she was diagnosed with Alzheimer's. Because Winnie's son, Paul, had been her dad's best friend, he felt obligated. But Anna couldn't help thinking the reason ran deeper than that. Her father had lost both his parents when he was young, and Winnie had lost her husband and son too soon. Mutual sorrow could cement a relationship.

Plus, Winnie had no one else to look after her. Since her dad passed away last year Anna had inherited Winnie's medical power of attorney.

"I don't expect you to do anything," Myra said. "We're out searching, and we called the police. I just wanted you to know. I'm sure we'll find her soon."

"Thank you," Anna said, forcing herself to take a deep breath.

Despite all the safety and security precautions they took at the facility, Anna understood that patients with dementia did take off unannounced from time to time. Myra did her best to create a safe and nurturing environment, but nothing was foolproof. Especially with Winnie, who'd turned out to have Houdini flair whenever she got agitated.

"Please text me when you find her," she told Myra.

"We will."

Anna ended the call and stared at the screen, daring the phone to interrupt her again. Problems were stacking up like Jenga blocks, one wrong move and the "to-do" tower would tumble in on her.

Dear Lord, she prayed jokingly, *please send me a clone.*

What she wouldn't give for a clone! She took another deep

breath and slowly let it out through her teeth. She'd find a way to manage everything. She always did. Where there was a will there was a way. Right?

"Mommy, Mommmmmmy!" Logan came tearing into the mudroom, tears running down his face.

"What is it, honey?" Anna crouched and opened her arms wide. "What's happened?"

Her three-year-old flew into her embrace. "Al-Allie!"

He sobbed, burying his face against her shoulder. On his heels, her ten-year-old daughter stormed into view. She wore a blue T-shirt with galloping horses imprinted into the material, denim shorts, and her curly red hair was pulled into a ponytail with a scrunchie.

"He came into my room, Mom, and he knocked my phone off the dresser. Look!" Allie flashed her phone in front of Anna's face. "He cracked the screen!"

There was indeed a hairline crack. Very tiny, but there.

"It was an assident," Logan wailed.

"I want a new phone. I need a new phone. He owes me a new phone!" Allie flailed dramatically.

"Allie, lower your voice." Anna got to her feet and leveled a calming gaze at her daughter. "We can discuss this without yelling."

Logan clasped his arms around Anna's thigh and shot his sister the side-eye.

Allie glowered at him. "Phone! Cracked! Brat!"

"Shh. You're upsetting your brother."

"You always take his side."

"He's three and he didn't mean to crack your phone. You're lucky you even have a phone. Many kids your age don't. Suck it up, buttercup."

The cell phone was a cost they could have waited a few years on. Allie had her own phone simply because Kevin adored gadgets and had buried Anna with research and articles on why it was good for children to have their own phones. Anna had been against it, wanting to wait until Allie was thirteen.

Kevin won when he said, "The GPS tracker will let you know where she is every moment of every day."

Begrudgingly, she'd agreed to the phone for Allie's tenth birthday. There were plenty of days when she couldn't pry Allie from her phone screen that she regretted the decision.

Allie scowled, folded her arms over her chest, and chuffed out her breath. "He's your favorite. It's not fair, not fair, not fair."

From her pocket, Anna's cell phone dinged and then rang.

Logan boo-hooed.

Allie stormed down the hall.

Kevin called, "What is going on?"

Did she have to solve everything? Fix everyone? *Yep, you're the mom. Comes with the job description.*

Well, she refused to feel sorry for herself. Enough of this nonsense. She had to break the mood and turn the ship around, or the entire day would be a wash.

Hmmm, how to get their attention, and snap her kids out of this mind-set? Anna searched the laundry room and her gaze fell on the cymbals.

Aha.

Prying Logan from her leg, she grabbed for the cymbals and clashed them together. Sang at the top of her lungs, "Seventy-six trombones led the big parade!"

Allie poked her head back into the mudroom. "Mom, what are you doing?"

"Line up!" Anna hollered. "We're going to march this out."

"Mom!" Allie rolled her eyes hard.

Anna clashed the cymbals.

Allie lined up behind Logan, who was already following her as Anna marched down the hallway.

"Knees high!" she called and started in on the lyrics again. "Seventy-six trombones!"

They proceeded past the master bedroom headed to the kitchen. The kids falling in step with her. Anna clashing the cymbals with resounded emphasis. Kevin came out of the bedroom to join them, making a silly drum major face and waving a golf putter like it was a baton. He got in front of Anna to lead the band.

Typical.

Let her get the party started and Kev showed up to take over as if it had been his idea all along. But Anna didn't care. She'd shifted the mood. They were laughing and singing and marching.

Score one for Mom.

The doorbell rang.

Logan left formation, ran for the door, and, before Anna could stop him, flung it wide open.

Anna halted, eyes on her son.

"Mom?" A confused expression crossed Logan's little face as

he looked at the visitor and then at Anna and repeated in a soft, befuddled whisper, *"Mommy?"*

She shifted her gaze from her son to the thin, spiky-haired, redheaded woman standing on her front porch holding a thick leather dog collar in her hand and appearing as if she'd just scaled Mount Everest to get it.

A complete stranger who looked exactly like *her.*

Anna's mouth dropped open and she blinked hard, trying to parse what she was seeing. But it was like the time she took calculus in high school. Nothing made sense no matter how hard she tried to understand it.

Her giggly mind said, *You prayed. God answered. Here she is. Your clone.*

Literally.

Yeah, be careful what you wish for because you just might get it.

The cymbals fell from her hands and hit the floor with a jarring clatter. Everyone jumped, including the clone on her doorstep.

Oh wait. Oh hey. Now she'd figured this out. She was still sound asleep and trapped in some kind of lucid nightmare. That was why it felt so real.

Soon, she soothed herself, soon enough the alarm would go off and everything would return to normal.

But deep inside, a part of Anna knew that nothing would ever be the same again.

CHAPTER FOUR

Amelia

The Mirror

Somehow, Amelia didn't expect Anna to look quite so much like her in person. She thought there would be differences, and there were, but they were cosmetic.

She'd studied Anna's features in her sister's social media photo posts, but to actually see herself looking back without benefit of a mirror was, well . . . slightly shocking.

Anna weighed twenty pounds more and had long wavy hair that fell to the middle of her back; her ears were triple pierced, and she had a small diamond nose stud, along with a small butterfly tattoo on her left upper arm.

Amelia's body pumped a flood of adrenaline. She was hot and cold, sweaty and dry all at the same time.

Anna was Amelia outside of her own body. Seeing her sister's face for the very first time was remarkable.

I'm not alone, she thought, and a crazy giddiness lightened her heart.

Finally, she was not alone, and it felt so glorious that instant panic wrapped around her throat like a thick fist.

It wasn't just that her mirror image was staring back at her, it was the entirety of Anna. A sister. At long last.

Amelia was overcome, both joy and fear tangling up inside her. They studied each other like zoo monkeys introduced for the first time.

Anna stared back at Amelia with the same dark chocolate eyes that Amelia used to peer at her. Friends, acquaintances, and even strangers had often commented on the purity of Amelia's eye color. It was just intense brown, no other hues, shades, highlights, or shadows. And at last, while looking into Anna's eyes, she got what everyone had been on about.

Pure deep brown eyes were mesmerizing.

In the quiet stillness after the cymbals fell now, she fully understood the concept of deafening silence.

Four openmouthed strangers blinked at her.

No one spoke.

Neither her twin, nor the man that Amelia recognized from social media sleuthing as Anna's husband, Kevin, nor their kids, Logan and Allie. A nice, normal family.

And she was here to blow up their world.

"Hello," she said as calmly as if she were interviewing for a job that she didn't care whether she got or not. "My name is Amelia Brandt and I know this is a shock, but I'm your sister. Your twin sister. Your identical twin sister. Might I come in?"

No one moved.

Then, her niece—it was the first time Amelia thought about the child in the context of being related to her—spoke.

"Why are you holding Cujo's collar? What did you do to

Cujo?" Her voice filled with preteen indignation. "Where is my dog?!"

The girl looked like her father, blond, Nordic, broad shouldered. She was almost as tall as her mother, five foot six. Amelia knew because it was her height, too, and something told her that muscular Allie was very good at sports

It surprised Amelia how much being misunderstood by this girl hurt. Especially since it had taken such a supreme emotional will for Amelia to rescue the Doberman.

Amelia extended the collar to Allie and watched small black bristles of dog hair drift to the doormat that said *Welcome, Y'all*.

Glowering, Allie snatched the collar away, her bottom lip trembling, her eyes fearful and angry. "What. Did. You. Do?"

"Allie," Anna finally spoke, gripping her daughter's shoulder. "You're being rude. Let her tell you what happened."

Allie folded her arms over her chest, the dog collar clutched in her fingers.

"The dog's collar got hung on the fence T-post and it was choking him. I took the collar off," Amelia explained as if it had been just that easy, instead of the most monumental thing she'd done since picking up the phone and calling Dr. Ellard for help.

Allie's eyes widened and her grip on the collar tightened. "Oh," she said, looking a bit sheepish. "I'm sorry. Is Cujo okay?"

Amelia nodded. "He's fine now, but you might consider a breakaway collar."

Allie flew past her, sailing down the steps and running over the cobblestone walkway toward the Doberman's pen, calling, "Cujo! Cujo! You poor boy!"

Amelia switched her attention back to Anna. The color had returned to her twin's cheeks, but she was still staring in stunned disbelief.

"You're my sister?" Anna asked, repeating what Amelia had said earlier. "My twin sister? My *identical* twin sister?"

Amelia waited patiently for it to sink in. She understood the shock. She'd gone through a similar reaction three days ago.

"Thank you for rescuing Cujo," the tall, handsome blond man said. Her brother-in-law, Kevin, was the first to recover equilibrium. "Won't you come in Miss? Mrs.? Brandt?"

Please and thank you. Polite Texas manners and hospitality. Politeness made Amelia twitchy. It felt like a cover-up for real emotions. Generally, she much preferred blunt honesty.

"It's Ms.," she murmured.

Kevin stepped forward and held out a hand.

She stared at it.

"It's safe," he said, mistaking her reluctance as concern about spreading germs instead of what it was. Social anxiety.

Warily, she took his hand.

He used the handshake to gently tug her over the threshold into the foyer with the rest of them, and she wasn't sure she liked that, either.

The boy, Logan, clung to his mother's hand and eyed Amelia suspiciously. "Who you?"

Was she supposed to explain it all over again? Amelia didn't know how to interact with children. She'd never been around them, not even when she was a child.

"You not my mommy." Logan widened his stance to match his father's, crossed his chubby little arms over his chest.

"No, I'm not."

"Puddin' pop." Anna crouched to her son's level. "Why don't you go help Allie check on Cujo?"

Logan stood there, glowering at Amelia distrustfully, his cheeks puffed out, his eyes narrowed.

"Take the cymbals with you," Anna instructed.

Logan picked the cymbals up off the floor, then finally, he nodded and darted past Amelia to follow after his sister, banging the cymbals together as he went—*clang, clang, clanggg*.

As the noise grew distant, Anna straightened, and Amelia spied a soft moistness in her eyes. Then Anna made a swift, sudden move, arms held wide, as if she wanted a hug.

Amelia panicked, held up both arms to keep her sister at bay. She could smell the dog on her skin. Or maybe it was the scent of her own fear. Either way, she needed space and time to collect herself before jumping headlong into this overwhelming relationship. Time for a little social distancing.

"Might you point me in the direction of the washroom? I'm afraid the dog salivated on me." She sounded too stiff and she knew it. *Drooled*. She should have said "drooled" like a normal person.

"Sure." Anna didn't seem the least bit deflated by Amelia sidestepping her hug. She didn't take things too personally. A quality Amelia admired.

"This way." Anna crooked a finger for Amelia to follow and led her to a small half bath off the hallway. Then she waved in the direction of her husband. "We'll just be waiting out here."

The two of them stared at her and it felt bizarre. "Um, thank you."

Amelia stepped into the bathroom, closed and locked the door, and switched on the light. Glancing around, she blinked in disbelief.

The bathroom was decorated almost identically to the half bath in her penthouse apartment, albeit with cheaper versions of the same items. Anna's white subway tiles were ceramic while Amelia had marble. The cabinetry was gray, Shaker style, but these were prefabricated whereas Amelia's were artisan crafted. Same light fixtures. Same oval mirror. Same fluffy gray bath rug. Same Revere Pewter wall color.

Her mouth dropped open and the hairs on her arms raised.

Uncanny.

How was this possible? Some kind of unsettling twin telepathy? Some inexplicably spooky DNA connection? She'd read similar stories about separated twins who'd been reunited.

Don't be fanciful. It's not that odd. It's a generic modern bathroom design. Blame Pinterest.

Amelia searched for something that wasn't like her decor at home. The bath towels were a slightly dustier shade of sage green than the ones she'd bought from Ralph Lauren and her hand soap dispenser was not a kitschy penguin, and the bathroom layout wasn't the same, but other than that, the rooms were eerily identical.

Goose bumps accentuated the raised hairs on her arms and as she met her startled gaze in the mirror, alarm bells chimed in her head. Or maybe it was just the kids slamming those cymbals.

But it didn't matter. Amelia had a jarring feeling this was only the first in a long line of surprises.

Softly singing "Happy Birthday" twice, she washed her hands in the bathroom sink. Amelia heard tension in the muted conversation outside the door.

Anna and her husband were arguing, even though she couldn't make out everything they were saying.

Closing her eyes, she whispered, "This is so much more complicated than I imagined."

She opened her eyes, dried her hands on the sage-green towel, blew out her breath, gathered her courage, opened the door, and stepped into the hallway.

Anna and Kevin paused midargument, something about sticking to a budget, turned, and gave her hawkeyed stares.

Amelia forced a smile. She knew it didn't look genuine, and she quickly dropped it in favor of her much more comfortable, blank-slate expression. A fellow musician had once called it her go-away-ain't-nobody-home-shuttered-window look. A bad date had dubbed it a cold-fish stare. Amelia called it loneliness.

"Sister," Anna said.

"Um . . . yes?"

Without warning, Anna sailed across the few steps of travertine tiles between them and folded Amelia into her embrace.

Stunned, Amelia squirmed, but Anna tightened the hug and held on. Hugging a stranger. One of Amelia's least favorite things.

Anna pressed her mouth to Amelia's ear and whispered this chant, "My identical twin sister, my identical twin sister, my identical twin sister."

Not knowing what else to do, Amelia stood completely still, her arms ironed stiff at her side.

While they might be identical twin sisters, they *were* strangers. In the best of times—and this was certainly not that—Amelia had trouble with intimacy. They'd been apart for thirty-five years. Spending nine months in a shared womb couldn't make up for that.

And still, Anna kept hugging her with a fierceness that had Amelia longing to run and she would have, but staying meant living.

Clang, clang, clang. Outside, Logan was still hammering those cymbals.

"What do you do for a living?" Anna asked, finally letting go and brushing a strand of hair behind her ear.

"I was a cellist," Amelia murmured. "For the Chicago Symphony."

"Was?"

"I retired two years ago."

"Retired? But you're so young."

"I have a trust fund."

Anna looked envious but tried for perky with a bouncy tone and overly broad smile. "So, you're a music lover. Me too!"

What was she supposed to do here? Encourage the small talk? Not Amelia's forte.

"I play the guitar," Anna prattled. "Ten years of lessons. I'm okay. No virtuoso, but I'm passable for party sing-alongs. All I really care about is having fun playing with my friends."

Amelia smiled. "It pleases me to think of you running scales on the guitar while I was practicing the cello."

Anna pulled a sad face. "Imagine if we'd been able to practice together. Hey." She snapped her fingers. "Did you bring your cello with you?"

"No."

"Oh."

They fell silent and things felt weird again. They were still standing in the hallway outside the bathroom, and that just seemed wrong. Anna's husband hovered in the background. Amelia wished he'd go away but didn't expect it. He looked as if he was put on earth for the express purpose of protecting Anna.

That, she liked about him.

"I always knew something was missing," Anna murmured and hugged her again. "And now I know that something was *you*."

This was too much, way too soon. Amelia broke free from Anna's hug. The hurt look on her twin's face punched her in the gut, but things were moving far too fast for her comfort. "I'm sorry. I need to g-go."

Anna blinked rapidly. "Wh-what?"

Amelia's heart pounded so loudly she couldn't think. "You need . . . I need . . . we need time to process this—*alone*."

"But you can't just come to my door and not explain what's

going on. Please, let's sit down and talk this out." Anna waved in the direction of the living room they'd passed earlier. "Kevin was just heading out on a business trip."

Shaking her head, Amelia searched for the right words. Anna wasn't wrong. She couldn't just show up, drop this bomb, and leave, but she desperately wanted to get out of there. In fact, a deep-seated dread took hold of her and burrowed in.

Anna reached for her hand. Her palm was warm while Amelia's was ice-cold. "Please, sit. I have fresh-squeezed lemonade and homemade chocolate chip cookies."

Of course, you do.

Interlacing her fingers with Amelia's, her twin led her to the living room. Amelia let her, even as her inner voice screamed, *Withdraw, retreat!*

In her mind, she heard Dr. Ellard contradict her. *You have to stop distancing yourself from people, Amelia. It served you in the past, but now it's the source of your greatest pain.*

Yes, well, easy for him to say, he hadn't grown up the way she had.

And here was Anna, all encompassing, and smiling relentlessly. Gung ho and cheerful in the face of adversity. Everything Amelia was not. Amelia owned her traits, both positive and negative sides. She was cautious and reserved and independent, and she was good with that. Until she was in the presence of a bubbly people person like Anna, and then she wished for a personality transplant.

Her sister settled on the couch, still holding Amelia's hand so that she had to either sit down with her or make things even more uncomfortable by pulling away.

The living room was clean in the way of people with children, dusted and vacuumed, but cluttered with toys and items of daily living. Awkwardly, Amelia perched on the cushion beside her sister, pressed her knees tightly together, stared at Anna's hand clasped with hers, and willed her sister to let go.

Kevin leaned his shoulder against the wall leading from the hall into the living room, watching them. That felt weird too.

"It was so kind of you to save Cujo," Anna said. "And I apologize for the way Allie lit into you. She's got strong opinions and she loves animals so much."

Amelia bobbed her head, wished she'd been that self-possessed as a child. "It's okay. It's good to know who you are when you're that young."

"We're all taken aback." Anna exhaled a wobbly laugh.

"Bowled over," Kevin mumbled.

"Understandable."

"I don't know where to start." Anna tightened her fingers around Amelia's.

"Start?"

"Getting to know you. I feel like I did on my thirtieth birthday when my best friend, Darla, dared me to go skydiving with her. As that single-engine plane climbed into the clouds over the drop zone, we held hands in solidarity."

"She scared the stuffing out of me," Kevin grumbled.

Anna held up their joined hands and offered Amelia another bright smile. "We leapt in tandem jumps with the instructors, Darla and me. One after the other. We just let go, trusting everything would turn out all right."

"Meanwhile . . ." Kevin snorted. "I was on the ground practically having a heart attack that the mother of my children was jumping out of a perfectly good plane. I'm in the insurance business. No one ever thinks that something bad will ever happen to them, but it does."

"Logan wasn't even born then," Anna tossed over her shoulder as an aside to her husband. To Amelia, she said, "Darla and I landed softly, safely, ran into each other's arms and did a jubilant dance, surprised and delighted to find the world was exactly the same, but deep inside, *we'd* changed forever."

"That must have been a life-affirming experience," Amelia said.

"Yes." Anna fixed her gaze on Amelia's. "Now, I feel like I'm leaping all over again."

Amelia's stomach flipped, and she felt her palm grow sweaty against Anna's. Her right eye ticked, a nervous twitch that her perfect posture couldn't contain.

"I'm just floored," Anna said. "Utterly."

"I didn't know how to warn you that I was coming. I tried writing a letter. I couldn't imagine calling you out of the blue. I thought about contacting you through 23andMe."

"Oh gosh," Anna said. "*That's* how you found me. I haven't even been on the website since I had the genealogy test done last year. I'm sorry. I'm so busy I never even thought to go back and check to see if I had new matches, and I must not have signed up for the alerts. When I went on before, the only DNA matches I had were with fourth and fifth cousins I'd never heard of."

"Why are you apologizing to me?" Amelia asked.

"Huh?" Anna blinked.

"You don't owe me an apology."

"If I'd checked the website regularly, we could have met sooner. I'm assuming you recently had your test done?"

Amelia nodded and eased her hand from Anna's grasp. "Yes, three days ago I got the report back, but you see, I already knew about you."

"Really?" Anna put a palm to her chest. "You knew about me? How?"

"I believed you were dead."

"Dead?" Anna blinked.

"Because that's what my parents told me."

"I'm not dead." Anna raised both palms.

"Clearly."

"How did your parents react when they found out about me? Did they come with you?" Anna glanced around as if expecting Sarah and Frank Brandt to walk through the door.

"My parents passed away two years ago in a car accident."

"Oh no." Anna's concern seemed genuine, and she pressed a hand to her heart. "That's terrible. I'm so sorry that happened to you."

"Everyone has sorrow." The last thing she wanted was sympathy. Amelia pushed up the sleeve of her lightweight summer jacket. That's when the bracelet that had been tucked underneath her sleeve dropped down to her wrist.

Anna's eyes fixed on the bracelet and widened. Her entire body tensed visibly.

"Where did you get that?" she croaked.

A cold, chalky taste filled her mouth and a hard shiver ran up Amelia's spine. She'd worn the bracelet on purpose, wondering if Anna had an identical one. It seemed, from the look on her sister's face, that she did.

"From my mother. She bought one for my sister, too, but it went missing the night we were born during a hurricane . . ." Amelia took a deep breath. "The night, I'd been taught, that my sister died."

Anna's gaze snapped closed around Amelia's like a steel trap. "I have an identical baby keepsake bracelet, except with my name instead of yours."

"What does this mean?" Amelia asked.

"I was hoping you could tell me."

They stared at each other.

"How did we get separated?" Anna whispered.

"Your mother?" Amelia had pondered this question for three days and kept returning to the most obvious explanation.

Anna leaned away from Amelia for the first time. "My mother what?"

Tread lightly. Amelia pondered a response that didn't cast Anna's mother in an unfavorable light.

"No." Anna shook her head vigorously. "No. Not my mother. She didn't do that. You're wrong."

"I didn't say anything."

"You didn't have to. It's written all over your face. My mother did *not* switch her dead baby in exchange for me." Anna hopped to her feet. "She didn't do that!"

"It's just one possibility." Swamped with more cortisol and

adrenaline than she could tolerate, Amelia leaped up, too. She hated conflict and avoided it at all costs.

"What are the other possibilities?"

"Stolen by fairies?" Amelia tried for humor.

"Changeling." Anna guffawed, except it wasn't laughter, but rather the sound of someone losing her grip.

Tension crackled between them.

"I should go," Amelia murmured. "Give you time and space."

"No, no." Anna reached out, grabbed her hand again, and clung to her. "Please don't go. We have to figure this out."

"Not in one day." Amelia tugged her hand away. "We'll talk later."

Out on the front porch, cymbals—*clang, clang, clang.*

"Please." Anna pressed her palms together beseechingly. "Please stay. We have a guest room."

Amelia slipped her purse off her shoulder, opened it up, took a business card from the gold-plated card case, and passed one to Anna. "Here's my contact information. I'll be staying at the Moonglow Inn on the beach. Call me tomorrow and we'll speak again. Right now, this is too much for either of us."

Anna moved as if to hug her again, but Amelia backed up, leaving her twin snatching at air. She couldn't be the one to comfort her sister. She simply didn't know how.

"Please stay." Anna sounded so lost.

"Anna," Kevin said in a scolding tone that made Amelia dislike him. "Stop being so needy and let the poor woman go."

CHAPTER FIVE

Anna

The Angry Husband

W hat the hell, Anna?" Kevin asked after Amelia left. He looked as if he'd been gut kicked, his eyes big as golf balls, and his hands fisted at his sides.

Yes, well, try having it happen to you, bucko. Identical twin you never knew about knocks on the door . . .

"I-I don't know."

"You have an identical twin sister?" He jammed his fingers through a thick thatch of blond hair.

"Apparently."

"How?"

Anna lifted her shoulders, her mind stuck in neutral, unable to go either forward or reverse. She couldn't find the words to express her feelings. It was like being reunited with a long-lost friend she'd never known.

Or finding a soul mate.

Never in a million years would she ever have thought she'd wake up one late spring morning, open her front door, and find herself standing there. How was she supposed to process this? Especially with Kevin glaring at her as if she'd been keeping secrets from him intentionally.

"I don't like this," Kevin hissed.

"Neither do I."

"Why didn't Amelia call first and break the news more gently?"

Anna settled her hands firmly on her hips. "You're starting to tick me off, big guy."

"How's that?" His face turned blustery.

"This is happening to *me* not you."

"Babe, when something happens to you or the kids, it happens to me, too. I wanna crunch something." He made a motion like he was crushing a beer can in his right hand.

Anna resisted rolling her eyes and instead recalled what he'd looked like in high school running down the length of the football field, his long blond hair streaming from beneath his helmet, a youthful Nordic god in all his glory, the football tucked into the crook of his arm, and grinning like he owned the world when he scored the game-winning touchdown.

She remembered how her heart had tripped over itself knowing she was his girlfriend and later that night she would be in his arms as he made love to her for the first time. The fire still burned after all these years, but sometimes, when he turned all caveman and possessive, she just wanted to kick him in the seat of his pants.

Anna shot him a look that she hoped said, *Rein it in, dude*. Even though the kids were still outside on the porch, he was talking loud enough for them to overhear.

"What is it specifically you don't like?" she asked.

"This 'twin' sister showing up out of nowhere." He gestured wildly, working himself up. "How do you know she's who she says she is?"

"Seriously?"

"Well?" He had the same expression on his face that he got whenever he suspected a client of insurance fraud.

Anna reached up and gently knocked her knuckles against the side of his head. "Duh, she looks exactly like me."

"You're naïve." He grunted and lowered his eyelids in a skeptical squint. "She could be scamming us."

Anna snorted. "What are you saying? That she's a total stranger who went through the trouble of having her appearance altered just so she could take us for the two hundred dollars and some change in our bank balance?"

"Wait, what?" He drew his head back. "Is the checking account that low?"

"You're getting sidetracked. Stay on topic. Amelia didn't come here to scam us. This isn't a soap opera."

"It sure feels like one. A twin sister you never knew existed shows up on our doorstep. How does that happen? I don't trust her any farther than I can throw her."

"I believe that she's my twin and while I haven't had time to fully explore and process what that means, I welcome her with open arms and I'm *glad* she's come to Moonglow Cove."

Kevin snorted.

She knew that snort. He was struggling to stifle his opinion. "What?"

"You'd hug Satan if he came knocking, bake him cookies, and try to redeem him."

His words hit her like road gravel dinging her minivan's paint job—not real damaging but annoying all the same. "I thought you liked that about me."

"I do. I do." Kevin quickly backtracked. "You're a kind and giving person and I love you for it, but compassion has an assigned risk."

This time, she couldn't help it. She rolled her eyes at Kevin's insurance jargon. She much preferred his sports metaphors.

"Meaning . . . ?"

"Bottom line? You collect people like strays."

"I do not." Her cheeks heated.

"Winnie," he said, holding up one finger like he was going down a checklist. "Case in point."

"Winnie's family."

He held up a second finger. "The Harmonious Housewives."

"We've been together since high school! We're like sisters."

"My point." A third finger went up. "Darla."

"Darla? She's my best friend and the most incredible employee I've ever had. She's family, too."

"That's what I'm saying. We've got enough family members without adding more."

"Kevin Jerome Drury, you can never have enough family." She sank her top teeth into her bottom lip.

Kevin had grown up in a house with six brothers and sisters and while he'd mellowed considerably since their marriage, he still clung to the not-enough-resources-to-go-around mentality.

Sometimes that trait led to a get-it-while-you-can outlook on life that Anna didn't care for.

"Not all of us were blessed with a huge clan the way you were," she murmured. "You take your family for granted."

He had the decency to look hangdog. "That was a lousy thing to say, Bean."

He called her by the nickname he'd given her in high school because she'd so adored jelly beans. It'd been a long time since he'd called her that and the word swept her up in memories back to Moonglow Cove High School when he'd given her a giant bag of Jelly Belly jelly beans, the size you can only get at big-box warehouse stores, and then he'd asked her to go steady.

She'd been sixteen and he'd been seventeen. He'd been her one and only ever since. Sometimes, she secretly wondered if she'd missed out by not dating a lot of guys, but from the very beginning, Kevin had been The One.

At the time, it was the happiest day of her life until it was eclipsed by their wedding and then later, the birth of their children.

"I'm sorry," Kevin said, coming over to rub her shoulders and give her that steady *look* that said *you-and-me-team-always*. "I apologize. I know you're still grieving your dad."

"Apology accepted." Anna tried her best not to hold grudges. Pouting served no one, and life was too short.

Kevin plowed a hand through his hair. "I'm still trying to absorb all this."

"Me too."

"It's mind-warping."

"Do you remember when I told you that I've always felt like I had this empty hole inside me that I couldn't fill no matter what?"

"Hmm."

"And that I had no idea why I felt that way because I have a terrific life?"

He nodded, but the guilty expression on his face told her he didn't really remember at all. Sometimes she got the feeling he didn't listen to her anymore. As if he thought he had her all figured out and was certain he knew what she would say or do before she said or did it. Frankly, his lack of attention was a little insulting.

"Why would you feel empty? You've got me and the kids. You've got your mom and Mike and his family. You've got my nutty but lovable family too. You have a bazillion friends. You're golden."

"I know." She glanced down at her hands. "I can't explain it or at least I couldn't until today. I have a twin sister, Kevin, and I lost her; and somewhere, in the depths of my soul, I *knew* it."

"Anna . . ." He shook his head, rubbed his temple with his thumb as if he were getting a migraine. "I worry."

"About what?"

"That woman. You."

She scowled. "What about me?"

"You're building a fairy tale around this. Twin sisters, separated at birth, and now reunited. Happy, happy, joy, joy. It's not that simple."

She notched up her chin. "What if I *am* building a fairy tale? Why is that wrong?"

"Because," he said, "fairy tales aren't real."

"Our romance was a fairy tale. We're living proof that happily-ever-after *does* happen."

His eyes met hers and she saw in them a harsh expression she'd never seen before. "Tell that to the folks who lost their homes in Oklahoma. Life's complicated, Anna. Mature people recognize that. Grow up."

Stunned, she opened her mouth to offer a counterpoint, but her phone vibrated in her back pocket, pulling her attention away from her husband. She yanked out the phone and checked the screen. "Mom."

Blatantly, he grunted.

Fearful that her legs wouldn't hold her, Anna moved to the kitchen table and plunked down in her usual spot to answer it.

Kevin didn't seem to notice because he was too busy pacing. She got it. He was freaked. So was she.

Keeping her voice as even as she could, Anna answered, "Hey, Mom."

"Where are you, sweetie?" Her mother's kind voice filled her ear. "It's ten to ten and you know it takes as least fifteen minutes to get to the salon from my town house. Are the kiddos out of sorts? What's up?"

"I . . . Mom." Anna's throat closed.

"Yes?"

There were so many things she wanted to say, so many damn questions she wanted to ask, but this confrontation had to happen in person.

Her mind swirled as she considered how to break the news

about Amelia. How did she form the words? Should she call a family meeting? Should Amelia be there when it happened?

"Could you please call the salon and tell them we have to cancel?" she asked.

"What is it? What's wrong?" Anxiety leapt into her mother's tone. Usually Robin Straus was even-keeled, but ever since Anna's dad had died last year, Mom's fears got triggered much more easily than they once did.

"I'll explain later."

"Are the kids okay? Tell me the kids are okay, and I won't worry."

"The kids are fine, Mom."

Shaking his head, Kevin left the kitchen. She heard his shoes slapping against the travertine tiles as he headed for the bedroom.

"Something's wrong. You don't sound like yourself."

"Just call the salon, Mom, and cancel. I'd appreciate it."

"Why?"

Anna couldn't find the words to tell her mother what had just happened when she hadn't absorbed it herself. She grabbed for an excuse. "Winnie's gone AWOL again."

"Oh. Is that all?" Robin sounded relieved. "Did they check the hospital? She's always drawn back to the L&D ward. I guess after spending four decades there as a midwife, it's like going home."

"I'm sure Myra's checked the hospital."

"I feel for Winnie, I really do, and I so hate that she's got Alzheimer's and doesn't have a family of her own to care for her."

"We're her family, Mom. I'm her legal guardian and I have her power of attorney."

"I know, sweetheart. It's just I hate to see you saddled with this." Robin sighed. "Never mind."

Anna knew what that sigh meant. Her mother was a tenderhearted person, but she'd never fully understood why Dad felt obligated to care for Winnie and why that burden had been passed on to Anna.

Kevin returned carrying his laptop. He plopped down next to her, opened the computer, and tapped on the keyboard.

What was he up to?

Looking at her handsome husband, Anna felt a mix of emotions. Wistful that he was headed out on the road again, and that she'd be left alone with the kids for weeks. Irritable that he was leaving her to deal with these new revelations by herself. And secretly a little relieved that she didn't have to juggle him, too, along with her mother, the kids, and her twin sister.

"I'll cancel our appointments," Mom was saying. "When should we reschedule?"

"I can't even . . . I'm too distracted to think about that right now."

"I'll handle it. Next Tuesday sound good?"

"Don't reschedule. We'll discuss this once I get Kevin on the road."

"Okay, but, sweetheart," her mother said. "I did want to talk to you about something. I've finally been strong enough to go through your father's things. New Hope called me looking for donations and I said yes."

Right now, Anna couldn't deal with giving away her dad's things. "Kevin's headed out the door. I need to see him off."

"All right then." Her mother sounded hurt.

Anna felt like a jerk, she'd been too abrupt. Softening her tone, she added, "I'll text you later."

Mom hung up without another word. She was ticked.

Yeah, well, I'm ticked, too. Mother, you've got some explaining to do. Biting back a heavy sigh, Anna switched off her phone and set it on the table.

"I want to show you something." Kevin pointed to his Google search.

Anna leaned over his shoulder. "What is it?"

"Nothing."

"Huh?"

"I googled your twin sister and there is nothing about her on the internet. There are over a dozen Amelia Brandts and none of them are her."

"Maybe her name's not spelled like that."

"I've tried several different spellings. Nada. Bupkis."

"So what if she doesn't have an internet presence? Big deal. It doesn't mean anything."

"Everyone under fifty has an internet presence of some sort."

"That's a sweeping statement."

Kevin scowled. "It's *shady*."

"While it might be unusual, I wouldn't go that far."

"I'll do an advanced search. Even if you pay some company to scrub your history, you can't completely delete your internet presence."

"No," Anna snapped. "Leave it alone, Kevin."

"I smell something fishy."

Anna stood up. "You have to get on the road."

"You're throwing me out?"

"People in Oklahoma need you."

"I've decided not to go."

"Excuse me?"

From the porch, Allie sang in her high-pitched melodious voice, "Seventy-six trombones," as she banged the cymbals rhythmically.

Why did the noise sound so ominous and when had her daughter gotten so good at keeping time?

Kevin jutted out his chin. "I'm not leaving you alone with her."

"Allie?"

"Don't play dumb."

"You can't stay home. We need the money."

"To hell with money." Since Kevin was an independent adjuster, he could set his own schedule depending on how much he wished to earn.

"We're not running up the credit cards again. Go to work."

Kevin's eyes narrowed. "Don't tell me how to take care of my family."

"Look, I appreciate you wanting to do this, but we're basically broke." She took in a deep breath, felt her throat tighten. "I need time alone with my sister. You can't cancel out this job with no notice. I'll be okay."

"What if something happens?"

"Nothing's going to happen."

"She could rob us blind. Harm the children. She's a stranger."

Anger pushed up through her, but Anna shoved it back. Kevin was just thrown for a loop, and he didn't know how to deal with his feelings. She was in the same kayak with him, no point paddling in the opposite direction.

Plus, he was by nature a worst-case-scenario kind of guy. He'd always been cautious. At least when it came to personal safety. Finances? Not so much. He did like to spend.

Like everyone else, they'd struggled in the aftermath of the pandemic, but Kevin, with his taste for the finer things, had found it hardest to rein in his spending. Money was the main thing they fought about and when she'd been on the brink of losing the bakery, things had gotten pretty rocky over his extravagance.

In the early years of their marriage, they'd been broke, and young love had been more than enough, but as they'd become more successful in their businesses, his drive for material things had increased along with their income. She supposed his need came from growing up in the middle of the pack of seven kids with frugal parents who aggressively pinched pennies.

Maybe she was at fault for indulging him when he gifted himself with expensive golf clubs or the latest electronic gadgets. He did work hard, and she wanted him to be happy.

As the economy slowly recovered, things between them had evened out, and they hadn't been fighting as much lately.

But now there was this twin thing.

"I promise, I won't leave her alone in the house or with the children. We can even meet outside the house, if that'll make you feel better. I think it's silly, but I'll do that for you if you insist." She studied her husband, closed the laptop, and handed it to him. "Be careful on the road. We are going to be fine."

He didn't take the computer. "I can't be gone for a month or longer the way I usually am."

"Then just stay a week."

"Three days." Kevin ground his teeth. "I'll be back on Saturday."

Anna started to argue, but she could see he was dug in. It would take him eight hours to drive to the town in Oklahoma, so that meant he'd work Wednesday, Thursday, and Friday and drive home on Saturday.

Three and a half days with Amelia should be long enough for them to work through the initial getting-to-know-you stage and give Anna enough time to decide the best way to break this disquieting news to her mother and brother.

While three days' worth of work wouldn't really earn them the money they needed, it would keep them from having to use credit cards to get by.

Anna dragged her nails across her bare arm, itchy from a mosquito bite she hadn't even realized she'd gotten. "Fine. Three days."

"If anything happens, you'll call me immediately and I'll come right home," Kevin said. "I'm here for you, Bean."

"Nothing is going to happen."

One eyebrow shot up on his forehead in that way of his that she usually found comical. "Don't let Amelia cause trouble between you and your mother."

Anna opened her mouth to argue, but let it go. He was a man, after all. His capacity for understanding the intricacies of female emotions and relationships was limited. No fault of his own, that's just how it was.

"Scoot." Feeling lighter, she playfully swatted his fanny like he was one of her children.

"There's that sunny smile I fell in love with." He grinned and kissed her before retrieving his luggage that he'd left in the hallway.

Anna folded her arms over her chest and followed him to the back door. "Tell the kids good-bye before you go."

"Will do."

"Oh, hang on. With all the interruptions, I forgot your care package." Anna bustled to the refrigerator for the large collapsible cooler she'd filled with healthy staples to lessen Kevin's temptation to hit the junk food while on the road.

She'd prepped several homemade Buddha bowls with rice, quinoa, sweet potatoes, fresh greens, and cruciferous veggies. She included baked edamame, chickpeas, and popcorn for crunchy on-the-go snacks.

"Here you go." She handed him the tote. "Please try to stay away from fast food. Your arteries will thank you."

Looking resigned, Kevin nodded.

"Cheer up, I did make a special treat." From the fridge, she took out a key lime pie.

"When did you make that?" he asked.

"Last night. I couldn't sleep." She slipped the pie into another tote bag.

"I don't need the whole pie," he said. "One slice'll do."

"Don't be silly, you love key lime pie."

"Honestly"—he sounded peeved—"I don't want the whole pie. Leave it for the kids."

"Take the pie. Share with your clients who need cheering up." She pressed it into his hands.

"Anna, no." His tone was a dagger, and his eyes flashed a warning.

She pulled back. "What is it?"

"You're anxious over this Amelia thing. I get it. But ease up, okay?"

"I baked this pie just for you," she said, alarmed to hear herself whimper. "I stayed up past midnight."

"I didn't ask you to do that."

"The diet is hard for you to stick to, so I thought why not give you something to smile about with your favorite pie." Anna tried to slip around his arm to open the tote with the Buddha bowls and snacks to slip the pie inside.

"Stop!"

She halted. Wow. He'd actually raised his voice over it.

"Look, here's the deal. I don't really like key lime pie."

"Sure you do. I made it for you when we were dating, and you said it was your favorite."

"Cards on the table? I lied. You were cute and sweet, and I wanted to sleep with you."

Stunned, Anna settled the pie onto the counter. "I've been making you this pie for eighteen years."

"Yeah, well, now you can stop."

She pressed a hand to her forehead, felt sick to her stomach. "I can't believe you've kept this from me for eighteen years."

"Don't overexaggerate. It's just pie."

No, no, it was not. The pie lie was a crack in the foundation of their marriage.

"Is there anything else you haven't told me?" she asked. "Anything more you need to get off your chest?"

"Now that you mention it, yeah. You've been pulling away from me for years and it hurts."

His words hit her like a punch. Had she?

"I haven't."

"You're up at four o'clock in the morning. You volunteer for too many clubs and organizations. There's Winnie. The band. Our mothers are raising our kids half the time because you're off doing community services. At night, you're too tired for sex more often than not."

Sex.

So that's what this was all about. It always came down to sex with men, didn't it? Dumbfounded, she stared at him. She had no idea her husband felt this way.

"And now you suddenly have this sister, who's come looking for another slice of your time."

"I iron your own freaking shirts, Kevin." She tightened her arms over her chest, barely keeping herself from saying the other "f" word that she really wanted to shout.

"You could just send them to the dry cleaner." He grunted. "Do you know what it feels like when you'd rather iron my shirts than take me up on a quickie?"

There were nine hundred responses flipping through her mind, but, honestly, she was too flabbergasted to say any of them.

"It makes me feel as if you are avoiding me. As if you'd rather iron than go to bed with me. It makes me feel inadequate and neglected."

"Kevin, I'm a busy mom. I have stuff to do."

"And now, with Amelia strolling into our lives, you'll add even more stuff on your to-do list. How come I'm never at the top of that list, Anna?"

"You're sounding like a big baby."

"I sound like someone who wants his wife back."

"And *you* told *me* to grow up?" Anger burned her skin. "Take your own advice."

Kevin looked like a man who'd made a decision he'd been weighing for some time. "You know what?"

"What?"

"I think we need a time-out from each other."

Her angry heart jumped into her throat. "What do you mean by that? You're going on the road. We won't see each other again until Saturday."

"Let's fully take a break. No texting or FaceTime or emails for the next three days unless it's an emergency. It'll give you space to think about what's most important." Tossing that over his shoulder, Kevin stalked out.

Stunned, Anna stared after him, mouth agape.

As the door clicked shut behind her husband, a big neon warning sign flashed in Anna's head and she thought, *Oh no, my husband is terrified I'm embarking on a new journey without him. How can he be so insecure?*

Furious, she turned to the pie, grabbed fistfuls of crust and sticky filling, and started jamming the entire mess down the garbage disposal.

CHAPTER SIX

Robin

Curiosity Killed the Cat

If there was anything Robin Straus had learned in her seventy years on planet Earth it was this: *love was not a straightforward affair.*

Romantic novels and movies, time-honored fairy tales and diamond engagement ring commercials led you to believe that when you met your soul mate, alchemy happened. You fell in love, got married, had babies, and lived happily ever after. It was a naïve fantasy so far removed from the truth that it'd be laughable if it wasn't so painful.

Life was so much more complicated, beautiful, and frankly poignant for such a simple reduction.

Love wasn't a direct line from meeting to forever melding. It had twists and turns, peaks and valleys, meandering paths and abrupt crescendos. No greeting card sentiment could ever capture the complex emotional quagmire that was real human relationships.

The hallmark of lasting love was not red roses tied up with raffia in a crystal vase. It wasn't expensive chocolates and bubbly champagne. It wasn't a lavish wedding ceremony or a honker of a diamond ring. It wasn't out-of-this-world sex—although that could be part of the equation—sex was sex and love was love. People could have great sex without love being involved and have great love with no sex.

Loving someone meant making sacrifices and putting their interests ahead of your own. But it also meant having strong boundaries and not letting your love for someone sway you from honoring your own needs and preferences. It couldn't be unrequited or one-sided, either, where one person did all the giving and the other all the taking.

That wasn't love. That was exploitation.

Love was a balancing act.

A delicate back-and-forth.

A gentle dance and sway.

And love meant that when your actions hurt someone you loved, you sure as hell better say you are sorry. True apology and real forgiveness were the essential ingredients in a long, lasting, layered love story.

Whether between partners, friends, parent and child, or siblings.

Since losing Heathcliff Robin often found herself thinking about the intricacies of love, her relationships and what they meant to her.

Especially today, as she sat among the piles of Heathcliff's things in the climate-controlled storage unit, pondering what was going on with her daughter.

Anna had canceled their hair appointment at the last minute, which wasn't like her reliable child. While Anna did have an impulsive streak, she was a people person, and when she disappointed others, she carried her guilt like a weight.

Robin had never known Anna to back out on a commitment without an exceptional reason. Something was wrong in her daughter's world. The tension in her voice had been unmistakable.

And Robin felt it in her bones.

Her instinct had been to jump in the car and drive over to Anna's house, but her son, Mike, was on the way over to help her clean out the storage unit and take his daddy's things over to the local nonprofit charity that serviced Moonglow Cove's needy population.

Dwarfed by the maze of possessions surrounding her, Robin heaved a thick sigh. It had taken her a year to get to this point where she could go through Heathcliff's belongings, but now that she was in the midst of it, grief wrapped around her like a clammy hand.

How had they managed to amass so much junk?

They should have thrown the stuff out or given it away when they'd moved to Arizona for Heathcliff's health five years earlier. Instead they'd rented the storage unit. Choosing a hundred-dollar-a-month storage bill over the pain of cleaning out the past. Their thinking? Once his health improved, they'd come back home.

But in the end, after Heathcliff's fragile lungs lost his battle against the coronavirus the previous year, Robin bought a modest town house in an over fifty-five community not far from where Anna lived.

Heathcliff's firefighter uniforms, even though he'd retired a decade before his death, were stacked on the floor at her right elbow. His suits and jeans, still on the hangers, hung from rods on rolling racks. His summer attire—cargo shorts, Hawaiian shirts, and crew-neck tees—was sorted into boxes to her left. Lined up in front of her were belts, ties, hats and caps. Beyond those accessories sat his shoes: running sneakers, dressy loafers, cowboy boots, steel-toed work boots, rubber boots, fishing waders.

Seeing her late husband's things lined up for disposal took Robin's breath away. The energy and determination that had galvanized to start the cleanup vanished like thin smoke.

Giving away Heathcliff's possessions was the final act of letting go. Admitting that he was gone forever.

Reality distorted and Robin felt as if her body were being pulled headlong down a dark endless corridor at warp speed.

Emotion flooded her in a hot swamp. Anger and sadness mixed with guilt and regret. Other, more complex feelings burst from her heart as a half-dozen images flooded her brain.

In her mind's eye, Robin saw her husband manning the backyard barbecue grill in the house they'd had on the beach, the house that Mike now owned and lived in with his wife, Gia, and baby daughter, Faith.

She saw Heathcliff flipping hamburgers in those blue jean shorts and a red shirt printed with vintage cars, adding a veggie burger just for Anna the year she turned thirteen and announced she was a vegetarian.

Everyone had teased her about it, but not Heathcliff. He'd shown he respected her decision by adding the veggie patty and then later, when Anna had gone back to the grill and asked if she could have a real burger, he'd cooked one without saying a word.

How Robin had loved him for that! He'd always been a caring, empathetic father.

His bespoke cowboy boots brought back memories of the time he'd taken her and the kids to M.L. Leddy's during a family trip to the Fort Worth Stockyards. The place smelled of leather and history and the guy behind the counter winked and asked Anna if she was her father's girlfriend.

Anna had chuffed out her chest and said in a loud, peevish, five-year-old voice, "Don't be silly, he's my *daddy!*"

The brown plaid bathrobe reminded Robin of the bedtime stories Heathcliff read to the kids and the blueberry pancake breakfasts he cooked using a Mickey Mouse mold. He'd topped the pancakes with melted butter and blueberry maple syrup.

To this day, Robin couldn't eat pancakes without melted butter and blueberry maple syrup.

He'd worn that navy pin-striped suit to Anna's second-grade daddy-daughter dance. Anna's dress had been mauve taffeta with a flare skirt, her shoes white patent leather, the song was "I Loved Her First."

Robin had gone along to watch, her heart overflowing with love for them both and that precious, special moment.

Anna had been so scared to waltz in front of so many people, so afraid she would mess up and make a fool of herself, but Heathcliff had smiled tenderly. "Put your feet on mine, sweetheart, and just keep looking into my eyes. I've got you, Anna. Never forget, I've always got you."

They danced to the same song again at Anna's wedding reception except that time he'd worn a rented tuxedo.

Funny how the bulk of her memories of her husband revolved around the kids, even though they'd been married for ten years before having Anna. Heathcliff had been an exemplary father. Robin couldn't have asked for more on that score. He'd been a good man, a tender lover, a great provider, but Anna's birth *had* altered their relationship.

Although it was a subtle shift, no one but Robin seemed to notice.

He'd become slightly more secretive, less open with her, and whenever Robin tried to broach it, he'd gaslight her, telling her it was all in her imagination. Because their life was so normal in every other way, she'd let it go, but something had changed between them thirty-five years ago, and she'd never been able to pinpoint exactly what it was.

The one thing she did know, and had resented, was the closeness he'd developed with Winnie Newton after Anna's birth.

If the midwife hadn't been twenty years older than Heathcliff, Robin might have suspected he'd been carrying on with her. He was over at Winnie's place often, mowing her lawn, taking her grocery shopping, doing little repairs around the house while neglecting his own home improvement projects.

All Robin could figure was that night during the hurricane bonded her husband to the midwife in a way she would never understand.

That realization didn't make her resent Winnie any less.

Overwhelmed by memories and emotions, Robin placed a hand to her heart. She probably shouldn't have parked herself in the middle of the storage unit. Getting up off the concrete floor was a bit of a challenge.

She shifted from sitting to kneeling, then, bracing her hand against the wall, pushed up. Grunted "upsa daisy" as her aching knees creaked loudly. Her head swam, her blood pressure dropping quickly. Orthostatic hypotension, her doctor called it.

Pausing, she waited for the sensation to pass, her flimsy knees wobbling, the scent of Heathcliff all around her. It was funny and unfair. He was long gone, but his fragrance lingered.

It made her feel as if he might walk through the door after playing dominoes at the community center with his retired firefighter cronies, give her a peck on the cheek, and ask her what was for dinner.

Robin swiped the back of her hand over her brow, glanced across the room at the old office desk and chair they'd stuck at the back of the unit. What was inside there? So much time had passed she couldn't remember if they'd cleaned it out or not before hauling it over here. Maybe she should look.

Forget it. There's too many boxes to step over.

True enough, but did she really want to have to come back here and do this again? Once was enough. She'd do it all today.

Pressing one hand to her lower back to brace her achy hip,

she picked her way around boxes, trunks, and crates. She had to squeeze through the narrow passageway between rows of stockpiled possessions.

Overhead a weak fluorescent light cast a sickly flickering glow across shadows of the past. The dusty boxes triggered a sneezing fit and she fumbled in the front pocket of her capris for a tissue.

Robin climbed over the dresser she'd gotten at a thrift store and refinished when Anna was a baby. Painting in the garage with the door open on a rainy spring day. Stenciling bunnies and chickens on the pale pink color after it dried. Later, she'd repainted it in Indian Ocean blue when Mike was born, boats and trains replacing the bunnies and chickens.

She spied the matching crib, collapsed and stacked against the wall. She should probably give the dresser and crib away but couldn't bring herself to let them go. She'd offered the furniture to both Anna and Mike, but her son, the carpenter, had hand carved the baby furniture for Allie, Logan, and Faith.

There were plastic boxes labeled in Sharpie with the contents in Heathcliff's precise handwriting—tax documents, "Xmas" lights, flower vases, electrical cords, knickknacks. She couldn't go through all these things. It was too much. Too soon. Why had she come over here today?

Because Anna stood you up and you didn't have anything else to do.

Yes, and then she was back, worrying about her oldest child.

Finally, she reached the old rolltop desk, wiped dust off the chair seat with a tissue, and sat down. She opened drawers and peered inside.

The narrow front drawer held pens and number two pencils,

erasers, paper clips, rubber bands, tape rolls, and Post-it notes. There were school photos of the kids. Mike at five on a rocking horse, flashing a grin showing off his first missing tooth. Anna at thirteen, in the gangly throes of adolescence, when her face had elongated, but her body hadn't yet caught up.

Robin pocketed the photos.

Mike had hit all his milestones right on time. Anna had been a late bloomer, not getting her period until she was fifteen. Robin had worried that something was wrong and took her to the doctor. The doctor assured her that nothing was wrong with Anna. It was just genetics.

At first, Robin didn't understand. She'd gotten her own period at twelve and that was the usual age for the women in her family.

But then she figured Anna had gotten the late-onset puberty from Heathcliff's side, the same place she'd gotten those chocolate-brown eyes and gorgeous red hair. Heathcliff's great-aunt Matilda gave her the hair, though Heathcliff had never told Robin about Great-Aunt Matilda until after Anna was born.

Oddly, none of his cousins seemed to remember Matilda; then again, Heathcliff's family hadn't been known for their unity. His own parents had been killed in a house fire when he was a teenager—the pain of that loss never really left him—and their deaths were the reason he'd become a firefighter.

Not having close family ties was why he and Robin had bonded so solidly. They'd been in the same boat, both only children, both orphans when they'd met. When she was eighteen, her mother died from pancreatic cancer, and five years later, her father, in the throes of clinical depression, had taken his own life.

The depth of her loss sank sharp talons into Robin, and for a moment she was overwhelmed.

Salty tears filled her mouth, overflowed her eyes. Dropping her head, she let sorrow overtake her. Fell into it. Felt it turn into a thick dark cloud. But she didn't cling to the emotions, just sat in them until the brunt wore off, and finally, the pain faded.

"Well," she said. "Well, enough of that."

Drying her eyes, she returned to her task. She dug through more drawers. Files. Owner manuals. Insurance documents. Bank statements. All a decade out of date. There were keys of various shapes and sizes, all unlabeled. She had no idea what they unlocked. A jar of coins, mostly pennies. She fished out the quarters and stuck them in her front pocket. Old birthday and holiday cards.

In the bottom drawer she found a small metal lockbox.

She leaned over to pick it up. She'd never seen it before. Had no idea what might be inside. Did she dare look?

Hauling in a long breath, she poked the latch with a trembling finger.

It didn't open.

Locked.

What secrets did Heathcliff lock away inside this box? The bigger question? Why was she so certain it contained anything mysterious at all? She and Heathcliff had a loving, trusting relationship.

Well, for the most part. She tried to tell herself not to be silly. It was most likely filled with sentimental items that would carry no secrets. But then why was it locked? Why the sudden flutter of fear flapping inside her heart?

Did any of the keys in the top drawer open the lockbox?

Frantically, she tried key after key, and finally, the last one she tried fit the lock. Holding her breath, she twisted the key and the lid popped open.

The box was empty except for one thing.

Another key.

It was labeled with a white circular tag left over from when they'd had a big garage sale before Mike went to college. Flipping the label over, she saw written in Heathcliff's hand: *Winnie's safe-deposit box, Moonglow Cove Central Bank. To be opened only in the event of her death.*

"Mom?" Mike's voice echoed down the corridor of the storage facility. "Are you in here?"

She swiveled in the chair, saw her son's head poke around the open door of the unit, felt her eyes grow as wide as his.

"What are you doing?" He stepped inside. "How did you get way back over there?"

"I took the easiest route." She waved him toward the path she'd taken to get to the desk surrounded by towers of boxes.

He picked his way around the stuff and sat down on the edge of the desk beside her chair. His butt rested right next to the metal lockbox that held the key.

Mike smelled of cedarwood shavings and the mild odor of shellac. He had been working, carving his handmade furniture he sold in his own storefront on Paradise Pier. He was one of the top independent furniture makers in the country, specializing in baby cribs, bassinets, and cradles.

Reaching over, she brushed sawdust from his hair.

He glanced down.

An urge to hide the metal box and key from him bulldozed her.

Stuff it down, put it away, ignore, ignore, ignore.

A bad habit she'd spent seventy years cultivating. She'd never been the sort to rock the boat. She was a take-life-as-it-came gal. She trusted people and believed in the basic goodness of mankind. Yet she couldn't help wondering what was in Winnie's safe-deposit box and why Heathcliff had the key.

"Mom?"

She blinked at her son.

"Are you all right?"

"Fine." Robin forced a smile and closed the lid on the metal box.

"What's that key open?"

Robin shrugged. "We better start loading things up."

He looked as if he might push for an explanation, but Mike was an agreeable son. His personality was a lot like hers in many ways.

Instead he said, "Are you sure you're ready to give away Dad's things?"

"I am."

He cocked his head, shot her a speculative glance.

"I need to get it done. It's been over a year."

"There's no rush."

"I feel like I can't move on with these things weighing me

down. Besides, I'm wasting money with these monthly storage payments and every dollar counts on a fixed income."

"Okay, Mom. Whatever you need."

"May I ask you something?"

"Anything."

"What's wrong with your sister?"

Mike's forehead crinkled. "What do you mean?"

"Something's eating Anna."

"She seemed fine yesterday when I stopped by the bakery. Why?"

"She canceled our hair appointment last minute. She wouldn't stand me up unless something was wrong."

Mike shrugged. "Maybe she and Kevin got crossways."

Robin splayed a hand to her heart. "Is there a problem in their marriage? What aren't you telling me?"

He raised his shoulders and his hands, palms held up. "Nothing, nothing big. I've just noticed that they seem to have been more at odds lately, but all married couples go through bumpy times. It'll blow over."

Robin didn't like the sound of that. Now she was more concerned than ever.

"Let's get this finished. Afterward, I'll take you for an early dinner."

"Just you and me?"

"Just you and me. Gia is working the church fundraiser and Shelley is watching Faith at the Moonglow Inn."

"Can we swing by the bank before?"

"Sure."

"And afterward, pop in to see Anna?"

"She's fine, Mom," he said in a measured tone.

Robin pressed her palms together. "Please?"

Mike let out a sound that was part sigh, part chuckle. "Okay, but don't blame me if Anna slices you like a Ginsu. She hates it when you hold her feet to the fire."

"Anna won't go off on me," Robin said confidently. "I'm her mother."

But deep inside she felt a stiff scrabble of fear. There had been something different in her daughter's voice that morning, a note she'd never heard before.

An ominous note that worried her more than a severe storm warning.

CHAPTER SEVEN

Anna

Getting to Know You

A nna barely slept.

Thinking of her twin, she kept drifting in and out of slumber, and eventually found herself getting up to scour the internet in the middle of the night for any mention of Amelia.

It took almost an hour, but at last, buried several pages deep into a search engine, she came across a short article about her sister's first cello solo with the Chicago Symphony.

This was a big deal. Big enough to warrant a Wiki biography page. But Amelia didn't have one. In fact, Anna couldn't find anything else about Amelia.

Why not?

"You sound like Kevin," she muttered when, bleary eyed at three A.M., she poured herself a cup of coffee and called Darla to tell her that she needed to take a few days off and to contact the college coed who worked part-time to see if she could help out at the bakery.

As did most bakers, Darla got up in the wee hours of the morning to bake for the six A.M. breakfast crowd. Anna did the same on Mondays, Darla's day off. The bakery was closed on Sundays.

Darla could tell something was up, but her friend didn't push for explanation. "On it. Let me know if you need anything."

Anna hung up, stared at her reflection in the kitchen window-pane, and muttered, "I have a twin sister."

Turning her back on her reflection, she closed her eyes and took a sip of coffee. She tried to be in the moment, savor the hit of caffeine, but she simply couldn't concentrate. She had to fig-ure out when and how she would break the news about Amelia to her mother and brother. They still dwelled blithely in the land of "before."

This was so hard. She had no idea how to start, but she was grateful that Kevin was out of town.

Yesterday, right at five, she'd taken the bake sale cupcakes to the church and her sister-in-law, Gia, had told her that Mike and Robin had dropped by the house to see her.

Thankfully, she'd been picking up the kids and missed their visit, but she couldn't keep dodging her family.

She had a plan for introducing them to Amelia, but first, she needed to get to know her sister better.

Picking up her phone, she yawned and then texted her mom. I'll B out of pocket for 2 days. Dinner party on Sat! Bring Mike and fam. 6 p.m. See U then.

After that, she texted her brother, Mike, and Kevin's mother, Veronica, a similar message, switched off her phone, and tossed it back on the table

With a fretful heart, she slipped into her son's room, curled up in the race car bed with her drowsy boy, and took a short nap.

* * *

AT EIGHT A.M. on Wednesday, June 2, Anna showed up at the Moonglow Inn with her kids in tow. She hesitated in the minivan, wondering if it was too early for Amelia to be up and about. She tended to forget everyone didn't wake up as early as she did.

You're here. Just do it.

She hustled the kids from the vehicle. Allie had her face buried in her phone screen, while sleepy Logan yawned and clung to her hand. She probably should have left them with a sitter, but the kids were a solid buttress against her footloose emotions, and she needed them with her.

As if they were on some cosmic timetable, Anna stepped into the foyer, just as Amelia descended the stairs.

That same jolt of recognition slammed through her at the sight of her twin, almost as impactful as it had been the previous day.

Amelia stopped halfway down the stairs and met her gaze.

Anna's heart and hopes jumped into her throat in one tightly packed knot.

Her sister stunned in form-fitting beige capri pants, a black top with a Peter Pan collar and three-quarter-length sleeves, gold Grecian sandals, and a French pedicure. Anna would look like a blimp in that outfit, but her twin appeared daisy fresh, and eye-catchingly gorgeous.

Anna stared down at her cutoff blue jeans, faded green tank top that had seen better days, ten-year-old Birkenstocks, and unpolished toenails. What had she been thinking when she'd gotten dressed?

Rhetorical question. She hadn't been thinking about clothes at all.

Their gazes fused.

A curtain of breathless dizziness fell over Anna. How did you go about reconciling that you had a long-lost identical twin? She had no idea.

When people saw them together, heads would swivel, and someone was bound to mention the sighting to her mother. Gossip spread like wildfire in Moonglow Cove.

Uh-oh. Things were quickly spiraling out of her control.

Hmm. It looked like she might not be able to wait until that dinner party to break the news about Amelia to her family.

"Morning," Anna said, putting as much cheer into her voice as she could scoop up.

"Good morning." That was it. Simple. Direct. A bit distant.

No worries. She got it. She truly did.

Anna crooked a finger at Amelia and inclined her head toward the beach. Without another word, she took both her kids' hands and walked out the front door, still struggling to catch her breath.

"Mom?" Allie asked. "Are you okay?"

Wham! Her daughter was too perceptive. Bringing the kids along wasn't such a hot idea after all.

"I want you and your brother to stay at the bakery with Darla," she said, letting go of her daughter's hand long enough to text her friend and ask if she could keep an eye on the kids for a few minutes.

Darla: Send 'em on.

Anna: Cookies, coloring books, and chocolate milk should keep them busy.

Darla: No sweat.

Anna hustled them across the street to the bakery and rushed back to the inn just as Amelia came out on the front porch, the screen door creaking closed behind her. She stood quiet, self-contained, watching Anna with a cautious gaze.

"May I have a hug?" Anna asked. "I *really* need a hug."

Amelia looked awkward and Anna got the impression she didn't get too many hugs.

Or want them.

Amelia moistened her lips, and finally gave a brief nod.

Touched, Anna gathered her sister to her chest and squeezed her hard. Stiff-armed, Amelia patted Anna on the back and pulled away.

Heavens, but they had a lot of work to do in order to bridge this gap and truly become sisters. Maybe they would never get there. That strummed a chord of sadness inside her.

She heard her brother Mike's steady voice in her head. *Give it time. You tend to rush intimacy, sis.*

"I have a younger brother," Anna said.

"Mike." Amelia nodded. "I looked you up on social media. You have pictures of your brother and his wife, Gia, and their adorable little girl, Faith."

"You looked me up?" Anna said, feeling both flattered and a little put off by the invasion of privacy.

Amelia had been spying on her, but was it really spying when she plastered her life all over social media for anyone and everyone to see?

Kevin was right. She *was* too open and trusting. And anyway, she reminded herself, she'd been doing some social media sleuthing herself. Except she'd found precious little, while Amelia had struck gold.

"I needed to know what I was walking into." Amelia paused, then added, "Turns out it was a fairy tale and I'm the big bad witch."

"Hush! Don't say that. Why would you say that?"

"It all seemed simple on the surface. Introduce myself. Get to know you and your family, but it's not that easy, is it?"

"Nothing worthwhile ever is."

Who in Amelia's life was affected by this? Anna knew next to nothing about the woman who'd upended her world, but she wanted to know everything. Every last detail.

It would take a while to catch up on the thirty-five years they'd spent apart, but she couldn't wait to get started, even with Kevin's dire warning to be careful.

You love too hard, too soon, Kevin once said to her when she'd had a falling-out with a new friend. She'd been shattered over the woman's betrayal. *Your heart is too big, Anna. You want to hold the whole world in one of your huge hugs. Not everyone warrants your love, Bean. Remember that.*

From his point of view, it had been logical advice, but Anna had wondered, Why not? Why couldn't she love everyone? Didn't even villains deserve love? Maybe they deserved it most of all. Wasn't the lack of love what had turned them villainous in the first place? And by withholding love from someone who'd hurt her, wasn't she in turn behaving just as badly as the person who'd doled out the pain?

Everyone deserved a second chance, right?

She'd actually taken that question to her pastor, thinking he'd be on her side, love thy neighbor and all that, but he'd quoted some Bible passage on discernment and mumbled something about casting pearls before swine.

Anna came away feeling disappointed and discouraged, but unable to stop following her heart, despite the dings she'd taken for being too open.

Her twin yawned twice. Amelia brought a palm to her mouth to hide it and yawned a third time.

Anna laughed. "You're not a morning person, are you?"

"How did you know?"

"Professional musicians tend to be night owls. At least the ones I've known."

"True. Musicians mostly work at night. Staying up late becomes a habit. When I was a little girl, I used to love getting up early and wandering the house before anyone else was awake. Now? I normally sleep in until nine."

"Oh, I'm sorry I came over so early."

"It's not your fault that my room faces east and the curtains aren't light blocking."

Anna flashed her thumb toward the Gulf. "Are you game for a walk on the beach?"

Amelia nodded.

They strolled side by side to the beach and didn't speak until they reached the water. There, Anna turned to her and said, "Thank you for being brave enough to come to Moonglow Cove."

"Don't thank me. I've done nothing to deserve your gratitude."

"Let me rephrase. I'm so thrilled that you came looking for me."

A pinched expression came over Amelia's face, and Anna had the strangest feeling her twin was hiding something.

The rising tide washed foam and seaweed over the sand. Ahead of them on the beach children slung bread at seagulls that flocked and squawked. Even farther down the stretch of sand another group of children flew colorful kites.

"I had to tell the lady who runs the B and B who I was," Amelia said.

"Shelley," Anna supplied. "Shelley is my sister-in-law Gia's older sister. She's supercool. I adore her."

"Yes, she told me about her relationship to you. The second she saw me she knew something was up. I had no idea about small towns where everyone knows everyone. I asked her not to tell anyone about us since you haven't told your family." Amelia paused. "Or have you?"

Anna shook her head. "I invited my mom and my brother and his family over for dinner on Saturday evening, along with

Kevin's parents. I thought we could tell them together. In person. Hopefully, Shelley won't spill the beans to Gia. But you never know. I'll talk to her when we get back."

"And what about your husband?" Amelia asked.

Anna bent to pick up a small perfect shell and slip it into her pocket. Allie enjoyed making seashell art.

"He won't be home until Saturday." Anna took a deep breath. "And he put a moratorium on contacting each other."

Amelia canted her head and narrowed her eyes. "What does that mean?"

"No calls or text or emails between us while he's gone. Unless it's an emergency." Anna crinkled her nose. "We had a fight."

"Over me?"

"Not only that." Anna exhaled loudly. "We just need space from each other."

Amelia pressed her palms together in front of her heart. "I'm so sorry for causing problems in your marriage. That was never my intention."

"I know." Anna rubbed her upper arms. "This runs deeper than you. We've been arguing more lately because he keeps spending money on frivolous things. I think Kevin is having some kind of midlife crisis."

That explanation was how she placated herself. It sounded better than *we're growing apart.* The conversation lagged as they walked to the water's edge.

After a bit, Amelia said, "I grew up with the view of Lake Michigan from the window of my parents' penthouse condo."

"No kidding." Anna pointed at the Craftsman-style bungalow

next to the Moonglow Inn. "I grew up right there. The house was once caretaker quarters for the town founders, the Chapmans. They owned the house that's now the Moonglow Inn. After World War II, the family sold off the bungalow along with half an acre of beachfront property. My dad bought it in 1981. My brother, Mike, lives there now."

"What happened to your dad?"

"He was a firefighter and in 2001 spent time at Ground Zero as a volunteer. He ended up with a chronic lung infection. A few years back my folks moved to Arizona for his health and they sold the house to my brother, Mike." Anna gulped. "We lost Dad last year to coronavirus."

"I'm so sorry for your loss." Amelia's delivery was matter-of-fact, obligatory.

Anna forced a smile. Talking about her father was still a tender topic. "It was a tough time, but you know what? Our family really got closer during it. There's always a silver lining if you look for one."

"It's a beautiful morning," Amelia said, cutting off that conversational thread.

She lifted her arms in the air, opening wide in a sun salutation backbend. As she stretched, her capri pants rose with her movements, the hem of her pants riding up on her calves, revealing numerous, deep, faded scars crisscrossing the backs of both legs.

Anna gasped. She'd been doing that a lot over the past twenty-four hours. "What happened?"

"Pardon?" Amelia blinked and dropped her arms. The pants hem slid back down to cover the scars.

"Your calves! They're mauled!"

Amelia waved a hand as if the disfiguring wounds were nothing. "Oh, that."

"What happened?" Anna blurted, then slapped a palm over her mouth. "That was rude. You don't have to answer."

"I don't mind talking about it. I was attacked by a dog in the park when I was seven." Matter-of-factly, Amelia shrugged.

"Omigosh! How horrific! You must be terrified of dogs now. Did you have PTSD?"

Again, the casual shrug.

"And yet, you saved Cujo yesterday. That took guts." Dang, she admired Amelia's bravery even more now.

"I had little choice. Your dog was going to die if I didn't do something."

"But to face your fears, after an attack like the one you suffered?" Anna stared at Amelia's calves. "That took true courage. Then Allie yelled at you because she thought you'd hurt Cujo. I'm so sorry for her behavior."

"I get it."

"What did your parents do when the dog attacked you?" Anna asked.

Amelia was so adept at schooling her features, she didn't show any emotion. "My parents weren't there when it happened."

"Who was with you?"

"No one."

Huh? Anna couldn't imagine letting Allie go to the park alone at ten, much less seven. "You were at the park all alone?"

"My parents . . ." She paused, locked gazes with Anna. "*Our* parents believed in what they now call free-range parenting."

Anna put a palm to her chest. She couldn't picture Amelia's parents as hers. "Meaning?"

"They were pretty hands-off in the child-rearing department."

"Tell me about them," Anna encouraged, plopping down on the sand.

Amelia glanced down.

Anna patted the spot next to her. "Sit."

Looking uncomfortable, Amelia crossed her ankles and slowly sank to the ground. She brought her knees to her chest and hugged them, while Anna stuck her legs out straight, planted her palms in the sand behind her, and leaned back to eye her sister.

"Talk." It dawned on her how bossy she must sound and she modified, "Please."

CHAPTER EIGHT

Anna

What Might Have Been

A minute passed.

It was all Anna could do not to rush to fill the silence. Instead, she kicked off her Birkenstocks and dug her toes in the sand.

After several quiet moments, Amelia swept a hand at the water. "I didn't have the kind of peaceful life you have here. I grew up in a Chicago penthouse condo so big that I could go a whole day without seeing my parents."

It should have been my life, too, Anna thought. It would have been if fate hadn't intervened.

Anna crashed her gaze into Amelia's. The reality of who she might have been was starting to sink in. She could have lived a glamorous, wealthy urban lifestyle with her twin sister. A concept she couldn't wrap her head around.

"What were they like?" Anna asked, then added tentatively, "*Our* parents."

Amelia drew her cell phone from her pocket, turned it on, flipped through photos, found what she was looking for, and passed the latest-model iPhone to Anna.

It was professional studio photograph. The middle-aged couple in the picture were impeccably posed and presented in an image of self-satisfied affluence.

The man, Anna's *real* father, stared at the camera with a hooded, brooding gaze and not even a ghost of a smile. His hair was chestnut, his brown eyes the same shade as Anna's and her twin's. He sported a thick Tom Selleck mustache and a dimple in his chin just like Anna and Amelia.

Now she knew where that dimple came from too. A shiver passed through her. Biologically, this man *was* her father.

He wore a tailored gray, pin-striped suit and a crisp white shirt with a mildly patterned steel-colored tie. A tie tack of his initials in Courier font, FB, anchored his tie to his shirt. He seemed slick, professional, curated. A powerful professional.

"His name was Frank," Amelia said.

Beside Frank sat a woman who looked so much like Anna and Amelia that all the air left Anna's lungs.

This then was her real mother.

A cold chill chased over her and she shivered hard.

"And what was *her* name?" Anna whispered, running a finger over the screen, tracing the curve of the woman's soft salmon-colored curls.

"Sarah," Amelia said. "Sarah Mae O'Leary before she married Frank. She gave me the same middle name. Your middle name was to have been Fae. Amelia Mae and Anna Fae. What middle name did your parents give you?"

"Caroline."

"That's pretty."

It was a dead girl's name.

Anna pulled her bottom lip up between her teeth, used her fingers to enlarge the photograph, homing in on Sarah's face, and cutting Frank out of the picture. Sarah's eyes were narrower, her chin small, her eyebrows perfectly groomed, and her cheekbones high. "She looks . . ."

"Dramatic?" There was an odd tone to Amelia's voice that drew Anna's gaze to her sister's face again.

"I was going to say 'fascinating.'" Anna tucked a strand of hair behind one ear.

"Sarah could be a bit . . ." Amelia paused, clearly measuring her words. "Self-absorbed. She could easily get lost in a project and forget I was there, and Frank was a workaholic."

"I see." Anna got the feeling it hadn't been a happy marriage. "What did Frank do for a living?"

"He was in corporate law."

"And Sarah was a stay-at-home mom?" Anna asked.

"No way. She was an interior designer and we had a showcase house to prove it. She said she'd rather die than stay home alone with me."

A shudder passed through Anna. "I work outside the home, too, but that's a cruel thing to say to a child."

"Sarah wasn't well suited to motherhood." Amelia pressed her lips together so tightly, her mouth disappeared. "It wasn't her fault. It's just the way she was."

"I don't know what to say." Anna rubbed her kneecap. "Your life sounds like something from a movie."

Amelia started to nibble her thumbnail but stopped. "Don't romanticize the poor little rich girl."

Had she been doing that?

"I wished I'd been switched instead of you," Amelia blurted, looked horrified, and slapped a palm over her mouth.

Anna had a feeling Amelia was rarely this straightforward and she actually appreciated the honesty, but she didn't even know her twin.

"I'm sorry," Amelia said. "That was unforgivable."

Anna stared at her sister, unsure how to respond. Twenty-four hours ago, her world had been pretty darn perfect, even though she might not have appreciated it at the time. Now, everything she'd believed to be true was all a bizarre lie.

"Don't apologize for how you feel," Anna said.

"It's stupid. There's no point yearning for a different childhood. It turned out the way it turned out." Her tone was philosophical, telling Anna that, for the most part, Amelia had worked through her past.

Respect and admiration for her twin's resilience touched her. Anna ached to dig into that past, and maybe she would have kept prying, but her sister stood abruptly.

Anna scrambled to her feet, still holding Amelia's phone.

It rang and Anna startled.

Not from the call, which the caller ID identified as "telemarketer," but from the ringtone. It was "Let It Go" from *Frozen*.

"We have the same ringtone!" Anna marveled, passing the phone to her sister, who looked at the screen and switched it off. "One more odd thing we have in common."

"Let's keep walking." Amelia took off down the beach, trotting as if trying to outrun something or someone.

Anna scurried after her, feeling like she'd done something wrong.

For a bit, they ambled aimlessly.

Idly, Anna noticed they walked in lockstep and it was such a weird sensation that their steps matched, she purposely lagged, throwing them out of sync.

"We both grew up around water," Amelia mused. "I know my way around a boat. I'm a strong swimmer and a decent sailor, but there's a difference between a lake and the ocean."

"What's that?" Anna asked. She hadn't spent much time exploring the world. She'd married young and while she loved her life, she couldn't help wondering if she'd missed out by staying so insular.

Her twin sister paused and turned her face into the wind. "There's something ancient and primal about the ocean. Something mysterious about the relentless ebb and rise of tide and the heavy brush of salty sea spray."

Ahh, Amelia had a lyrical bent. But of course, she was a professional musician and a creative. Anna liked to think she was a creative, too, but with baked goods instead of music. While she loved playing the guitar and being in her band from high school, it was absolutely just for fun.

When she got right down to it, her real passion was people. She loved making others happy. Whether the form took baking, playing music, or gardening, most of her hobbies and interests centered around relationships.

Most?

Okay, all.

Anna joined her sister as she gazed out at the Gulf and felt the wind ruffling through her hair. Hope fluttered inside her, and rose shakily, longing to soar with the kites sailing the sky. One persistent, worrisome question took root in her mind.

What if, what if, what if?

What if she and Amelia could be sisters for real? What if Amelia moved to Moonglow Cove? What if this turned out to be one of the best relationships of her life?

She'd harbored fantasies of it all night. Picturing them shopping together, taking the kids to the park, throwing backyard barbecues. She dreamed of styling each other's hair and giving mani-pedis and taking quilting lessons together.

Silly stuff, really. Sweetly mundane, ubiquitous sister activities. Sadness filled her as she yearned for all they'd missed by not being raised together.

But one look at Amelia, so sleek and self-contained, killed those fantasies. *Dream on.* Amelia didn't seem like the domestic type who appreciated the simpler things in life.

Feeling anxious, Anna fingered the delicate keepsake bracelet at her wrist, caressing the tiny smooth pearls and small sharp diamonds as if they were prayer beads. She'd taken the bracelet out of her jewelry box that morning and put it on before coming over.

Amelia tracked her movements. "You found your keepsake bracelet."

"I did."

Amelia turned her own bracelet on her wrist so that the medallion faced up. They lined their hands up at the wrist, side by side. Identical except for the names.

"Together again," Anna whispered.

"Together at last."

"This is our proof."

"Never mind that we look exactly alike." Amelia's laugh was light, but genuine.

And then suddenly it was as if a dam had broken and they started talking at once. The matching keepsake bracelets, it seemed, had given them permission to relate as sisters.

"I love your haircut by the way," Anna said. "So cute."

"An impromptu change."

"You did it because you were coming to see me?"

"Yes." Her smile was full of wisdom and left Anna feeling as if she'd missed out on an insider joke. "My hair used to be as long as yours."

"Now I'll know what I would look like if I got a pixie." Anna touched her hair and imagined whacking it short. Kevin would flip. He loved her hair. "I wonder what else we have in common."

"Through 23andMe, I learned that I am an ultraprocessor of caffeine," Amelia said. "How about you?"

"Me too! I can drink a pot of coffee at ten P.M. and still sleep like a baby." Well, normally anyway. Last night had been an exception. "It drives Kevin berserk. He can't touch a drop of caffeine after noon or he's up all night."

"I'm allergic to penicillin. I found out when I got stitched up for this." Amelia plucked the material of her pants leg and lifted one calf to give Anna a closer look at her scars.

"Get out! I discovered I was allergic to penicillin when I had strep throat."

"I had strep throat, too. When did you have it?"

"Nine."

"No way! In the summer?"

"Yes. June."

They stared at each other and simultaneously said, "Wow!"

"I'm sixty percent Irish," Amelia said. "I assume you are too?"

"Yes, with twenty percent Italian thrown into the mix," Anna said. "I was confused about that at the time, because I've done genealogy on my dad's side and they were all Ellis Island Germans who came to America at the turn of the twentieth century. And while Mom's family went back to the original Virginia colony, they were from England, mostly."

"And now we know that's not your heritage at all."

Whoa. It struck Anna then just how much of her life had been a lie.

Basically, all of it.

"You know," she said. "This whole thing is wildly absurd. Me being switched with a dead baby. Us getting separated."

"Surreal."

"It's like a story you'd see on *Dateline* or *20/20*." Anna reached down to pick up a rock and skip it over the ocean waves. "It's going to get a little crazy when people in Moonglow Cove find out about us."

"Maybe we should tell your family sooner rather than later?"

Anna screwed up her face. "I had this perfect plan . . ."

"About the dinner party?"

Anna nodded. "I had this notion of how I wanted it to go. At my house. On home turf. You stay stashed in the guest bedroom until everyone gets there. I sit them down, tell them what happened. You walk into the room. We make civilized introductions and have a nice dinner. I'll cook my specialty. Chicken marsala with homemade garlic toast and a big fresh salad."

"Chicken marsala is my absolute favorite dish in the whole world."

"Mine too."

Their gazes welded again, and Anna felt an instant bond so strong it scared her. The other two times in her life she'd felt anything this monumental, she'd been looking down into her children's newborn faces.

"You've given it a lot of thought." Amelia folded her arms.

"All night."

Her sister shook her head. "I've upended your life."

"Not your fault."

"I shouldn't have come," Amelia said, seemingly more to herself than to Anna.

"No," Anna scolded gently and reached for Amelia's hand. "Don't say that. Never say that. I'm glad you're here. You are wanted. *Always.*"

The look her twin gave her jerked Anna's heartstrings like a rip cord. The vulnerable, hopeful expression in her eyes said, *Really?*

Up ahead one of the kites dove on a sudden wild current and smacked hard into the ground. *Thunk.*

Anna felt the impact in her gut. She put a hand to her stomach, startled.

There was a commotion on the beach; a mature, full-figured woman in a skirted swimsuit ran toward them, waving her arms.

"Help! Help! I can't find the lifeguard and there's an elderly lady floundering in the water! I can't swim! I don't have my phone! Please, someone, call 911!"

Immediately, Anna rushed to the distraught woman, and took her by the shoulders. "Slow down. Take a deep breath."

The woman tried but failed as anxiety shook her from head to toe. "She . . . she . . ."

"Tell me what lady you're talking about and where she's at," Anna said.

"I-I-" The woman gestured helplessly toward the waves. "She was wearing a nightgown and socks but no shoes. She looked demented. At first my girls thought she was a ghost."

Winnie!

The thought exploded in Anna's brain. Myra Marts had never called her back and in the craziness of yesterday, she'd forgotten to check in with the director of the memory care facility. She turned to tell Amelia about Winnie, but Amelia wasn't there.

While Anna had been trying to calm the excited woman and get the full story, Amelia simply acted.

Without hesitating, her twin kicked off her sandals and went running into the ocean toward a lone figure bobbing so far out on the waves that Anna could barely make the figure out.

In the dizzying love of a mad insta-crush, she thought, *My shero.*

Her twin dove underwater at the same moment a large waved crashed, tossing Amelia savagely about. As the strong current yanked her sister from Anna's sight, her crazily pounding heart jolted to a standstill.

CHAPTER NINE

Amelia

The Rescue

The wave smacked hard into Amelia, sending her tumbling and spinning underneath the water, and knocking her breathless.

Doggedly she shook off the stun, drawing on the inner strength that had gotten her through a lonely childhood. An inner strength that had gifted her with the capacity to turn off worrisome emotions and do what was necessary.

Ignoring her seizing chest, Amelia swam.

Her body might be weakened from end-stage renal disease, but she was mentally tough, and she swam daily, albeit at a much lessened pace and length than before her illness.

Privileged kid that she'd been, she'd learned to swim in her parents' penthouse swimming pool when her mother had thrown her into the deep end at age three. The sudden terror of being airborne before her head went under was her earliest, and most vivid, childhood memory.

She'd done it, though. She'd swum. She'd survived. And

she'd been swimming ever since, even though sometimes the waters were very deep indeed.

Salt water filled her mouth, her eyes, and her ears, but Amelia pursued her mission with the same determination that earned her a seat on the Chicago Symphony. Compartmentalizing, she felt nothing beyond this single mission: rescue the drowning woman.

Kicking through the surf, she battled the incoming current as it coyly shoved her back toward the shoreline. She thought she heard Anna calling her name, but it didn't really register. She peered through blurry eyes at the solitary figure bobbing on the waves fifty yards ahead of her. Thankfully, still afloat.

Good. She was in time.

In her head, she hummed Pachelbel's Canon in D, the song that never failed to soothe her, and kept moving. By the time she reached the elderly woman, every muscle in her body quivered. Exhaustion, heavy as the water itself, pulled at them both.

The woman fought.

Frantically, she tried to grasp Amelia's short hair. Amelia ducked and slipped her arms around her. The woman locked her hands and dropped her arms around Amelia like a noose. Amelia's head went under several times and her legs, which were the strongest part of her, felt shockingly worn out.

She had to calm the woman, or they were both going to drown. She didn't dare look around to see how far away the shore was, terrified that if she knew the distance, she'd lose the will to get back.

You've got this, she lied to herself, something she'd grown very adept at over the years.

"Help!" the woman gurgled. "Help!"

That's what I'm trying to do, she thought but couldn't say because speaking used up too much energy. Amelia bobbed beside the elderly woman, spitting water from her mouth, and shaking it from her eyes.

"Easy," she whispered, shocked at how soft her voice sounded. "I've got you. It's going to be okay."

Terrific. Now she was lying to the woman, too.

The older woman mewled like a kitten as a fresh wave battered her frail body.

Amelia positioned herself on her back and secured her arms around the woman's armpits. The woman, also on her back, floated above Amelia as she towed her toward the shore. After a few seconds, she stopped struggling and went limp. Amelia couldn't tell if she'd lost consciousness or not.

Someone met her halfway, slogging through the water, arms reaching out to take the woman from her.

Amelia turned her head and saw that it was her twin. Their eyes met and they shared a bond, a momentary link looping them together. Stone-cold respect for her reflected in Anna's eyes.

That look gave Amelia a shot of raw adrenaline and she helped drag the elderly woman to the shore.

"You can let go now," Anna said gently. "I've got her."

Relief spread through Amelia's achy limbs, and she relinquished the woman to her sister. Someone else came sprinting into the shallow surf. It was the lifeguard, a bit late to the party. The three of them carried the woman to the sand.

Anna and the lifeguard took the woman's arms, Amelia went for her feet. Amelia stumbled over her own feet, dropping to her knees as Anna and the lifeguard stretched the woman out on the ground.

"Winnie!" Anna cried and clasped the woman's hand. "Speak to me."

Apparently, her sister knew the woman whose eyes were shuttered, but thankfully Winnie was breathing.

"I'll get my first aid bag," the lifeguard offered and sprinted off.

People gathered around them, murmuring with concern. Someone draped a beach towel over Winnie in her thin, soaking wet nightgown printed with blue posies.

Amelia crawled to the spot in the sand at Winnie's right that the lifeguard had just vacated.

"Winnie?" Anna lightly patted the woman's cheeks. "Please, speak to me."

The woman moaned but didn't open her eyes. Her face was the color of ashes and her lips were tinged blue.

Anna gripped the woman's hand. "It's me, Anna. I'm here and I love you."

Winnie's eyes fluttered open, she turned her head. "Anna?"

"Yes." Anna glanced at Amelia with tears in her eyes. "You saved her."

Ahh, there it was again. That tingly boost Anna's admiration stirred inside Amelia.

She only admires you because she doesn't know you, hissed the voice in her head that sounded exactly like Sarah Brandt. *You sure have her fooled. Good on you.*

Sidestepping that thought, Amelia said, "Who is she?"

"This is Winnie Newton," Anna explained. "She's the midwife who was there when we were born."

Well, that seemed pretty coincidental. Amelia was not the kind of person who looked for "signs," but if she was, she'd call this one a big red sign, like the kind that pointed you to the theater exits.

Winnie looked from Anna to Amelia and stared wide-eyed. "Amelia?"

How did she know her name? Ahh, she had raised her hand to wipe wet hair from her forehead and the bracelet medallion with her name on it was facing the woman.

"Yes," Anna repeated. "This is Amelia."

"Twins!" Winnie clapped her hands so lightly it made no sound. "Together again."

"Together again," Anna echoed.

Winnie raised trembling arms to reach up and cup both their cheeks in her palms. "Together again."

"We found our way back to each other," Amelia said.

"Finally." Winnie breathed and let her hands drop. "Together again."

After you separated us, Amelia thought and met Anna's gaze. They stared at each other, sharing that special twin connection, reading each other's minds.

"She did it," Amelia said to Anna. "She really did it, didn't she?"

Her sister nodded.

But why? And how? Those were the questions.

Winnie clasped her hands together in a beseeching prayer and raised them toward Amelia. "Please forgive me."

"There's nothing to forgive," Amelia murmured. Holding a grudge served no purpose.

"Forgive me," Winnie begged.

"You've done nothing to me."

"Please, please, please forgive me." The woman's eyes rolled back in her head until all Amelia could see were the whites of her eyes and she began a low keening unlike anything she'd ever heard.

Torn apart by Winnie's emotional suffering, Amelia did something she would never have ordinarily done. She leaned over and embraced the older woman. "It's okay, it's all right. Shh, shh."

Winnie encircled her arms around her neck, buried her head against Amelia's chest, and in a frantic, mangled chant wailed. "*Forgimmeforgimmeforgimme.*"

Awkwardly, Amelia patted the woman's back. "I forgive you."

Winnie raised her head with so much relief in her eyes.

"I need to get in here." The lifeguard was back, nudging Amelia out of the way so he could strap a blood pressure cuff around Winnie's thin arm.

"What happened?" Anna asked Winnie. "Why did you go into the ocean?"

Winnie gave them a Cheshire cat grin and said nonsensically, "'Tis in my memory lock'd, and you yourself shall keep the key of it.'"

Wait. Amelia recognized the passage. The woman's strange mutterings were an Ophelia quote from *Hamlet*? Did the quote hold some deeper meaning for the midwife? What was she trying to say?

Anna got up to come around and wrap a beach towel around Amelia's shoulders. She didn't know where her sister had gotten it, but assumed the towel belonged to a bystander.

"Are you okay?" Anna asked.

A good-size crowd surrounded them now and for the first time since coming ashore, Amelia snapped fully back into her body. She heard sounds more acutely. Seagulls. The wind. Curious conversations rising like the tide as it floated around them.

Anna has a sister.

Twins.

Identical twins.

Who? What? When? Where? Why? How?

Good questions. Questions Amelia had been asking ever since she'd learned that Anna had lived.

Beach patrol showed up, along with EMTs and paramedics. Anna gave them a rundown of Winnie's medical history, but the medical personnel seemed to know all about her. They loaded Winnie into the back of an ambulance and carted her off to Moonglow Cove Memorial Hospital.

Leaving Amelia alone with her sister and the gawking bystanders.

"C'mon," Anna said, wrapping her arm around Amelia's shoulders. "She's safe and we should let them do their job. Let's go find some dry clothes."

* * *

AT THE MOONGLOW Inn, Amelia changed and quickly blew her hair dry. She would have offered Anna some of her clothes, but her twin wore a size eight whereas Amelia was a size two.

Shelley, one of the inn owners, gave Anna a floral cotton maxi dress from the gift shop.

Within a quarter of an hour, Anna and Amelia had regrouped. Anna had asked Darla to keep Logan and Allie at the bakery for a little while longer, and the sisters were in Anna's minivan, headed toward Moonglow Cove Memory Care Center to get the things Winnie needed for a hospital stay.

"You're incredible under pressure," Anna chattered. "Just amazing. So calm and controlled. I'm envious of your ability to hold it together."

Amelia had noticed Anna had a tendency to talk too much when she was anxious.

"Not always," Amelia murmured. Under certain kinds of stress, she did thrive, but other times she was an epic failure, like when she'd lost Robert and her parents in one swoop.

She reminded herself that even the strongest person would collapse under that grief, which brought her to the reason she was here in the first place. She needed a kidney. But now was not the time for *that* conversation.

"I want to be clear about something," Anna said.

Fear tickled Amelia under the chin. Had Anna somehow figured out why she was here? Twin telepathy?

"What's that?" Amelia asked evenly, although her pulse was quick and thready.

"After we're done with all this, we're checking you out of the Moonglow Inn and you're coming to stay in my guest room. End of discussion."

Amelia opened her mouth to speak.

Anna cut her off. "No argument. It's time we got to know each other in earnest and the best way to do that is by spending time together."

"But your husband . . ."

"You let me handle Kevin. He's not home right now anyway."

"Your moth—"

"Really, I'm not listening. I need you there."

"Why?"

"This incident with Winnie escalated my timetable. For one thing, this is a small town and we're about to be the main source of gossip. Too many people know about us. Word is bound to get back to my mother within the next hour if I don't beat the gossips to the punch. The conversation with my family might not look how I imagined it going in my head, but we've got to tell her sooner rather than later. Like after we get Winnie's things and take them to the hospital."

"All right." Amelia agreed.

"Good! I'm so glad." Anna reached across the seat to touch

Amelia's hand briefly. To reassure her? "I can't tell you how thrilled I am you're here."

"I don't suppose that we'll ever know for sure what exactly happened that night we were born since Winnie has dementia," Amelia mused.

"Probably not."

"Unless your mother knows something."

"She doesn't." Anna's voice was adamant, and her grip tightened on the steering wheel.

Anna's thick auburn hair was damp from the ocean, and she'd plaited it into a single side braid at the Moonglow Inn. She'd slipped on oversized, cheap sunglasses and the diamonds in her bracelet caught the sunlight, casting little prisms around the car.

"We haven't had a chance to talk privately and we've got so much to learn about each other," Anna said. "I can't wait to find out everything about you."

You say that now.

"Here we are." Anna turned into the parking lot of the memory care facility.

When they walked in through the front door, their twinness immediately drew attention from the people in the common area. Heads turned from the TV tuned to an old black-and-white western and focused squarely on them.

Sunlight spooned down the pale blue walls, illuminating the blank stares of the memory impaired. The air smelled of Lysol and old age. Unlike the chaotic minds of the residents, their surroundings were serene, peaceful. Someone had taken great care with the environment: a gurgling wall fountain, a large saltwater fish aquarium, and several vases of flowers, which were probably plastic but looked real, placed around the room.

Anna greeted the residents, some who seemed to recognize her, others who did not. "Is Myra in her office, Trudy?" she asked the young woman at the reception desk who was barely past girlhood.

"I think she's with a patient down Corridor Two." Trudy flopped a strand of hair, dyed goth black, over her shoulder. She waved at the PA system. "Want me to page her?"

"Just text her. Tell her we'll be in Winnie's room collecting her things for a hospital stay," Anna said. "Myra can meet us there."

"Gotcha." Trudy pulled her phone from her pocket.

Feeling out of place, Amelia followed her sister down the long corridor filled with rooms housing more patients, many of whom were bedridden, she noticed from quick glances through open doors.

The farther they went, the deeper Amelia's feeling of inexplicable dread. Amelia couldn't say what she was afraid of, but it felt as if each step they took away from the bright, cheerful lobby, the closer they were to being pulled into a maelstrom.

Amelia lagged, fighting against the oppressive feelings overwhelming her.

Anna slowed, waiting for her to catch up. "Are you okay?"

Amelia nodded.

"I want you to know one thing," Anna said.

"Oh?"

"No matter what happens, you and I are in this together."

It was such a kind thing to say. Anna was such an open book. A welcoming person willing to trust Amelia and take her at face value. Guilt was a spider, crawling down the back of Amelia's neck. She needed to tell Anna why she was really here and soon.

"Anna . . ."

"Here we are." Anna gave her one of her cosmic smiles and pushed open the door to the last room on the left. Her sister started inside but halted in the doorway.

Amelia almost ran smack-dab into her twin, stopping just in the nick of time. She whipped her head around to see what had stalled Anna.

There was a stylishly dressed older woman rummaging through Winnie's dresser drawer with her back to them. Leafing through the closet was a handsome, thirtysomething man dressed in jeans and a simple black T-shirt that showed off his muscular shoulders, buff torso, and tanned skin. He looked as startled to see them as they were to see him.

"Mom! Mike!" Anna exclaimed. "What are you doing here? And why are you searching through Winnie's stuff?"

"Anna, I can explain . . ." The woman lifted her head and turned toward them. In her hand was a picture frame. Her gaze fixed on Amelia, and her eyes widened as her mouth fell open.

Then Robin Straus made a sudden strangled cry and dropped the photograph.

The frame hit the tile floor and shattered, the sound of breaking glass reverberating sharp and brittle in the cramped, airless room.

CHAPTER TEN

Anna

DNA

I'll get something to clean that up," Amelia said calmly, efficiently, and ran away.

Anna didn't blame her twin. She, too, yearned to escape, but her family was teetering on the brink of falling apart and only she could save them.

And the first step on the road to putting her family back together was to discover why her mother and brother were searching through Winnie's things.

Delicate hand, Anna, delicate hand. It was her father's voice inside her head, telling her how to handle Robin.

Her mother's eyes were glazed; her breathing shallow and her skin pale.

"Mom?" Mike asked. "Are you all right?" From where he'd been standing near the closet, Mike picked his way around the broken glass to their mother. Gently, he took her arm. "Let's sit you down before you fall down."

Anna winced. *For shame.* She should have been the one to

reach out to Mom. Normally, she would have hopped right to her mother's side, but today?

Well, truly she was ticked off, the blunt edge of her anger a pointy surprise.

"Mind the glass." Waving at the sharp shards, Anna sucked in her breath through clenched teeth.

Her brother waltzed Robin around the mess and eased her onto the edge of Winnie's full-size bed, covered with a hand-made patchwork quilt.

Robin drew in a shuddering breath.

"Mom?" Anna skirted the foot of the bed and came around to the other side. "Are you all right?"

"It's a memory quilt," her mother murmured, running her fingers over the cloth. "I made it for Winnie along with some of the Quilting Divas, the ones whose babies Winnie delivered. We sewed this as her retirement present. The squares are from our children's baby blankets and clothing."

"You never told me that." Anna's gaze latched on to her mom's face.

Robin studied her with confusion on her face. "Didn't I?"

Anna could see the navy flecks in the blue of her mother's eyes, and the skin folds wrinkling at the corners. "No."

"I'm sure I did." Robin traced a blue square. "This was from Mike's first onesie. And this . . ." She shifted her hand to a pink square near the border. ". . . was from the baby blanket we brought you home from the hospital in."

Why was Robin talking about this blanket instead of Anna's identical twin showing up out of nowhere?

"Mike, do you remember me telling you about the quilt?" Robin asked her brother.

Mike stuck his hands in his front pockets and hunched his shoulders. Classic Mike when he didn't want to get into something. "Um-hmm."

"See? Mike remembers," her mother said as if her brother's hedging was ironclad proof.

Anna let it slide. The quilt didn't matter, and she wouldn't be sidetracked. "Forget the quilt, I want to talk."

Just then, Amelia came back with a broom and dustpan.

No one spoke.

Anna stared at Amelia. Amelia stared at Robin. Robin stared at Amelia. Mike stared at Anna. Amelia stared at Mike. Amelia stared at Anna.

Full circle.

And still, no one uttered a word.

Finally, Anna moved toward her twin, held out her hand for the broom and dustpan. "I'll sweep up."

Silently, Amelia handed the cleaning tools to Anna.

"Let me do it." Mike took the broom.

Did her younger brother realize she was on the verge of falling apart? Did she look that fragile? Or did he just want something to do with his hands?

Probably the latter.

Anna started to protest. She wanted something to do, too, but she decided to let it go. If Mike wanted to sweep, let him sweep. There were bigger fish to fry here than a busted picture frame.

As Mike swept, Anna crept over to pick up the photograph.

She shook the picture over a wastebasket to dislodge glass fragments off the surface.

She stared at a snapshot of Heathcliff Straus and Winnie looking at each other with a conspiratorial expression. The picture was as new to her as the knowledge that Robin had helped sew Winnie's quilt. Where had this photograph come from? She'd never seen it here before and she came to see Winnie every Sunday after church.

From the cars in the background, and the youth of the subjects, the photograph had been taken some time in the early nineteen eighties. Before Anna and Amelia were born. Her father and Winnie stood posed against the railing at Paradise Pier, grinning into the camera in beachgoing clothes, arms thrown around each other as if they were close as mother and son, even back then.

It was a sweet picture.

A poignant picture.

A picture that unsettled Anna in a way she couldn't describe. She plopped down beside her mother on Winnie's bed and extended the photograph toward her.

Robin took it.

"Where did you get this?" Anna asked.

"I found it in the closet." Mike splayed a palm to his nape.

"Who took the picture?"

"I did!" Robin exclaimed and then she tore the photograph right in two.

Anna gasped. "Why did you do that?"

"*She's* ruined everything."

"Is that why you were here snooping through Winnie's things? To tear up a forty-year-old photograph?"

Robin didn't answer.

Anna swung her gaze to her brother. "Mike?"

"Mom asked me to bring her by so she could ask Winnie something, but Winnie wasn't here." Her brother looked sheepish, protecting Mom.

Anna narrowed her eyes. "Winnie's in the hospital. She almost drowned in the Gulf this morning."

"Oh no!" Robin clutched her chest. "Is she going to be okay?"

"They're keeping her for observation." Anna touched her mother's knee. "What was it you came looking for?"

Robin shifted her gaze to Mike.

Her brother shrugged. "Might as well tell her."

"Not now. That'll keep." Robin beaded a hard stare at Amelia, who hovered at the threshold, waved a hand at her. "We've got *this* to deal with."

Mike smiled at Amelia, grabbed a metal folding chair from the closet, opened it up, and waved for her to sit. Thank heavens for her easygoing brother. He might be an accomplice in her mother's scheme, which she'd yet to figure out, but Anna could trust Mike's sense of fairness.

From where she sat, Anna could see through the window to the hummingbird feeders dotted with red-throated hummingbirds. Flowers bloomed in the well-tended beds. Some patients sat sunning in their wheelchairs, while more active groups tossed horseshoes or played shuffleboard.

Outside everything looked nice and normal. Inside, they were all quietly ignoring the elephant in the room.

Anna cleared her throat and grabbed this particular elephant by the tusks. "Amelia, this is my mother, Robin Straus, and my brother, Mike. Mom, this is my identical twin sister, Amelia. We met through 23andMe."

"No." Mom's voice croaked.

Anna studied her mother's face for shame or guilt, but all she saw was pure shock.

Expressionless, Mike stepped closer to the wall as if hoping the Sheetrock could absorb him.

"No." Her mother shook her head fiercely. "No. No. *No!*"

"Yes." Simultaneously, as if perfectly choreographed, she and Amelia crossed their legs and leaned toward Robin.

Startled by their unconscious mirroring of each other, Anna stared at her sister for a long moment and something inexplicable passed between them.

That twin connection again. It was almost as if Amelia was inside Anna's head and she was inside Amelia's.

Eerily, the hairs on Anna's arms lifted and she felt a surge of acceptance and longing so strong it terrified her. How could she feel this deeply for someone she didn't even know?

"No!" Her mother's voice came out harsh and adamant. "It's not true. You are *not* Anna's twin. You can't be."

Stunned, Mike, Amelia, and Anna blinked at Robin in disbelief.

"Mom." Anna infused her tone with tenderness and patience. "Look at her. She's my twin sister. There's no doubt of it."

"No." Robin shook her head like Logan when he didn't want to do something. A rapid back-and-forth, moving so quickly that her iron gray curls quivered. "People have doppelgängers. You hear about it all the time on the news. They say we all have a double. This woman is *not* your sister."

Amelia shifted and reached for the purse she'd settled at her feet. "I have the DNA test right here, Mrs. Straus, if you'd like to see it."

"I do *not* want to see that." Robin clasped her hands in her lap. She had a round youthful face and usually looked a decade younger than her age, but right now with her skin so pale and her mouth drawn tight, she looked every one of her seventy years.

Her mother was in shock.

Anna felt bad. Why did things have to be this way? She fingered the medallion on her bracelet and noticed her twin was doing the same, so she stopped.

"Look here, we have matching keepsake bracelets."

"So?" Mom's chin went up defiantly. "Anyone could get a jeweler to make a similar bracelet."

"Now how would that happen?" Anna asked. "How would Amelia know what my bracelet looked like? It's been in my jewelry box since you and Daddy gave it to me on my wedding day to wear for something old."

"Social media. You probably posted a picture of it and she . . ." Robin pointed a shaking finger at Amelia. "Saw it."

"I didn't post about it," Anna assured her.

"You forgot you did it."

"Mom . . ." Anna started to say at the same time Amelia said, "Mrs. Straus?"

Anna gave Amelia a helpless smile. "You go first."

"No!" Robin's bottom lip quivered. "No one goes first. We aren't having this conversation. I won't hear of it."

She fisted her hands and burrowed them into the pockets of her paisley print A-line housedress, looking so vulnerable it broke Anna's heart.

"I understand how unsettling this must be for you, Mrs. Straus," Amelia said.

"You understand *nothing*." Her mother's voice shook with whispered rage.

"I understand that Anna is my twin sister." Amelia extended the DNA reports to Robin. "If you don't trust your own eyes, it's right here in black and white."

Robin thumped the papers with her thumb and forefinger but wouldn't look at them. "This is nothing but gobbledygook. Just numbers on a page."

Amelia withdrew the reports and sat back in her chair, her eyes hooded, revealing nothing about her feelings. "I imagine this hurts you a great deal, but facts are facts. DNA doesn't lie. Anna is my twin sister."

"No, DNA doesn't lie, but slick scammers do. I read the AARP. I know there are devious criminals out there running cons on people."

"Why would I con you, Mrs. Straus?" Amelia asked.

"I don't know. You want my money."

"Ma'am," Amelia's voice was kind, and patient, but her composure rubbed Anna the wrong way. "I am very well off. I don't need your money."

Robin's eyes widened. "I bet that's how you made your money. Scamming poor old ladies like me!"

Amelia looked hurt but struggled not to show it.

Anna darted a glance at her brother, hoping for backup.

But Mike had taken out his pocketknife and the small block of wood he carried with him and started whittling.

Watching her brother adeptly carve the head of a figure, Anna experienced her big sisterly love as a tight and fragile thing. People often commented on how dissimilar she and her brother looked. Anna with her red hair, pale freckled skin, and chocolate-brown eyes. Mike with dark hair and piercing blue eyes. He was the one who resembled their mother's side of the family.

No, not *their* mother. *His* mother.

Mike wasn't her biological brother.

Reality hit her so hard she could barely breathe. Anna felt torn in two pieces and confused about her split loyalties. She knew so much about Mike, but he wasn't even her blood brother. She didn't know this stranger who looked exactly like her, but they'd shared a womb.

Sarah Brandt's womb.

The bottom dropped out of Anna's stomach, out of her entire world, and a tiny squeak escaped her lips. She empathized with her mother's inability to accept the truth. She wanted to deny it, too. Things would be so much easier that way.

But she could not.

The pain on her mother's face was almost more than Anna could bear. Her mother had lost so much: her husband, her parents when she was young, and now she was forced to confront another truth—she'd also lost her biological daughter.

A child she should have grieved thirty-five years ago.

No wonder that she couldn't take it all in.

Amelia stood up, her pitying gaze on Robin. "I should go and give you time to process this." She shifted her attention to Anna, extended the DNA profile. "Should I leave the reports?"

"No!" Robin jumped to her feet.

Anna saw a stark fear in her mother that she'd never seen before and, frankly, it terrified her.

"Take those reports with you!" Robin screamed, then brushed past Amelia as she fled the room.

"I better go after her," Mike mumbled, pocketing his knife and wood carving. With a tight smile, he ambled from the room.

Leaving Anna and Amelia staring at each other.

Amelia's face offered no emotion. She folded the report and placed it on the bed beside Anna. "I'll call for a ride."

"Please don't go."

"Your family needs you now."

"You're my family, too," Anna said.

Amelia's eyes widened. "You really feel that way?"

"Don't you?"

Barely nodding, Amelia blinked. "I'm so sorry about all this. I didn't mean to cause so much trouble."

Anna eyed her, still unsettled by seeing herself reflected in her twin's eyes. Her mirror image. "Didn't you?"

"I realized there would be fallout." Amelia notched up her chin in the same way that Allie did when she stubbornly dug in her heels about something. "But I didn't fully appreciate just how much this would wound your mother."

"You're brave." Anna's pulse quickened, and she was confused by everything she was feeling—love, anger, guilt, distrust, remorse, and fear. She was scared of the way things were bound to change. Her family spinning out of balance. First with Kevin, now with her mother and brother.

"How so?" Amelia murmured.

"Coming to Moonglow Cove all alone without advance notice. I don't know if warning us would have made it any easier. Maybe. Maybe not. I'm not sure. But it's true this is taking a toll on my mother."

"And you, too." Amelia said it as a statement, not a question.

Anna ignored that last part. "Mom's been pretty fragile since Dad died last year. They had a storybook love affair and losing him just about killed her."

"I really am sorry for your loss," Amelia said.

"I'm sorry you got caught up in my mama drama."

"I'm the *cause* of your mama drama." Amelia lifted her hands and gave a rueful laugh.

Holy donuts, Anna thought, that was *her* laugh, note for note, and she got a fizzy feeling deep inside her lungs. It dizzied her head as quickly as if she'd inhaled champagne.

"Although I wanted you to come stay with me, maybe you're right to stay at the Moonglow Inn. Let me talk to Mom. If that goes well, we can meet up tomorrow. I've got a lot of things to straighten out."

"I understand." Amelia nodded. "I'm comfortable where I'm at. Don't worry about me."

Myra Marts, a convivial brunette RN in her midforties who wore her lipstick too dark and her scrubs too tight, came barreling into the room.

She got a good look at Anna and Amelia and halted in her tracks, her mouth flying open. "Trudy was right. You're identical!"

After they informed Myra about Winnie, Amelia took a car back to the Moonglow Inn.

Anna gathered the things Winnie would need in the hospital, slippers, clothes, her favorite blanket, and took them to the hospital.

The charge nurse on the floor told Anna that Winnie was getting an IV for her dehydration and resting comfortably. It turned out she might not even need her things because they'd probably dismiss her back to the memory care facility the next morning if she continued to do well.

Anna dropped by Winnie's hospital room, but she was sound asleep. She covered the elderly woman with the blanket she'd brought and tiptoed out the door.

* * *

ANNA PICKED UP her kids from Darla and went over to her mother's town house, in the over fifty-five community.

She opened the back gate, told the kids to play on the swing set, and went inside through the sliding glass patio door that her mother never bothered to lock.

The house was eerily quiet except for the ticking of the grandfather clock in the hallway. "Mom?"

No answer.

Her mother's car was in the driveway, but she could still be with Mike in his vehicle. She'd already texted her mother three times, but she hadn't texted back.

"Mom?" She moved through the house toward the master bedroom. Tapped on the door. "Mom?"

No answer.

Anna cracked the door.

The room was dark. Curtains drawn. Her mother was piled in the middle of the mattress with the covers pulled over her head.

Anna's heart lurched. She kicked off her shoes, padded over to the bed, slipped between the covers, and spooned against her mother's back.

Robin's body shook softly as she cried. Her mother was in raw, animal pain.

"Mom," Anna murmured, tightening her grip. "Mommy?"

Robin turned in her arms and Anna cradled her like she did her children. The same way she'd comforted her mother when her dad had died.

"If . . . if . . ." Robin hiccuped on her tears. "That test . . . if she really is your twin . . ."

"She looks just like me, Mom. Forget the DNA test for a minute and just believe your own eyes."

"*If*," her mother reiterated. "If she's your twin, what does that mean? How did you get separated?"

"You don't know?" Anna leaned her head back on the pillow so she could fully see her mother's face.

"How would I know?"

"You were there when we were born."

"There was a hurricane that night. The lights went out. We were bathed in darkness. I'd lost a lot of blood and then I lost consciousness. I lost track. I don't remember anything."

"Mom," Anna whispered, fingering the jewelry at her wrist. "Tell me about the keepsake bracelet. Where did you get it? When did you buy it?"

Robin rolled away from her, sat up against the pillows. Anna did the same, turning on the lamp so she could look into her mother's eyes.

Snatching tissues from a box on the bedside table, Robin avoided Anna's gaze as she dabbed away tears. "I've told you this story before."

"I need to hear it again."

Robin cupped her chin in her palm, stretched her fingers along her jawline, and turned her face away from Anna. Sighed.

"I know this is hard on you, but please, tell me what happened that night I was born." She rested a hand on her mother's shoulder.

Another big sigh.

"After you were born, that time was fuzzy for me. I had to have several pints of blood. I was in the hospital for almost a week. My thinking was foggy. I couldn't even nurse you."

"Give me your hand."

Robin shook her head. "What?"

"Give me your hand, please" she repeated.

Slowly, Robin extended her right hand.

Anna took off the bracelet and dropped it into her mother's palm. "When did you buy this?"

"You know that your father bought it. The bracelet was for what you girls nowadays call 'push presents.'"

"If it was a push present for you," Anna asked, "why was it a gift for me?"

"Because . . ." Mom met Anna's challenging stare head-on for the first time and she hauled in a deep breath. "Your father understood that all I ever wanted was *you*. You came first, Anna. Always. Heathcliff knew that any present for you was a present for me."

Well, that was a sweet answer, but it seemed like an excuse.

Guilt gnawed her and she felt like a jerk for badgering her mother, but she had to get to the bottom of this. Had to understand how thirty-five years had gone by without knowing she had a twin sister.

"Remind me what Dad said when he gave you the bracelet. How did he explain the name on the medallion?"

"It's true that I'd planned on calling you Caroline," she said, gazing over her shoulder at the picture of Anna's father sitting on the dresser. "After my mother."

"How did you feel when Daddy gave you this?" Anna touched the bracelet's medallion that spelled out her name. "What did you think?"

"He told me that the minute he saw you he knew you weren't a Caroline. Even though we'd never talked about calling you Anna, he said that's what you looked like to him. Based on the *certainty* that you should be Anna, he had Bosch's Jewelry commission the bracelet just for you while I was recovering in ICU."

"In retrospect, don't you think that seems a little fishy?"

"No, not at all. You father was always surprising me in unexpected ways. It was one of the things I liked most about him. He kept life interesting."

You could say that twice.

"What was your reaction when he gave you this bracelet and essentially told you he'd changed my name while you were unconscious?" Anna rubbed the spot between her eyebrows. A gesture of frustration she'd picked up from years of living with Kevin. She stopped, stared pointedly at her mother.

"I told him I loved the name Anna and that he was right. You looked exactly like an Anna and that was that."

Anna squeezed her eyes closed so tightly she saw a burst of white stars and felt a panic seize her from the inside. Ever since she'd met Amelia, she'd been dancing away from this new reality. This hidden truth.

And she understood that she was so close to falling off the edge of reason, just like Mom had.

"Anna?" her mother whispered. "Are you all right?"

Her eyes flew open. "No, Mom, I'm *not* all right. Amelia has a completely different story about the bracelets."

"Amelia." Her mother spat out the name like she tasted a spoonful of wasabi she'd mistaken for mashed potatoes.

"Yes, *Amelia*. She was told by her parents that her twin sister, Anna, had died during childbirth at Moonglow Cove Memorial during a hurricane."

"But . . . but, that can't be."

"They told her that they'd bought an identical bracelet for her sister and that Anna's bracelet had gone missing that same night the babies were born."

"Nooo!!!" Her mother wailed like a wounded animal, clamping her hands over her ears. "It's not true, it's not true, it's not true."

Anna didn't want to believe it, either, but the evidence was as glaring as a Times Square billboard. Anguish sank vicious teeth into her, shredding her to a million savaged pieces. She didn't want to say it, but she had to.

Her entire body quivered from the force of her emotions. There was only one explanation that made sense. Only one deeply disturbing account of what fit the evidence.

"It is true, Mom, and we need to face facts."

"What truth? This Amelia person's truth?"

"The *honest* truth."

"No, no, no," Robin mewled.

"I'm *not* your biological daughter."

Robin's blue eyes flooded with tears, and her face twisted in suffering. It took everything Anna had inside her to say what she had to say. She loved her mother more than life itself and the last thing she wanted was to hurt her, but as much as she might like to forget this, she couldn't hide from it.

"Your baby didn't survive. Caroline died." Tears rolled down Anna's cheeks, too, hot and sorrowful. .

The loss was almost too much to bear. The reality unthinkable. Robin Straus, the woman who'd cooked and cleaned for Anna, held her hair back when she puked, taught her how to ride a bicycle and master the smoky eye, cheered louder than any other mom at her college graduation, was *not* her mother.

"No." Robin whimpered, fisting the baby bracelet in her palm and raising it to her heart. "No. You're wrong. You *are* my baby. You didn't die."

"I didn't die, but I didn't belong to you."

"Who did you belong to?" In that moment, her mother looked younger and more helpless than Logan.

Anna's next words were like a sword, cutting off all hope that Amelia had indeed made a terrible mistake. "There's only one explanation that fits. Only one possibility that bears up under examination."

"No, no, no." Robin's bottom lip quivered.

She'd spent all night thinking about it and her theory came out fully formed.

"Daddy loved you so very much that when your little girl died, in the craziness of the hurricane blackout, somehow he switched the babies. He stole me from the Brandts, and in my place he left them your dead Caroline. And I suspect that Winnie was in on it and has known all along."

CHAPTER ELEVEN

Robin

The Truth Hurts

For thirty-five years, Robin had denied the dark doubts that occasionally sneaked into her mind in the wee hours of the night. A vague unnameable dread she'd kept locked down, fearful of the secrets lurking in her subconscious.

Now, here was Anna confirming something Robin had never been able to explain or accept. She'd never quite felt like Anna was "hers," the way Mike had been, but she could never say why.

"I'm hungry." She grabbed another fistful of tissues from the box on her bedside table and scrubbed the tears from her face.

Tossing the tissues in the wastebasket, Robin swung her legs over the side of the bed and popped to her feet.

She was the mother. It was her place to comfort Anna, not the other way around. But damned if she could do that right now.

"Mom? Are you okay?"

Robin didn't answer. She rushed from the bedroom but then paused as she passed by the living area. Through the sliding glass door, she saw her grandchildren playing in the backyard. Allie was pushing Logan on a swing.

They aren't my grandchildren, she thought, sudden anger mingling with her grief, and her heart shattered more violently than the picture frame she'd broken in Winnie's room. *Heathcliff, what have you done to me?*

"Mom?" Anna came up behind her.

She didn't want this, not any of it.

Not Anna's pity.

Not the truth of twins.

Not the idea that the baby she'd carried in her womb was dead. She couldn't accept the truth. Not yet. Without a word, she headed for the kitchen.

Anna trailed after her.

Robin opened the bottom drawer next to the sink, pulled out two aprons, passed one to Anna, and tied the other around her waist. It said: WORLD'S GREATEST GRANDMA. Fresh tears pressed the backs of her eyelids, but she blinked them away.

"What's the apron for?" Anna asked.

"Put it on."

Raising her eyebrows, Anna slipped the canvas navy blue apron over her head and tied the back sash. This apron said: WORLD'S GREATEST GRANDPA.

Tears blocked Robin's throat. To chase away her grief, she hummed the first song that popped into her head, "Chattanooga Choo Choo." A silly song her mother used to sing to her when she was a girl.

Anna stared at her as if she'd lost her mind.

Maybe she had.

Robin stepped to the pantry and started pulling out

ingredients—flour, brown sugar, granulated sugar, salt, vanilla, baking soda, chocolate chips. "Could you get out an egg and two sticks of butter from the fridge."

"Mom, what are you doing?"

"Why, I'm making cookies of course. The children need an afternoon snack." She went back to humming as she carried the ingredients to her KitchenAid stand mixer.

"String cheese will do. Don't make cookies."

"Should we add walnuts?" Robin canted her head. "Or pecans?"

"Neither, Mom."

Mom.

That word sounded like a weapon now, a sharp katana slicing right though her. *Mom.* Another flare of anger, hotter this time.

"Egg and butter, please." Robin held out her palm.

Silently, Anna fetched the ingredients, set them on the counter with the other supplies, then folded her arms over her chest, leaned against the cabinet, and watched Robin with concerned eyes.

Carefully, Robin measured the flour, spooning it into a cup, leveling it off with the back of a butter knife, and dumping it into the mixing bowl one, two, three times. "Why do you suppose that woman came to Moonglow Cove to ruin our lives?"

"Please don't be hostile toward Amelia. I understand you're beyond hurt, but she is my sister."

"You mean she's your only real family."

"I didn't say that. You will always be my mother, no matter what some DNA test says. You don't need to be blood related to love someone." Anna looked pained. "Please don't be like this."

"I don't have a right to my feelings?"

"Of course you do, but you're such a kind person, can you spare some empathy for Amelia?"

Robin's heart ached. Anna was appealing to her higher self, but right now it felt as if her "higher self" had climbed on the Choo Choo and taken off for Chattanooga.

"Could you hand me a teaspoon, please?"

Sighing, Anna pushed off from the counter. She searched the drawer for measuring spoons and passed them over.

"Thank you. Could you whisk the egg?"

Anna cracked the egg in a bowl, tossed the shells in the wastebasket, then whisked the egg while Robin browned the butter in a skillet. They worked together as they had thousands of times before, sharing their passion for baking. But it felt different this time.

Off.

Imbalanced.

Tension ran through the room like a live electrical wire.

The jolting silence reminded Robin of Anna's challenging teenaged years, but this wasn't like those tiffs and pouts. This wasn't just hurt feelings and misunderstandings. This shift between them was monumental and permanent. They could not unknow the truth.

Anna no longer belonged to her.

Fresh pain jabbed Robin. Reality hadn't changed, just her understanding of it. *She's never belonged to you.*

Somewhere deep down inside her where she'd never dared tread, Robin had known something was off. About Heathcliff's behavior with the baby who'd looked nothing like anyone in their family and about his strange deepening attachment to Winnie after Anna's birth.

She'd accepted his excuses because she'd so badly wanted that baby, so desperate for her happily-ever-after.

But now she was left with the rumble of her husband's misdeeds, mocking her with the truth. There was no such thing as happily-ever-after. Eventually you got your heart smashed to silt no matter what.

"Why don't you pour us a glass of wine?" Robin added melted butter to the sugar in the mixing bowl and attached the wire whisk to the mixer to cream the ingredients.

"Day drinking, Mom?"

"I just got the second-worst news of my life. Pour."

"Do you honestly believe that me finding out I have an identical twin is a bad thing?"

She shot Anna a look. "Not for you."

Anna looked distressed. "C'mon, Mom, it could be great if you let it. Think of the situation as gaining a daughter instead of losing one."

She glowered. "I'm appalled by your thoughtlessness."

Anna staggered back. "W-what?"

"Do you realize I haven't had time to grieve my biological child? What if it were *you* and you'd just found out Allie wasn't your baby?"

"Oh, Mom." Anna plastered one palm to her forehead and the other to her belly as if she were feeling sick.

"This news is fresh to me. It's happening here and now, not

thirty-five years ago. You might be able to handle this, but I cannot."

Anna's face crumpled. "I'm so sorry I was so clueless."

"You can't really expect me to welcome Amelia with open arms until I've had time to process all this."

"No, no. You're right."

"It's too much, too soon."

"Amelia says——"

"I don't want to talk about her," Robin said, realizing she'd forgotten to preheat the oven. She leaned over to punch the controls with the knuckle of her index finger, preserving her manicure.

Anna said nothing, just opened the wine, doled out a generous pour, and passed it to Robin. The pulse at the hollow of Anna's neck ticked rapidly.

She'd upset her daughter, but Robin couldn't seem to pull out of her mental tailspin. "You're not having any wine?"

Anna shook her head.

"Suit yourself." Robin took a big sip. Bigger than she intended. Her mouth filled with more wine than she could swallow, and she had to spit it into the sink.

"Feel better?" Anna added a slice of sarcasm to her voice.

Not answering, Robin rinsed out the sink, but she didn't meet the heat of Anna's stern stare. She washed her hands, dried them on her apron, then added flour to the creamed butter and sugar as if nothing had happened.

"You forgot the leavening ingredients." Anna held out the baking soda, powder, and salt.

"You finish the cookies up." Robin topped off her wineglass and wandered into the backyard, as a dozen different emotions shifted and converged. So many damn feelings she couldn't label them all.

The door closed behind her with a soft click.

She moved to the chaise lounge underneath a colorful sun umbrella and stretched out to watch her grandchildren. She still wore the stupid apron. Setting her wine on the side table, she leaned forward, untied the apron, took it off, wadded it into a ball, and set it beside her wineglass.

There.

She sipped the wine and studied the children, noticing how much Allie looked like Anna. No question where that DNA came from.

The kids were playing hide-and-seek. Allie covered her eyes with the crook of her elbow, while a giggling Logan hid behind the juniper bush. He was wearing the flip-flops Robin tried to warn Anna weren't good for his feet. She could see his little toes wriggling underneath the branches.

"Ready or not," Allie called. "Here I come."

In a breathless rush, Robin was transported back to her childhood, hiding in the dark in the early 1960s while the neighborhood kids searched for her, calling her name as she pressed her chest hard against the cool ground, and feeling the rapid pounding of her heart.

She'd not been good at a lot of their youthful games. She'd been a klutzy kid, always daydreaming and not watching where she was going, but when it came to hide-and-seek, she was a champion. One time, the kids had given up without finding her, drifting home to their dinners and leaving her lying flush against the rich red Texarkana soil, concealed behind a prickly hedge of yaupon holly.

Lonely and alone but feeling startlingly free until her mother came looking for her.

Robin's heart pounded the same way now as it had then, heavy with fear and a strange ripple of excitement.

Allie met Robin's eyes, pointed at the juniper bush, and winked. "Where oh where are you, bubba? You are the best hider in the whole wide world."

Aww, that was so sweet of Allie to pretend to be flummoxed by Logan's amateur hiding skills. Anna and Kevin were doing such a great job of raising them to become kind and conscientious adults.

She watched them for several minutes, taking pleasure in her grandkids until a fierce wistfulness washed over her. She hadn't been blessed with siblings of her own but had longed for them almost as much as she'd longed for children.

Anna's not yours.

No, but Mike was.

Then a terrible thought occurred to her. What if Mike wasn't hers, either? Winnie had been there when he was born as well. What if Winnie and Heathcliff had switched him, too?

"Good batch, Mom."

Munching on a cookie, Anna came out of the back door,

balancing a plate with more cookies in her hand. Under her arm, she carried three juice boxes. Anna was back to her usual good-natured self, having let go of the kitchen tension.

Robin breathed a sigh of relief. She hated being crossways with her children.

"Feeling better?" Anna asked.

"I don't think I'm going to feel better for a very long time."

"I get that." Her daughter settled into the chair next to the lounger and put the cookies and juice boxes on the table between them. She poked a straw into one of the juice boxes and took a long sip.

Robin reached for her wine.

Anna studied her but said nothing.

Yes, she shouldn't be day drinking. Normally, she didn't, but ever since Heathcliff died, she'd reached for wine more and more often to soothe herself. Unnerved by Anna's stare, she put the glass back down.

"You're judging me."

Anna shrugged. "I'm not. Do what you need to do. This twin thing is unsettling for everyone."

Robin circled the rim of the glass with an index finger. "It's more than unsettling. There's been a giant rip in the fabric of our lives."

On the back lawn, the kids had switched roles. Logan was now covering his eyes, Allie hiding underneath the slide so her brother could find her easily.

"She's a great older sister." Robin nodded.

"She is."

"So were you. You were so much help with Mike when he was a baby." Robin took a sip of wine. "Today was hard on me."

"I understand."

"I'm so mad at *that* woman."

"Amelia?"

"No." Robin took another sip, saw Anna frown, but she didn't stop. "Amelia is fine considering the difficult situation we're all in. I'm talking about Winnie. She's the one putting us all through this. It's all her fault."

"Mom, she has dementia. She's ninety."

"She didn't have Alzheimer's when you were born." Robin knew she sounded like a petulant three-year-old blaming everyone and anything for her meltdown, except her own actions, which wasn't like her at all, but she didn't know how to rein herself in.

Not yet anyway.

Anna sat with her hands in her lap, not saying a word.

"Winnie is the reason you were separated from your sister. Why I never got to grieve my baby." Then, to her horror, Robin burst into helpless sobs.

Anna hopped from her chair and threw her arms around her. "Oh, Mom! I've been so selfish. All I've been thinking about is myself and Amelia. I've been so self-centered. It never occurred to me that you're just now grieving the daughter you lost."

"I didn't even know I'd lost a daughter. But that's not all. Don't you get it? You're not *mine* anymore."

"Of course, I'm your daughter. I will always be your daughter, no matter what." Anna pulled a tissue from her pocket and dabbed Robin's face the same way she wiped away her children's tears.

"This wine is giving me a headache." Robin pulled back.

"I don't think it's the wine, Mom. I think it's emotional stress, but it's probably a good idea to slow down." Reaching over, Anna nudged the wineglass from her grasp.

"I am so mad at your father I could pinch his head off. He died and left me with his mess."

"May I ask you a question?"

"Do I have to answer?"

"No."

"Fire away then."

"You never suspected I wasn't yours? Not at all. Not even a tiny bit? Not even somewhere in the back of your mind?"

"No." Robin shook her head so vigorously, denying the deep suspicion she'd never allowed to bloom. "Never."

"Don't be mad at Daddy. He did what he did because he loved you and wanted you to have the baby that you'd tried so hard to conceive."

"Maybe he wasn't involved," Robin mused. "Maybe it was just *her*."

"Because of the keepsake bracelets . . ." Anna shook her head. "I don't see any way around it. Daddy *had* to be involved in the baby swap."

"What is it that the military calls situations like this?" Robin tapped her chin with an index finger.

"FUBAR?"

"I'm not sure that's it." Robin frowned as she chased that thought down an empty alley of her mind.

"Fucked up beyond all recognition."

"Don't swear," Robin said automatically, in mom mode. "But yes, it is FUBAR. Still I thought there was another set of initials."

"SNAFU?"

"What does that stand for?"

"Situation normal: all fu—"

"No, no, you were right the first time. It's the FUBAR one. Our situation is not normal in any way."

"No, it's not." Anna's soft smile was so gentle it literally hurt Robin to look at her.

Robin stared at her hands. She'd chipped her manicure when she'd cleaned out the storage unit.

Somewhere, behind a fence, a lawn mower started up.

"You were both such good parents," Anna murmured. "You and Daddy wanted me, and you loved me with all your hearts. From the little that Amelia has told me about her parents, getting switched at birth was the best thing that ever happened to me and we should be grateful to Winnie for pulling it off."

Robin bit down on her bottom lip. "My head says that's true, but in my heart, I'm so mad at them both."

Anna kept a hand on Robin's thigh, maintaining physical contact. "It's okay to be angry. There's nothing in the world wrong with that. It is a lot to process."

"I feel like I did when the doctor told me that they'd have to put your father on a ventilator, and we weren't allowed to be with him as he died." Her mother doubled up her fists. "I wanted to punch something—the doctor, the wall, the coronavirus. I didn't care. I was losing the love of my life and there was nothing I could do about it. Do you know how helpless that feels?"

"You're not losing me, Mom."

"I know this sounds selfish, but I *do* resent Amelia. The time that you used to spend with me, you'll be spending with her now."

"My extra attention to Amelia is temporary, Mom. I'm just trying to get to know my twin. Soon, Amelia will go back to her life in Chicago and things will return to normal."

"You promise?"

"I swear it."

"How soon?"

"We haven't discussed it, but I doubt Amelia will stay longer than a couple of weeks."

Robin swiped away a straggling tear. Enough self-pity. Time to be the parent. "You can take the children home now. I'll be all right."

"First, there's something I need to talk to you about." Anna dusted cookie crumbs from her fingers, leaned forward in her chair.

Robin tensed, knowing she was not going to like this conversation.

Logan counted as the sun slipped closer to the horizon and a whippoorwill called. "One, two, free, four . . ."

"Why were you and Mike searching Winnie's room?" Anna asked.

Unable to bear the intensity of Anna's stare, Robin studied her grandson. "You used to mispronounce 'three' when you were Logan's age."

"Mom?" Anna's voice changed timbre and without even looking at her, Robin knew she was frowning. "Why were you search-ing Winnie's room?"

Clearing her throat, Robin straightened. If they were going to have this conversation right now, she needed the rest of that wine. She reached for the wine and Anna didn't stop her.

"Mom?" Anna wasn't going to let this go. "Why were you in Winnie's room?"

"Mike and I went to talk to Winnie," she said.

"Don't lie to me. I'd told you Winnie had gone AWOL and wasn't at the memory care center." Anna wasn't letting her off the hook. "You *knew* Winnie wasn't there."

"I didn't know that for sure." Robin finally met her daughter's pointed stare. Yes, she sounded defensive. She was defensive. "For all I knew they'd found her."

"You were hoping she wasn't there."

"Maybe."

"Why?"

Realizing she was cornered, Robin took the key she'd found in Heathcliff's lockbox from her dress pocket and passed it over.

Anna studied the key, flipped the label tag over, and read it out loud. "Safe-deposit box, Moonglow Cove Central Bank. To be opened only in the event of Winnie Newton's death."

She speared Robin's gaze. "Where did you get this?"

"I found it in your father's things when I was cleaning out the storage unit."

"You've never seen this key before?"

"No."

"Did you take it to the bank?"

Sheepish, Robin nodded.

"Why? It says right here the safe-deposit box should only be opened when Winnie dies."

She heard the tone in Anna's voice, accusatory and indignant. They were sitting on opposite sides of the table, the cookies between them. The yellow daylilies in the flower bed swayed in the breeze as they closed up. Smoke from the next-door barbecue grill drifted over the fence.

"I didn't open it." Robin brushed a lock of hair back on her forehead.

When doctors were encouraging people to touch their face less, she'd almost broken her anxious habit of fussing with her hair whenever she felt stressed. Quietly, she rested her hands in her lap.

"Why not?" Anna asked. "If you went all the way to the bank? What stopped you from crossing that line?"

"Turns out two keys are needed to open the safe-deposit box. I figured Winnie must have the other one."

"So you dragged Mike into your *I Love Lucy* scheme, and you went looking for it."

No point in denying it, Anna had her dead to rights. Robin notched up her chin. "So what if I did? It's my right to do what I wish with my dead husband's things."

"Why didn't you bring the key to me instead of Mike?"

"I was afraid you'd tell me I shouldn't open the safe-deposit box."

Anna toyed with the key, twisting the label around her index finger and tapping the metal tip against the glass table, *tap, tap, tap*. "What do you think is inside?"

"Before I went to the bank, I thought maybe it was Winnie's will. But now?" Robin started to rake her hand through her hair, stopped herself. "Since Amelia showed up, I think it might be a confession."

Anna sucked in a deep breath so loud it rattled Robin. "Me too."

"Do you know where the other key is?"

Anna shook her head. "And even if I did know where the other key was, I wouldn't feel comfortable opening the safe-deposit box while Winnie is still alive. Dad wanted whatever is in that box to stay a secret until Winnie is gone."

"I feel like I don't even know who Heathcliff was. Forty-five years of marriage and he's suddenly a stranger. If you're right and he and Winnie switched babies . . ." Betrayal bit into her and only the thought of her daughter's pain and her grandchildren playing hide-and-seek kept her emotions in check.

She had to snap out of this funk. She'd already been too selfish today. Anna was the one this was happening to. Her daughter needed her support right now. Robin didn't have the luxury of self-pity.

Anna had the string of the label wrapped so tightly around her finger that it was turning dusky.

"Sweetheart." Robin reached across the table to touch Anna's hand. "You're cutting off your blood supply."

"Oh!" Anna blinked and unraveled the string.

For the second time since Robin had found out about Amelia, she saw tears in her daughter's eyes. Her child was hurting.

She wrapped Anna in her arms. "It's going to be all right. We'll figure this out."

"Will we?"

"Remember how bleak things looked last year when we lost Daddy?"

Anna nodded.

"That was much worse than this."

"Mom?" Anna cupped Robin's cheek. "You're shaking like a leaf."

"I'm scared."

"Of what?"

"That you'll leave me behind."

"Never. Ever." Anna hugged her tightly. "Amelia needs me right now. I have a feeling no one has ever loved her completely and unconditionally. I need time with her, but please don't be jealous. My love knows no bounds. There's room for everyone in my heart. And you will always and forever be my mother."

For the rest of her life, Robin would remember every nuance of this moment under the umbrella in her backyard, with the scent of honeysuckle in the air, and the taste of dry white wine on her tongue, and the sound of the children giggling as they chased after lightning bugs, oblivious to what was happening on the patio.

And as Robin's world collapsed, a whole new beginning she'd never thought to imagine was unfolding. Now all she had to do was open her heart, let go of her prejudices and misguided beliefs, and accept the changes as they came.

CHAPTER TWELVE

Anna

Differences of Opinion

On Thursday morning, June 3, two days after Amelia first appeared on her doorstep, Anna went to fetch her sister from the Moonglow Inn and bring her home.

She'd dropped the kids off with Kevin's mother, Veronica, and started to text Kevin to update him on everything. Then she reminded herself that he'd insisted they take a three-day break. He'd not contacted her and if she hadn't had her mother and Amelia to distract her, she might have obsessed with wondering what he was thinking and doing.

It took everything she had inside her not to at least text him emojis or gifs, but she resisted. After she left the kids, she went by the memory care facility to see Winnie, who'd just been dismissed from the hospital.

Ignoring the temptation to search Winnie's room for the mystery key, or to interrogate her about her role in the baby switch—she knew it was futile with the woman's dementia—Anna left after a quick visit and went to the bakery where she told Darla everything that had transpired over the last two days. Her friend commiserated, told her not to worry about the bakery, and promised to hold down the fort while Anna took time to sort out her family issues.

At 9:30 A.M. Anna walked across the street to the Moonglow Inn, carrying two large coffees and chocolate croissants.

She didn't know how her twin took her coffee, so she brought it black and stuck creamer packets and a variety of sweeteners in her pocket. Anna preferred her coffee unaltered.

So, as it turned out, did Amelia.

Maybe she should start with the assumption that she and Amelia were more alike than not. That thought pleased her inordinately.

They sat in rocking chairs on the front porch of the Moonglow Inn watching traffic go by on Moonglow Boulevard as they enjoyed their breakfast.

"To something else we have in common." Anna raised her paper cup. "Coffee black."

"Purists."

They toasted and grinned at each other.

After a bit of sipping and noshing, Amelia asked, "How'd things go with your mother yesterday?"

Anna shrugged, trying to not let on how worried she was about Robin. "It's taking her a while to process this. Understandable."

"I like that about you," Amelia said.

"What?"

"How you cut people slack."

"She's my mother."

"You do it for everyone. I think it shows what a great mother Robin is."

"Aww, Amelia, that's very nice of you to say."

"How are *you* doing during all this?" Amelia asked.

"Conflicted," Anna admitted.

Amelia nodded, sipped her coffee, and shifted her gaze back to the boulevard. On the seawall, in front of the inn, four-seater bicycle surreys passed by. Smiling families pumped their legs in lazy unison.

"I love people watching," Anna said. "Do you ever make up stories about them? Kevin and I do. We call it Guess Who."

"No, not really." Amelia paused. "But I could try . . . for you."

Anna's stomach jolted. It was nice of her to try, but it didn't seem much fun if Amelia wasn't into the game. "You don't have to."

"Let me give it a shot. Blue surrey. Dad behind the wheel. Hawaii shirt. Paunchy belly. Middle-aged cliché. He's got a dull job. An accountant or insurance agent. He dreams of owning a red Ferrari but instead he puts the money in his kids' college fund and is having an emotional affair online but doesn't realize he's actually being catfished by a couple of guys from his office. They live in Akron. Mom stays home, longs for the dancing career she gave up, and does mountains of laundry for those three boys, Larry, Moe, and Curly."

"Wow." Anna whistled. "That took a dark turn."

"I botched it." Amelia dusted the croissant crumbles from her fingers, wadded up her white paper napkin with the Moonglow Bakery logo on it. "I'm not much good at reading people."

"No, no. You were actually quite good at the game, just a little pessimistic."

"Show me how it's done." Amelia waved at the next surrey that bicycled by, the fringe on the canvas top bouncing jauntily.

Looking at the passengers, a young man and woman in their midtwenties, Anna said, "Newlyweds on their honeymoon. They were high school sweethearts who got engaged right after graduation but waited until they finished their college education before getting married. He's a pediatric intern who cares more about saving children's lives than making money. She's a tech whiz who works at a nonprofit because it give her a sense of fulfillment. They've just bought a nice starter home and have a five-year plan for a family."

"And now with crushing student loan debt so astronomical, they won't dig out of it until it's time to send their kids to college."

Whoa boy. Was that how Amelia truly saw the world? Through such a clouded lens full of trouble, dissatisfaction, and strife? "In some ways we are pretty different, you and me."

Amelia nodded. "You're an extroverted optimist."

"What's wrong with that?"

"Nothing's wrong with that. It's fine. I was just making an observation."

"Does that make you an introverted pessimist?"

Amelia shrugged, gave a small grin. "I prefer realist."

Anna uncurled the rolled edge of the cardboard lip on her empty coffee cup, ironing it flat between her finger and thumb. Something had happened to Amelia to color her view of the world in such somber and muted tones. Anna wanted to take cake frosting and paint her sister's world in sweet, bright, primary colors.

Hopping up from the rocking chair, Anna said, "C'mon. Let's load up your luggage and go to my house. We've got two full days together until Kevin gets back on Saturday evening and I don't want to waste a minute of it."

* * *

FIFTEEN MINUTES LATER, Anna and Amelia were tooling down Moonglow Boulevard headed south away from the bakery and the inn and toward Anna's house. The mood was a little lighter than it had been on the porch after their revealing game of Guess Who.

But Anna still had trouble sitting with Amelia's frequent silences.

So she talked. A lot. Anna chattered about the town, acting like a tour guide and trying not to think about how upset Kevin would be when he found out she'd moved Amelia into their house.

Kevin had been the one to issue that no communication crapola or she would have told him about Amelia and how moving her twin into the house was the right thing to do. Kevin could just suck it up.

Phooey on him. Anna didn't care.

Well, okay, yes, she *did* care what Kevin thought. She hated when they were on the outs, which granted wasn't often, but because their true fights were so few, when they did have them, their differences of opinion stuck out like neon signs and they'd learned to tiptoe around those issues to keep the peace.

Like Anna's tendency to mother any- and everyone who would let her. From stray pets—that was how they'd come by Cujo—to the neighborhood kids, to Logan and Allie's classmates, to the people who came into the bakery, to her band the Harmonious Housewives, to Winnie and Kevin's family. Her husband felt as if she gave away too much of herself and he was quick to point out that not everyone appreciated her kindness and generosity and she shouldn't waste it on such people.

Their first big fight on that issue came when Darla divorced her first husband, and Anna had spent the entire evening consoling her friend on what was her and Kevin's fifth wedding anniversary.

Yeah, lousy timing, but Darla was her best friend and she'd been in need.

She'd told Kevin he was acting selfishly, and he'd said it was a sorry state of affairs when his wife would rather dole out advice and sympathy to another woman than go out to dinner with her man on their fifth anniversary.

She accused him of being jealous.

He'd called her thoughtless and that made her cry, because all she ever wanted was to make other people happy.

They'd worked through it. They'd both apologized and the next day Anna cooked his favorite meal—filet mignon and duchess potatoes with baked Alaska for dessert—to make up for missing their anniversary date.

He told her he didn't want to limit her world, that he just

wanted her to remember that he was a vital part of that world. His confession touched her so much she vowed to show him how much she loved him in little ways every day like spray-starching his dress shirts and making him key lime pie.

Now, though, Anna was starting to see how giving too much was driving a wedge between them. Especially when he'd never asked for those particular gifts from her.

She did love her big, blond Viking and wanted their marriage to thrive, but to this day, there was that underlying current of resentment when she spent too much time doting on others. Personally, she didn't see it as taking away from Kevin. She saw it as growing love like a garden by sharing it with as many people as possible. The more love you created, the more you had to give away.

Right?

Her parents had taught her that. Her family had been the ones who spent Thanksgiving and Christmas feeding the homeless, celebrating their own holidays either the day after or the day before. They headed food drives and volunteered at the animal shelter. They hosted foreign exchange students and donated to the Red Cross and Salvation Army. Her folks instilled humanitarian values that Anna cherished and was proud of.

"You don't know when to stop helping," Kevin grumbled from time to time whenever she got overloaded. "Nor do you ever stop to think if people even want your help."

That stung.

For now, Kevin didn't need to know Amelia was staying at their house. He'd forgive Anna. She believed with all her heart that they had the kind of relationship that could weather any storm. She knew it to the marrow of her bones.

Which might explain why sometimes she ignored his advice.

He was suspicious of her twin. It was the protector in him, and she loved that he looked out for her and the children, but soon enough he'd see that he could trust Amelia. This would all work out. Things always did when love was at the core of her motivations.

"You told me the other day that you'd retired from the Chicago Symphony," Anna said, switching off the air conditioner and rolling down the windows. It was a balmy day. Not yet too warm and the smell of sea air lifted her spirits. "Do you have another job?"

"Not at the moment."

What did Amelia do with herself all day? No spouse, no kids, no job, no parents to look after. Anna couldn't fathom that much freedom. She'd never in her life been alone. She'd gone from living with her parents, to living with roommates in college, to living with Kevin.

Amelia said, "I do a lot of swimming and horseback riding."

"Omigod! You love horses? I adore horses and Allie does too. She's absolutely horse crazy. We were thinking about buying her one for her eleventh birthday, but stable boarding is so expensive."

"I could pay for that," Amelia offered.

"No, no, that's too far generous." Anna shook her head.

"I apologize. I didn't mean to offend you."

"You didn't."

"Having money insulates you and it's easy to forget that when you offer to pay for things you might be stepping on toes. Some people think you're trying to buy them. That's not what I intended. I just wanted to do something nice for you and Allie."

"You don't owe me anything," Anna said. "I don't want you to feel as if you do. If anything, I'm the one who owes *you*." She stopped. Her feelings were still so raw she didn't think she could express them adequately.

"I understand."

"Maybe we could ride horses soon. Me, you, and Allie."

"I'd like that." Amelia gave a small smile.

Another long moment passed where neither of them said a word. They were at a red light, the engine idling with a soft purr.

"Do you have anyone special in your life?" Anna asked, going through the list of questions that had been stacking up in her mind since they'd first met. There was so much they needed to discuss.

"No," Amelia stared down at her hands intertwined in her lap. "There's no one."

Her sister had a habit of interlacing her fingers whenever she didn't want to talk about something, Anna noticed.

"No boyfriend? Oh, wait, I shouldn't assume anything about your sexuality. No significant other?"

"I'm straight and no, no boyfriend."

Why not? Anna wanted to ask but didn't.

After a long pause, Amelia cleared her throat. "I was engaged once. Robert died two years ago in the same car crash that killed my parents."

Wow! That was rough. "I'm so sorry."

"Everyone has pain," Amelia said it as matter-of-factly as if she was ordering pizza delivery. "I'm not special."

"No, but losing three loved ones all at once? That's a terrible blow. I lost my dad last year and it just about killed me."

"You were close to him."

"Very."

"I wish we didn't have losing parents in common," Amelia whispered.

"What was Robert like?" The light changed and Anna hazarded a quick glance at her twin before easing the minivan forward.

A soft smile flitted across Amelia's face. "Romantic. Intelligent. A risk taker."

"Was that what attracted?" Anna asked. "The risk taking? I mean, since you're pretty cautious yourself. Seems like a daredevil might be a big draw."

"Could be."

Angling her head, Anna shot Amelia another glance. She still wasn't used to the fact that there was someone in the world who looked exactly like her. Would she ever grow accustomed to it?

Amelia said nothing.

"I want to get to know you better," Anna said. "I want us to be *real* sisters."

Amelia stared down at her hands.

Anna wished she'd bitten her tongue and swallowed that soppy sentiment whole. Apparently, from the aloof expression on her twin's face, it had been the wrong thing to say.

"Your family doesn't seem to feel the same way about me," Amelia murmured. "Your husband, your mom, your brother. I see the way they look at me."

"Give them time. They're just in shock."

"And you don't need time?"

Anna was elbow deep in honesty, no backing out now. "We've already wasted thirty-five years. I don't want to spend another second without knowing you inside out. We're *twins*. We're supposed to be close."

Amelia blew out a short puff of air. The strongest reaction Anna had gotten from her today. "Anna, there's something you should know—"

"Oh! Oh!" An idea hit Anna like a lightning bolt in cloudless sky. In the middle of traffic, she made a sudden U-turn.

Amelia slapped both palms to her chest and let out a startled "Eep!"

"Sorry for the abrupt change of direction, but I just had a fantastic thought!"

"Um, all right." Amelia grabbed the dashboard with both hands. "Where are we going?"

"Back to Paradise Pier."

"Why?"

"Sisterly bonding time." Excited tingles. Anna loved amusement park rides. She'd always been an adrenaline junkie, although motherhood had tempered that somewhat. "We're going to do the things we never got to do together as children."

"We are?" Amelia might have paled. It was hard to tell since her coloring was already so fair. She needed more sun.

"Yep." Anna turned into the Paradise Pier parking lot thronged with cars.

"Um, I'm really not much of a carnival person."

"You'll love it. C'mon." Anna knew she was steamrolling her twin, but she felt justified. She had a plan. Anna guided the minivan into a parking spot and killed the engine.

Amelia had a death grip on her seat belt.

"Wait, are you afraid of amusement rides?"

"I'm afraid of a lot of things," Amelia mumbled.

"Seriously?" Anna shook her head. "I don't believe it. You looked like such a badass and the way you saved Winnie yesterday, impressive."

"Badass?" Amelia laughed hollowly. "Not in the slightest."

"You will be after today."

"Now *that* sounds ominous."

"We've got three hours before I have to pick up my kids from my mother-in-law. Let's make the best of it. First stop, the Juggernaut. You'll love it. Best wooden roller coaster in Texas."

CHAPTER THIRTEEN

Amelia

The Juggernaut

Anna, Amelia decided, loved just about everything and everyone.

As they strolled the boardwalk, passersby did double takes, and at least a half-dozen times people stopped Anna to ask who Amelia was.

Message received. They were a sideshow.

The nosy curiosity didn't seem to bother Anna. Her face lit up whenever she introduced Amelia as if she were inordinately proud of her. Anna's eyes turned sincere and shiny as she chattered about finding her long-lost twin.

Well, you didn't find me. I came looking for you. But only because she had ulterior motives.

That thought made her miserable.

Anna was so nice and kind and loving and truly wanted a real relationship.

Guilt piled up inside Amelia. She needed to tell her twin why she was really here. The sooner the better, before Anna started spinning untenable sisterly fantasies.

Although from the looks of it, she was already too late.

The roller coaster was at the back of the pier, and right on the Gulf of Mexico. They passed a pub filled with revelers singing "Happy Birthday to You." To this day, Amelia couldn't hear the song and not think about washing her hands for twenty full seconds. A wall of mirrors outside the Fun House tent distorted their images going from fat to thin, squat to tall. It was the first time Amelia had seen herself in a mirror with her twin at her side. The resemblance *was* unnerving, especially with squashed altered features

"Anna!" A woman behind a funnel cake kiosk waved to them. "Over here!"

They strolled over.

The woman stared at them gobsmacked. "You have a twin!"

"Can you believe it? A secret twin. Just like a soap opera." Beaming, Anna flung her arm around Amelia's shoulder. "Am I the luckiest person alive or what?"

Amelia forced herself not to tense at her sister's touch. She couldn't decide if Anna was just nervous or if she was one of the most relentlessly positive people that she'd ever met. Overwhelmed, she casually sidestepped, forcing Anna to drop her arm, and then Amelia could breathe again.

But she could still feel the pressure on her shoulder where Anna's arm had rested.

"How come you didn't know about each other?" asked funnel cake lady. Her thick mane, dyed a lovely maroon color, was shoved up underneath a hairnet. She wore a neon pink T-shirt a size too small, emblazoned with KEEP CALM AND EAT FUNNEL CAKES. From the fryer came the crackling sound of bread dough cooking at a high heat.

"It's a mystery, Roberta." Anna slung her arm again over Amelia's shoulder. "We're still trying to unravel how we got separated."

"Funnel cakes on the house," Roberta said. "It's not every day someone finds a long-lost twin."

"That's so sweet of you!" Anna exclaimed. "But we just had chocolate croissants."

"It's a standing offer," Roberta said. "Two free funnel cakes for the reunited twins whenever you want."

"Have a great day. We're off to the Juggernaut." Anna waved good-bye to Roberta and linked her arm through Amelia's.

Ugh. She dreaded this Juggernaut thing, but Anna seemed determined.

To tell the truth, Amelia had never even ridden a roller coaster. They looked dangerous and moved too fast on those crazy dips and whirls. Her mother said amusement parks were nasty and plebian and wouldn't let her attend them.

As a kid, she'd felt she'd missed out, but she'd never had a real urge to rectify the oversight.

They reached the Juggernaut. Amelia craned her neck *up, up, up* to see the top of the tracks. Passengers screamed like maniacs as the cars zipped by, clacking on the wooden rails, but they did look as if they were having fun.

"Two tickets please, Oscar," Anna told the man at the booth.

They had to go through the whole twin thing again with Oscar, whose voice held the timbre of a bass oboe, an oddly high, light tone for such a stout man.

Others gathered behind them. It worried Amelia that they were holding up the line.

Oscar not only gave them free tickets, he gave them fast passes so the attendant at the door ushered them to the head of the line.

Although Amelia was accustomed to preferential treatment, having been raised with money and the privileges that came with it, the fast pass thing made her uncomfortable and she said as much to Anna. "I don't like cutting in line."

"Oh," Anna waved a hand. "Don't worry about that. You're new to Moonglow Cove."

Amelia cocked her head. "Meaning?"

"Here, people do little favors all the time for each other. The town embraces the pay-it-forward concept." Anna pointed at a sign on the waste barrel that literally said, PAY IT FORWARD. KEEP PARADISE PIER CLEAN.

Amelia glanced around. It was a pretty clean pier.

"I gave Oscar twenty bucks a couple of weeks ago to get his bicycle tire fixed when it blew out in front of the bakery and for Roberta, I sent apple strudel to her house when her in-laws came to visit from Germany. I sent it over in the pan that I baked it in so that she could pretend she'd made it. Her mother-in-law is very exacting on what constitutes a good wife. Apparently, strudel-baking skills are highly prized in her family."

"You're very kind," Amelia said, but secretly thought that her

twin's generosity left her wide open for manipulation by unscru-
pulous people.

"Hey." Anna beamed and nudged her gently with her elbow.
"It's the Moonglow Cove way. Stick around. You'll see. Ooh,
we're up next."

A roller-coaster car slid into place and the automatic bars
raised, allowing the current passengers to disembark on the opposite side of the platform. Next to the roller coaster was a carousel, playing oompah-pah organ music as the colorfully painted
horses bobbed up and down on their poles. Amelia wished they
were going on that ride. Something nice and sedate.

"Maybe we could go on that instead?"

"Oh, you!" Anna laughed and guided her into the front car.
"The carousel is too slow paced even for Logan. Take a walk on
the wild side, sister."

Wild side.

If Anna only knew!

Amelia was far too familiar with the wild side. She'd run a
marathon of wildness in her past. That was why she preferred
the carousel now. The wild side could go oh-so wrong and it
was laughable that Anna considered a roller coaster a reckless
adventure. Her twin was overprotected and didn't even know it.

In the nitty-gritty of real life, a roller-coaster ride was about
as dangerous as a church picnic, but she wouldn't prick Anna's
safe little world. Amelia had learned a long time ago it was best
to keep her opinion to herself. Far less fallout that way.

"Here we go!" Anna giggled and reached for Amelia's hand as
the bar went down to hold them in place.

Suddenly, her roller-coaster scoffing felt like the raw bravado it was.

The hunk of metal moved on the rails, shooting forward down the track. Amelia thought of news stories she'd read of amusement park ride disasters and her mind started spinning runaway stories the way it did when she was obsessing.

On the upside, if she was killed in a roller-coaster accident, she wouldn't have to ask her sister for a kidney. *Okeydokey, Debbie Downer. Just grit your teeth and get through this.*

The roller coaster sped up, gaining enough momentum to zip around a loop where the car turned upside down, *oh hello!*

Amelia squeezed her eyes closed and clung to Anna's hand.

Anna screamed laughter at the top of her lungs.

She'd had one helluva week, facing several fears. She'd freed the Doberman. Knocked on the door of her long-lost twin. Upset her twin's family. Saved a demented elderly midwife from drowning and now this wild roller-coaster dive. Way too much stress in such a short amount of time.

But then something interesting happened.

The dip and flip of her stomach exhilarated her. Danger without too much risk. Like a cheesy horror movie.

Her heart skipped and her skin prickled, and she felt more alive since, well, she couldn't remember when she'd felt so present, so in the moment.

Probably the last time she'd picked up a cello.

Anna's hand was locked around Amelia's, her palm soft and slightly sweaty. It felt nice having someone to hold on to.

Melancholia stole over her as she thought of all they'd missed out on. The car took another loop, shaking off the mood and bringing her back into her body as a fresh thrill shot through her.

She heard a scream of delight and realized the sound came from her as the coaster dashed into a tunnel and all went dark.

Anna never let go of her, not once. They were in this together.

How did her sister do it? How did Anna open her heart so easily? How did she accept their twin bond without hesitation or fear?

"That was awesome," Anna crowed. "What did you think?"

"Terrifying," Amelia declared. "But in a positive way."

"Told you. The Juggernaut rules!"

The car slowed, sliding back to the platform; the sound of Anna's laughter buoyed her heart and Amelia started to wish she could stay here forever, just like this, making up for lost time. The two of them stared into each other's eyes, knowing they had an irrevocable connection like no other, and for a moment, it was glorious.

* * *

THEY SPENT THE next three hours hitting the rides at Paradise Pier and when they went to pick up Anna's children, Amelia met Kevin's parents.

Veronica and Pete Drury were what Sarah Brandt, with a sniff, would call corn-fed hayseeds.

Ruddy-cheeked, hardworking farm folk. In Pete Drury, Amelia saw where Kevin got his fair good looks. Pete wore denim overalls, a plaid shirt, and muddy work boots. He didn't say much, but just kept shaking his head and muttering, "Twins, huh?"

Veronica wore mom jeans and a work shirt that matched her husband's. Her hands were rough and calloused, her blue eyes intelligent. She smelled of lilacs and vanilla. On the wall in the living room was a beautiful quilt with the squares containing names and pictures of her children and grandchildren.

Veronica brought out iced tea and Oreos. Pete had a beer. They gathered in the living room, sitting underneath that wall quilt. The conversation was stilted and weird and went on for far too long, but the kids were having fun jumping on the trampoline with their cousins in the backyard, so they waited that out.

On the way home, Anna announced she didn't feel like cooking and they headed for a restaurant chain. Amelia, who had to be careful of her salt consumption because of her renal failure, ordered a salad.

"Come on, you need to eat more than that," Anna said, gently nudging her in the ribs with her elbow.

"I'm good."

Anna sighed and shook her head as she dove into a pile of macaroni and cheese. "I wish I had your willpower."

After dinner, they went back to Anna's house. They unloaded Amelia's luggage and Anna showed her to the guest room.

"Mom leaves her things here for when she comes over on Mondays at three A.M. to stay with the kids while I go into the bakery. Mondays are Darla's day off. Ordinarily, I don't go into the bakery until six."

"No problem," Amelia said. In all honesty, she'd rather have stayed at the Moonglow Inn, but Anna seemed determined to have her in the house.

It won't last long, she told herself and being here would give her the opportunity to broach the topic of a transplant. Maybe she'd do it tonight once the kids were in bed.

The children were wound up from their outing and reluctant to get their baths and settle in for bedtime stories.

Anna told Allie she could stay up and watch *Frozen* as long as she remained quiet in her room. It took two readings of *The Velveteen Rabbit* and *Goodnight Moon* to draw a yawn from Logan's sleepy lips. Amelia curled up in a chair at the foot of Logan's bed, listening as Anna read to him.

"You read to him every night?" Amelia whispered after Anna tucked her son in and they'd tiptoed from the room.

"Unless Kevin is home, then we take turns," Anna said.

"Wow."

"Your parents . . ." Anna paused and added with a wince, "*Our* parents never read to you?"

Amelia shook her head. "They weren't big on reading for pleasure. I'm not sure where I picked up the habit."

"What do you like to read?" Anna asked.

"Mostly nonfiction. Biographies are my favorite."

"Me too! And survival stories. I love survival stories."

"Those are the best. Did you read the one about the couple lost at sea for three months? It's been on the *Times* list for weeks."

"I just finished it. Big question, why did the wife agree to sail around the world in that tiny boat when she and her husband couldn't get along in their three-thousand-square-foot home?"

"I know, right?"

They looked at each other and grinned.

"As far as fiction goes," Amelia said. "I'll read two or three thrillers a year, if someone recommends them."

"Oh, I love thrillers, too. Do you ever read romance?"

Amelia shrugged. "I'm not a very romantic person."

"Happily-ever-after gets me every time." Anna plastered a hand over her heart. "Call me sentimental, but I like things to end on a positive note."

It was a nice thought, but Amelia had never found happily-ever-after to be very realistic.

Anna chuffed out her breath. "I don't get nearly as much time to read as I would like, so I've taken to listening to audio. Time-saver."

"I still like the feel of holding a book in my hands."

"Wait until you have kids. You'll become an audiobook convert. Mark my words."

Yes, well, given her age and her medical condition and lack of an available partner, children most likely were not in the cards for Amelia. She and Robert had talked about it, but . . . well, never mind ancient history.

"I'm going to open a bottle of wine," Anna said, trailing into the kitchen. "Do you want a glass?"

Amelia shook her head and held up a palm. "I'm good."

"You sure? I was hoping for a wine and a gabfest on the back patio, but if you're too tired, we can have a rain check."

"Don't mind me. Enjoy your wine. You've earned it."

"Nah, that's okay. If you're not going to have any, I won't either. Iced tea?"

Again, Amelia shook her head. She had to watch her fluid intake, or her feet would start swelling. "I think I might just turn in. It's been a big day."

"I get it. It's too much, too soon." Anna held up her palms and chuckled ruefully. "You need your space. Hanging out with children when you're not used to little ones can get pretty intense."

Amelia moistened her lips. "It's not the children."

"It's me, isn't it? I'm coming on too strong. I have a tendency to rush relationships. I'll try to back off."

"I—"

"Don't feel like you need to explain," Anna interrupted. "It's good to have strong boundaries. Kevin nags me about that. He says I give too much of myself away."

"There's boundaries," Amelia mused. "And then there's castle walls. With moats. And alligators."

Laughing, Anna fetched a glass and filled it with iced tea. She wandered out to the patio, sat at a deck table next to the pool.

Amelia followed and settled into the chair across from her sister.

The full moon slid behind a column of clouds, dripping the pool in shadows. A mockingbird squawked from the moonglow pear tree at the neighbor's orange tabby cat sitting atop the wooden privacy fence, rhythmically swishing its tail.

The mockingbird fluttered off the knotty branch where Amelia suspected it must have a nest, hovering a bit above the tree, as if hung on indecision whether to abandon her babies in favor of chasing off the interloper or to stay put. Clearly, the cat had had run-ins with the mockingbird before.

The bird dive-bombed the cat.

With a backward look over its shoulder, the tabby turned and scaled down the other side of the fence.

"Do you want to talk about those castle walls?" Anna murmured.

"I—" Amelia paused, bit down on her bottom lip.

Anna waited patiently for her to continue.

"I didn't have the kind of life you have here." Amelia swept a hand around their surroundings.

"We were thinking of moving."

"Why? It's a beautiful home and the gardens are amazing. You have such a green thumb."

Anna's nose crinkled. "I do love the gardens, but the house is small."

"It's cozy."

"Cozy. Real estate code word for cramped." Anna laughed. "Seventeen hundred square feet, the kids are growing, and we've kicked around the idea of a third baby."

"You're thinking about another baby?"

"Kevin's keen on it. Me? I would be good either way. I feel fortunate that both kids are healthy. Sometimes I think, why push my luck? Besides, we'd have to build up our bank account before we went down that road again. Last year sure did a number on our finances and we still haven't fully recovered."

"You're a good mother," Amelia said and meant it.

Anna blushed prettily. "Enough about me. I want to get to know *you*."

"I'm pretty boring."

"Not in my book. That's why I wanted you to stay here. I want us to become sisters in the truest sense of the word."

That felt like a big obligation. One Amelia had no business committing to for so many reasons.

Anna's face was animated. "I want to do as many things together as we can while you're here, go horseback riding, take long walks on the beach, hang out at the bakery cooking up fun stuff." She snapped her fingers. "Oh, and I'm in a band. We're playing in a summer concert in the park tomorrow evening. I'd love for you to come. Can you please come?"

"Um—"

"I won't take no for an answer."

Amelia lifted her shoulders. "In that case, how could I refuse?"

"Yes!" Anna paused and then looked slightly alarmed at having gotten what she asked for. "Although don't expect much. Our band is just four former high school band geeks. We're not professionals. We just like to have fun, drink wine, and make music."

"A passion for music surpasses skill every time. Skill you can develop. Passion? That's something you can't fake."

"Not true, but generous of you to say so. Anyway, I'm so glad you're coming. Finally! I have a sister!"

Sadness overtook Amelia. She and Anna could never be real

sisters, no matter how much she wished it were possible. Far too much lay between them for that to ever happen. Too much time. Too much distance. Too much baggage.

At least on Amelia's part.

And once Anna learned the truth about Amelia's past and why she was here, she didn't know if her sister would even speak to her at all.

"And maybe, no pressure here, just throwing it out there, you might consider playing a set with us at the concert?" Anna curled her fingers into her palms and brought her hands to her chin, looking for all the world like Allie when she got excited.

The idea of playing the cello again struck both terror and yearning inside of Amelia. It had been so long since she'd performed that part of her wanted to yell, *Yes!* But the perfectionist in her said, *There's no way, you're not in concert shape.*

"I don't have a cello."

"If I could find one?"

"Maybe. I don't know." Amelia shook her head. "Let me think about it."

Anna's phone, which was sitting on the table between them, buzzed. Anna glanced at the screen. Groaned.

"If you need to take the call, go ahead," Amelia invited.

"Do you mind? It's Mom. She needs extra attention right now."

"No, not at all."

"I'll be right back." Anna lifted the phone to her ear at the same time she pushed away her chair. She wandered off into the darkness, headed to the garden path lighted with solar lamps and sweetened with the scent of roses in full bloom.

In awe, Amelia watched her sister walk away. How did her twin manage to juggle all the balls in her life and look so graceful doing it?

Glancing up, she saw Logan standing at the back doorway in his pajamas, looking at her with a blank stare.

"Hey, buddy," she said, not really knowing what else to say because she wasn't that great with kids.

He didn't answer, just walked right past her as if in a trance and headed for the backyard swing set.

"Logan?"

He toddled across the damp lawn without even looking at her. It hit her then that the boy was sleepwalking.

What should she do? Amelia scratched her chin. She'd heard you shouldn't wake up a sleepwalker. Or was that just an old wives' tale? And if it were true, what were you supposed to do? Certainly not allow a three-year-old to traipse around outside in the dark barefooted.

She searched for Anna, but her sister had disappeared into the shadows. She couldn't even hear her talking on the phone.

"Logan," she whispered.

He didn't answer, just moved methodically toward the swing set. Thank heavens there was a locked gate around the pool.

Amelia trailed after the boy, watched him climb onto a swing, grab hold of the chains with both hands, and kick his legs to build momentum.

The moon passed from the clouds and silhouetted the boy.

He lifted his face to the sky. Giggled.

"Are you awake?" Amelia drifted over.

Rubbing his eyes, Logan nodded and yawned.

"Do you want me to take you back to bed?"

"Uh-huh."

She crouched to pick him up. He threw his arms around her neck, rested his head on her shoulder, and started sucking his thumb. She got to her feet with Logan clutched in her arms.

Dizziness swamped her the way it had before she'd gotten her diagnosis and she hadn't known what was wrong. Holding tightly to the boy, she swayed unsteadily, struggling to get her bearings.

Too much. Today had been too much activity.

She waited for the dizziness to abate, Logan's sweet little-boy breath warming her neck. Tightening her arms around him, she headed into the house, kicked off her shoes, and tiptoed up the stairs with him.

In his room, she settled him into his race car bed. She covered him with a Star Wars blanket, looked down at his angelic face, and felt her heart crack open.

She would never have one of these of her own. Even if she got a kidney transplant, she'd have to stay on antirejection drugs for the rest of her life. She was already thirty-five. Children were an impossible dream that she was better off not dreaming.

Before now, she'd not thought much about having children. Robert had been on the fence and she'd never had any real maternal urges. First, her life had been busy building her career, and then the death of Robert and her parents had flattened her, and later, her own failing health took precedent.

Why was baby hunger hitting her now? The longing slammed into Amelia so hard and fast it took her breath away.

You don't deserve to have children. You'd just screw it up like everything else.

"Auntie?"

Amelia's heart lurched. He'd called her Auntie. "Uh-huh?"

He sat up, stretching to kiss her cheek. "Night."

Logan.

And his adorable little boyness. That was what triggered these fantasies, these useless hopes. She had other, more essential things on her mind, like staying alive.

Once she was certain Logan was sound asleep again, she went back outside to see her sister emerging from the gardens. Anna slipped her phone into her pocket.

"How's your mom?" Amelia asked.

"She was having a bit of a meltdown. She saw a program about the coronavirus, and it brought back bad memories. It took me a while to get off the phone because I didn't want to tell her I was with you. She's still upset about what happened."

"Understandable." Amelia paused, then told her about Logan.

Anna rubbed a palm over her forehead, looked distressed. "He was sleepwalking?"

"I put him back to bed, stayed with him while he fell asleep again."

"That was so kind of you." Relief filled Anna's eyes. "Thank you. You're a lifesaver. What can I do for you in return?"

Now was the time to tell her. Put it out there. *If she's not willing*

*to give you the kidney, no harm, no foul, you can go back home and wait
on the transplant list.*

Jutting out her chin and inhaling deeply to bolster her courage, Amelia said, "Anna, there's something you—"

But before Amelia could finish, Anna wrapped her in a lung-squeezing hug that left her feeling overwhelmed again.

"Listen, I'm just going to be the first to say it," Anna declared. "And please don't feel like you have to say it back to me yet. I know you'll get there."

"What's that?" Suddenly, Amelia was petrified and aching to run away before her sister said something irrevocable.

Too late.

Anna's eyes turned dreamy and Amelia knew she was sunk.

"Never, ever forget this, Amelia Brandt. I am your sister and I love you."

CHAPTER FOURTEEN

Anna

Hello, I Love You

Anna had jumped the gun by telling Amelia how she felt about her. The shock and dismay on her sister's face were all too easy to read.

"I—" Amelia backed up, twisting from Anna's embrace. "I-I think I'll retire for the night."

Feeling like a fool, Anna dropped her arms to her side. "Yes. Sure. You're right. We need to get to bed. It's almost ten and I'm usually asleep by nine thirty."

"Anna—"

"Night!" In a rush, Anna picked up her tea glass, hurried to the kitchen, and dumped the tea into the sink.

Her heart pounded and her palms sweated, and she felt . . . well . . . stupid. She'd gone out on a limb and Amelia had sawed it off.

Hitting the ground shamefaced was not fun.

It's okay, it's all right. Don't be embarrassed for being you. There's no shame in leading with your heart, Anna. Her father's voice was inside her head as she brushed her teeth and got ready for bed.

Yeah? Easy for him to say. He was the one who'd separated her and her sister in the first place, and he'd died without ever having to explain himself.

"I'm so mad at you, Daddy," she muttered into the darkness.

Undone, she buried her face in Kevin's pillow, inhaled his scent for comfort as she often did when he was on the road and she felt lonely. Tonight, pillow-sniffing didn't work. Both her husband and her father had betrayed her.

She thought of her mother, and guilt slapped down her spine one vertebra at a time. She'd been pretty rough on Mom, and she felt guilty.

The consequences of what her father, and she assumed Winnie, had done thirty-five years ago had ripples that extended far beyond just her and Amelia. Mom was affected. Mike. Kevin. Her kids.

Logan and Allie.

They were young and they would bounce back, but she couldn't underestimate the effect this was having in their lives. Emotionally, she'd shoveled them aside, going about their daily routine by rote, too caught up in her own upheaval to give much thought to how their little lives had been impacted.

Do better, Anna, dammit.

Unable to sleep, Anna got out of bed. Whenever she couldn't sleep, she cleaned, and now she started up on a long-procrastinated task: to rearrange the kitchen drawers. She'd been putting it off for months and things were in a jumble. Maybe if she'd get her cutlery drawer in order, and Marie Kondo the hell out of it, she could get her life back on track.

As she bent over the drawer, tension pulled her shoulder into a spasm. It hurt so badly, she stopped in her tracks and did some yoga moves on the kitchen tile floor.

She hadn't been to yoga class since Amelia had shown up on her doorstep and her muscles were telling her all about it. She did a few quick sun salutations, wondered if there was such a thing as moon salutations and if she should be doing those instead. Anna ran through the sequence they practiced in her studio's vinyasa class. Salute to the sun. Standing forward fold. Low lunge. Plank. Chaturanga. Up dog. Down dog.

Butt in the air, arms in front of her, elbows facing forward, she peered between her legs. Good grief, was that dried ketchup on the baseboard? She hoped it was ketchup and not blood.

The glamorous life of a mom. Sighing, she ended her short yoga workout, grabbed a rag and some pine cleaner, and attacked the baseboard.

"Mommy?"

She looked up to see Allie standing in the kitchen doorway shivering, and rubbing her eyes, her pajamas soaked at the crotch. "I wet the bed."

"Oh, sweetie." Anna hopped to her feet. It had been years since Allie had wet the bed.

"I-I didn't mean to."

"I know, honey, I know." She hugged her daughter, not caring that she got pee on her own clothes. "It's okay. It happens."

"I haven't pee-peed the bed since I was five," she wailed.

"My fault. I shouldn't have let you guys drink so much lemonade at the restaurant." She wrapped her arm around her daughter's shoulder and guided her into the Jack and Jill bathroom she shared with Logan.

Turning on the shower, she helped Allie out of her wet pajamas. "You shower while I go strip your bed and put the sheets in the washing machine."

Silently, Allie nodded.

She kissed her daughter's head. "It's nothing to be ashamed of. Don't give it a second thought."

"But I'm too big to wet the bed."

"Sometimes our bodies just do what they do," she said. "We clean up the mess and move on."

"Like when you have the flu?"

"Yes. Just like that."

Allie looked marginally better and climbed into the tub, pulling the shower curtain closed behind her.

"I'll bring you some fresh pj's for you to put on and make a dry bed for you to crawl into." Anna left the bathroom and went into the mudroom to find the urine remover they used when Cujo had accidents on the carpet.

She stripped the sheets, sprayed the cleaner on the mattress, and wished she'd never taken off the mattress protector. She put down a plastic garbage bag over the wet spot and made the bed with fresh sheets. Tomorrow, she'd finish cleaning up the mattress strain. Tonight, all that mattered was getting Allie back into bed.

Allie got out of the shower and dressed in clean Hello Kitty pj's that were getting too small for her. Anna made a mental note to donate them and buy her daughter replacement pajamas.

"Grandma is mad at Aunt Amelia, isn't she?" Allie asked out of the blue.

"She's not mad at your aunt. She's just upset about the way things are."

"That you're not really her daughter?"

"I am her daughter, Allie. Just like you're mine. It doesn't matter if she's not my biological mother, she raised me and loved me and I'm hers."

"It's like you're adopted, but no one knew it."

"Yes, it's like that." *Dad had known.*

Allie looked her point-blank in the eye. "Am I adopted?"

"Heavens no. Why would you think that?"

"You didn't know you were adopted. Maybe you don't know that I'm adopted too."

"Honey, you've seen the pictures of your birth. I was there, your dad was there, your grandmothers were there. Four people, besides the hospital staff, saw me give birth to you."

"And no one saw Grammy give birth to you?" Allie asked.

How did she explain this without casting her father in a bad light? Especially since she wasn't sure what had really happened. Maybe her father was innocent, and it had all been Winnie's doing.

"There was a hurricane the night Amelia and I were born. The lights went out in the hospital. It was chaotic."

"Could I have a twin out there somewhere?" Allie asked. "Could she just show up one day, expecting us to be sisters and change everything?"

"No, that's not going to happen."

"How do you know?"

"Because I have a picture of you in my womb. Remember the sonogram photograph in your baby book? There was only one baby in there."

"I'm so glad," Allie said. "While it would be nice to have a sister, I would want to know her from the very start. Not have her show up when I was old."

Anna suppressed a grin at the "old" comment. "You have nothing to worry about, sweetheart."

"But you do. Ever since Aunt Amelia showed up Dad's been mad at you and Grandma's been mad at you and my cousins and friends keep asking me stupid questions about how come you didn't know you had a twin sister." Allie gnawed her fingernail. A habit Anna thought she'd broken.

Was this why she'd wet the bed? Distressed over what people were saying? Allie was a sensitive soul and a disruption in her routine affected her more deeply than it would for some children. A fresh guilt stabbed through Anna. She'd been neglecting her daughter, self-absorbed with her own drama.

"You can tell people that if they have questions, they can come ask me or Amelia. Will you do that?"

Allie nodded and offered up a tiny smile.

"I love you more than anything, you know that, right?" Anna brushed a lock of hair from her daughter's face.

"I love you, too, Mommy."

See, Amelia, that's how it's done. I say I love you. Then you say it back. So easy a ten-year-old can do it.

Anna hugged her daughter tightly, guided her back to bed, tucked her in, kissed her forehead, and turned out the light. As she padded back to her room, she vowed to do a much better job as a mother, daughter, and sister.

And for Amelia, that meant giving her twin breathing room.

* * *

THE NEXT MORNING, Friday, June 4, Amelia acted as if nothing had happened the previous evening, which was A-okay with Anna. Sweep that declaration of undying love right under the rug, where apparently it belonged. She had a new goal. She'd show her sister firsthand what it was like to be part of a loving family.

They had breakfast in the kitchen. Anna served blueberry pancakes with real maple syrup and crispy bacon.

"You made Grandpa's favorite breakfast." Allie wriggled happily, last night seemingly forgotten.

"Whip cream, whip cream!" Logan announced, struggling to open the refrigerator for the Reddi-wip.

A few minutes later, Anna managed to get everyone seated around the table. "Let's join hands and say grace."

"At breakfast?" Allie asked.

"Yes, ma'am. We want to thank God for Amelia coming into our lives." She held out her left hand to her daughter and offered her right hand to her sister.

Amelia hesitated.

Anna had gotten the impression that the Brandts weren't

churchgoing people. This was probably making her twin uncomfortable. Great. Now what? She couldn't back out of the prayer at this point. Allie had already taken her hand and Logan's.

Logan had his little palm extended toward Amelia, just as Anna did.

Amelia stared down at her plate, raised her gaze, slipped into a small smile, and took their hands.

Whew, okay.

Anna bowed her head, determined to keep the prayer short and sweet. "Dear Heavenly Father, thank you for bringing Amelia into our lives and thank you for these awesome blueberry pancakes."

"Amen!" Logan sang out.

Everyone dropped hands and tackled their pancakes.

Allie drizzled a generous amount of syrup over her plate, cut off a bite of pancake with a fork, and promptly burst into tears.

Instantly, Anna set down her fork and went to her daughter's side, placed a hand to her back. "What is it? What's wrong?"

"I miss Grandpa!" Allie turned and sobbed against Anna's shoulder.

She squeezed Allie tight, kissed the top of her head, and wished like heck she'd made oatmeal instead of her father's signature blueberry pancakes.

"Oh, sweetie, I miss him too. It's okay to feel sad. It's okay to cry."

Glancing up, Anna checked on Logan, who was busy squirting the Reddi-wip over his pancakes oblivious to his sister's distress, and then she let her gaze drift over to her twin.

Amelia sat impossibly straight. Emotionally controlled. Isolated. Calm. Cool. Collected.

But behind those measured brown eyes, Anna saw a flicker of emotion. An emotion that punched her right in the heart.

Stark, abject yearning.

"Allie," Amelia said.

"Yes?" Allie pulled back, sniffled, swiped her hand over her nose.

Anna fished in her pocket for her tissue, passed it to her daughter, and wondered what her sister would say next.

"Would you like to go buy a horse?"

* * *

"You can't buy Allie a horse," Anna murmured after they'd finished breakfast and were loading the dishwasher together. She'd sent the children to walk Cujo, and to get them out of earshot of the conversation. "Why did you offer to buy her a horse?"

"She was crying."

"And?"

Amelia passed her two coffee mugs. "I didn't want her to cry."

"When the kids are upset, we don't run out and buy them expensive gifts. We soothe them instead and show them how to channel their emotions in an appropriate manner."

Amelia's face flushed. "I apologize. I overstepped."

"You did."

"I still want to buy her a horse."

"No." Anna shook her head.

"All right, I'll go tell her."

"Let me be the bad guy. She's my daughter. I'll tell her."

"How about this? What if I buy the horse for me? I pay for the boarding, and Allie can ride her whenever she wants."

"You're still rewarding her for crying. That's not a message I want to send."

"But you aren't sending it. I am."

Anna ran a palm over her mouth. She was miffed at her twin for what she'd done, but also touched and deeply saddened that Amelia thought the way to a child's heart was to shower her with expensive gifts.

"That's how your parents showed you love, isn't it?" Anna asked.

"What?"

"Frank and Sarah Brandt didn't teach you how to handle life's curveballs. They just threw money at problems. Threw money at you."

Amelia pressed her lips into a thin flat line, and barely nodded. Moisture glistened in her twin's eyes, and it was the first time Anna had ever seen her near tears. It sent her heart reeling.

Quickly, Amelia blinked away her feelings, tacked up a tattered smile. "How about this? I buy a horse for me and board her nearby and Allie can muck out the stalls and brush the horse in exchange for riding her whenever she wants."

"You're getting a mare?" Anna asked, understanding she'd already lost this battle. As mild as Amelia might appear on the outside, on the inside her sister was forged of steel.

Amelia nodded. "Is it okay if I let Allie name her?"

"Sure." *Might as well throw in the towel.*

"Thank you." Amelia looked so gratefully earnest that Anna felt bad for thwarting her.

Anna put the last dish in the washer, loaded it with soap, and punched the start button. Straightening, she noticed Amelia studying her with a serious expression.

"What is it?" Anna asked.

"There's something else I need to discuss with you. Something important."

Gulping, Anna dried her hands on a kitchen towel. Uh-oh.

"About last night—"

That's exactly what she was afraid Amelia was going to bring up—Anna's foolish declaration of love.

Awkward.

Amelia would either try to tell her why she wasn't ready to say she loved her in return, or worse, fake it and say she loved Anna, too, when she didn't really feel it yet.

"Let's leave the somber discussions for another time. We just have one more full day together before Kevin comes home and we've still got so much to catch up on."

"But I—"

"Please?" Anna pressed her palms together and met her sister's eyes. "Can we table anything that might cause a problem between us and just enjoy the moment?"

Solemnly, Amelia bit down on her bottom lip and nodded.

"Great!" Anna said, knowing she sounded way too cheerful. "Let's round up the kids and go find you a horse!"

CHAPTER FIFTEEN

Amelia

Reality Check

They bought the horse.

The animal was a small twenty-year-old roan gelding, and Allie named him Heathcliff, after her grandfather. They took the gelding to a local stable to board. It turned out to be the most perfect morning. The weather was balmy, and the sky was overcast just enough to provide great shade without producing any rain.

Allie was in heaven. She keep hugging the horse around the neck and cooing to him.

"She's happy," Anna murmured to Amelia. "I know I was a bit of a Scrooge over the horse, but thank you."

"I'm glad she likes him."

"Are you kidding? She *loves* him."

"Anna," Amelia said, gathering her courage. "I really *do* need to talk to you about something important."

"Okay, but later." Anna waved away her comment like an apple with a worm.

Sighing, Amelia bit back the truth she'd been aching to tell her sister. *I'm here because I need one of your kidneys.* Swallowed the words whole. Her mouth filled with the taste of bile and worry.

Even though Allie loved the horse and Amelia wasn't sorry she invested in it for her niece, she wondered if it would look like a bribe when Anna discovered the real reason that she'd come to Moonglow Cove.

Was it a bribe?

No. Yes? She hadn't meant it to be one. Not consciously, but in the back of her mind . . . maybe?

"Tomorrow," Anna said. "We'll have a long talk tomorrow before Kevin comes home."

All right. That gave Amelia some time before things irrevocably shifted between herself and Anna, and she was determined to milk every ounce of joy from the marrow of this moment because it wouldn't last long.

"Remember, tonight is the concert. You're still coming to that, right?"

"Yes," Amelia said.

"And you'll play a song with us?"

"If you can find a cello on such short notice."

"Yay!"

"Aunt Amelia!" Allie said. "Watch this!" Then the amazing child jumped onto the horse bareback without a boost up.

Nope, not a bribe at all, and the horse was worth every penny Amelia had spent to put a smile that big on her niece's happy face.

* * *

THAT EVENING, THE concert was held in an outdoor amphitheater in the park near the beach. They'd packed a picnic basket and swung by to pick up Winnie at the memory care facility for the amateur event in the park.

Robin met them there.

The program started at five. Anna's band didn't go onstage until six, but they got to the park early to find a good spot near the stage.

Robin eyed Amelia leerily.

Amelia offered her a smile that she hoped said, *Truce?*

"Mom," Anna said. "Could you help me spread out the blanket?"

"I'll help," Amelia offered.

Looking flustered, Robin inclined her head toward Winnie, who was crouched on the sand, putting broken seashells in her pockets. "Why did you bring her?"

"Mom, she's cooped up inside all day. It's the nice thing to do, and maybe a few outings here and there will dissuade her from running away from the facility."

"Or give her a bigger taste of freedom."

"Mom, please be nice."

"She's more of a handful than the kids." Robin waved at the children who were playing with glow sticks on the sand.

Amelia anchored her corners of the blanket with the picnic basket on one side, the Igloo cooler on the other. The cooler made her think of transplants and thinking of transplants reminded her she was running out of time . . .

But now was not the moment.

Tomorrow, she'd tell Anna the truth. No more delays. Tonight, she would enjoy the music and her sister before their relationship changed forever. It didn't matter whether Anna agreed to give her the kidney or not. Things would be different between them and there was nothing she could do about that.

Winnie eased down in the middle of the blanket, stretched her legs out in front of her with the skirt of her dress hiked up around her thighs. In her lap she had a bouquet of sea oats she picked up from somewhere when no one was paying close attention.

She pulled the oats off the stalk, recited, "She loves me, she loves me not."

"Goodness." Anna dropped on her knees beside the elderly woman. In the kindest voice, she said, "Winnie, we don't want to harm the sea oats."

Nodding, Winnie extended her bedraggled little bouquet to Anna and whispered, "She loves me not."

"She loves you very much, silly." Anna leaned across Winnie's outstretched legs to envelop her in a warm, cumbersome hug.

Amelia's chest clutched. Anna was so kind, so caring, so generous. She knew her sister would give her a kidney in a heartbeat, but because of Anna's endless capacity for love, she didn't know if she should ask. Maybe she should just leave town and never come back.

Winnie started crying then, her frail body shaking as she chanted, "Loves me not, loves me not, loves me not."

Amelia glanced over to see Robin staring at her and not in a good way. She turned from Robin's harsh gaze and sat beside Winnie and Anna. Lying on her back, she pointed up at the fluffy clouds painted pink by the setting sun.

"Ooh look," Amelia said to distract Winnie. "A family of kittens."

Winnie's tears dried and she peeked over Anna's shoulder at Amelia. "Kittens?"

"Yes, a basketful of white kittens, can you see them?"

Giving Amelia a grateful smile, Anna brushed the sea oats off the blanket and helped Winnie onto her back so she could cloudgaze with Amelia. Carefully, she tucked Winnie's dress around her legs to keep her from exposing herself to concertgoers.

"The kids have wandered too far," Robin said. "I'll go get them."

"Thanks, Mom." Anna lay down on the opposite side of Winnie. They watched the clouds filter and shift in the breeze blowing off the ocean. They called out the images they saw in the sky.

It was a peaceful moment. Far too short-lived, but Amelia made a point to enjoy it and she heard Dr. Ellard's voice in her mind. *Live your best life now.*

Hmm, sometimes, Dr. Ellard sounded a lot like Oprah.

The crowd thickened as the sky darkened. Other families arrived, staking their claims and setting up blankets and camp chairs. As the music started, Robin returned with the children.

Amelia helped Winnie sit up, while Anna opened the picnic basket and passed out ham and cheese sandwiches, potato chips, and bottled water.

Fifteen minutes before six, Anna got up and dusted her palms on the seat of her shorts. "I'm off for our set."

"Yay, Mommy!" Allie clapped, and Logan clapped because his sister was doing it and echoed, "Yay, Mommy!"

They hopped up and gave their mother a kiss for good luck.

It was such a precious moment, Amelia found herself longing again for children of her own.

Grinning, Anna leaned in and whispered in Amelia's ear. "I found a cello."

"What?" Amelia blinked, remembering her excuse for why she couldn't join Anna's band.

Laughing, Anna wiggled her fingers and disappeared behind the amphitheater with the other members of her musical group.

Amelia couldn't settle herself. Her heart skipped and her stomach fluttered.

Anna had a cello.

Her twin wanted Amelia to play with her band. And darn it, Amelia *wanted* to play, but she hadn't picked up the cello since Robert and her parents had been killed and the cello had become a symbol of everything she'd lost.

In her mind's eye she could see Dr. Ellard, smiling wisely and saying, *Maybe it's time you picked the cello up again.*

Maybe what was once lost is now found?

Heady thought.

Scary thought.

She'd gotten comfortable in discomfort.

After the current band finished, the emcee came onstage to introduce the Harmonious Housewives. He was totally bald, sported a full beard, thick and black, and moved with quick, lithe steps that belied his bearish build.

Anna was the lead guitarist. She took her place at the front of the stage, her guitar strapped around her neck. The drummer and bassist assembled behind Anna and the lead singer.

Pride for her sister swelled in her chest. Sniffling, Amelia crinkled her nose. Pollen, she told herself, but that wasn't true.

They were so different, she and her twin. Anna, extroverted, clearly blooming in the limelight. While Amelia loved playing the cello, she hated solos. Anna stepped forward with a long guitar riff.

The song ended, but instead of the band seamlessly blending into the next number, the bearded emcee—who looked as if he should be announcing a wrestling match—skittered back on-stage with his microphone.

"Ladies and gents, we have a very special guest in the audience tonight," he said.

Anna took off her guitar and disappeared backstage.

Going after the VIP guest? Amelia wondered.

"Please put your hands together." The emcee demonstrated. "And let's give a big round of applause to cellist Amelia Brandt, who's come to our little hamlet all the way from the Chicago Symphony. Amelia is the identical twin sister of our very own Anna Straus Drury!"

Goose bumps spread up Amelia's arms. Anna really did expect her to play? *Oh my.* She was both delighted and distressed by the thought.

Anna returned carrying a cello. She grinned big and waved wildly at Amelia.

The crowd erupted in hearty applause and heads swiveled as people turned to stare as if she was a big deal.

Anxiety, that mean boa constrictor, wrapped around Amelia's lungs. She wanted to make music with her twin, but her feet seemed welded to the earth.

"Sister." Anna held out the cello. "Will you do us the pleasure of accompanying us for our next number?"

The crowd started clapping and chanting, *"Amelia, Amelia, Amelia."*

The drummer kept time to the beat of their chant.

She couldn't leave her twin hanging. If it meant facing her past and that damned cello, then that's what she would do for Anna. The sister who loved her.

Amelia stood up and cupped her hands around her mouth and hollered across the park. "Who says I know the song you're going to play?"

Anna strummed a few chords to the *Frozen* theme song, the ringtone for both of their cell phones. "Let It Go."

Amelia's heart pulled forward, even as her legs balked.

"Do it, Auntie." Allie gave her a little shove.

"Amelia, Amelia, Amelia!"

Anna strummed her guitar. The bassist joined in. The crowd shifted the chant to *Let It Go! Let It Go! Let It Go!*

Everyone was looking at her as if she was a big deal, and it felt so good that she could hardly breathe.

Ha! Little do they know. The voice in her head was pure Sarah Brandt.

Anna clasped her hands together in prayer pose, and her eyes misted with tears as she mouthed the lyrics.

The lead singer held up the cello.

The drummer positioned a folding chair in the center of the stage and motioned for her to come up.

Amelia's feet sprang forward, carrying her to her sister and the stage.

To the cello.

The instrument that had gotten her through a lonely childhood. Playing the cello was the only time in her life when she'd been part of something bigger than herself and she'd been away from it for two long years.

The next thing she knew, Amelia found herself sitting onstage, the beautiful cello in her hands, and she was making it weep in a way that she herself didn't dare.

She peered out at the audience, saw Robin jumping up and down, grinning and raising her fist in solidarity. Allie and Logan joined in, hopping like pogo sticks. Even Winnie looked engaged, her eyes wide, her lips moving as she sang along.

Amelia caressed the cello.

Home! She was home and it felt wonderful.

The band moved back, giving her the solo. At first, she was startled, but the music was inside her pouring out as she expertly manipulated the instrument, stirring the emotions of the crowd.

Everyone was on their feet, dancing on the beach, some singing off-key and boisterously, "Let It Go."

She absorbed their collective energy, channeled it, and allowed it to inspire her. She closed her eyes and played for all she was worth.

A moment later she felt someone move to her left, and glanced over to see Anna standing beside her, keeping pace with her on the guitar. If she shifted gears, could her sister follow? Could the Harmonious Housewives keep up?

Give them the chance. If they can't keep up, they can leave the music to you. Her pulse galloped. *Do it.*

Boldly, she eased into Vivaldi's "Winter," borrowing the fast-paced finale from the great classical master stylized in the fashion from the group Piano Guys.

Anna didn't miss a trick. She was right there with her. Totally getting where Amelia was going. It was as if her twin was inside her brain, instantly reading her thoughts and giving her just what she needed exactly when she needed it.

The bassist and rhythm guitarist backed off, giving the two of them their duet. Behind them, the drumbeat underscored their musical fusion.

Slowly, she flitted from Vivaldi back to "Let It Go." Anna and the drummer went right along with her. The bassist and lead singer/guitarist came back in to wrap up the piece with the final strains of the song.

It had been years since she'd experienced a collaboration like this, and she was speechless at the flawlessness of their performance. Once in a while, life did dish up the perfect moment and this was one of them.

The audience went insane, clapping, cheering, and flooding the stage.

The next thing Amelia knew the crowd surged, lifting her up. She found herself carried along by the audience as they passed her from person to person, mosh pit style. Strange hands gripped her. It was terrifying and at the same time thrilling. Like the Juggernaut.

Confused and confounded she looked around to see that Anna was also crowd surfing.

What a high!

It felt like total acceptance.

In the end the groups carrying them along deposited them on their feet on the beach in front of each other.

"Wow!" Anna breathed heavily, sounding exhilarated.

Amelia wondered how she must look with mussed hair and flaming cheeks, panting and victorious.

Their gazes locked.

They grinned at each other.

"I'm glad you encouraged me to do that," Amelia said. "It was therapeutic."

"I thought you weren't going to and then I realized too late that you never really agreed to do it. You said 'maybe' and I took it for a yes and located a cello. That wasn't fair."

"I should have said yes to begin with. I let fear hold me back."

"I felt lousy springing it on you."

"You warned me." Amelia chuckled. "I just need to remember that in your world, maybe means yes."

"You could have refused."

She kept holding on to Anna's gaze, felt a hard thrill go straight through her bones. "And leave you hanging? No way. We're twins, right?"

"And look how it turned out!"

"The best collaboration ever," Amelia said. "Move aside, Lennon and McCartney."

Anna flushed prettily. "How about we ask Mom to take Winnie back to the center and then watch the kids for a couple of hours so that you and I can really savor this time together? Our first collaboration only happens once."

* * *

AMELIA'S ENERGY LAGGED from the adrenaline comedown after the concert, but she was determined to hide her tiredness. It had been a beautiful evening, and she wanted it to go on for as long as possible.

After sending Robin off with Winnie and the kids in Anna's minivan, they strolled the beach toward the jetty that extended out into the Gulf. Robin had left the keys to her Camry for them to use when they were ready to come home.

"It was amazing the way you seamlessly shifted into Vivaldi's 'Winter.' Totally inspired," Anna said.

Amelia shrugged. "I took a chance. I didn't know if you knew the piece or not."

"I'm so glad you did. I get the feeling you're not a gambler," Anna said. "But OMG, you're an astounding musician, Amelia. What a rush to play with someone of your caliber."

"Thank you." Amelia's cheeks heated.

Anna reached for her hand.

Startled, Amelia drew back.

Anna pressed her lips together, glanced down, and dropped her hand.

"You caught me off guard." Amelia reached for her sister's hand. "I'm not used to people touching me."

"I'm sorry, I'm too handsy."

"It's not a flaw. You just have to give me time to get used to you."

"I can do that."

Amelia squeezed her sister's hand.

Anna squeezed back.

"Tonight was very special for me, too." Amelia smiled kindly.

"I'm just blown away by your talent. You knew when to blend the songs, and on what note." Anna sighed. "I'll never be that good."

"But you followed where I led."

"Yes, but on my own?" She shook her head. "I couldn't have gotten there. Together, we had a phenomenal rhythm. It's like we were totally inside each other's heads. Almost as if we were the same person."

Moistening her lips, Amelia slashed a sidelong glance at her sister. It was too true to be comfortable. From the amphitheater behind them they could hear another band onstage, the music vibrating into the night.

"I feared it was a mistake," Anna said. "When I saw the look on your face after the emcee asked you to come onstage."

Amelia stopped walking, forcing Anna to stop walking, too, or drop her hand, and her sister didn't seem the least bit inclined to let her go. "Why?"

"Why what?" Anna looked confused, her dark eyebrows dipping low.

"Why did you want to play with me?"

"Who wouldn't?" Anna looked so earnest.

"No ulterior motive?"

"None."

They'd arrived at the jetty.

Quaint marine streetlamps lit their way. Water lapped against the jetty's stone wall. Out on the water, lighted boats cruised. In the far distance, oil rigs glittered. Without talking, they strolled to the end of the jetty, still holding hands, but Amelia's palm grew sweaty at the secret she'd been keeping from her twin.

The time had come to tell her sister the truth, even if it meant ruining the most perfect day. Out on the far end of the jetty, the wind was stronger, whipping their clothes around their bodies and their hair into their faces.

"This is probably my ego getting the better of me," Anna said. "But do you think we could play together again sometime? Maybe you could even join our band?"

"Maybe," Amelia hedged.

"Oh, wow! That would be so awesome."

Bewildered, Amelia stared at her. *Remember, to Anna a "maybe" means yes.* "But I'm not going to be around for that long."

"Why not? You said yourself you have nothing in Chicago. Consider moving to Moonglow Cove."

A hard shiver ran through Amelia's body as her gaze locked with her twin's. Anna wanted her to stick around. She loved her. She'd confessed it last night.

And it was more than Amelia could handle.

The jetty vanished and, weirdly, it seemed as if they were

suspended between sea and sky, embraced by wind and water, the elements an integral part of what was passing between them. The soothing notes of the band still playing in the distance, a soundtrack punctuating everything. Music, the link between them that forged a quicker intimacy.

Amelia closed her eyes, floated for a luxurious half second, inhaled deeply, and then said what she should have said on Tuesday. Dropping her sister's hand but holding tight to her gaze, Amelia sucked in a deep breath.

"I came to Moonglow Cove for only one reason."

"I know. You came to meet me." Anna's eyes were so bright and happy and here was where Amelia was going to go and ruin everything.

"Not really." Amelia breathed in deeply. This was the moment; she couldn't avoid it any longer. She owed Anna—big-hearted, kind, welcoming Anna—the full truth. "I came here because I'm in renal failure."

Amelia watched her words sink in.

Anna's eyes widened and she fingered her keepsake bracelet and then she took a step backward. "Wh-what?"

"My kidneys are failing."

"Y-you're dying?" Anna hiccuped.

"Without dialysis or a transplant, yes, I will die, and the sooner I get a kidney, the better. But with AB negative blood, my chances are extremely low unless . . ."

Anna hauled in a deep breath and crashed her gaze into Amelia's. The expression in her eyes said she understood immediately what was at stake. "Unless I give you one of mine."

CHAPTER SIXTEEN

Anna

Difference of Opinion

The news that Amelia was dying and only Anna could save her was a lot to absorb.

As was the fact that her identical twin sister, whom she'd known less than a week, had come to town solely to ask her for a kidney.

That's why Amelia was here.

A kidney.

Not for some big family reunion or sisterly lovefest.

Anna felt sick to her stomach. No wonder her sister had seemed so rattled when last night, Anna had told Amelia that she loved her. How could Amelia tell her she loved her back, when she only wanted one thing?

Anna's kidney.

"W-why didn't you tell me before?" Anna asked, struggling to control her hurt.

Shamefaced, Amelia glanced down at her clasped hands. "I tried a time or two but we got interrupted and then I didn't know how to start. Not once I got to know you and your family.

How could I ask a perfect stranger for a gift that precious? How could I ask you to make such a big sacrifice for me?"

"Then why did you stay in Moonglow Cove?" Anna put a palm to her belly, terrified she was going to puke. "Why didn't you just leave?"

"We were having so much fun and I was getting to know you and it was really nice . . ."

"No." Anna folded her arms across her chest. "I want the honest truth." Staring down the length of the dark, stone jetty, the short distance between them felt like a yawning chasm.

"I—"

"If it was too hard for you to come right out and ask me for a kidney," Anna went on, trembling with anger, "why did you *really* stay? You could have left. Maybe you should have left. I would have left under those circumstances."

"I-I had no one else to turn to. Nowhere else to go."

"What do you mean? You're rich. You could go anywhere. Why not just *buy* a kidney?" Anna slapped a palm over her mouth. Why had she said that? It was hurtful and she didn't mean it.

Amelia winced. "Money is *all* I have, Anna. I have no family. No job. No close friends. Not anymore. Just a few hangers-on who are there for what they could get. But you . . . you welcomed me with open arms. You didn't hesitate. You accepted me right off the bat. No questions asked."

Balling her hands into fists, Anna tried to reconcile the emotions churning through her—anger, sadness, hurt, betrayal, but at the end of it all was forgiveness.

Yes, she was ready to forgive Amelia anything, because in the end, she *was* her twin sister. They had a biological connection that Anna had with no one else on earth. Not her mother, nor her brother, not even her own children. Allie and Logan were half Kevin.

But she and Amelia?

They were identical twins. The closest any two human beings could be. Turning her back on her sister would be like turning her back on herself. But they had to work through this.

"I defended you. Kevin suspected you were up to something, but stupid, gullible me, I didn't want to believe him."

"You're not stupid." Amelia wrung her hands. "And you're certainly not gullible. You're kind and generous and thoughtful. Don't blame yourself. Don't beat yourself up. This is all on me. I mishandled everything."

"You accepted my hospitality. You came into my house with ulterior motives. You caused problems between me and my mother. You caused problems in my marriage." All Anna's pain came spilling out.

The face in front of Anna's was as familiar as her own, but Amelia's skin paled, her cheeks reddened, and her lips were a dusky blue as if she wasn't getting enough oxygen.

"There's so many things I could say," Amelia murmured. "So much that needs to be said, but I'm so afraid I'll hurt your feelings."

What? Was she accusing Anna of having a fragile ego? *Gee, sis. Thanks for another stab in the gut.*

From the minute they'd clamped eyes on each other in Anna's foyer, it had been love at first sight for Anna, but now this relationship had all the earmarks of a rough breakup with a selfish boyfriend.

Fear clutched Anna at the thought she could lose her twin forever, and just when she'd found her!

"My family is everything to me, Amelia. You do understand that there is nothing you could ever do or say that could truly hurt me . . ." Anna bravely raised her chin, speaking her truth. "Beyond walking away and cutting me out of your life completely. Now *that* would kill me."

Amelia's brown eyes turned bleak as if she had been thinking of bolting from Moonglow Cove right now, tonight. "I don't know that we would even be friends, if we weren't twins."

Another fresh kick to the teeth. "Why do you say that?"

"We're so different. Yes, we look alike, and have the same bathroom decor and love of horses and music, but that's all superficial. At the core, we've got nothing in common. Our lifestyles are polar opposites. Our values. Our personalities, too."

"So? You think Kevin and I have tons of things in common beyond our kids? We're different and we get crossways with each other at times, but we're still nuts about each other."

"I don't—"

"Please. Not right now." Anna raised both palms. "Maybe you *should* go back to the Moonglow Inn. I'll pack up your things and have an Uber bring them to you."

"Yes, you're right. Absolutely. That'll work."

Amelia was so calm, so unphased that Anna wanted to scream

at her. Instead, she turned and walked away, stumbling down the jetty in the dark, headed for her mother's car in the parking lot.

Amelia did not come after her.

Sadness shook Anna's body. From her hair—which she'd pinned in a bun atop her head—all the way down to her sandals, she trembled.

Driving home in the darkness, tears spilled down her cheeks.

People dotted the boardwalk, laughing and smiling as they wandered the souvenir shops or strolled in and out of restaurants. Eight P.M. was early for a Friday night, but bone-deep exhaustion wrapped around Anna.

While Robin's Camry idled at the traffic light, Anna shuffled through her thoughts, trying to reconcile everything that had happened, and came up with the three items she knew for certain.

One: Her twin's appearance in Moonglow Cove had not really been to reconnect with her.

Two: Whenever he found out about Amelia's renal failure, Kevin would crow victoriously, "I told you so."

Three: If she wanted more time with her sister, she had no choice but to give her a kidney and that's what she wanted more than almost anything right now . . . more time with her sister.

Leaning forward in her seat at the traffic light, Anna pressed both palms to her back, one hand over each kidney.

Which one would they take? Left? Or right? Was Amelia's kidney condition hereditary? Did Anna have an increased risk of developing kidney disease herself? What if sometime in the future, Logan or Allie needed a kidney and she couldn't help because she'd already given one to her sister? What if something happened during the surgery? What if she died? Who would mother her children?

She could say no of course. That was her right. She didn't owe Amelia a kidney. She didn't owe her anything really. Even if it *had* been Anna's father who'd switched her out at birth, it wasn't Anna's fault. It didn't obligate her to Amelia.

You can't let her die when you have the power to save her.

Torn in two opposing directions, Anna had absolutely no idea what she should do. She and Amelia had just found each other, and while they had a lot of things to work through, they couldn't do that if Amelia died.

By the time she got home, Anna was a total basket case, and she prayed her mother had put the kids to bed. She didn't want her children to see her this anxious and freaked-out.

And what about her mother? Robin was bound to notice that she was wrecked.

As it turned out, neither her children nor her mother was an immediate issue because parked dead center in the middle of the driveway was Kevin's car.

Home an entire day early, her big, blond husband was leaning against the trunk, arms folded over his chest, face like a thundercloud, looking hell-bent on a fight.

Weak-kneed, Anna got out of the Camry.

She did not need this right now.

Kevin straightened and came for her. His blond hair was mussed from repeatedly raking his fingers through it in frustration. He moved like a bull intent on goring the matador who'd been taunting him. Head lowered, leading with his broad shoulders, nostrils flaring, he swaggered down the driveway to where she'd parked.

Her heart jumped off a cliff and died at her feet. She'd never seen him so angry. What in the world had happened on the road? Instant dread filled her.

"Kevin . . ." Her voice came out so tremulous it terrified her.

"What the ever-loving hell, Anna?"

She drew down deep to the base of her courage. Dug inside her gut and hauled up her outrage with a deep exhale. "Do not curse at me, Kevin Durant Drury."

His tone softened, but his eyes did not. "I'll do my best to keep my temper under control, and the curse words out of my vocabulary, but I can't make any promises."

"Those are my boundaries," she squeaked, hugging herself against the shiver running through her that had nothing to do with the cool summer night breeze coming off the Gulf. "Do not raise your voice, and do not say any words that you wouldn't say in Sunday school."

"You're in no position to make demands." He growled low in his throat.

"I'm barely holding it together here, and I don't need you yelling at me."

"All right." He lowered his voice and intentionally spoke slower. "Let's discuss."

"Why are you home a day early?"

"To save you from doing something stupid."

What was that supposed to mean? "Oh," she said. "You're here to *save* me."

"Hell yes."

She raised her eyebrows and widened her eyes at him. "Excuse me?"

He snorted. "You're my *wife*, Anna."

"Meaning?" She rested her hands on her hips, felt her own anger rising to match his simmering tempo.

"You twin sister, Amelia Brandt, is nothing but trouble."

"You're entitled to your opinion, Kevin, but don't you dare say anything against my twin sister."

"I'm not going to bad-mouth her, Anna, but I am not going to shy away from the truth, either. You need to hear what I have to say."

"And what truth is that?" She knew she sounded snippy and stressed, but she hadn't fully processed Amelia's confession yet and her husband wasn't making things any easier.

"This morning I learned that your twin sister has renal failure and I'm guessing she's come here to ask you for a kidney. As soon as I found out, I cut the job short and drove straight home."

An uneasy feeling overcame her. How had he learned about Amelia before she had? "How did you find out?"

"You know? She told you?"

"Yes. Tonight. You didn't answer my question. How do *you* know?"

Kevin's blue eyes pierced her, hard-edged and unrelenting. "I have my sources. I do my research. Did you think I was really just going to drive away and leave a stranger with my wife and kids?"

"I'm feeling undermined."

"I also know how she lost her kidneys." He paused, glared harder. "Do you?"

"I-I didn't ask." Why hadn't she asked? Now he had something up on her.

"Maybe you should call her now." He trod closer. A twig crunched beneath his business loafers, cracking sharply in the dark.

Anna jumped.

"Are you scared of me, Anna?" He sounded stunned and his eyes suddenly filled with an incredulous pain, as if she'd betrayed him in some fundamental way.

"N-no." Not really. She'd never felt threatened by Kevin before, but right now? She was feeling high-strung and not handling this well.

"Do you think I would *ever* hurt you?" He blinked hard as he wadded his hands into tightly clenched fists.

"Not intentionally."

"I put your needs and the kids' needs ahead of my own all the time."

She did know that. He was a wonderful provider, but the way he was looming over her right now was unsettling. He seemed barely able to hold on to his anger. It seeped from his pores, full of indignant testosterone.

"Why can't you do the same for me?" He didn't raise his voice. He didn't curse. He sounded calm and controlled, leaving her no reason to take him to task.

Kevin wanted to win and if she didn't want to come off looking like the crazy one, she had to match his tempo and pace. The urge to walk away was overwhelming, but she didn't. For one thing she wanted to know what he knew, for another she liked winning just as much as he did.

"What are you talking about?" she asked.

"You. Putting your sister ahead of our relationship."

"That's not what I'm doing."

"No?"

Okay, she'd jumped into this thing heart-first, but she'd no intentions of putting her family second and she didn't like him insinuating that she was.

"You're trying to take something very complicated and put it in a box," she said. "It doesn't fit."

Having no contact with each other since Tuesday had been a very bad idea. Anna saw that now. Kevin had been brooding since he'd been gone.

"I knew from the beginning there was something fishy about your sister."

"Kevin," Anna warned again. "Do not diss Amelia."

"Is it wrong of me to want to take care of my wife?"

"No," she said. "But it is wrong to stand in the way of my relationship with my sister."

"That's not what I'm doing."

"Oh, then please." Anna threw her hands in the air. "By all means, tell me. What *are* you trying to do?"

"You're seriously thinking about giving your sister a kidney, aren't you?"

"I don't know yet. But if I do, it'll be because it's something for my sister. It's got nothing to do with you."

His face darkened, and sweat popped out on his brow. "It's got *everything* to do with me. If you give her a kidney and you die during the operation, what am I supposed to do?"

"She's my sister."

"And I'm your husband."

"She needs a kidney to live a long, healthy life. We have a rare blood type. I'm the only real chance she has."

Oh wow, she'd made up her mind. *Just like that*, Anna realized. And it wasn't in response to Kevin's goading. Anna was the only real chance Amelia had and she couldn't ignore that.

"What if I told you she blew out her kidneys using heroin? She's an addict, Anna. Your sister is a drug addict."

A pinch in her chest. Fear in her belly. She heard the words, but they didn't sink in. Amelia? A drug addict? She couldn't believe it. Amelia didn't even drink.

"Why are you making up lies about her?"

"I know this is hard for you to hear, sweetheart." His tone turned so tender that she wanted to punch him right in the breadbasket. But his eyes seemed so earnest. "But it's the truth."

Disbelief pummeled her. Kicked her right in the teeth. "You never answered my question. How do you know all this?"

He looked so ashamed that Anna knew she wasn't going to like the answer. "I called Steve."

Steve Couts was a private investigator who worked for the same insurance companies Kevin contracted with. They played golf together at the Moonglow Country Club. Steve had access to information that other people did not. If Steve couldn't find the dirt on someone, there was none; and Steve *always* found dirt of one kind or the other.

"Wh-what?" she asked, not because she hadn't heard him, but because she couldn't believe he had gone behind her back and hired Steve to investigate her sister.

"I had to protect you, and the kids. I wasn't able to be there in person, but I take care of my family——"

"And you didn't think I could take care of myself and our children?"

"That's not it. I just know what a generous heart you have, and how easily you open up to people. In all honesty, Anna, how did you expect me to react? Just let you bring a heroin addict into our home?"

Anna took a deep breath to control her response and answered in a measured tone. "You don't trust me."

"Of course, I trust you——"

"If you trusted me, you wouldn't have gone behind my back. You would have told me about your concerns and what you planned. You would have been up front about it."

"I tried. You blew me off."

Anna thought about her parents and the secrets they'd kept from each other and the trouble it had caused. So much suffering. So much pain.

"No, Kevin, you don't get to do that, you don't get to make this my fault."

"What would you say, Anna, if I told you that *I* was going to give my kidney to a stranger who lost his shooting up dope?"

"For one thing, Amelia isn't a stranger, I trust her, and you should respect my feelings," Anna said, both defensive and protective of her twin.

But Kevin was dead right. If he'd ever told her he wanted to donate his kidney to a drug-addicted stranger, she would lose her ever-loving mind.

That was the thing. She might not know Amelia very well, and they might have been separated for thirty-five years, but they'd shared a womb. The same DNA coursed through their veins. It wasn't the same thing at all, and she resented Kevin for the comparison.

She stared into her husband's eyes, the man she loved from the first time he waltzed her out onto the dance floor at the junior prom, her heart in her throat with excitement, and she felt wildly adrift. Right now, he seemed like more of a stranger than Amelia.

"Your twin sister is a drug addict who ruined her own kidneys. Face facts! If you give her your kidney, it would be like throwing it into the trashcan."

"Even if what you say is true, she's beaten it."

"Has she? Heroin is notoriously hard to kick."

"But not impossible. She has grit and determination."

"How do you know if she's truly beaten it?"

"They wouldn't put her on a transplant list if she hadn't."

"All right, let's roll with that, she's a recovering drug addict, who damaged her kidneys, got clean, and now she expects you to save her from her bad habits?"

"Everyone deserves a second chance," she said, but inside, she knew he'd made a good point. "And she doesn't *expect* it, she just asked. That's all."

"I don't care. I don't want you to do this."

"You're asking me to choose between my sister and your male ego?"

"This isn't about my ego." His voice was so low Anna could barely hear him.

He sounded so resolute in his convictions, so intractable. Her anger confused him. She saw it in his eyes. All he wanted to do was protect her.

Her heart wrenched. "You can't protect me from this."

Torment flared in his gaze. "What about our children? What if something happens to you? What then?"

Kevin knew where her soft underbelly was, and he'd gone straight for it. Using their children as leverage. It was the major thing that gave her pause.

"What if one day, our children needed a kidney from you, and you couldn't give it to them because you'd already given it to Amelia?"

"We've never had the kids' blood typed. I might not even be able to give them a kidney anyway."

"What if you were a match?"

"What if the polar ice caps melted tomorrow? I can't base today's decisions on what might happen years from now."

His eyes narrowed and his chin turned to stone. "It's clear where your priorities lie."

"What's that supposed to mean?"

"Your sister means more to you than your own children."

Anna lost it. Fury at her husband slammed through her. For more than half her life she'd loved this man. Devoted herself to him and their children and the one time she needed his support he fought her.

"No, no." She shook a finger at him. "You do not get to do that. It's unfair. I get that you're scared out of your mind. Me too! But that's emotional blackmail."

He ducked his head, dropped his hands, backtracked, and mumbled, "I didn't mean it like that."

She jumped back into her mother's car and barked, "Take care of your kids."

Then she drove away, a mental snapshot in her rearview mirror of Kevin standing in the dark with hangdog eyes, his hands stuffed deep into his pockets, and his mouth hanging open in shocked surprise.

CHAPTER SEVENTEEN

Anna

Truth, Brownies, and Consequences

Two hours later, after driving aimlessly around town trying to make sense of the mess her life had become, Anna pulled into the parking lot behind the Moonglow Bakery.

Inside the dim, silent interior of her mother's car, she sat listening to the engine click as it cooled down and she slumped back against the headrest.

Palm trees waved shadowy leaves underneath the glow of the security lamp. She craned her neck so she could see the boardwalk across the street and hear the tame ocean sending soft waves to the shore. Light traffic cruised the boulevard on a Friday night and far out into the Gulf, oil rig lights twinkled.

This was her usual world, totally normal, nothing out of place, but she couldn't shake the feeling that she'd stepped into some bizarre Twilight Zone where everyone was exactly the same except for her.

Who was she? Wife, mother, daughter, sister?

There it was. The change. The difference. The paradigm shift of epic proportion. She hadn't had time to absorb that implication. Not really. She'd been fighting so hard to keep her life on an even keel, but now she had to face facts.

Her life was never going to be the same again and she needed to shed those illusions that she could go right back to who she was before Amelia came to town. Whether she gave her twin a kidney or not, Anna was forever transformed, and no amount of denying reality could erase that.

She was still uncertain how to confront Amelia. Part of her prayed Kevin was wrong, but another part of her feared it was true. That her sister really was a heroin addict.

There was only one way through the misery—face it head on.

Hitching in a deep breath, Anna got out of her vehicle, hit the key lock, stuffed the key into her pocket, and strolled across the street to the Moonglow Inn.

It was after eleven and all the lights were out in the Victorian. Anna hesitated on the front porch.

If she knocked, she'd wake the household and that didn't seem fair. When she was a kid and her family lived in the cottage next door to the inn, she and the oldest Clarke sister, Madison, used to sneak out of their bedrooms and go for late-night walks along the beach.

Spurred by the memory, Anna went around the side of the house to the window of what used to be Madison's room but was now the guest room where Amelia was staying. In the rock garden, she picked up a handful of pebbles and, as she'd done twenty years ago as a teenager, gently lobbed small stones at the pane to wake her sister without arousing the rest of the B and B.

Tick.

The first stone hit the window and fell back down on her head. She'd tossed it so gently she barely felt the pelt. She waited.

No Amelia.

Thunk.

The second pebble hit, the sound a little louder than the one before.

C'mon, sis.

Nothing.

Well, sugar cookies, now what?

Maybe Shelley had given Amelia a different room when she'd come back and this one was vacant.

Or maybe Amelia was just a really sound sleeper.

Anna curled the final stone in the crook of her index finger, pulled her arm back, and adding just a tiny bit more force, chucked it.

Thud. Crack.

Where the rock had landed, a thin fracture spread the forked lightning over the pane. Anna slapped a palm over her mouth. *Oh shit,* she'd broken the window.

The curtain flapped and the window went up. Her sister stuck her head out of the screenless window and blinked down at her.

Anna motioned for her to come down. Tomorrow, she'd explain to Shelley about the broken window and pay to have it fixed, but for now, her focus was on her sister.

"What is it?" Amelia whispered.

"We need to talk."

Amelia nodded and closed the window. Anna paced the side yard, waiting for her to appear.

Her sister came around the side of house, eerie in her restrained calmness and long white sleep shirt that fell past her knees. She wore beach flip-flops and a thin white sweater that covered her arms. In that moment, except for her short pixie haircut, Amelia looked like a Dickensian novel heroine—wan and thin and mysterious.

Amelia said nothing, just looked at Anna expectantly.

"Do you know how to bake?" Anna asked.

Nodding, Amelia said, "Robert had a sweet tooth."

"C'mon, then."

"Where are we going?"

"My bakery." Without waiting to see if Amelia would follow, Anna took off toward the crosswalk at Moonglow Boulevard, wondering why she felt so breathless.

She heard Amelia padding behind her and stopped for her to catch up. Anna felt Amelia settle beside her as they waited for the light to change.

There was no traffic.

"We could just cross," Amelia said.

Yes. Break the rules. But Anna was such a rule follower, she shook her head. "It'll change soon."

Amelia raised her eyebrows but said nothing. She waited patiently, accepting Anna's nonsensical insistence on waiting for the light.

The Walk sign lit up.

They moved at the same time. Their tandem rhythm seemingly ingrained into their DNA. Anna looked over at her twin.

Amelia was studying her.

Automatically, she put on a smile, but she couldn't even convince herself she was happy and dropped it. With a bob of her head, she indicated for Amelia to follow her around the corner of the building.

She slipped the key into the lock and opened the back door into a hallway that led to the bakery kitchen.

They went inside. She turned on the lights. The kitchen gleamed. Darla was as good a cleaner as she was a baker. The place was spotless. But Darla, as she frequently did, had forgotten to turn off the satellite radio and music whispered across the butcher board counter. Anna cocked her head, listening to puzzle out the tune. Identified "Let It Go."

Timely.

Was it a sign?

Goose bumps ran up her arm and she shuddered. *Let it go.* A message that had seemingly become her theme song.

Should she just let it go and not even ask how her sister had lost her kidney function? Did it matter in the long run?

Anxiety twisted Anna up inside.

Amelia's gaze met hers.

In her sister's face, Anna saw that her twin understood what this meeting was really about, but neither of them wanted to come right out and say it. Amelia hated admitting vulnerability and Anna?

Well, she hated hurting other people's feelings.

Tell the real truth, Bean. It was Kevin's voice, sarcastic in tone, rattling around in her head.

Anna clasped both palms over her ears. *Get out of my brain.*

Okay, the reason she didn't just come out and ask, *Are you a heroin addict?* She really didn't want to know.

Let it go.

Overwhelmed by her feelings, and not knowing how to deal with them, she reached for her mother's favored method of conflict resolution—food.

Soundless, she gave Amelia an apron.

Her sister put it on without a word and waited for further instruction.

"Brownies," Anna said. "Preheat 375."

Amelia flew to the oven, set the dial. "What else?"

Her sister looked at Anna with eyes so eager it hurt her heart. Her twin was desperate to please her.

Yeah, desperate for a kidney.

"I'll get the dry ingredients," Anna said. "You get the wet."

Amelia blinked.

"Eggs, vanilla, butter." Anna ticked them off on her fingers.

"On it." Amelia leapt to the refrigerator.

Grinning, Anna ducked her head.

Her twin gathered everything in her arms and brought her bounty to the counter where Anna arranged flour, baking soda and powder, salt, sugar, and cocoa powder. Anna's gaze landed on Amelia's elbow where she'd tucked a box of European butter.

An elbow covered by a sweater.

Her sister always kept her elbows covered, wearing some kind of cover-up or longer sleeves even in June. Before, she'd just thought Amelia chilled easy because she was so thin. Now she understood there was possibly a darker reason why she never bared her arms.

Fear flooded her then, and she didn't quite understand it. Her hands shook so hard she could barely spoon flour into a measuring cup. Why was she suddenly so scared?

Amelia stood watching her, the ingredients still cradled in her arm.

"You can set those down," Anna mumbled, hearing the breathless anxiety in her own voice.

Cautiously, Amelia unloaded the items onto the counter beside Anna. "What next?"

"Could you cream the butter and sugar?" Anna nodded at the industrial mixer.

"How much of each?"

"Our brownie recipe is posted on the inside of the cabinet door beside the mixer."

Amelia opened the door, read the recipe, and set to work.

Anna usually baked in this kitchen five days a week, but today it felt new, different, almost exciting—because Amelia was here with her. She enjoyed it so much, she slowed down, wanting to savor the moment.

She stirred the dry ingredients with a kitchen whisk, while Amelia scraped the creamed butter and sugar off the side of the stainless-steel mixing bowl. They were moving in tandem again, just as they had when they walked on the beach. Using the same small circular motions to fold things in evenly. She slowed down to break the pattern, but then Amelia slowed too.

On purpose? Anna wondered. Was her sister intentionally trying to match her rhythm to create a connection?

She straightened.

So did Amelia.

Her twin's guileless gaze searched Anna's face. "What is it?"

"You don't know?"

"Know what?"

"We were moving like synchronized swimmers."

"Were we?" Amelia blinked. "That's weird."

"Very weird."

They stood looking at each other across the kitchen island between them. The overhead light shone in stark contrast against the deep darkness outside the windows.

Inside the bakery was silent, save for the swishing tail of the Felix the Cat wall clock.

It was as if they were stranded on an island with no one else to turn to except each other. To shake off the unsettling feeling, Anna finished off the brownie prep and popped the dough in the oven to bake.

"Tell me more about being a cellist," she said, still unable to say what she'd brought Amelia here to tell her. It was so hard to be forthright. "How did you get into that career and why the cello?"

A happy little half-moon smile lit up Amelia's face.

"It's all about the sound." Amelia sighed dreamily. "The rich sound of the cello is at the heart of any musical ensemble. Balancing the sound of the higher-pitched violin and viola, bringing the music back down to earth."

Outside on Moonglow Boulevard, a car slid by, bathing the room in headlights for a moment, but Anna was enraptured by the expression on Amelia's face and the way her fingers pantomimed playing the cello.

"There's no other instrument like the cello. It is a workhorse, capable of performing multiple roles, and carrying the orchestra on its back." Amelia's smile deepened as if she was giving a university lecture, and Anna could see she was obsessed with it. "If the cello were a person, it would be a doting mother."

"You're crazy about the cello."

Amelia's cheeks pinked. "I am."

"So why aren't you in the symphony anymore? What happened? It seemed you were poised on the edge of greatness."

"Long story."

Did that story include heroin addiction?

Anna fingered the delicate pearl-and-diamond bracelet at her wrist. "I do remember you. Not here." She tapped her forehead with an index finger, and then moved a palm to her heart. "But *here*."

Amelia moistened her lips, looked stricken. "That's so sweet, but . . ."

"What?"

"You brought me here in the middle of night to discuss something. Let's discuss it."

Tension invaded Anna's shoulders. She was trying to tell Amelia everything that was in her heart, but it seemed she'd lost all sense of timing and finesse.

Her sister had given her an opening, so she grabbed it, and blurted, "You're a drug addict."

So much for the subtle approach.

Amelia didn't flinch. Her face seamless. "*Recovering* drug addict."

There it was. The truth.

Snoopy Kevin was right. Damn him.

The smell of baking chocolate filled the room. Brownies. Her favorite comfort food. But suddenly, sugary brownies were the last thing Anna wanted. What she wanted was for her sister to say Kevin was wrong.

The silence hurt. It was that heavy.

Anna cleared her throat, shifted her hips, trying to look casual and unshocked by Amelia's answer. "Heroin?"

The oven timer dinged.

"Brownies are ready." Amelia slipped on an oven mitt and bent over to take them out of the oven. She straightened, the pan of piping hot brownies in her hands, steam rising up.

All the color left her sister's face, which wasn't easy since her twin was already as pale as a cotton ball, and Amelia let out a soft little cry.

She was going to pass out.

Snatching up a kitchen towel, Anna ran to save her.

CHAPTER EIGHTEEN

Amelia

Sisterly Bonds

Instantly, Anna was at Amelia's side, snatching the brownies from her hands with a kitchen towel, just as Amelia's knees buckled.

In one fluid movement, Anna tossed the brownies on the stovetop, towel and all, then swooped to where Amelia had collapsed on the tile floor. The back of her head rested against the warm oven door and the smell of melted chocolate filled her nose.

"You fainted!" Anna fanned her with a hand as if that would help.

"I d-didn't." Alarmed by the extent of her weakness, Amelia could barely push the words over her lips. "Just got dizzy and lost my balance."

"Does this happen often?"

Amelia nodded. "More and more lately, as my condition worsens."

With a trembling hand, Anna fingered her bottom lip. "We need to get you back to the Moonglow Inn."

That short journey across the street felt like a million miles at this juncture. Amelia drew in a deep breath. "Give me a minute, please."

Anna frowned. "Your skin is cold and clammy. Should I call an ambulance?"

Amelia shook her head.

Her sister pulled a phone from her pocket. "I'm calling an ambulance."

"No." She wrapped a hand around Anna's wrist. "Please don't. I'm fine." Taking one look into her sister's skeptical eyes, Amelia raised her shoulders in a half shrug and added, "*ish*."

"Hmph." Anna folded her arms over her chest and drilled down her gaze as if staring at one of her children when they were in a stubborn mood.

"How about those brownies?" Amelia asked. "May I have one?"

"Now?"

"Isn't that why we made them? To bond over chocolate while I tell you the tragic tale of how I ruined my kidneys?"

"Good point." Anna popped up.

Amelia shifted, leaning her back against the kitchen counter. The tile floor was spotless, she noticed, unable to find a single crumb to focus on.

Anna bustled around and a minute later, she was sitting beside Amelia, the pan of chocolate brownies resting on the kitchen towel she spread over her lap. She held up two spoons. "Let's go old-school."

Uncertain what her twin meant by that Amelia took the spoon Anna handed her.

"Dig in," Anna encouraged, dipping a spoonful of gooey, warm brownie from the center of the pan.

Apparently, "old school" meant throw manners to the wind. Amelia followed her sister's lead and scooped up a brownie that oozed cakey goodness over the rim of her spoon.

Amelia took a bite. "Oh my goodness, these are the best brownies I've ever put in my mouth."

"If you'd met me sooner, you could have turned to brownies instead of drugs and you wouldn't need my kidney." Anna laughed.

"If only," Amelia said, not really meaning to sound sarcastic, but Anna must have taken it that way because she let out a hard bark of laughter.

"Yeah." Anna gave a rueful shake of her head. "Who am I to rescue you? I can't rescue my own marriage."

"I . . ." Amelia wasn't good with comforting people. She'd had no role models for that growing up and had been too caught in her own emotional turmoil to even consider it was skill she actively needed to cultivate. "You . . . um . . ."

"Don't mind me." Amelia waved her spoon. "Things will work out with Kevin. We've hit potholes before."

"This time, *I'm* the pothole."

"Nooo." Anna denied it, but Amelia knew the truth.

"I'm upsetting your life. I never meant to disrupt your life, Anna, or cause trouble in your marriage."

"Didn't you?" Anna's tone was frivolous, but her question was serious. "I mean, you did come here for my kidney. That's a pretty concrete and deliberate goal. Not to mention ghoulish. How could you think that wouldn't upset my life?"

Well, look at her sister, getting feisty. Amelia liked it when rebellion sparked in her twin's eyes.

"Why are you grinning?" Anna tilted her head.

Amelia stuffed a spoonful of brownie into her mouth and chewed to keep from answering.

"Cheater." Anna went in for another bite. "Ooh, these are some damn good-ass brownies."

She also liked her sister's foul mouth. Generally, she avoided cursing because Sarah Brandt's vocabulary had been liberally sprinkled with four-letter words and Amelia had come to associate cursing with animosity.

But when Anna cursed, it was good-natured and honest, and she didn't use the words as weapons, just a means of self-expression.

Emotion swept through her, taking Amelia by surprise. She usually felt warning tingles in her fingers and toes to let her know when unwanted feelings were sneaking up on her and she should yank them out by the roots. Dr. Ellard had taught her to identify how emotions showed in her body and she'd learned to listen.

But this? This was a tidal wave of fear, panic, regret, guilt, and anger, coming at her all at once. There was no running, no hiding, no freezing in place. The torrent was upon her and she flashed back to childhood.

The raised voices, the broken glass, the bruises . . .

On her father's face.

Just that short glimpse, a flash of her past, her father with a bloody nose and black eye at the hands of her mother, left Amelia gasping.

"That's it." Anna picked up her phone from beside her on the floor. "I'm calling 911."

"No, no, please." Amelia touched her sister. "I'm having a moment, but seriously, I'm *fine*."

"You don't look fine." Anna glanced down at Amelia's hand on hers.

Amelia fought a powerful urge to move away but resisted it. People connected through touch and as hard as it was for her to casually touch people without an anxious thought, she sensed her sister badly needed the contact.

You need Anna more than Anna needs you.

Yes, Dr. Ellard, thank you so much for that. After a year of intensive therapy three times a week, it felt as if her psychiatrist was permanently embedded in her brain.

All right. She'd admit it. She needed Anna, literally couldn't live without her. *Happy now, Dr. Ellard?*

Anna was still holding the phone. Her body angled forward.

"You were right. Coming here for your kidney *is* ghoulish and I wish I'd found you three years ago before things turned so dark. I can't change what I did, and I'm deeply ashamed. That's what's bothering me. Not my physical health."

"I'm not convinced." Anna pressed her lips together.

To show her sister that she didn't need to go to the hospital, Amelia dug into the brownie again. "Mmm."

"I don't know how you were raised, or what you went through

growing up, but you're my sister." Anna squeezed her hand. "You're family. And in this family, we have each other's backs. I suspect you don't fully understand what that means."

That last bite of brownie got caught her in throat. Amelia massaged her neck and blinked against Anna's heartfelt sentiment.

Gulped.

"I'm here for you. Now, forever, always. No matter what," Anna said staunchly, completely invested.

"You're right," Amelia said. "I don't fully understand what that means."

"I don't want to speak ill of the dead, but you know," Anna said, "I don't think I like your parents very much."

"They did the best they could. They were . . ." Amelia paused, searching for the right way to say this. "Family ties just weren't a big priority for them."

Unlike you.

"I need some milk." Anna plopped the brownie pan in Amelia's lap and got up. "Do you want some milk?"

"I really can't drink milk with kidney failure. Too much protein and potassium."

"But brownies are okay?"

"Sugar and chocolate are safe."

"Hooray for that. Coffee?"

"In a heartbeat."

Anna set the brownie pan on the counter, put on coffee, and then extended her hand to help Amelia up.

Once she was on her feet, Amelia grabbed hold of the counter in case she got dizzy again, but she didn't.

Anna hovered, her hand at Amelia's back.

"It's okay. I'm good."

"Let's take our coffee and brownies into the dining room." Anna passed two cups of black coffee to Amelia, picked up the pan of brownies, and led the way through the bakery storefront to the dine-in tables.

Anna didn't bother to turn on the overhead light. There was enough light from the kitchen and the streetlight slanting through the partially opened window blinds. She parked herself at the bistro table in the center of the room, her face draped in shadows.

Taking the seat across from her, Amelia felt nervous all over again. The darkness helped, but she knew it was time to tell the story she'd been avoiding ever since she came to Moonglow Cove.

Anna reached over, covered Amelia's hand with hers, and gave her a reassuring smile. "Tell me what happened."

Five minutes passed before Amelia could melt her defenses enough to get started.

Anna waited, her attention fully focused on Amelia. She didn't squirm. She didn't speak. She just waited.

Unlike Amelia who couldn't seem to get comfortable on the wooden chair that rubbed against her butt bones.

Anna didn't look away.

Unlike Amelia who stared unseeingly at the shadow-drenched pastry display case.

Anna wasn't distracted.

Unlike Amelia who was mentally checking out by playing Pachelbel's Canon in D in her head.

Her sister was as open, relaxed, and accepting as Dr. Ellard.

That terrified Amelia, and a maddening urge to flee pushed at her hard. If she went back home, she could stop having to feel so much.

But could you? Could you really?

No, which was why she sat in this chair, loony with the need to come clean to someone who wasn't a doctor, counselor, or therapist.

Felix the Cat ticked off the seconds, his plastic tail swishing in time to the ticks. *Tick. Swish. Tick. Swish. Tick. Swish.*

Steady, even, unbroken. Reliable as time.

Amelia sipped the coffee gone tepid and cleared her throat.

Anna leaned forward, rested her elbows on the table, and settled her chin into her upturned palms.

"It started innocently enough," Amelia said, feeling both respected and conflicted from being watched so intently by her twin.

If they'd grown up together, they would've shared many intimate conversations such as this. But as thirty-five-year-old strangers, with nothing more than a DNA connection, it felt intrusive.

Anna expected too much from her. She wanted emotional closeness and bonding. It was her price for a kidney. Intimacy was her currency. It was a price Amelia had difficulty paying.

"First it was just wine with dinner. Nothing wrong with that. Then it became a few cocktails afterward. Robert was a cosmopolitan man and a corporate lawyer. We entertained his clients. He had a lot of job stress. He drank and I drank with him."

"How long were you two engaged?"

"Four years."

"A few too many drinks on occasion is a long way from a heroin addiction serious enough to ruin your kidneys." Anna's voice was even-keeled, nonjudgmental, more curious than anything.

Her twin had lived a simple life, in a small beach town, surrounded by people who loved her.

Amelia wasn't sure she could fully explain the whys of how she'd gotten trapped in the world of drugs. At least not in a way that Anna could understand.

"I had a prestigious but stressful job, too," Amelia said. "A coveted position. Someone was always after your spot. There's a lot of pressure to top yourself with every performance."

"You started taking drugs to cope with job stress?"

"Not really. Not a lot." Amelia closed her eyes briefly and took a deep breath. "At least I don't think so."

"The addiction snuck up on you." Anna was so earnest it was almost cute.

Nodding, Amelia placed her palms together and brought them to her lips, her thumbs hooking underneath her jaw. If anyone saw her, they might think she was whispering a prayer into her hands, but it was actually a stalling technique to give her time to plan what she should say next. She'd picked up the ploy from Dr. Ellard.

"Between my work and Robert's, we went to a lot of parties. Most nights of the week we were out on the town or hosting guests. There were celebrities and VIPs. Along the way, someone offered cocaine as a pick-me-up. Robert and his friends made it seem so glamorous."

Anna let out her breath in a long loud whoosh. "Peer pressure. I get it."

But Amelia understood that using drugs to disconnect from emotional pain wasn't something her wholesome twin could really understand. Anna would wonder why brownies and hugs weren't enough.

"Cocaine made me feel invincible. I already had an issue with shyness and social anxiety. Cocaine made socializing so much easier. But even so, I didn't like how jittery it made me, so I didn't do it all that much. I'm jittery enough on my own, thank you very much."

"You don't look jittery on the outside."

"High-functioning anxiety."

Anna reached for her hand and squeezed it tight. "I'm so sorry that you felt like you had to do drugs to fit in. That must've been tough."

A lump clogged Amelia's throat. She couldn't believe her twin was so understanding, so accepting. Kindness and compassion were not the world she'd grown up in. She found it strange and simply too good to be true.

"How long did this last?" Anna asked.

"Maybe a year. Things were going well, terrific even. I got my first cello solo during the time I was getting high. I told myself the drugs boosted my creativity, and maybe they did. At the time, I still had a modicum of control. If I decided not to do drugs for a week or two, I could hold to that commitment. My ability to step away when I chose convinced me I didn't have a problem."

"What happened for you to lose control?"

"Robert ran a red light. An eighteen-wheeler was coming in the opposite direction, and T-boned his Bugatti, killing him and my parents who were riding in the back seat." She got the story out in a matter-of-fact tone. It was what happened. No need to embellish the story.

Good job, Amelia.

"I can't imagine what that must've been like," Anna murmured. "Losing them all at once. Even though I lost my father last year and it was the worst thing that ever happened to me, we knew it was coming."

It was sweet of Anna to try and make her feel better. But it didn't work.

"For years, Dad suffered lung problems related to his career as a fireman," Anna went on. "So he was vulnerable."

Oh great, the guy who stole babies was also a hero. All hail Heathcliff Straus.

Dr. Ellard opined inside her head. *People are complicated.*

"While it was horrible watching Dad waste away, we did have time to prepare. We got to say everything that needed to be said, and he had all his affairs in order."

Yes, that would have been nice if Sarah and Frank and Robert had had their affairs in order.

"Although . . ." Anna shook her head. "In retrospect, maybe not. He took the secret of my birth to the grave. That's not a guy who has made peace with what he'd done. Why didn't he tell me when he knew the end was near? That would have been the prime moment to come clean."

"Maybe he was protecting Winnie?"

"From what? She's ninety and has Alzheimer's."

"Maybe he was protecting her reputation. From what I can tell, she seems pretty beloved by the patients she attended."

"Maybe." Anna took her hands in hers and Amelia didn't resist. She *wanted* Anna to hold her hand. "I just can't imagine losing both parents and my fiancé in one tragic accident. I don't know how you coped. Under those circumstances, I might have turned to drugs too."

"You wouldn't have," Amelia said. "You're too good of a mom for that."

"Those babies do anchor me." Anna got a rapturous expression on her face at the mention of her children, but she quickly shifted her attention back to Amelia. "That must have been such a terrible time for you."

"I was in a fugue. I couldn't function. At the funeral, I fell down the steps of the church and hurt my back. I took a leave of absence from the symphony. To help me through it, my family physician gave me Percocet, and that's when I *really* went off the rails."

"How I wish I had been there! How I wish I could've helped you! I hate that you were so alone through all this. You didn't have anyone at all?"

"Colleagues at work, but because my job was so demanding and competitive, I'd had trouble making friends, and I wasn't really that close with anyone. And my old friends? My drug use had pushed them away."

"No grandparents? Aunts or uncles? Cousins?"

"I have distant relatives, but we don't keep in touch. There was nobody to hold my hand in the dark and eat brownies with."

"Shameful." Anna clicked her tongue and looked forlorn.

"Don't feel sorry for me, please. I *liked* my life. That is, until I couldn't function anymore. I couldn't make myself play the cello if my life depended on it. In fact, until playing with you at the concert, I hadn't picked up the cello in two years."

"You're kidding. You were amazing!"

"I guess it's like riding a bike."

"You're so talented."

"So are you."

Anna waved a hand. "I'm a housewife with a bakery that turns a small profit, but I'm cool with that. You, on the other hand, were on top of the world."

"Until I wasn't." Amelia toyed with the medallion on her bracelet. "In those days after my parents and Robert died, I went to a very dark place. I did awful things to get drugs. I went from Oxycontin to heroin. I blew through that stuff like a freight train. I *loved* it. When I was on heroin, I didn't feel a thing. It was bliss . . . until it wasn't."

Anna took a deep breath, but she didn't make a negative comment. She just listened, showing up for Amelia in a way no one other than Dr. Ellard had ever shown up for her before.

"I ended up hanging around some very sketchy people. Then one night, in a shooting gallery—"

"Shooting gallery? What's that?"

Oh, her sister was so naïve. "It's an abandoned house where addicts gather to shoot up drugs."

Anna gasped. "That sounds terrifying."

"Yes, it is. On that night, a hotshot cellist from the Chicago Symphony ended up on the wrong side of town, in a place where she had no business, overdosing on heroin."

Amelia heard sniffling and realized Anna was crying for her. Her sister leaned across the table and hugged her so tightly Amelia had trouble catching her breath.

"I am so sorry, so very sorry that happened to you." Anna clung to her hands.

"It's not your fault. Please don't take responsibility for my problems."

A flash of concern. Her twin took on the issues of others, as if by shouldering their burdens she could eliminate their pain. But no amount of emotional weight that Anna piled onto her own back could untangle the mess that Amelia had made of her life.

Anna intensified the hug. "I'm so grateful we found our way back to each other, even if the circumstances are dire. I couldn't imagine not having you in my life."

Guilt, that heavy, odious stinker, overtook Amelia.

"Can I ask you something?" Anna said.

"What is it?"

"You don't have to——" Anna gulped and stared at Amelia's elbows.

"Show you my scars?" Amelia asked, reading her twin's mind. She pushed up the sleeves of her sweater, exposing her arms.

Anna couldn't look at them though. Nor could she hold Amelia's gaze.

Getting too real for you, sis?

Anna still kept her eyes averted. "Heroin is a hard drug to kick. How do you know you're done with it forever?"

Ahh, here it was. The question Amelia feared. The one for which she had an unsatisfactory answer.

"I've been clean for over a year and I spent six months at an intensive rehab program that focused primarily on heroin addiction. I've avoided the people and behaviors that got me into that situation in the first place. I have a therapist I see thrice a week back in Chicago, and I belong to Narcotics Anonymous. But you're right, I can't sit here and tell you that I'm done with heroin forever. There's no guarantee I won't relapse. I wish I could promise you otherwise, but I can't."

"You're a better risk than you give yourself credit for," Anna said.

"How's that?"

"You have an identical twin sister who'll be there for you no matter what." Anna looked so earnest.

It felt as if a giant screwdriver had been inserted in the center of Amelia's chest and someone was twisting it tighter and tighter.

"You can't rescue me from life," Amelia said.

"I don't have to. Once I give you a kidney, you can rescue yourself."

That touched Amelia far more than she could say. Nervously, she plucked at her sleeves, pulling them down.

Anna held out a restraining hand. "Wait."

Hesitating, Amelia felt herself sink back against the chair. It was almost as if she wasn't in charge of her own body.

Anna leaned over and lightly kissed the old track marks dotting the bend of Amelia's elbow.

At the feel of her twin's warm lips against her cool skin, Amelia turned to stone. She felt too much!

"You're so brave." Tenderly, Anna kissed the scars on her other arm, too. "You've been through so, so much."

A rush of grief at Anna's tenderness hit Amelia like a huge wall of water, knocking the air from her lungs as surely as the surf had tossed her around the day that she'd pulled Winnie Newton from the Gulf.

Anna kept kissing her the way Amelia had seen her kiss her kids when they got bumps and scraps.

Tears gathered in her eyes, but Amelia couldn't trust herself to express them.

"'She conquered her demons and wore her scars like wings,'" Anna quoted.

"Atticus," Amelia said to keep from crying.

"What?"

"Atticus. He's a Canadian poet. The poem was framed on the wall at the rehab center."

"Oh, Darla has that as a tattoo. I didn't know it was a famous quote."

Amelia laughed too loudly, startling them both, and the moment got awkward and weird.

Anna tugged down Amelia's sleeves to cover her elbows. "Thank you for showing me your scars. I know that was hard for you."

She nodded.

"Can I have another hug?" Anna asked, but didn't wait for an answer. She embraced Amelia.

Overwhelmed, Amelia sat with her arms at her sides not hugging Anna back. Not because she didn't want to, but precisely because she did. Amelia wanted to let loose her love and pour it onto Anna as much as Anna poured her love onto Amelia, but she simply didn't know how.

"Amelia?" Anna whispered.

"Yes?"

"You're going to live. I'll make sure of that. Tomorrow, at the dinner party, oh wait, that's tonight now." Anna looked at her phone. "Damn, Darla will be here at three."

"You're still hosting the dinner party for your family?"

"Yes, and together, we're going to break that news that you need a kidney and that I'm going to give you mine."

"But you haven't discussed it with Kevin."

"Leave Kevin to me. For now, though, we should get you back to the Moonglow Inn. You need sleep." Anna kissed Amelia's cheek. *Smack, smack.*

That's when Amelia realized something monumental.

Anna believed that with enough love, she could fix anything. Even more importantly, her sister apparently believed that Amelia was salvageable. After seeing herself reflected through the rosy world of Anna's eyes, Amelia was starting to think that maybe she was.

CHAPTER NINETEEN

Anna

The Dinner Party from Hell

Anna decided to bake a cake for the dinner party. Italian cream. Kevin's favorite. It was a tricky cake to keep moist, but she enjoyed the challenge.

Or that's what she told herself.

Truthfully, it was a peace offering to her husband. Then something occurred to her.

What if he didn't really like Italian cream cake? What if he'd been lying to her all these years like he had with the key lime pie? If he lied about pie, what else did he lie about?

And what if these small, inconsequential lies actually hid much bigger ones?

The question was a thorn in her heart. She missed her husband. Missed his woodsy scent and the feel of his strong arms around her. Missed his laugh and the way he mussed her hair when he kissed her.

She yearned for him and ached to make love to him.

But she knew the only way she could get to that space with

him in his current state of mind was to tell him she wouldn't donate a kidney to Amelia. And she simply couldn't do that.

Amelia.

Another love that caused her so much pain.

Husband versus sister. Why did she have to choose one over the other and when had she and Kevin gone so far off course?

It was handy, under the circumstances, to blame Amelia's arrival for their communication breakdown, but that was an excuse. Somewhere along the way, through the ups and downs of family life, they'd drifted away from each other and hadn't even realized it. Amelia's appearance in their lives had merely shone a flashlight on their problems.

They simply weren't communicating.

When she'd gotten home after her time with Amelia, Kevin was not in their bedroom. She searched the house for him, found him asleep on the chaise lounge beside the pool. She left him there, but she didn't go to their king-size bed.

Instead, she crept upstairs and got in bed with Logan, pressed her nose against his head to inhale the comfort of his little-boy scent, and fell into a hard sleep. When she woke at seven thirty feeling dazed and poorly rested, Kevin was gone, and he hadn't left a note.

Anna texted him while she took her coffee on the patio, staring at the Kevin-size imprint in the cushion on the chaise lounge. He couldn't have been gone long.

Where R U?

It took him an hour to reply. Mom & Dad's.

She waited fifteen minutes. It was the longest she could hold out. She hated being at odds with him. With anybody, actually. Texted: You and your folks will B here for the dinner party, right?

The reply came immediately. A thumbs-up emoji.

That was optimistic. Yes?

She thought about texting him again but resisted. There was an Italian cream cake that needed baking.

Anna turned the cake into a symbol. If the cake turned out moist and delicious, then the party would be a smashing success. Get the cake right and everything else would fall into place. The cake she could control. Other people? Not so much.

The party was scheduled for six P.M. Invited: Mom, Mike, Gia, and their baby, Faith. Kevin, and his parents, Veronica and Pete.

Amelia was due to arrive at four to help prepare and Anna wasn't sure if her help was a blessing or a curse.

She finished baking the cake. It was too dry. She threw it in the trash and started over, metaphorically rolling up her sleeves. This time the damn cake was too moist. She'd overdone the buttermilk and the result was sticky cake with a gummy mouthfeel.

Ugh.

"Third time's a charm," she sang out to Logan, who was sitting at the dining room table coloring.

He'd been so good today. Allie was still in bed and Anna let her sleep. It was summer vacation and a Saturday, although if

Robin knew Allie was in bed at ten A.M., she'd give Anna one of her silent, motherly looks that said, *Not the way I'd do things.*

Anna made a third cake and this one was perfect. Right track. This was all going to work out.

From there, she moved onto prepping the rest of the meal. Assembling a green salad and stashing it in the fridge. Brining the chicken. Making doughs for homemade pasta and Italian bread. The house filled with the homey smell of yeast, garlic, and lemon zest.

Nostalgia pulled at her chest and she yearned for her uncomplicated past before she learned she was a twin, when cooking a delicious meal was her main concern.

At eleven o'clock, Allie stumbled into the kitchen, eyes bleary, and her gorgeous red hair tousled every which way. Yawning, she poured herself cereal and plunked down at the table beside Logan.

"Earth's too tiny and too far away," Allie said through a mouthful of Froot Loops.

What was she talking about? Anna straightened from where she stood making icing for the cake and looked over the counter to the breakfast nook.

Allie was leaning over Logan's shoulder peering at his drawing.

Logan lifted his shoulders and curled inward to protect his creation from her prying eyes. He wore an indigo T-shirt and swim trunks with baby sharks on them. She'd told him they could go swimming once she had everything prepped for dinner.

"It's not Earth," he said.

"What is it then?" Allie sounded truly curious and not just asking with big-sisterly contrarianism.

"Me."

Allie canted her head, and stared at his drawing. "You're a tiny blue blob in outer space?"

"No," he said. "It's a picture of my dream."

Drying her hands on a kitchen towel, Anna moved across the room to see what Logan had drawn. The entire page was scribbled in black crayon, except for a small, blue lopsided circle on the very edge of the page. The shape of the circle felt sad. As if it had once been a vibrant balloon that had deflated.

Anna pulled out a chair and sat beside her son. He was in emotional pain. It was there in his drawing for her to see. She leaned over and kissed the top of his sweet little-boy head.

"Tell me about your dream, sweetheart."

Rolling her eyes, Allie pulled out her cell phone and started texting while still munching Froot Loops. She dribbled milk on the table. Anna pointed at it and motioned for her to get a hand towel, but Allie just swiped it up with the hem of her sleep shirt and kept texting.

Anna almost told her to put the phone away, but Logan needed her full attention right now and she didn't want a dustup with her daughter, so she settled for a motherly glower that Allie ignored.

Logan kicked his feet against the rung and Anna felt the vibration coming up through the wooden chair. Her son's feet got restless whenever he was nervous.

Ducking his head, he picked up the black crayon and scribbled in more darkness, humming under his breath the Star-Wars-Darth-Vader's-in-town song "Imperial March."

Her baby was scared, and she hadn't been paying attention. Pain pierced her heart. Shame on her!

She wanted to scoop him into her arms and cover his little face with kisses, but as she leaned in, she felt his body tense. Reeling, Anna backed off.

"Where are you?" she asked. "In this picture? In your dream?"

He propped one cheek in his palm, gave her the side-eye, and tapped the end of his crayon against his chin the same way Kevin used a pen to tap his chin when he worked at his desk.

"It's the sky," Logan clarified.

"Who's there with you?"

"Nobody. No one."

"Where's Daddy?" she asked, trying to keep her voice light, casual, pretending she didn't care whether he opened up or not.

Sometimes, if she was too overeager, her son had a tendency to earn the nickname his father had given him. Turtle. He'd slow down, withdraw, zone out. As a parent, when you had a quiet kid who didn't usually rock the boat, it was easy to let him spend too much time in front of a screen.

She leaned closer. "Buddy?"

"Daddy's on the road." Logan spread a few more aimless scribbles across the paper.

"Where's Allie?"

He narrowed his eyes at his sister, who was obliviously texting away. "She's onna phone."

Hmm, were we being literal?

Anna spread her palms out on the table in front of her, stared down at her wedding ring, and waited a full minute before asking, "Where am *I*?"

His ocean blues eyes met hers.

She held her breath.

He studied her for the longest moment, then finally, in a voice so tiny she could barely hear him, whispered, "I dunno."

* * *

AT FOUR, AMELIA showed up looking anxious and way over-dressed. She wore tailored black slacks as she had on the first day, an aquamarine sweater set with three-quarter-length sleeves, and trendy black-and-aquamarine ballet flats. She had on pearl earrings and a pearl necklace and at her wrist, the keepsake bracelet.

Anna fingered her own bracelet as she waved her sister inside. How long were they supposed to wear them? The bracelets were fragile, dainty. If they wore them all the time, the metal was bound to wear thin and they risked the chain breaking. But she feared taking it off, in case that sent a message to Amelia that she didn't intend.

"How are you doing?" Amelia asked, crossing the threshold.

"I was about to ask you the same thing."

They held each other's gaze and Anna felt a surreal moment of true connection. There was one secret less between them. Last night, learning about the real reason Amelia had come to

Moonglow was painful to hear, but now they could be fully honest with each other.

It felt good. Optimistic.

"I'm nervous about this party," Amelia said.

"Me too."

"Where are the children?" Amelia asked and opened her oversized tote bag and took out a sack imprinted with the logo of a high-end local store.

"They're getting changed. They just got out of the pool."

"I have presents."

"You don't have to bring them expensive gifts." Anna shook her head. "That's not the way to win them over."

"Oh." Amelia looked uncertain and slipped the bag back into her tote. "I'm sorry. I should have asked your permission first."

"No, no, it's okay. It's just that I already struggle against Kevin who is overly generous with gift giving. I don't want them to equate love with material possessions."

"I understand." Amelia clicked the snap on her tote closed.

"That's how you were treated," Anna said. "In place of love and affection you were given things."

Amelia winced. "Yes."

Why had she said that? *Oh, for a filter!* Anna peered at the sack. "What did you get?"

"I got Logan a die-cast race car."

"He'll love that. Sometimes I fear as much as that boy loves race cars, he's bound for NASCAR." Anna chuckled, trying to ease the tension.

"For Allie," Amelia said, "I got pink paddock boots for when she goes to see Heathcliff."

Momentarily, Anna was confused when Amelia said her father's name. Oh yes, the gelding. Allie had named the horse after her grandfather. She'd completely forgotten about the horse.

"You can give them the gifts," Anna said.

"You changed your mind?"

Anna shrugged. "Something just occurred to me."

"What's that?"

"I've been reading this book about love languages." Trying to get a bead on what was wrong with her and Kevin, but she wasn't going into that. "Gift giving is your love language. I gotta respect that and let you be you."

Looking mildly contrite, Amelia said, "I'll tone down the gift giving after this."

"Thank you." Anna linked her arm through Amelia's. "Now get in here, sister, and help me get ready for this shindig. In case you haven't figured out by now, acts of service are my love language currency."

* * *

Two HOURS PASSED in a buzz of sisterly conversation as they prepared for the dinner party. It would have been so much fun if Anna wasn't wound up in knots over having to break the news to her family that she was giving Amelia a kidney.

Mike, his cute blond wife, Gia, and their one-year-old, Faith, were the first to arrive. Yay! They were the safest. Anna didn't know how her mother and Kevin's family would handle the news, but she was fairly confident Mike and Gia would be on her side.

But why did there have to be sides? Why couldn't everyone be supportive?

In the kitchen, Anna introduced Amelia to Gia and Faith, and left them chatting, while she took her brother by the sleeve and pulled him into the dining room where Amelia had set a beautiful table using Anna's good china.

"I have an agenda," she told her brother.

Mike jammed his hands in his front pockets and hunched his shoulders the way their father used to do when he felt put on the spot. "I suspected."

"I'll need a backup."

"For what?"

"I can't get into it right now." She cast a glance over her shoulder to see Gia handing the baby to Amelia. Her twin looked wide-eyed with surprise. "Please, just be on my side."

"I'm not liking the sound of this."

"Kevin's going to fight me, and I suspect so will Veronica and Pete and maybe even Mom."

"Good Lord." Mike's brow furrowed. "Are things that bad between you and Kevin?"

Yes. Yes, they were, and her heart ached with the pain of their emotional separation, but she couldn't fix her and Kevin. Not now. Not yet. She had to fix Amelia first.

A knock sounded at the back door.

"That'll be Mom," she said, recognizing the way her mother knocked and turned the doorknob at the same time.

"Yoo-hoo. I brought wine!" her mother called out.

"Just back me up, brother, please. I need support." She pressed her palms together, beseeching.

Mike nodded, but just barely. He was a considerate person and didn't make promises lightly. "Okay, but if your husband never speaks to me again, it's on you."

"Hi!" Mom came to the dining-room doorway, waving a bottle of wine. She was overdressed as if she knew something big was afoot. Stylish clothing was Robin's armor whenever she felt nervous. "Can we open this?"

"Sure." Anna took the bottle and led her into the kitchen.

Amelia was still holding Faith and looking only slightly less terrified. Gia had brought a tray of crudités, and she was busy rearranging the food from where it had shifted on the drive over.

"There's my baby girl!" Robin cooed at Faith and held her arms out.

Looking deeply relieved at the sight of her grandmother, Faith reached for Robin. "Maw-Maw."

Robin smiled at Faith's enthusiasm and took her from Amelia, who looked just as relieved as Faith.

Anna met Amelia's eyes and she gave her a warm smile.

Amelia smiled back, inexorably linking them with that slight lift of her lips. Her sister didn't throw around smiles easily, but when she did, it felt like a tremendous gift.

She heard the back door open and the sound of Kevin's footsteps on the mudroom tile. *He's home!*

Anna's pulse kicked, and her legs wanted to fly to him. Her heart wanted him to wrap his arms around her and hold her tight and tell her everything would be all right. But she also wanted respect and understanding. Using their last fight as a guidepost, she didn't believe he would offer her those things.

Her heartbeat, which had galloped at Amelia's smile, slowed, slogged until she could hardly tell that it was still beating.

"The wine?" Mom nudged.

Blinking, Anna pulled her mind back into her body and glanced down. She had the corkscrew in one hand, the wine bottle in the other. Robin, with Faith on her hip, was staring at Anna with thirsty eyes.

She set about stabbing the corkscrew into the cork, but all her attention narrowed to the sounds in the mudroom. Pete Drury's laconic voice asking, "What's for dinner?" as he came in through the back door that creaked on its hinges. Veronica's breezy laughter that signaled she was in a good mood.

Kevin hadn't spoken since entering the house. Was he expecting her to come to him as she usually did when he returned home from a trip?

Going through the motions but not really registering what she was doing, Anna uncorked the bottle and poured her mother a glass of wine. Her ears stayed tuned to the mudroom as Logan and Allie rushed downstairs to greet their father and grandparents.

"Could you take this little bundle?" Robin asked, swapping wine for the baby.

"Now . . ." Her mother took a big sip of wine and did a twisty little dance step. "Let's get this party started. Where's the music? We need music."

Mom was trying way too hard. Talking too loudly, forcing a smile, searching for distraction. Anna recorked the wine bottle, and asked the AI personal assistant device to play classic sixties rock. Steppenwolf filled the room, "Magic Carpet Ride."

Anna held Faith against her chest, but the one-year-old swiveled her head around, eyes on her grandmother.

Grinning, Robin raised her glass in salute and turned the twisty little dance step into full-on body gyrations. Let it be known, that at seventy years of age, Robin Straus didn't need no stinkin' hip or knee replacement.

The baby squirmed against Anna, wanting down. Gently, she patted the baby's back.

"I think she needs a clean diaper," Gia said. "I'll take her."

Gia took the baby into the bedroom for a diaper change while Mike wandered off to speak to Kevin, Veronica, and Pete.

That left only Anna, Robin, and Amelia in the kitchen. Amelia lurked in the corner, watching without a word.

God, how I wish I had a tenth of her emotional self-control.

Robin kicked off her shoes and danced like the barefooted hippie she'd been once upon a time.

Yay, go Mom!

In the past, Anna might have joined her mother in the dancing and wine drinking. Anna loved when Robin acted spontaneous, free and uncensored, showing her sassy side. This was an aspect of her mom's personality she rarely saw.

Watching her mother now, even knowing Robin's spunky

behavior was anxiety fueled, she admired her spirit. Mom's determination in the face of adversity, while still wearing her red lipstick, said a lot about her.

It hit Anna like a slap that she really didn't know her mother outside of the label of "Mom." Once she'd become a mother, Robin nobly wrapped up her own bright light so that her children could shine. And while it was terrific for a child to have such an attentive, giving mother, she saw for the first time the exacting toll that living her life for her children had taken from Robin.

What youthful dreams had gone unfulfilled?

When Anna was a kid, Robin loved telling her and Mike that being a wife and mother was all she'd ever wanted.

Really, Mom?

What about when you were thirteen? What did you dream of then? What did you whisper in prayer when you got on your knees, seven and selfish and supposing that God was your personal wish-granting genie? What did you wish for when you blew out candles on birthday cakes and threw coins into fountains? What did you want so badly you could taste it?

Was it just wedding gowns and baby cribs?

Or was there more to you?

Robin hummed along with the music. "I lost my virginity to this song."

"Mom!" Scandalized, Anna covered her mouth with her hand.

What would people think? But then she thought, *What the hell?* They were all family here and it was past time to be emotionally honest and open with each other. If you wanted more intimacy, you told the truth.

Kindly.

That's how you made connections. You showed your vulnerability and accepted the other person's damages because those were foibles you shared as members of the human race.

Wounds.

Battle scars.

Half-baked healing.

"Well, I did." Robin laughed waltzing around the room, dipping and swirling so quickly Anna feared for the wineglass in her hand. "It was summer and somehow he got someone to loan him a small sailboat and he took me sailing in the bay and—"

"This was with Daddy?" Anna asked. She'd heard more times than she could count how Heathcliff and Robin had been each other's first, last, everything, just like her and Kevin, so she wasn't sure why she asked the question.

Mom's smile slipped but only for a fraction of a second. So briefly that Anna believed she'd imagined it.

"Of course, with Daddy," Robin said.

She's lying.

The thought flashed across her mind so startling that Anna actually took a step back. Another thought piled onto the back of that one.

You'll never really know your mother until she stops lying to herself.

Followed immediately by a third, far more disturbing thought. In what ways did Anna lie to *her* children?

CHAPTER TWENTY

Robin

A Change of Heart

She shouldn't be drinking along with the Xanax the doctor had prescribed for her last year after Heathcliff died.

Robin had popped the antianxiety pill in the car after arriving at Anna's house, because she had a bad feeling about this "dinner party" and wanted to be prepared. Now, as the family gathered at the dinner table, passing around salad bowls, the garlic bread basket, and a platter of chicken marsala, she knew she was right to be worried.

With the chicken marsala, Anna brought out the big guns. It was her specialty dish. The recipe she served for birthdays or other celebrations. Celebrations meant good news of some kind. News meant change.

Robin was bone-tired of things changing.

When she was young, she believed that when you got old you stopped changing. Ha! Nothing was further from the truth. It just seemed that way because the more things changed, the more they stayed the same.

No one at the table spoke and there was only the sound of

glasses and silverware clanking. The food was delicious, but Robin couldn't eat. She felt the tension in the room as a steel band tightening around her throat.

Something was up and despite the chicken marsala on the menu, Robin feared it was not a celebration.

Anna and Kevin sat on opposite ends of the big family dining table. Kevin at the head, Anna at the foot. They hadn't once looked each other in the eye. Nor had they spoken to each other.

Robin had been watching and she wondered if anyone else had noticed. She shifted her gaze across the table to Kevin's parents. She'd always liked Pete and Veronica. Salt-of-the-earth folks. Oh sure, Veronica could drone on about her quilts and her many grandchildren, and getting full sentences out of Pete was a Herculean task, but they were good people.

And so was Kevin.

He'd been a supportive husband to Anna and a loving father to Robin's grandchildren. He and Heathcliff had played golf together. He and Mike went deep-sea fishing from time to time. He was an all-American boy, with both the strengths and flaws that went with it.

Meaning, he could be a bit shallow and stubbornly opinionated at times.

He provided a good living for his family and he loved her daughter and he was kind to Robin. He didn't seem to mind that she was over at their house often, but sometimes, as a mother, she wished a different life for Anna.

One that had not looked so much like her own.

Yes, she'd loved being a wife and mother—both were the

greatest joys of her life—but sometimes . . . Well, it didn't really matter now, did it? Water under the bridge.

Mike and Gia sat on the same side of the table as Robin. The three kids, Allie, Logan, and Faith, were at the kids' table in the adjacent kitchen and Gia kept craning her neck around Mike's shoulder to keep an eye on them.

Sitting next to the Drurys, as far on the opposite side of the table from Robin as she could get, sat Amelia.

They were halfway through the meal, Mike had started small talk about moving his furniture business from Paradise Pier into the building next door to the bakery, when Anna tapped her iced-tea glass with the side of her knife.

"Could I have your attention?"

Everyone turned to look at Anna. Even Allie had left the kids' table to come stand in the doorway.

"Thank you all for coming tonight." Smiling, Anna glanced around the table, making eye contact with everyone individually.

Except her husband.

"It's always a joy to have you in our home."

Everyone mumbled something trite in response. Despite Anna's sweet words, anyone could see joy was not what she felt in this moment. More like trepidation.

Anna straightened up taller in her chair and reached over to take her sister's hand. "Amelia and I have important news you all need to hear."

That's when the alarm bells went off. That's when the dread that had been nibbling at Robin night and day since Amelia had come to town wrapped around her like a weight, pulling her down into a place she didn't want to go.

Finally, Anna met Kevin's gaze.

Robin felt the jump of anger between them. The hostility in Kevin's eyes caught her in the gut, and she wished she hadn't eaten so much.

What was going on here?

"Amelia has renal failure." Anna said it so matter-of-factly it sounded as if she was reading her grocery list. "And she needs a kidney transplant as soon as possible to give her a chance for a normal life. And if everything checks out with my health, I'm giving her one of mine."

Kevin's gaze was frosty. "You're really going through with this?"

Anna lifted her chin. "I am."

Tension was a spike, sharp and steely.

"Against my wishes?" Kevin's face darkened.

Veronica and Pete stared at their son.

"S'up?" Pete asked.

"Why are you against Anna giving her sister a kidney?" Veronica gave her son a look.

Kevin turned his cold glare on Amelia. "You want to tell them, or should I?"

Gia hopped up from the table and shooed the kids from the dining room. "I'll take them outside," she called over her shoulder. "This is grown-up talk."

Robin felt guilty for not being the one to take the kids outside and a bit regretful that Gia had beaten her to a good excuse for dodging this conversation. She considered excusing herself from the table, pretending to go to the restroom, but instead just getting into her car and driving home.

"Tell us what?" Robin heard herself ask even though she hadn't intended on saying anything.

"Amelia . . ." Anna started to say, but Amelia reached over and touched Anna's shoulder. Nodded. They exchanged a knowing glance.

"I lost my kidneys to drug use," Amelia said. "I was addicted to heroin for almost a year."

Shocked, Robin stared at Amelia. She was a heroin addict? A druggie who'd ruined her kidneys and now wanted to harvest one from *her* only daughter?

She clenched her teeth and her hands, and Robin's mind flooded with a hundred different ways she could reply, but before she got a word out, Kevin hopped to his feet.

"No!" He slammed his fist against the table. "I forbid it."

"Excuse me?" Anna said in a voice hot enough to fry a turkey.

Robin twisted her fingers in her lap.

Her son-in-law quivered from head to toe. He sounded so angry, but when Robin looked into his eyes, all she saw was stark fear. He was terrified of losing Anna.

Yes, well, so was she.

"I won't let you do this," Kevin said. "She made her bed." He pointed a finger at Amelia. "Let her live with the consequences of her choices."

Robin swung her gaze to Amelia. She agreed with Kevin one hundred percent. In fact, at this moment, she was so on his side, if Kevin had decided to run for public office, she'd put his campaign sign in her yard, and she hated the noisy clutter of campaign signs.

She resented Amelia for coming here, for putting Anna on the spot, for expecting a kidney from her daughter after she'd ruined hers. Amelia had ruined Robin's life as well—her daughter wasn't truly hers . . . her husband had lied to her for years.

But with Amelia sitting there, looking so much like Anna that it physically hurt Robin's soul, something shifted inside her.

Anger directed at Amelia was anger directed at her own child. In a short time, Anna had found a love for Amelia that Robin couldn't fathom. Not because she didn't want to, simply because she didn't have a twin. It was a relationship beyond her knowledge.

She felt left out, cheated somehow, and was immediately ashamed for her pettiness. She should be glad her daughter had such a special connection. She just wished that tight connection was with her and not some stranger.

Whoa! Where had that come from?

Amelia and Anna were holding hands, huddled at that end of the table. Amelia was looking at Anna as if she'd painted the moon and stars in the sky.

She loves her, Robin thought, and goose bumps raised across her arms. *Amelia loves Anna.*

Jolted, she pushed away her plate. She didn't want Anna to give Amelia a kidney, but Robin knew from experience that when that determined look came into Anna's eyes there was no dissuading her.

If this was what Anna wanted, then Robin would back her up.

No matter what.

Yes, she was scared as hell for her child. Yes, the idea of Anna going through major surgery sent icy fingers of dread closing around her spine. Yes, standing on the sidelines watching the situation play out was damn hard for an involved mother.

But . . .

Anna needed her support.

Robin truly only wanted one thing for her children and that was happiness. Giving to others made Anna happy. Even from the time she was three and gave Mike, as a newborn infant, her chocolate cookie because he (real quote here, she'd even put it in Anna's baby book) "looked hungwee."

If giving Amelia a kidney made Anna happy, so be it.

Ahem. A kidney is not a chocolate chip cookie.

No, but Anna wasn't three anymore, either, and she was in charge of her own life.

Kevin was not on Anna's side and from the looks on Veronica's and Pete's faces, neither were they.

Robin's heart went out to her daughter. This was the worst dinner party ever and going downhill fast.

"You're doing this thing, aren't you?" Kevin growled at Anna. "You made up your mind one hundred percent."

"I have."

His face was flushed redder than Robin had ever seen it. He was still standing, his stature and anger looming over the entire table. She was so glad that Gia had had the presence of mind to get the kids out of earshot.

In the moment, nostrils flaring and neck veins bulging, Kevin truly resembled a vanquishing Viking. "You're doing it no matter what I think. No matter what I want. No matter what is best for our family."

"Yes," Anna said so softly it was alarming. But it was not a cowed whisper of passivity, rather deep, unshakable conviction. "Amelia is my family too."

"No," Kevin said, getting louder the quieter Anna became. "You've chosen her—a stranger—over your own family. She means more to you than the kids and I do."

"That's not fair to Anna," said Mike, who was sitting beside Robin.

"Amelia needs me." Anna looked calm on the outside, but Robin knew her daughter. Kevin's accusations were ripping her up inside.

"I need you. Logan needs you. Allie needs you." Kevin's tone was practically begging her.

Anna's face flushed, and Robin felt her child's guilt in her own gut. "That's playing dirty, and I'm not going to let you make me feel bad about this."

"Please," Veronica interjected. "Think of your children. What will happen to them if you die on the operating table?"

"All of life is a risk, Veronica," Anna told her mother-in-law. "Some risks are worth taking."

Kevin glared down the table at Anna, a look so hurtful Robin wanted to jump up and box his cheeks. "Decision made?"

Anna let go of Amelia's hand, pushed back her chair, and got to her feet. Putting her hands on her hips, she affirmed, "Decision made."

"Fine. Then you can do it without me. I'm taking my folks home and then I'm going back to Oklahoma."

Had Kevin just told Anna he was leaving her? Robin put a palm to her forehead, trying to quell the pitch of her stomach.

Pete stared blankly. "Huh?"

Veronica blinked as if blindsided. "Kevin?"

Kevin wadded up the pretty linen napkin and tossed it onto his plate. Robin watched as the cloth soaked up the marsala wine sauce. The stain would be hard to get out of that white material.

"Mom, Dad. Let's go." Kevin headed for the kitchen and the back door beyond.

"But there's cake . . ." Pete waved at the Italian cream cake on the sideboard.

Veronica took hold of her husband's arm. "I'll make you cake at home."

"Anna's cakes taste better."

"Of course her cakes taste better, she's a professional baker. Come on, now." Veronica got Pete out of his chair, linked her arms through his, and guided him around the table.

Pete's gaze locked longingly on the cake.

"Hold on a minute, Veronica," Anna said. "I'll get Pete a to-go slice."

Pete's eyes and smile widened spontaneously. "Yes. That."

"Mom, Dad," Kevin hollered from the kitchen. "I'm leaving."

Robin didn't like the way Kevin was pushing people around. What had gotten into him? Normally, he wasn't so demanding. Then again, this wasn't a normal situation.

Anna bustled around, opening the sideboard's cabinets where

she kept a stash of cake boxes and extra silverware. She cut Pete a generous chunk of cake and slipped it into the box.

"I'm not sharing this with Kevin," Pete whispered conspiratorially.

"Mom! Dad!" Kevin hollered again. Followed by the sound of the mudroom door slamming closed.

Something came over Robin then. Mama bear instincts in high gear. A punching surge of anger and grief that she hadn't felt since Heathcliff died.

Faster than her seventy-year-old self should be moving, she was out of her chair and flying toward the kitchen, muscling Pete and Veronica away from the back door.

"Kevin!" she shrieked, knowing she sounded like a loon, but someone had to put a stop to his petulant behavior. Her daughter was suffering, and he was letting her down by acting like a total jackass.

Kevin stopped in the middle of the driveway on his way to the family car, his back to her.

It was just before twilight, the sky awash in soft pinks, oranges, and purples. The air was scented with the smell of barbecuing meat on neighbors' grills. A seagull cawed in the distance.

"Kevin," she said, less frantic this time.

He spun around and glared at her, anger as fierce as her own radiating off him in scorching waves. Ironing his arms flat to his sides, he leaned forward, face still beet red and his chin quivering.

"What is it, Robin? What do you want from me?" His voice sliced her viciously.

Typically, in such situations, Robin would put up her hands, raise the white flag, and back off. Especially when she was wearing Easy Spirit pumps and pearls. Not that such confrontations happened often.

"What the hell, Kevin?" She jammed her hands onto her hips, opened her mouth again, and was about to let him have it with both barrels when she saw his face.

The pain in his eyes was so raw, so visceral, that she caught it like a tossed ball, cradling it in the heat of her belly.

His gaze locked on hers and in that moment, she could literally see what he was thinking but unable to say to her. *I'm terrified of losing her, Robin.*

"Me too," she whispered to his unspoken confession, unnerved by the telepathy, her heart splitting wide open at his vulnerability.

"I can't . . . I can't." He splayed his palm to his nape, paced in circles. "I can't even."

"You've gotten yourself worked up," she said in what she intended to be a soothing tone.

He scowled.

Up went her hands. "But with legitimate reasons. Just take a big deep breath, okay? I don't want you passing out."

He didn't look happy about it, but he did it.

"Again," she prompted.

He shot her the side-eye. "I'm good."

She let it go. Robin became aware, without turning her head to verify, that Pete and Veronica were standing behind her in the driveway.

"You have to let Anna do what she needs to do."

"Fine." He snorted. "She can do whatever she wants without me. She didn't even bother to tell me first. I can't stand by and watch Anna get duped by a drug addict. I'll leave that to you."

Kevin motioned to his parents, who jumped in the car with surprising agility. Doors closed and they drove away without another word.

And it wasn't until they were out of sight that Robin glanced up and saw Allie hiding in the oak tree overhead peering down at her. The girl had her hair pulled across her face, using it as a mask.

Robin's heart sank. The child must have heard the entire exchange.

"Hey there, kiddo. What are you doing in that tree?" she asked, putting extra softness in her tone.

"Hiding from the yelling."

That was a hard tug on the heartstrings.

"Maw-Maw?" Allie asked.

"Yes, sweetheart?"

"Exactly what is it that Mama needs to do that makes Daddy so mad?"

No way was she touching *that* with a ten-foot pole. "Come on, sugar bear, get down. I do believe your mama has cake."

"You're not going to tell me, are you?"

"No, no I am not. If you're big enough to ask questions, you're big enough to ask them of your mother. You shouldn't keep secrets from her. Now climb down. I thought I saw lightning bugs in the garden. Let's go get your brother and chase them."

Chasing lightning bugs used to be one of Allie's favorite

summer pastimes, but she shook her head. "It's no fun without Daddy."

Robin took her granddaughter's hand and led her to where the honeysuckle bloomed, its sweet scent a melancholy undertone. Ahead of them the night lit up with the blinking phosphorene glow of lightning bugs. Fireflies they called them in other parts of the country, but here in Moonglow Cove it was lightning bugs.

"Maw-Maw?"

"Yes?"

"Can I ask you something?"

"Surely." *Hope I don't have to lie.*

"Are Mom and Dad . . ." Allie hitched in a breath and hugged herself in the shadows, the lightning bug show forgotten. "Getting a divorce?"

"Oh, no, no, no. They love each other very much, honey."

"But my friend Jojo's mom got divorced and she said sometimes love just isn't enough to save a marriage."

Allie shouldn't have to think about this. Robin wanted to physically shake Kevin and Anna both and tell them they needed to get on the same page for the sake of their kids.

"That's Jojo's mom's experience. It's not the same for your mom and dad."

"So everything's going to be okay?" Allie's voice lightened.

"Everything's going to be okay," Robin assured her, but as she wrapped her arm around her granddaughter, she couldn't help worrying, *Would it?*

CHAPTER TWENTY-ONE

Amelia

My Little Runaway

After a dinner party as depressing as Rachmaninoff's "Isle of the Dead," all Amelia wanted was to go back to the Moonglow Inn, jump in bed, yank the covers over her head, and sleep for a week.

She'd been running on straight adrenaline since Tuesday, and her emotional tank was empty. Introvert that she was, a hot bath and good book sounded like the most appealing thing in the world.

Robin had offered to keep the kids until Monday so that Amelia and Anna could have time alone to discuss the surgery. Anna packed an overnight bag for the children and, now, she and Anna were standing in the driveway watching Robin's car disappear from sight.

After they left, Anna turned to Amelia. "Please come back to stay here."

Amelia twitched. "Kevin doesn't want me here. I don't think it's right for me to stay. I wouldn't feel comfortable staying since he feels about me the way he does."

"Forget Kevin. He's the one who left."

"I don't want to disrespect him."

"You're not." Anna took both of Amelia's hands in hers and looked her squarely in the eyes. "*I* need you. Stay. *Please*."

Amelia inhaled deeply.

"You're right." Anna raised a palm. "I shouldn't pressure you into staying. I understand. You need your space."

Amelia wanted to leave it at that, but the expression on Anna's face beneath the glow of the security lamp told her that her sister needed her to say yes.

Exhaling a sigh, she said, "Shelley and Sebastian are going to have to put in a revolving door for me."

"Yay! Thank you." Anna wrapped her in a bear hug.

Amelia absorbed the hug, but couldn't hug her back, torn in two by her urge to flee and her yearning to stay.

"Let's go check you out of the Moonglow Inn again?" Anna asked, stepping back and lifting an inquisitive eyebrow.

"I feel horrible coming between you and your husband," Amelia confessed.

"It's not just you or the kidney transplant." Anna waved a hand. "Things have been rocky for a while. I just hadn't wanted to admit it. We went through a lot of financial stress last year and we lost my dad. It's been the toughest time for our marriage."

"And then I come along." Amelia wanted to comfort her, but she didn't really know how. Awkwardly, she lightly patted Anna's shoulder. "And blow it all up."

"Wow, that sure is a fatalistic look on your face."

Was it? Amelia smiled to prove otherwise.

"Please, don't worry about us. As upset as Kevin is, he loves me, and I love him, and we'll find a way through it."

Amelia wanted to say, *What if you don't?* But why rock Anna's world any more than she already had? Her sister was a good person. She deserved to hang on to her optimism.

"When it's all over, Kevin will be glad I gave you a kidney. He's a kindhearted person. I know it doesn't seem like that right now, but honestly, he's just scared of losing me."

So am I.

The thought burst into her mind so passionate and vehement, Amelia startled. It was true. If something happened to Anna during or after the transplant, she'd never forgive herself.

"You know," Anna said, "I have to respect that Kevin spoke his mind and set boundaries."

"Is that what he did?" To Amelia, Kevin's behavior had seemed more like a temper tantrum, but maybe that was her own skewed view of anger considering Sarah Brandt had been a world-class tantrum thrower, and as a result, whenever conflict reared its head, Amelia withdrew into her solitary world of music, reading, and horses.

"Yes." Anna nodded as if to convince herself.

"His position sounds less like setting healthy boundaries and more like control tactics to me."

Anna paled and Amelia wished she'd kept her big fat mouth shut.

"But I've never been married," she amended quickly. "What do I know?"

"Kevin loves me."

"I'm sure he does."

Anna hiccuped and Amelia was terrified that she was going to cry, but no, her twin rallied.

"It's going to all work out," Anna said, channeling Mary Poppins with a chirpy voice and brilliant smile. "It *will*."

"I'm sure." Amelia nodded, but she wasn't sure at all.

* * *

IT WAS AFTER ten P.M. by the time they collected Amelia's things from the Moonglow Inn and returned to Anna's house. The place was eerily quiet without the children in it.

Amelia took her suitcases and headed for the guest room, but Anna said in a soft, lost voice, "Would you mind sleeping with me tonight?"

"In your bed?"

"It's king-size."

"Where Kevin sleeps?" The idea did not appeal.

"You're right." Anna waved a hand. "Dumb idea. I just thought . . ."

Amelia cocked her head, waited.

"When I was a kid and felt scared or lonely, Mom and Dad would wave me into their bed. It's where I felt the safest. Really connected to them, you know. But I understand that makes you uncomfortable, so please forget I asked."

Terrific! Good night!

Except Amelia couldn't forget it. "I guess I could use some safety and connectedness too."

"Oh, thank you!" Anna threw her arms around Amelia's neck and hugged hard.

All right, it didn't feel so horrible being hugged by her twin. In fact, it felt nice and Amelia was going to miss this closeness when she went back to her regular life.

"We can talk about kidney transplantation and what all's involved," Anna said, sounding efficient now. Her twin seemed to function best when she had a project and for the present, Amelia was that project.

It's what you wanted. It's why you came here.

Yes, but that was before she fully understood what was at stake for Anna.

Guilt crept up by degrees, starting first as a tingling in her toes, and turned into an anchoring numbness. What if something *did* happen to Anna during the surgery? Her nephrologist told her that transplants were harder on the donors than the recipients.

"Would you think less of me if I had a glass of wine?" Anna asked.

Amelia burst out laughing.

"What's funny?" Anna sounded confused.

Her sister didn't see the irony? Truly, Anna was a treasure with her wide-eyed, empathetic worldview. How did she stay so sweet and wholesome?

"I'm a recovering heroin addict, sister. I'm in no position to judge anyone."

"Oh, thank God." Anna made a beeline for the kitchen and Amelia followed. "I don't *need* alcohol to take the edge off, but after tonight, I would definitely enjoy a glass. Except I didn't want to make you uncomfortable."

"Addiction is my issue, not yours," Amelia said. "Don't re-arrange yourself to suit me."

Anna clucked her tongue, a pitying noise that bugged Amelia, although she wasn't quite sure why. Had Anna agreed to give her a kidney because she longed to "fix" Amelia? Was that what this generous gesture was all about?

Hmm. And was that motive emotionally healthy? She didn't know. She'd have to ask Dr. Ellard.

Anna poured herself a glass of wine, and Amelia got a spar-kling water from the fridge. They sat in the front porch rocking chairs and listened to the mockingbird making late-night racket in the crepe myrtle bush.

One of the neighbors must have been having a party. The sounds of soft laughter and music rode the air, along with car doors closing, and occasional headlights flickered through the trees as guests slowly departed.

That party seemed far more successful than the one Anna at-tempted tonight.

"My favorite rosebush is going crazy. If rose petals were money . . ." Anna used her bare toe to point toward the rose-bush in the flower bed so overpopulated with blooms that the branches drooped. "I should cut back on the plant food."

Oh, Amelia knew this game. Trite and inconsequential. Her parents had been experts at it. Pretending things were good when the world was crashing down around their ears. Denial was one damn grand river.

The part of Amelia that loved the psyche deep dive ached to push Anna to talk about her feelings. *Hey, Dr. Ellard, look at me. No hands.* But the part of her that had learned to go inward and shut out the world in order to survive curled up into a tight little ball and said nothing.

Her sister's marriage was in trouble and it was all Amelia's fault.

Anna might be playing it cool, but Amelia was an expert at that game. Keep things light. *Got it.* Skim the surface like a water strider.

"What's the name of the rosebush?" Amelia asked.

"I Love You Always."

Startled, Amelia shot Anna a sideways glance. "What?"

"The rosebush, it's called I Love You Always."

"Oh."

"You thought I was telling you I loved you again, didn't you?"

Umm, yes.

"Kevin bought me the rosebush for Mother's Day two years ago." She paused. "He's very good at gift giving. Maybe that's actually an issue."

Amelia was not going to comment. Another long silence stretched out between them.

"It's hard for you, freely accepting love." Not even a rhetorical question, just a plain statement of fact. Anna had figured her out.

Amelia lifted her shoulders in a perfunctory shrug. Now who was avoiding the deep psyche dive?

Several minutes passed with nothing but the creak of their

rocking chairs and dwindling sounds from the party next door to punctuate the silence.

Finally, Anna brought up the topic they'd been dancing around. "So, I googled kidney transplantation, but I didn't have time to delve deeply into the topic. Let's cut to the chase and just tell me what I need to know."

Amelia wanted to tell her she should continue with her research, but Anna seemed to want her to deliver the answers, so she did. For thirty minutes, they talked about the transplant. What it would entail, how long was the recovery time, what to expect afterward for both Anna and Amelia.

"We would do this in Chicago?" Anna asked, taking her last sip of wine.

"Ideally," Amelia said. "Since that's where I live and where my doctors are. But I understand if Chicago is too much of an effort. I'm sure my doctors would recommend specialists in Houston so you could be near home."

"Having the surgery in Chicago would be faster and easier for you, would it not? Since you've already formed a relationship with your doctors and they know your case, it makes the most sense."

"You're giving me one of your kidneys, Anna. You get to call the shots."

"Chicago it is." She slurred the last word but only slightly.

"I'm exhausted," Amelia said, telling the straight-up truth. "A quick hot shower and I'll be ready for bed."

"Me too." Anna put a palm over her mouth to hide a yawn.

Amelia showered in the guest room bathroom while Anna

was in the master bath. She considered staying in the guest bedroom and just hoped Anna would let her get away with it, but a part of her wanted to share a bed with her sister, the way they hadn't been able to do when they were children, giggling, sharing stories, and telling confidences.

Amelia felt a pang in her heart and she tried to find a dozen excuses for it as she stood under the hot water—indigestion, muscle strain, referred kidney pain . . .

A wrenching sense of loss.

Yes, there was that, too. Unwanted emotions crashed in on her as her mind filled with images of things that had never been. She and Anna taking their first steps together, learning to ride bicycles and horses, graduating from high school. She tasted salt as tears backed up inside her head. She had an urge to sink down onto the floor of the shower and bawl her eyes out.

But she wouldn't.

Compartmentalize.

That central word had gotten her through her life, but it no longer worked. She simply couldn't shove Anna into any kind of box.

Her sister was too magnificent to be contained. She was such a people person. So kind and thoughtful. A bit naïve and far too trusting in Amelia's estimation—she agreed with Kevin on that account—but Anna was deeply lovable to a degree Amelia had not expected when she'd started this journey. From Anna's social media feeds, Amelia judged her as a vacuous housewife with not much going on in her life besides exalting her family.

How wrong she'd been!

What she'd found was a sweet, complicated, profane, supportive, openhearted, pushy center of the community. Anna was supremely special in her ordinariness.

Amelia got out of the shower, toweled off, and put on her pajamas. She took her time applying night cream and brushing her teeth, giving Anna time to fall asleep, now wanting to avoid her twin because her heart was too full of unexpressed feelings.

Hauling in a deep breath, she went to the master bedroom just as Anna was coming out of the bath in pj's, her long red hair brushed to shining and a soft smile on her face. How could she look so peaceful with all that was going on?

"Just imagine." Anna was rubbing hand lotion into her skin. "A month from now this will be in our rearview mirror. We'll be healing together and planning a family vacation. We deserve it. Where should we go?"

"The French Riviera is marvelous this time of year," Amelia said without thinking. Seriously? She sounded like a snob. Cringing, she bit down on her bottom lip. *Be more considerate.*

Anna's eyes were saucers. "You've been to the French Riviera?"

"My parents . . . our parents . . . vacationed there every year." *Great*, she thought, *still elitist.* "Not that it's any big deal."

Oh no, had that made it worse? Ah, anxiety. Hello, here you are again. Second-guessing everything. Fretting and stirring and tightening her chest.

"Wow," Anna said. "The things I missed out on!"

"You missed out on *nothing*." Amelia's tongue landed hard on the last word.

"I missed the French Riviera!" Anna squealed as if she was thirteen.

Amelia raised a shoulder, and not wanting Anna to feel deprived, said, "Eh, you've seen one beach, you've seen them all."

"Don't disrespect the French Riviera."

"Maybe we'll go someday," Amelia mused.

"Really." Anna tossed the hand cream on the dresser and clapped her hands. "When all this is over, we'll still be friends?" Anna's smile was like a little girl who'd just been told she was having tea in Cinderella's castle.

"What? You thought I was going to just take your kidney and ride off into the sunset?" Amelia joked.

Five days ago, that's exactly what she'd intended. She'd thought she'd meet her sister, have some good conversations, tell her about the kidney, get the transplant, and go back to her life. In retrospect, that sounded incredibly selfish.

You should be ashamed of yourself. You worthless girl. You're the one who should have died. Your sister is the one who should have lived. The good one.

Amelia splayed a palm to her chest overcome by the vitriol in her own head. In her mother's voice.

"Amelia?" Anna put out a hand to her. "Are you okay?"

"Your family might not have been wealthy," she said, grateful to hear her tone come out normal. "But you had something I didn't. Parents who truly loved you. And I'd swap all the money in the world, all the summers on the French Riviera, all the Christmas ski trips to Aspen to have what you have."

Anna laughed nervously. "Easy for you to say. There's not a stack of bills sitting on your desk that you're not sure how you're going to pay."

Amelia stabbed Anna with her gaze. "Don't do that."

"Do what?"

"Minimize what you have. You've got a good husband. He loves you and wants to protect you. You've got two beautiful healthy children. You've got friends and family who would do anything for you. You've got an entire community that rallies around you. You've got your own business, a bakery that's always busy. I could see it from the window of my room at the Moonglow Inn. Understand this, Anna, when people come into your bakery, baked goods aren't the real reason they are there."

"It's not?"

"They come for *you*, Anna. People love the way you make them feel. They love how kind and generous and caring you are. You ask about their children, and their jobs and their health. When someone is sick, you take them food. When someone passes away, you're the first person there to hold their family's hands and tell them how sorry you are for their loss."

"Shelley and Sebastian told you all that," Anna said.

The innkeeper and her husband had indeed told Amelia that. "You are an incredible person, Anna Drury, and I am so very proud to call you my sister."

"Oh, Amelia." Tears misted Anna's eyes. "If you only knew how unremarkable I really am."

"I know things don't always seem rosy in your world. I know you have problems with Kevin and I'm not trying to minimize them, but you need to understand exactly how special and lucky you are."

"*You're* the special one," Anna said.

"No." Amelia shook her head. "No, I'm not. Not in the ways that count."

"You were a cellist with the Chicago Symphony and when the most unimaginable thing in the world happened to you, when you lost three loved ones in one tragic accident, when your world came crashing down around your ears, when grief dragged you through the muck, you still climbed out of it."

"I'm no hero."

"You fought your addiction and you won. Heroin is a hard drug to kick, but you did it. And now finally, you're getting a transplant, and you're going to have the life you deserved all along. A rich life, filled with family and friends and love and laughter." Anna reached for her, pulled Amelia into her arms, and hugged her. "I'll see to that."

Anna made it sound so beautiful, as if all Amelia had to do was close her fist around the dream, clutch it to her heart, and believe.

What a wonderful fantasy.

What magical hope.

But Amelia was a pragmatist. Her twin sister was the cock-eyed optimist. It was a sweet fantasy, but that's all it was. A fairy tale. So domestic. This fairy tale. And it was just what Amelia had never wanted before.

"It's getting late," Amelia murmured.

"Yes." Anna nodded. "We should get some sleep."

Anna hopped into the bed, but Amelia hesitated, thinking again, *This is where Kevin slept. He's not here and I'm sleeping in his bed.*

"The sheets are fresh if that's what you're thinking." Anna mugged a grin from where she was propped up in bed. "I changed them while you were in the shower and I'm sleeping on Kevin's side."

"It's not that I thought the sheets were dirty." Amelia waved a hand. "Hey, I've slept on crack house floors."

Anna winced.

Apparently that joke was too soon. "I feel guilty about Kevin."

Anna blew out her breath, picked at lint on the blanket. "I regret that he's taken the stance he's taken, but he's in the wrong."

"I bet he thinks you're in the wrong." Amelia lifted her shoulders to her ears, held out her hands.

"I'm sure he does. But he *is* wrong."

"Having never been married, I'm letting that slide on by." Amelia got under the covers.

"We have our ups and downs like any relationship." Anna asked the AI personal assistant device to turn off the lights and the room went dark.

"Anna?"

"Yes."

"What if Kevin doesn't get over this?"

"He will."

"How do you know?"

"He loves me."

"And you trust that love so much you're willing to test it to this degree?"

Manually, Anna turned the light back on and sat up. "You've never had anyone love you like that?"

"Well, not to the degree that I wasn't afraid he'd walk out if I screwed up."

"So, this fiancé, what was his name again?"

"Robert."

"This Robert character had you worried that he was going to dump you if you didn't toe the line?"

"Not exactly." *It was that exactly.*

"What is it exactly?"

"It wasn't that bad."

"Not that bad? The guy was controlling you!"

Amelia asked the AI device to turn off the lights again. If she was going to cry—which she desperately hoped she wasn't but couldn't guarantee—she didn't want her sister to see.

Anna was right. Robert had been controlling. Just like her mother.

It was her inability to stand up for herself that had made her such a pushover. To follow so blindly his lead. And the drugs? That was just one more way to withdraw from the world, a sad attempt to eradicate her pain.

She saw now, with utter clarity, that she could not accept her twin's generous gift. Her own flaws and mistakes had brought her to this point. It was time to pay the piper for not being brave enough to face the truth before.

Leaving Moonglow Cove was the only decent thing to do. Get out of Anna's life before she destroyed her sister.

"It doesn't matter now," she said. "Robert is dead."

Anna made a noise like she wanted to say something more, to argue, to rail, but she didn't. Instead, she said, "Mistakes are how we learn."

Yes. In fact, while coming to Moonglow Cove had clearly been a mistake, Amelia had learned something very important from this trip. Mistakes were road maps to the dead-end cul-de-sacs, the "no outlet" streets. You took a wrong turn and doubled back to the beginning, starting afresh, maybe short of gas, but none the worse for having taken the detour.

Her trip to Moonglow Cove had been just that. A sweet detour. It was time to get back on the road, back to reality, back to her solo life.

It took a bit for them to settle in and stop talking. At half past midnight, according to the digital clock on the nightstand, Amelia heard Anna's deepening breath slow. She waited another ten minutes to make absolutely sure her twin was asleep.

Then Amelia tossed back the covers, and as quietly as possible, dressed in the clothing she'd worn earlier in the day, collected her suitcases from where she'd left them in the hallway, crept into the kitchen, and wrote a note for her twin sister on the magnetic notepad stuck to the fridge.

Dear Anna,

Your courage, heart, and generosity inspire me more than you can ever know. I'm so deeply grateful for your offer to give me one of your kidneys, but I simply cannot accept it.

I'm returning to Chicago and resuming my life. I hope you

can understand and forgive me for this abrupt departure. When you told me you loved me, I wasn't able to say it back. It wasn't because I didn't feel it, because surely, I did.

In my experience, when people say those words, they don't really mean them. They use love as a weapon for manipulation and control. So, you can imagine, when you told me you loved me after you'd just met me, I was taken aback.

But the more I'm around you, the more I see love in action. I see that you are purehearted and mean what you say. I don't throw the word "love" around lightly. It means too much to me to speak it frivolously.

Know this, Anna. I do love you. More than you can ever know. And that's why I have to leave. I refuse to disrupt your life and come between you and Kevin. Your happiness is all I want. I love you, forever always.

With all my heart and soul—Your twin sister, Amelia

She'd called for a ride to the airport in Houston before writing the note and her phone app dinged to tell her the car had arrived and was waiting for her at the top of the cul-de-sac. Stuffing her phone into her pocket, she took a deep breath, grabbed her luggage, and headed for the back door.

In her haste, the keepsake bracelet got hung on the levered door handle at the same time she jerked the door closed behind her. She felt a ripping sensation at her wrist, heard the sound of diamonds and pearls as they hit the concrete patio and rolled away into the dark.

Oh no! The keepsake bracelet had broken!

Stomach reeling, Amelia fumbled for her iPhone, turned on the flashlight feature, and scanned the ground.

One diamond winked at her, and she retrieved it, but in the darkness, it was all she could find without turning on the porch light.

At the top of the cul-de-sac a horn honked.

Please stop that! Yikes. Don't panic.

Another scan of the area with the iPhone light, but no more glittering gems. She did find part of the platinum chain and stuck that in her pocket along with the sole diamond.

Honk. Honk.

Then her cell phone buzzed with a text from the limo company driver. Leaving in 2 minutes.

Torn, she looked mournfully at the patio, then raised her head to the cul-de-sac above the garden valley of Anna's home.

If she wanted to leave before Anna woke up, she had to get out of here now.

Grieving the loss of the bracelet, Amelia shouldered her luggage and trudged up the hill, feeling as if something completely irreplaceable had been lost to her forever.

CHAPTER TWENTY-TWO

Anna

Brokenhearted

When Anna woke on Sunday morning and found Amelia's note, her heart imploded. She stood over the kitchen sink, stuffing leftover Italian cream cake into her mouth and sobbing around the glop of cream cheese frosting stuck to her upper lip.

Amelia loved her.

And Amelia left her.

What kind of freaking message was that to scrawl on a refrigerator notepad for your long-lost twin to find?

No. No.

Anna tossed the spoon into the sink, swiped the back of her hand over her mouth. Amelia didn't get to do that. To tell her that she loved her on paper and then just run off before they had a chance to talk about it.

Juiced by anger, Anna snatched up her cell phone that was charging on the bar, and punched Amelia's number. She was facetiming her sister, dammit.

The phone rang.

And rang.

And rang.

She tried several times. Never got an answer, not even voice mail. Then a gut-wrenching thought hit. Had Amelia blocked her number?

Outside, she'd found the pieces of Amelia's keepsake bracelet strewn across the patio as if Amelia had ripped it off intentionally and left Anna to pick up the pieces. Swallowing back more tears, she picked up all the pieces she could find, including the platinum medallion that said *Amelia*.

She brought the medallion to her lips, kissed it, and whispered, "What did I do to offend you so badly?"

* * *

UNABLE TO REMAIN in her house without either Kevin or Amelia in it, Anna went to join the kids at Robin's and asked if she could stay with her until Kevin came home, even it meant she'd have an extra fifteen-minute commute to the bakery. The homeowners' association at her mother's over fifty-five community wasn't happy with the situation and on the third day, Tuesday, left a snotty notice on Robin's door reminding her that grandchildren's overnight visits were restricted to a week's duration.

Anna assured her mother that was all the time she needed to get her act together, but it was a hollow promise. To distract herself from her problems, she hung out with Winnie at the memory care facility, taking her on long walks, bringing the senior her favorite oatmeal raisin cookies, rereading *Lonesome Dove* to her for the fourth time.

No matter how hard she tried, Anna couldn't forgive Amelia for running away in the middle of the night. From the very beginning, from the very first moment she'd seen Amelia and understood that her identical twin was the missing puzzle piece in her life, Anna took it for granted that they'd develop a close and caring relationship.

Because it was what *she* wanted.

She'd fallen in love with Amelia instantly, but her cautious twin didn't seem to have the same capacity for headlong love. Perhaps that was a healthier way to be, but Anna couldn't help how she felt.

And it was a knife through her heart that her sister had blocked Anna's phone number. She was cutting all ties.

The painful thoughts rarely left her.

On the fourth day after Amelia left, Kevin showed up at Robin's door, with a bouquet of daisies—Anna's favorite because she believed they were the friendliest flowers with their sunny centers and fresh white petals—a bag of Jelly Belly jelly beans, and an apology that never got off the ground.

She took one look at her contrite Viking standing there, flowers in hand, and was ready to forgive him anything.

"You came home," she whispered, hope overflowing her heart. He'd come to ask her forgiveness and she would grant it to him, oh yes, yes, yes.

"I couldn't stay away from you, Bean," he murmured.

She accepted the bouquet, smiled, and waved him inside. She couldn't fix Amelia, but she could fix her marriage. Kevin was here in the flesh, looking earnest and ready to make amends. Plus, daisies and Jelly Belly. He knew the way to her heart.

He smelled good, too, like the expensive basil shaving soaps she bought him as a stocking stuffer for Christmas and his face was clean-shaven. She liked a little stubble, but she also liked when his cheeks were smooth and softer. The contrast. The change. She found it appealing.

Last year, he'd grown a full beard and while he'd looked sexy as hell, she'd been relieved when he'd shaved it. The beard had come to represent hard times somewhere in the back of her mind.

They stalled in the hallway, staring at each other, Anna still holding the daisies and jelly beans.

"Can I give you a kiss?" he asked, looking as frightened and fumbling as he had that day in high school when he asked her to go steady.

She hadn't texted him or tried to contact him after Amelia left. She'd needed time to process her feelings and he'd certainly given her the space and not contacted her, either. They'd been at an impasse and she hadn't expected him to return home until the job in Oklahoma was over.

Part of her didn't want to kiss and make up until they'd worked through their problems, but another part of her didn't care about resolutions. All she wanted was to have her husband back.

She settled the jelly beans and daisies on the foyer table and turned back to him, but before she could tell him they needed to have a long serious talk first, he scooped her into his arms.

It was heady, she'd admit it. The giddy feeling surfing through her as he pulled her close and dipped his head. His kiss tingled and excited her in a way it hadn't in a long while.

There in her mother's foyer, Anna's body betrayed her, and she melted into Kevin's arms.

He kissed her as passionately as he'd kissed her in high school, letting her know she was *his* girl. Back then, she'd loved the idea of belonging to him.

Now? She felt uneasy with that concept. Especially in the face of their marital problems.

His lips were hot, and he held nothing back.

Objectively, wowza, what a kiss!

Just like old times, he lit up every nerve ending in her body. Who knew? Maybe it was because they'd had an argument and had been apart that the kiss felt so wild and wonderful.

He kissed her thoroughly, tumultuously, her body aching for him so badly that if they hadn't been in Robin's house, she might very well have taken him to bed.

Her lips were as hungry as his, their need pushing past all their arguments and misunderstandings. Kevin had always been an excellent kisser. Her husband tasted of peppermint and he smelled like sea air, basil, and citrus.

He rested his big palm on the small of her back, pulling her even closer.

She didn't resist.

Who cared that they hadn't worked through their differences? In this sweet slice of *now* all that mattered was his mouth on hers, making her feel better than she'd felt in over a year.

Okay, that was selfish. And misleading. If she kept kissing Kevin, she was essentially telling him that it was okay to storm away in a huff and she'd accept that kind of behavior from him.

But heavens, did his mouth light her up!

Put the brakes on. You can't do this until you've properly ironed out your problems and made up. You couldn't have makeup sex without the makeup part.

She tried to pull away, but Kevin had other plans.

He deepened the kiss, holding her tightly against him, exploring her with his tongue. Helplessly, she sighed into his mouth. Weak. When it came to her masculine Viking, she was so damn weak.

Her fingers swept up his nape and into his hair, threading through the silky strands. As Kevin took her breath away, she felt reborn in a fresh and fascinating way, and for the first time in a very long time, she fully inhabited her body, experiencing every twitch and tingle.

Her body, pulsing and throbbing with Kevin's energy, felt like a strange and curious thing, as if she hadn't known and trusted him for more than half her life.

The foyer just vanished, and, weirdly, it seemed as if they were suspended in the narrow hallway. She closed her eyes, floated on the precious moment, knowing it was swiftly coming to a close.

And yet, Kevin's kiss was endless, wrapping her in a hallowed cocoon of heat and hum as from the backyard, she heard their children playing.

Slowly, she opened her eyes and saw that Kevin was peering at her, an epicurean smile on his face that said he'd tasted the most amazingly delicious dish and she was it.

His blue eyes stirred her in ways they had when she was sixteen and head over heels for him. He took her hands in his and her pulse beat so loudly in her ears she could no longer hear the children's voices.

"How did you know I was here?" she asked.

"You weren't at home. Where else would you be?"

As if she were so predictable, he could set his watch by her. His smile was a bit too smug, and the goodwill he'd earned with the excellent kissing ebbed.

"I could have been off giving Amelia a kidney."

"Robin called me," he confessed. "She told me Amelia refused to accept your kidney and that she went home to Chicago. Thank God for that. I've got newfound respect for her."

Anger spread over Anna like a heat rash. "That's why you came home?"

He nodded as if he'd done a noble thing. "I came to comfort you. You take it hard when people reject your help."

She stepped back, stared at her husband. "I don't want your comfort. If you can't be there for me when I really need you, then I don't need you."

"Anna," he said sharply, a deep frown cleaving his brow. "I'm here *now*."

"Right. Supporting me when the situation suits you. I'll not soon forget that you left me because I wasn't giving in to your anger."

"I didn't leave you." His eyes narrowed and his voice darkened.

"I went back to work. We're on shaky financial ground. I was trying to provide for my family and you're raking me over the coals for that?"

She gaped at him. He truly believed his own bullshit. She was knocked so off guard she couldn't think of a quick comeback.

The sliding glass door slammed closed.

Anna jumped, brought from the mountaintop of her anger back into her mother's foyer. The sound of running feet and then the children were there with them.

"Daddy!" Allie hollered and launched herself into Kevin's arms.

"Daddy!" Logan echoed and grabbed hold of his father's leg.

Anna's gaze met Kevin's.

Robin came around the corner and suddenly five people in the foyer were three too many. "Oh thank heavens, he's come back."

"You set this up." Anna glared at her mother.

Robin shrugged, looked guilty but not penitent.

"Kids," Anna said. "Give your father a big hug and a kiss, and then go wash your hands. Your dad and I will be right back."

"We will?" Kevin looked like someone who'd urgently rushed up to a pharmacy two minutes after closing time and they had let him in.

Without waiting to see if he was going to follow, Anna turned and walked out the front door.

She heard Kevin's footsteps as he trotted after her. She marched down the front steps, and across the green lawn.

"Anna, slow down!"

She stopped and slowly turned to her husband.

Kevin was red-faced and breathless. He wore the crisp white shirt with the Toad's chili stain that she'd wanted to relegate to the rag heap, and he looked vulnerable and utterly endearing. Why did she have to love him so damn much?

"I'm sorry for what I said in the foyer. I can see now that I sounded like a jerk."

"On point, Drury."

"Sometimes I trip over my own ego." He hung his head. "I'm an idiot."

Her heart just rolled right over. *Don't go easy on him. He didn't stand by you when you needed his support.* "What do you want from me, Kevin?"

"I want to work things out. I want to find *us* again. I want to put our family back together."

"I'd like that too," she said, interlacing her fingers and staring down at her hands. "But it's not that simple."

"What can I do to make it simple?"

"I don't know that you can."

A soberness in his eyes pulled his expression down like a window shade. "Anna, I—"

"You were the one who left me."

"My job—"

"You used the job as an excuse. Do me a favor and own that."

"I was hurt," Kevin mumbled, pushing up the sleeves of his shirt higher on his forearms. "It felt like you were choosing Amelia over me and the kids."

"Don't you think I was hurt when you wouldn't stand by me? I never took you for a coward, Viking, but you ran out on me when I needed you most. That's not something I can just brush aside like it never happened."

"You called me Viking." He lowered his voice. "You only call me Viking when you're in a good mood." Hopeful eyebrows hopped up on his forehead. "Does that mean you're forgiving me?"

"Force of habit. Don't read anything into it."

He looked like a kid who had left his favorite toy in the driveway and someone had backed over it, breaking it to smithereens, and he was pathetically trying to glue it back together with Elmer's.

The wind blew Anna's hair from her messy bun into her face. She tucked the loose strands behind her ear. "You disappointed me in a fundamental way. It's going to take time for me to trust you again."

"And I am sorry for that. Truly." Kevin puffed out his cheeks. "I was hurt and jealous of Amelia. There. Is that what you wanted me to admit?"

"It's a start." She folded her arms over her chest.

"If you let me, I'd like to make amends." He was saying all the right things, but it didn't feel sincere.

"I need time."

"How much time?"

"I don't know." She shifted her weight. "I can't rush it."

He looked irritated and bit down on his bottom lip. "I see."

"You *did* teach me something."

"What was that?" he asked, digging his heels into the ground the way he did when he was nervous. Logan had picked up the habit.

"That I need to set stronger boundaries with you, the way you did with me."

His eyes narrowed in surprise and his lips flattened. "Huh?"

"Yes. You stood by your values and beliefs and when I didn't go along with it, you left."

"Wait. What? But you were mad at me for leaving."

"I'm mad at you for expecting us to take right up where we left off just because Amelia refused my kidney and went back to Chicago. I don't blame you for being upset and confused. This identical twin stranger appears in our lives, and I instantly want to make her part of the family. Maybe I was wrong to do that, but I can't help who I am. I love her, Kevin, and I won't apologize for that. You weren't here to really get to know her. It was a difficult situation for everyone and instead of hearing me out, you issued an edict and walked away."

"I—"

"I'm not the same person I was a week ago, Kevin. I didn't know it was possible to change so quickly in such a short amount of time, but I *have* changed, and you've helped me understand how I've been putting everyone else's needs ahead of my own. Especially yours, so thank you for opening my eyes."

Kevin gulped as perspiration popped out on his forehead. "That sounds ominous."

"No," Anna said in the most cheerful voice imaginable. "Not ominous. Redemptive."

"Meaning?"

"If you want to come home—"

"I do!" He pressed his placating palms together. "I do want to come home!"

"Slow down." She held up a palm. "I have a few rules first. Boundaries of my own. We need a start fresh."

"What does that mean?"

"It means that you were right, I was acting like a martyr. I was getting my identity from sacrificing myself to help everyone else. Well, I'm not doing that anymore. I'm going to stop giving away too much of myself too cheaply. I'm going to start honoring *me*. If you're good with that, come on home. If not—" She shrugged. "Read between the lines."

"Okay, okay."

"And one other thing."

He paled and bounced on the balls of his feet. "What?"

"I'm going to Chicago to convince Amelia to take my kidney and if you really mean what you say, you'll come along too."

CHAPTER TWENTY-THREE

Amelia

The Grand Gesture

D id I do the right thing by leaving Moonglow Cove?"
Dr. Ellard tapped his pen against his notebook. He still liked doing things the old-fashioned way, preferring pen and paper to the computer.

Amelia got that. She liked things simple too.

He peered at her over the rim of his reading glasses. He was a handsome, African American man in his late fifties with a full head of gray hair. Distinguished and reserved, he'd been a steady lifeline when she'd had no one else.

She owed him not only her sobriety, but her sanity. He'd pulled her back from the brink more times than she could count, but for the first time, it occurred to her that he did not have all the answers.

Especially when it came to *her* life. She needed to develop her own internal support system. Claim her power. Find her own path.

It was Monday, June 21, two weeks after she'd sneaked away in the middle of the night. Not only that, even though it had killed her to do it, she'd blocked Anna from her phone so she wouldn't have to deal with her pleas to return. Her twin was a force to be reckoned with, and Amelia simply didn't have the emotional strength to resist.

"Do *you* think you did the right thing?" Dr. Ellard asked.

"Was it cowardly of me to slip away in the night the way I did?" Amelia reached for her wrist to fondle the keepsake bracelet that wasn't there. She missed that stupid bracelet so much.

"Do *you* feel it was cowardly?"

"Yes, kind of, but what was even more cowardly was blocking her phone. I'm sure that hurt her." Amelia winced.

"From what you tell me about your sister, it sounds like personal relationships are very important to her, so I suppose she is hurt. How does that make you feel?"

"Like the world's worst sister."

"Could you let yourself off the hook a little?" he asked.

"What do you mean?"

"You haven't had much practice being a sister. In fact, this was your first time dipping your toe into the sibling waters. I'd say you did pretty well under the circumstances."

"Are you giving me an out?"

"Do you need an out?"

"You helped me so much when I first came here," she said, studying the man across from her.

A bemused expression lit his face. "And now? Not so much?"

"I think I might have outgrown you." She shocked herself by saying that.

He closed his notebook, sat up straighter in his chair, the bemused expression widening into a true smile. "I think you might be right."

Amelia felt almost giddy. "I'm healing."

"Psychologically, yes," he said. "But physically? Now that you've turned down Anna's kidney, what next?"

"I'm scheduled to begin dialysis in two weeks. Sooner if my lab values worsen."

"And you're at peace with that?"

Amelia nodded. "I am."

"I don't guess I'll be seeing you next week."

"I don't think so."

"Are you still going to Narcotics Anonymous?"

"Yes. Three meetings a week."

"All right then." He sounded matter-of-fact, but happy for her progress. "Feel free to call me anytime if you should need a tune-up."

"I will." Amelia stood up and extended her hand toward Dr. Ellard.

Smiling, he stood and hugged her instead of shaking her hand and it felt really good. He'd never hugged her before. "Psychiatrists live for days like these."

"The day the patient takes off the training wheels?" She stepped back and smiled up at him.

"The day she realizes she has the tools to handle whatever life throws at her. Good luck, Amelia. It's been my pleasure to help you on your journey and I wish the very best for you."

"If it hadn't been for you, I would've never gone to Moonglow Cove. You gave me the key to open a whole new world, Doctor."

His eyes saddened, but he kept smiling. "Even though things didn't turn out quite the way you planned?"

She smiled back, surprised by the bittersweet moment.

"I have a good feeling that no matter what happens, Amelia, you're going to be just fine."

"Compare that to the shape I was in when you first met me." A rueful laugh.

"You've come a long way, and I'm very proud of the hard work you've done. You should be too."

"I am. Thank you."

He gave her another hug then, quick, but warm. "I'm rooting for you."

She waved and walked from his office with a hopeful heart. She strolled Chicago's Magnificent Mile. The sky seemed bluer and the soft wind ruffled through her hair. She would start dialysis soon and she was on the transplant list, beginning the long wait for a kidney. But despite it all, she felt oddly happy.

She had a twin sister who loved her very much, and that made all the difference. Once life settled, she'd call Anna again, and make things right between them.

Humming "Let It Go," Amelia entered the building that housed her penthouse condo. At the security desk, the guard on duty put up a hand in greeting.

His name was Haskell, but she knew next to nothing about him. He'd been working in her building for four years and every year at Christmas, she gave him a lavish tip and a gift card to Amazon, but it was perfunctory without any real sense of connection to the man.

Thinking of Anna and how she would treat the man, Amelia stood at the desk. "What's your first name, Haskell?"

He looked taken aback, his mouth dipping in surprise. "Marlon."

"Are you married, Marlon?"

"Yes'm, I am. My wife's name is Freda and she's from Germany. Berlin. We've got two little girls. Yolanda, we call her YoYo, because she got so much energy that she bounces up and down like a yo-yo. And Olivia, who insists we don't give her a nickname."

"Tell them hello for me, will you? Freda, and YoYo and Olivia."

"Yes'm." He lifted his cap and grinned wider than she'd ever seen him grin. It seemed to be a day for gathering smiles. "Will do."

She turned toward the elevators.

"Oh, Ms. Brandt," Marlon Haskell called her.

"Yes?"

"There was a lady who came looking for you. She seemed really nervous, like she was brewing trouble."

A chill passed through her as she feared someone from her druggie past had come looking for her. The shadows of addiction would probably follow her for the rest of her life. She couldn't deny it, and she was grateful she lived in a building with strong security.

"What did the woman look like?" She braced herself for the answer. "Was she young? What was her hair color?"

"She was an older lady. Seventyish, and stylish with genteel southern ways. Wore purple and pearls."

Goodness, that sounded like Robin Straus. Her heart sped up. Had her twin's mother actually come looking for her?

"What did you tell her?"

"That you weren't here," Marlon said. "I hope that was all right."

"Did she say anything? Leave a message?"

"She said they would come back in a couple hours."

"They?"

He shrugged. "I didn't ask about that."

"When she does return," Amelia said, feeling wildly giddy, "could you please direct her, or them, whichever the case, up to the penthouse?"

"You got it," he said.

Perplexed, Amelia grabbed the elevator, curious as to why Robin Straus had come to Chicago.

* * *

AN HOUR LATER the doorbell rang.

Heart pounding, Amelia opened the door. She was expecting Robin, so she didn't look through the peephole.

But it wasn't Robin standing there.

Instead, Amelia found herself looking into a pair of chocolate-brown eyes that exactly matched her own.

"Hi," Anna said, sounding breathless.

Happiness rushed over her and Amelia did something she would not have done three weeks ago. She made the first move and embraced her sister.

Then they were both crying.

"You're crying," Anna said. "You don't cry . . . or initiate hugs."

"I missed you," Amelia said, far more than she knew until she was face-to-face with her twin again.

"I missed you, too!"

"Please, come in." Amelia stepped aside, her heart beating in a weird little rhythm, jumping along like a kid on a hopscotch grid, *thump, thump, thump-thump, thump.* It felt both odd and wonderful to have her sister inside her home.

Anna followed her, eyes widening as she glanced around at the art deco architecture and vaulted ceilings. "Wow, this is some crib."

"I inherited it." She waved her hand. "It's not something I earned on my own."

"Doesn't matter," her twin said, her grin a beacon, shining light all over Amelia. "The place is amazing!" She walked to the window overlooking the lake, hands planted at her lower back. "Now this is living."

"Said the woman who lives in a fairy-tale cottage with a magical garden near the beach." In her white kitchen with the industrial sink, she waved Anna to the island barstool and invited, "Have a seat."

Anna sat.

"What would you like to drink? I have coffee, flavored water, tea . . ."

Her sister studied her intently and in a low, concerned voice murmured, "Never mind the drinks. How are *you* doing?"

Amelia didn't want to talk about it. "I'm all right, but I need something to do with my hands. Coffee? Tea?"

"Tea is fine."

"Great."

In the quiet silence following that, Amelia filled a kettle with water and placed it on the stove to heat.

"How is everyone else in Moonglow Cove?" Amelia asked.

"Doing well. Missing you."

"And Winnie?"

"She's been so much happier since you came to town. It's like by finding each other, we gave Winnie closure, even with her fragile memory. Myra says she doesn't try to run away anymore, and she gets a lot of joy out of looking through old picture albums."

"I'm glad she's found some peace."

"Have you . . ." Anna trailed off. Her gaze fixed on Amelia's arms.

Amelia hugged herself. "Started dialysis?"

Anna nodded. She wore a pastel-green summer shift dress, sleeveless with a scoop neck, her hair was freshly styled, and her makeup impeccably applied as if she'd been eager to look her best.

"Not yet. But I go in for the surgery to have the fistula put in next week, but it takes a while for the fistula to develop. They'll dialyze me through a port in my neck until then." It was a day surgery that entailed connecting an artery to a vein in her arm for dialysis access. Although in her case, since her veins weren't in good shape, they might have to use a plastic graft.

"You should be having a transplant instead."

"No." Amelia shook her head. "I'm on the list. I'll wait."

Anna moistened her lips. "I looked it up. Getting a transplant before you go on dialysis is much better for your overall health long term."

"But not yours," Amelia said. "If you came here to try and talk me out of my decision not to take your kidney, you could have saved the airfare."

"I didn't fly," Anna said.

"No?"

"I took a bus."

"Why?" Amelia winced the second she said it. She should be more sensitive. Anna was on a tight budget; of course she didn't have the money to fly up here.

Anna's eyes twinkled. "*I* didn't come here to talk you into it. *They* did."

"They?"

Her sister got up and walked to the window that overlooked Lake Michigan, seemingly mesmerized.

It *was* a killer view.

Amelia studied the back of her sister's head, her straight shoulders, sturdy legs, and generous hips. Anna was a woman of substance. Solid. Dependable. Anna wasn't afraid of the world.

Around her, Amelia often felt like an ethereal puff of smoke.

"I can see why you like living here. It's beautiful. Can I move in?"

"What would Kevin and the kids say?"

"Oh, them." Anna laughed and waved a hand. "I suppose they'd want to tag along."

"Did you and Kevin . . ." Amelia arched speculative eyebrows to punctuate the question. "Work things out?"

"We came to an agreement."

"The fact that you're here tells me you won."

"'Win' might not be the right word, but I'm here, once again, to offer my kidney to you, sister."

"I simply can't accept." Amelia shook her head. "Even if something did cause Kevin to realign his thinking."

Anna laughed at that. "Why not?"

"The cost is too dear. I can't take the chance something might happen to you. You're a mom with two little kids. I can't be responsible for taking a mom away from her kids."

"You're acting as if giving you a kidney is a death sentence. It's incredibly rare for the donor to die. I looked it up. Odds are we'll both be fine and then once this is behind us, we can set about fully learning who we are as sisters. Until then . . ." Anna shrugged. "I don't think we can ever truly connect."

"But we've already connected."

"That's what I thought and then you snuck out of my house in the middle of the night, leaving only a refrigerator note behind like you were a rather considerate one-night stand."

They stared at each other.

"Remember when I told you that the only way you could hurt me was to completely cut me out of your life?"

Cringing, Amelia nodded. Yes, she remembered how Anna had put her vulnerability out there on a platter and Amelia had upended it.

"It broke my heart when you blocked my phone calls."

Shamefaced, Amelia ducked her head. "I had to," she whispered. "I couldn't bear to hear your voice pleading with me to reconsider. Don't you think I want to take your kidney? Don't you think I want to live?"

"Sometimes . . ." Anna shook her head. "No. I don't think you do want to live. I think you're too invested in the poor-little-rich-girl story. I think you like punishing yourself. I think you don't value who you are."

All the air left Amelia's body in a short hard puff, the way it does when you blow out birthday candles.

Guilty on all charges and deeply mortified that despite how hard she'd tried to hide her feelings and compartmentalize, Anna has seen right through her.

The kettle sang and Amelia turned off the gas burner. It gave her space for a deep breath to settle the anxiety building inside of her. She was feeling a little ambushed at the moment.

"You're denying me the chance to give you a healthy life, and I don't understand why."

No, Anna wouldn't. She'd grown up with a mother who loved her unconditionally and Amelia was so, so glad for that, so happy that her twin had escaped her upbringing.

"I want to do this for you. Not because I'm some great altruistic martyr. Selfishly, I want my sister around. I want to watch our kids play together. I want to grow old with you."

Amelia stared at the steam rising up from the teakettle. "Anna, I—"

"How do you think that makes me feel when you rejected me?" Anna said. "Have you given any thought to that?"

Yes, every sleepless night since she'd been back in Chicago. "I upended your life. I had no right to do that. You have a family—"

"So do you."

"Be honest—and this is not just me feeling sorry for myself—no one really wants me in Moonglow Cove except you."

She'd made up her mind to tell Anna to please go back home. They couldn't go on pretending that thirty-five years raised apart was not an insurmountable hurdle to building a solid sisterhood. There was simply too much baggage to ever unpack it all.

"No one?" Both Anna's voice and eyebrows went up. She stepped closer to the window and signaled someone down below with a wave.

Amelia cocked her head. Who was down there? Robin?

Then Anna crooked a finger at her. "Come look."

Cautiously, Amelia ambled to the window.

A yellow Moonglow Cove school bus sat parked at the curb—in a no-parking zone. Marlon was bound to come out and tell them to move at any moment. As she stood at the window beside her sister, another yellow bus drove up behind the first.

And then another.

"Wh-what's going on?" Amelia put a hand to her throat as a fourth bus pulled up. Moonglow Cove Independent School District was taking up half the block.

She still couldn't figure out what it meant, even as people started pouring out of the parked buses. Feeling anxious because they were in a no-parking zone, Amelia fretted, but Anna seemed not only content that they were breaking the rules, but excited about it.

They were carrying signs like protesters, but unlike protesters they were smiling. Dozens of colored poster boards, decorated with Sharpies, stickers, and glitter, spelled out their message.

Slowly, Amelia understood what was happening and her heart filled with a wondrous kind of dread.

Moonglow Covians descended on downtown Chicago, each carrying his or her own poster board sign. People kept piling out of the buses and, in an orderly fashion, walked across the street with their signs to line up on the opposite sidewalk, giving Amelia a better view. She started counting them, but lost count at two hundred.

Her heartbeat quickened.

From the last bus came the Moonglow Cove High School marching band, playing a tune that sent shivers down Amelia's spine.

"Let It Go."

She hugged herself hard against the goose bumps and tears. *Don't cry, don't cry, don't cry.*

She spied Robin holding hands with Logan and Allie, juggling posters underneath her arm, as they walked. The sidewalk across the street quickly filled, passersby stopping to watch as posters rose into the air.

We Love You Amelia!
Choose Life!!
Accept Anna's Gift!!!
Say Yes 2 Transplant!!!!
Come Back Home to Moonglow Cove!!!!!

And below the posters were the faces of the Moonglow Cove townspeople, transported by school buses to the Windy City.

She saw Roberta from the funnel cake kiosk on Paradise Pier, and Oscar, the Juggernaut operator. There was Darla, Anna's employee from the bakery, and Shelley and Sebastian from the Moonglow Inn. Pete and Veronica Drury were there as well. Mike and Gia, too, holding Faith, who was waving up a storm. The Harmonious Housewives joined in with the marching band, and there was Myra Marts playing the piccolo.

The swell of the music grew . . . "Let It Go."

All these people from Moonglow Cove had gotten on a school bus and driven up here to convince her to accept Anna's gift?

It was so illogical, so surreal, so unbelievable that so many people would do that for her, that she started looking for the catch. Was this a dream?

When she'd been on heroin, she'd had some wicked real dreams. Maybe she was having a flashback?

Kevin was the last person to get off the bus. He didn't carry a sign, but he was there and took pictures of the crowd. Then he turned and gave a thumbs-up to Amelia's penthouse window.

"They want you," Anna said.

"They want *you*," Amelia corrected.

"We all want you."

Amelia's body shook as she fought back the tears. For her entire life, the only thing she'd ever wanted was to be loved and accepted for who she was, flaws and all. She'd never had that kind of unconditional love from her parents.

But she had it now . . . because of Anna.

Amelia peered into her sister's eyes. "Seriously, it's you they want."

"Don't you get it? You're part of me and I'm part of you." Anna patted her lower back at her kidney.

"How did you get them all to show up?"

"I do things for people all the time, and they do things for me."

"This is beyond a favor, Anna. How did you afford it?" Amelia knew Anna's finances were on shaky ground.

"GoFundMe."

"How?" Amelia still couldn't wrap her head around how her twin had coaxed over two hundred people to drive more than a thousand miles in school buses just to show their support.

Anna stared out the window and let out a wistful sigh. "This has been my life's work, Amelia. Cultivating relationships. For better or worse, it's what I do."

"You're using your skills against me." Amelia smiled through the mist blurring her vision. "Bringing me into your fold."

"No, Amelia." Her voice was clear and strong. "I'm using it *for* you."

"But why?"

"Because I *love* you and I want you to be in my life more than anything else in the world. Plus, I was terrified if I just showed up here by myself, I still couldn't convince you to accept my gift. So . . ." She waved a hand at the people below. "I improvised."

"You're not giving me an out, are you?"

Anna shook her head. "Nope."

"I still don't understand why you went to all this trouble for me."

"Because," she said. "You needed to see for yourself exactly how much you are loved simply for being you. Not for your musical talents, not for your money, not for any material thing you can own or gain. I see you and I love you just as you are."

And that's when Amelia fully experienced the incredible power of having been born a twin. It was a knowledge that rattled the crumbling foundations of her deep-seated loneliness.

When you had a twin, you were never really alone.

CHAPTER TWENTY-FOUR

Anna

The Reversal

L aw enforcement arrived to shoo the buses from the no-parking zone. Anna got a text from Darla, who'd ramrod-ded the bus trip, assuring her that she'd round up everyone and get them back to Moonglow Cove safely.

But not everyone left.

Robin, Kevin, Mike, Gia, and the children all stayed behind. Anna had planned on having her family stay in a hotel, figuring she'd put it on her credit card and sort her finances out later, but Amelia insisted they all stay at the penthouse.

Since the five-thousand-square-foot penthouse had five bed-rooms, that arrangement worked out just fine.

And just as she'd prayed it would, Anna's grand gesture con-vinced her sister to agree to the transplant. Pete and Veronica had offered to keep Logan and Allie during the surgery and while Anna recovered, but she wanted her children nearby so that when she woke up, she would see their sweet little faces.

Nothing could heal a mother faster than that.

In the meantime, the kids would stay at Amelia's penthouse

with Robin. While Anna and Amelia spent the next week visiting doctors, getting tests done, and preparing for the surgery, Kevin, Robin, Mike, and Gia took the children sightseeing.

In the end, the surgery was scheduled for Monday, July 5. That gave them the weekend together before things changed forever. They'd planned to go to the city's Fourth of July celebration on Sunday, but after an overwhelming week, Amelia simply didn't have the strength to attend.

Anna sent her family on to enjoy the holiday, while she stayed behind with Amelia. Darkness found them sitting around Amelia's rooftop pool sharing mocktails as the night sky lit up with fireworks.

"No food or drink after midnight," Anna said, reading from the preoperative list the transplant surgeon's office gave them.

Amelia raised her virgin cosmopolitan. "We have three hours. Cheers!"

"We should be in bed long before that," Anna said.

Amelia nodded. A string of fireworks whistled and popped, showering the sky with an umbrella of bright, streaking lights.

They sat in silence for a bit, which Anna considered a good sign. They were comfortable together not talking.

"Thank you," she said.

"For what?" Amelia sounded puzzled.

"Accepting my gift. It means the world to me. *You* mean the world to me."

"I feel the same way about you." Amelia smiled. Her teeth shiny white in the darkness.

More fireworks burst and there was another long silence, but this one wasn't quite so comfortable.

"Are you scared?" Anna murmured.

"Terrified. You?"

"Petrified."

Amelia reached over the gap between their lounge chairs and took her hand.

Surprised, but happy, Anna grinned and interlaced their fingers. "It's going to be okay."

"Is it?" Amelia's voice was light, but underneath, Anna heard a ripple of worry.

"Don't do that," Anna whispered.

"Do what?"

"Be a realist." Anna inhaled quickly. "I'm hanging by a thread here. I could use some optimism, even if it's the fake-it-till-you-make-it type."

"In the end, it'll be fine."

Anna almost laughed. Amelia was doing her best to be positive and she appreciated her for it. Anna was the perky high school cheerleader who'd married the running back. She couldn't expect her sister to be something she wasn't.

"This will bond us in an irrevocable way." Amelia's face softened as she looked at her.

"Why do you think giving this kidney to you means so much to me?"

"I think I need a hug," Amelia said.

Music to Anna's ears. She hopped up too quickly for the hug, tangling her feet in her sister's chaise. She fell onto Amelia's lap and the chaise, knocked off balance, tipped over on its side by the edge of the pool.

"Eeek!" Amelia exclaimed and grabbed for Anna before she rolled off into the water.

They ended upside down on their backs with the chaise on top of them, their necks dangling off the concrete lip of the pool, Anna's long red hair dragging in the water.

"Good thing those were mocktails." Anna giggled.

"Are you okay?" Amelia asked.

Anna sat up, her long hair soaking down her back. "Now I know why you have short hair."

"Until three days before I came to see you, my hair was as long as yours." Amelia pushed the aluminum chaise away, rolled over onto one side, and slowly pushed herself up.

Anna couldn't help noticing how much weaker her twin had become since she'd been in Chicago, but she said nothing. The surgery was in a few hours. By this time tomorrow, it'd be over and done and they'd be golden.

"Then," Amelia went on, "I got the 23andMe report and was so freaked out that my sister wasn't dead, I went looking for scissors and instead found the gardener's pinking shears and I just started whacking off locks."

"Why?" Anna whispered, fingers to her mouth, imagining that scene. *Wait, she hired a gardener to tend the plants in the rooftop garden? Nice.*

"I don't know." The wind gusted and Amelia shifted.

More fireworks burst in the sky—*pop, pop, pop.*

Anna waited.

"I guess . . ." Amelia paused. "I was punishing myself."

That seemed like a really raw spot, so Anna steered the conversation back to lighter shores. "Hey, remember that time in the womb when you kicked me, and I punched you?"

"Wow . . . what? You remember when we were in the womb?" Amelia wrinkled her brow in confusion.

"Joke. Since we don't have any shared childhood memories, I figured I'd make up some."

"Even though I can't remember our life in the womb, there was a part of me that always was aware of you," Amelia said. "As if you were some great dream I once dreamed."

"I felt that too!"

Amelia's voice lowered, a balancing tonic to Anna's excitement. "There's something we need to discuss. Shall we go back inside?"

Amelia took a deep breath and motioned for Anna to follow her into the condo. Curious, she followed.

Amelia found her tote bag and brought it into the living area.

Anna sat down on the couch, watching her sister with a sidelong gaze.

From her bag, Amelia took out the neat separate compartments and stacked them up on the couch cushions around her until she found what she was looking for. Flat. Blue——the color of a bluebird egg. Legal size. It was an envelope made of silicone like the muffin molds in Anna's bakery.

"While we've been visiting doctors and hospitals, I put my lawyers on this," Amelia said.

Lawyers? As in more than one.

Yikes. Anna was out of her league. Seeing her twin's lavish lifestyle up close and personal was a tiny bit overwhelming. Amelia had a housekeeper, a gardener, and someone who came in twice a week to tend the huge-ass aquarium built into the wall. She had to be filthy rich to maintain all this, especially after not working and battling a heroin addiction. Anna couldn't even wrap her mind around what it must be like to have so much money.

Logan had fallen in love with the aquarium and wanted to know the names of all the fish. When Amelia told him they had no names, he begged to name them. Amelia said, "Sure," and for the past three days Logan would wake up, run to the aquarium, and say, "Good morning, Blue One. Good morning, Red One. Good morning, Yellow One."

Okay, so Logan wasn't particularly creative at naming fish, but Anna found it so adorable, she'd recorded him that morning. She planned on turning it into a ringtone.

Amelia handed her the silicone envelope.

Anna eyed it warily, and an uneasy feeling wriggled around inside of her. She did not take it. In fact, she put her arms behind her back. "What's in it?"

"My will."

"You made out a will?" Anxiety did a tap dance up her neck bones. Damn, why hadn't *she* made out a will?

"You didn't?" Amelia seemed genuinely puzzled.

Hey, sis, not everyone has on-demand lawyers. "I guess I was just optimistic. I have Kevin . . ." As if being married explained everything.

"Oh."

How freaking lame, Anna. How arrogantly self-confident. She just assumed that everything would be okay. Hadn't let herself consider that dying might be a real possibility. One big downside to seeing the world through rose-tinted glasses.

"Don't mind me. You do you. I'm just overly cautious and being prepared quells my anxiety."

"I should write something out. In case I don't make it." Anna crinkled her nose, full-on worrying now. She tried to think about how to divide things up in case of her death and she freaked. The thought of leaving Kevin and the children alone hit her hard. And Winnie, who would look after Winnie if something happened to Anna?

"You're not going to die," Amelia said.

"Neither are you."

Amelia slipped the envelope into Anna's purse that was sitting on the fireplace hearth.

"I don't want to see it. We don't need it. We're going to be fine." But a small voice in the back of Anna's head whimpered, *What if you aren't?*

* * *

IN THE PRE-OP holding area of a premier private hospital in Chicago, Anna and Amelia lay side by side on gurneys each with their own medical team preparing to take them to separate operating rooms. They'd said good-bye to their family, who settled anxiously in the surgical waiting room. They were hooked up to monitors and given IVs.

The time had come.

On either side of them stood two nurses.

Amelia's nurse was a petite, no-nonsense woman who looked and sounded a bit like the actress Rosie Perez. She wore trendy eyeglasses and had perfectly groomed brows and a name badge that said *Felicity Roman*. Anna had drawn the tall, willowy white dude who looked barely old enough to qualify for his job. Both nurses held syringes in their hand, waiting for the last good-byes to medicate their patients.

"Y'all ready for this?" asked the male nurse who'd spent time chatting with Anna and was teasing her about her Texas accent.

"Let's do this thing!" Anna sang out, then recognized she sounded far too cheerful for the occasion. Oh well, wouldn't be the first time.

Nor the last.

How was that for positive thinking? She was coming out of this surgery like a boss, ready to heal and bond with her sister in a whole new way.

"We're in this together," Amelia said.

"Did I really sign up for this?" Anna giggled.

"Getting cold feet, sis? You can still back out."

"Nope." Anna stuck her feet out from under the covers, raised her left leg into the air, and showed off the toe socks that matched

Amelia's. Robin had gifted them with the socks the night before. "Toasty warm."

"I want you to know one thing." Amelia rolled over onto her side so she could see Anna better.

"What's that?" Anna moved on her side as well, so they were staring each other in the eyes. Anna's heart tugged with so much joy she could hardly think. Such fiercely abiding love she felt for her twin sister!

Amelia's gaze locked on hers. "I promise to take good care of your kidney. I won't do anything to harm it."

"I know."

The air smelled of antiseptic and an underlying burnt odor. Somewhere beyond the double doors they heard muted voices as the staff prepared for their arrival. This was scary stuff, but Anna didn't think about that. She pictured Kevin and her kids and her mother and all her friends in Moonglow Cove and she just knew everything was absolutely going to turn out just fine.

How could it not? She had so much to live for.

"I need to ask you something very important," Anna said.

"Anything."

"If something happens to me . . ."

"Nothing is going to happen to you."

Yes, yes, Anna was sure of that too. "Just in case I don't wake up from this, I need you to promise me something."

"Absolutely." Amelia nodded. "Say the word."

"If anything happens to me"—Anna lifted a finger—"and don't roll your eyes, please help Kevin look after Allie and Logan."

"I'll say yes because I know that's what you need from me, but nothing is going to happen to you, Anna. We've got decades ahead of us as sisters."

It sounded nice, and Anna was all for nice, so she didn't contradict her twin. Emotionally, well, she was feeling a little panicky, but the only way to deal with that was to get through this thing.

"Thank you." She smiled at Amelia and Amelia smiled back, and Anna felt brave again and ready to go.

"Any last words before we send you off to dreamland?" Nurse Felicity asked.

"Yes," they said in unison. "Take care of my sister!"

Looking at each other, they laughed.

"We're on it," Nurse Felicity promised. "Now onto your backs."

"Next thing you know," the male nurse said, "you'll be waking up in post-anesthesia recovery hollering for pain meds."

"You do know I have a substance abuse issue," Amelia said. "It's what landed me here in the first place."

"No worries. We've got a solid treatment plan to help you control your pain with minimal risk of a relapse. Your doctors are on the ball."

"You're gonna come out of this on the other side," Anna said. "And your life is going to be better than ever."

"*Our* lives."

Anna laughed. "I'm glad you're finally seeing things my way, sister."

"This is it, ladies, say good night." Amelia's nurse slipped the syringe into the IV tubing.

The male nurse did the same with Anna's IV.

Anna reached out her left hand through the bed rails. "Put 'er there, sister."

"Let's do this thing, twin." Amelia clasped her sister's hand with her right.

United.

Together.

Their hands joined in solidarity.

It was the last sure thing Anna remembered.

CHAPTER TWENTY-FIVE

Amelia

All Is Lost

Four and a half hours later, Amelia regained consciousness.

She was slowly aware of the nurses moving around her, the moaning of the other patients, the acrid, hot-metal smell of the surgical suite clinging to the sheets, the sharp pains in her body.

But only one thought stood out in the lingering fog of anesthesia.

How was Anna?

She tried to speak, but her tongue wouldn't work. Although maybe it wasn't her mouth that wouldn't work. Maybe it was her brain. She reached up her hand, or thought she did, but her fingers seemed welded to the sheets. Again, she tried to speak, but all that came out was a grunting sound.

A nurse came over to her. "Oh dear, your pulse is too fast. Hang on, I'll get you something for pain."

Amelia tried to tell her no, she didn't want oblivion, but it came out like "nnnnn."

The nurse came back, rustled around somewhere at the side of her bed, and then Amelia was out again.

When she roused a second time, the room was quieter, the pace less frantic. She wondered how much time had passed.

Was Anna out of surgery?

This nurse was different. Or maybe she was remembering incorrectly. Everything had been so fuzzy before and every nerve ending in her back and side throbbed with pain.

She heard someone say, "Will you look at that urine in her catheter bag! It's the Little Kidney That Could. That's the second time I've emptied the bag this shift."

Amelia opened her eyes and blinked. The lights were dimmed. And she realized she was in a different room. "Wh—"

"Hello, Amelia," the nurse said in a cheerful voice. "You're in the ICU. I'm Cheryl. I'll be taking care of you this evening."

Evening? The surgery had been at seven that morning.

"Where—" Her lips were so dry, her throat abraded. It was all she could do to wrap her tongue around the words. "Is . . . my sister."

"Don't you worry about that right now. You just concentrate on getting better. Would you like some ice chips?"

Vigorously, Amelia shook her head. "Anna."

The nurse looked across the room, and Amelia realized someone was sitting in a chair next to her bed. Cheryl darted her gaze back at Amelia. "I'm afraid your sister hasn't woken up yet, but she's out of surgery."

Amelia tried to turn her head to see who was sitting there.

A chair creaked. Someone moved and then Amelia found herself gazing into her brother-in-law's face.

"Hey," Kevin said gruffly. "How you feeling?"

"Anna?"

"I'll leave you two alone." Nurse Cheryl slid out of the room.

Kevin looked serious. "Anna's been a little slow to wake up."

"Where is she?"

"She's in a different ICU."

"Why?"

The nurse bustled in with ice chips. "Here we are."

"Why?" Amelia repeated never taking her gaze off Kevin's.

"She's in the neurological intensive care unit."

"Why? What happened?"

"They can't say for sure—" His voice cracked.

Fear, deeper than anything Amelia had ever experienced in her life, grabbed hold of her. No, it couldn't be true.

But the grim look on Kevin's face said it was absolutely true. There was no denying it. Because her sister had given her a kidney she was in a coma.

"And?"

"If she dies . . ." His face flushed with fury. "I'm holding you responsible."

* * *

FIVE DAYS LATER, after they discharged Amelia from the transplant ward, Anna was still in a coma.

Kevin came to Amelia's room when she was about to leave.

Mike and Gia had taken the kids back home with them to Moon-glow Cove, leaving just Robin and Kevin in Chicago. Robin hadn't come to see her at all. She was holding vigil at Anna's bedside, according to the nurses.

This was the first time Kevin had spoken to her since he told her he held her responsible for Anna's condition.

She couldn't blame him for that. She held herself responsible and she deserved every ounce of his disdain.

"I've come to take you home," he announced. "Because it's what Anna would've wanted."

Her brother-in-law couldn't even look at her. That was fair. She couldn't look at herself. Whenever she peered into a mirror, all she saw was Anna.

"Kevin, I—"

"Please, I don't want to talk to you."

She nodded. Misery, guilt, and depression dogged her like a hungry stray. Part of her wanted to say, *I didn't want her to do this, she's the one who got a bus tour to convince me*, but that was victim blaming and it was the sort of thing Sarah Brandt would have said.

Shame burned her ears and misery carved a hole in her heart. None of this was Anna's fault.

In her head, she heard Dr. Ellard. *It's not your fault either.*

But it *was* her fault. She was the one who'd chosen to use drugs. She was the one who'd damaged her kidneys and now her beautiful, loving, kind twin sister—the good twin—was paying the price for Amelia's sins.

Now she was alone with Kevin, absorbing the brunt of his

anger. What minuscule punishment. She would accept his rage. Shoulder it. Welcome any animosity he brought her way.

Because she deserved it.

All of it.

"I'm not going home," she said.

Kevin stared stone-faced. His arms folded over his chest. Legs anchored wide apart. Impenetrable. He said nothing.

"I'm staying here until she wakes up."

Kevin grunted. "Suit yourself."

The nurse, who was waiting in the wings with a wheelchair, clicked her tongue. "You shouldn't stay at the hospital. You should go home and get some rest. We've already got your home health care scheduled."

"You can cancel it, right?"

"We could, but should we? You'd be more comfortable at home." What the nurse didn't understand was that Amelia's home was here, in that ICU bed, fighting for her life.

"I'm not supposed to be comfortable!" Amelia barked, relishing the pain.

"I'll cancel the home health then," the nurse said.

Anguish washed over Amelia, and she closed her eyes, fully aware that Kevin was glowering at her. If anything happened to Anna . . .

A memory swept over her. The sweet blissful oblivion of heroin and in that moment, she longed for its embrace, but she would not allow temptation to take her down. If she ever let that ugly idea take seed in her brain, Anna's gift would be for nothing.

She'd promised to take care of the kidney and she'd promised Anna that if anything happened to her . . .

Not even finishing that thought.

She would survive this, and she would do good things to honor her sister. That was what she would spend the rest of her days doing, finding ways to honor her sister who gave so much to everyone.

Opening her eyes, Amelia saw that Kevin was gone and the nurse was staring at her pensively.

"Look at it this way," she told the nurse. "If anything happens to me, I'm in the best place to get help."

"Yes," the nurse grumbled. "But I'll be the one scooping you up off the floor."

"I can't leave Anna," she said.

Nurse Cheryl sighed. "Fine. I'll wheel you to the waiting room with your brother-in-law."

"No." Amelia touched the nurse's arm and tried not to show her pain. "Please, I need to see Anna first."

* * *

ROBIN WAS SITTING at Anna's bedside, holding her daughter's hand, when Nurse Cheryl wheeled Amelia into the small darkened room.

Amelia's gaze strayed to her sister, and her heart reeled in her chest. Anna was completely still, covered by a light white sheet and one of Robin's homemade quilts. Tubes and drains snaked from her body. Machines beeped and flashed and whooshed in a mesmerizing rhythm. Her twin was on a ventilator, unable to breathe on her own.

Terror struck her. Knocked her down like a jaw punch. Her body trembled, and her breath came in short, quick pants.

Across the bed, she made eye contact with Robin. Amelia's heart pounded so hard and fast that her palms grew sweaty.

Nurse Cheryl vanished.

Down one ally, Amelia gulped. "H-how is she?"

Robin studied her for so long that Amelia figured she wasn't going to answer. Her face was inscrutable.

Her pulse gathered speed, shifting from a canter into a full-blown gallop. Robin had every right to hate her.

Absolutely.

Robin's stare held Amelia pinned to her wheelchair. Was Robin about to tell her that she was pond scum and didn't deserve to be loved by such a wonderful person as Anna?

"How are you?" Robin's tone was kind.

"Healing. The kidney is working great."

"I'm glad."

Amelia didn't know how to respond, so she didn't say anything.

"She's happy that you're here." Robin took a deep breath and let it out slowly, added in a tone several notes higher than before, "And so am I."

Excuse me? Amelia blinked, confused. Anna was unconscious. How could she be happy?

"Please." Robin nodded to the opposite side of Anna's bed. "Take her hand."

Amelia scooted her wheelchair closer, careful not to hit the IV stand with the big wheel.

Robin watched her.

Feeling as if she was taking some kind of test, Amelia reached for Anna's right hand, discovered there was a rolled-up washcloth stuck in between her closed fingers. She glanced over at Robin.

"That's to keep her from getting contractures while she's in the coma."

Amelia wasn't sure what that meant.

"Take the washcloth out," Robin instructed. "And hold her hand."

Okay . . . Amelia slipped the washcloth from her twin's hand and substituted her own hand in its place.

"Touch her fingertips with yours." Robin nodded, encouraging her with a smile.

Amelia slid her palm down a little so that her fingertips overlaid Anna's and instantly felt her sister's pulse hot and fast jumping from Anna's fingertips into hers. Amelia's own pulse throbbed with the power of the exchange.

Startled, she jerked her hand back, and peered over at Robin.

"She's in there. She knows we're here. You can tell by the pulse in her fingertips. She's strong and she's going to pull through. Don't doubt it. I don't."

The vigor of Anna's life-force pulsing so vibrantly through her hand seemed to suggest as much, but part of Amelia wondered if Robin was simply deluding herself. She wanted Anna to be okay, so she took the pounding pulse as a good sign.

Amelia put her fingertips to Anna's again, and *boom*, *boom*, *boom*, the startling energetic stamina. It was as if every ounce of Anna's life-force was in her fingertips. It felt both eerie and hopeful.

"When I first sat down and took her hand right after the surgery, her pulse in her fingertips was so weak I could barely feel it," Robin said. "But as I sat and talked, her pulse grew stronger and stronger. Then Kevin insisted I go back to your condo and get some rest, but when I came back the next day, her pulse was weak again, and I knew I couldn't leave her all alone. They got me a cot." She nodded to the metal cot folded and pushed against the far wall. "That's why I didn't come to see you. I was scared to leave her. It seems the longer I sit with her, the stronger she gets."

Amelia tried to imagine her mother sitting at her bedside and simply couldn't picture it. Sarah Brandt would have hired a sitter and gone on about her business.

"You're an amazing mother," Amelia said, alarmed to hear unshed tears in her voice.

"Anna is an amazing daughter. I'm so blessed."

Amelia clung to Anna's hand, absorbing her pulsing heat, overwhelmed with emotions.

After a long moment, Robin said, "I've been blaming Winnie for switching babies. I've been so angry with her, but as I've sat here with Anna, I realized something important."

"What's that?"

"If Winnie hadn't done what she did, I wouldn't have had the honor of being Anna's mother for thirty-five amazing years. I would have been left with empty arms and a broken heart. I'm not condoning what Winnie did, but I'm so grateful for it."

Amelia hauled in a deep breath, felt tremors run through her body.

"I also realized something else."

Moistening her lips, Amelia whispered, "What's that?"

"It could have just as easily been you."

"What could have been me?"

Robin patted Anna's arm. "You could have been the one who got switched. It was the luck of the draw."

Amelia blew out a long, audible breath through her mouth.

"*You* could have been my daughter," Robin whispered. "I remind myself of that whenever negative thoughts creep in. I don't hold you responsible." Tears glistened in her eyes. "Not for any of it."

A tear slipped down Amelia's face. *Oh no!* She didn't cry. She wasn't a crier. Robin needed her to be strong, not to break down like some blubber baby.

Another tear followed the first. Then another. And another. She grabbed for a tissue from the box on the bedside table, sopped her face.

Stop it. Stop crying now. The voice in her head was Sarah Brandt's impatient and disgusted.

"It's okay to cry," Robin murmured. "It's okay to feel. It's normal. Don't be ashamed."

Robin read her like a book.

"I . . . she—"

"No. Don't blame yourself. I won't put up with it. You are my daughter's twin and I love you."

I love you.

The words that had always been so hard for Amelia to hear and believe. So hard for her to say in return.

"I hope one day you'll come to love me, too." Robin's smile was gentle. "You know, it's not too late for me to be your surrogate mom."

Robin got up, came over, crouched in front of the wheelchair, and pulled Amelia, who was still sobbing, into her arms and held her for a long, long time.

CHAPTER TWENTY-SIX

Amelia

The Gauntlet

For three days, Amelia, Kevin, and Robin kept around-the-clock vigils. They took eight-hour shifts, one of them sitting at Anna's bedside at all times. Amelia generally stayed at night, sending Kevin and Robin to her condo to get some sleep. She was a night owl, after all, the musician who'd stayed up into the wee morning hours.

It was draining, but she'd been through much worse. Sheer will kept her going. She *would* be there when Anna woke up. To that end, when Amelia wasn't at the hospital, she got plenty of sleep, did mild exercise, and ate a well-balanced meal. It helped her heal quickly, even as the vigil went on.

The nurses babied Amelia. They checked on her, set up her cot, brought her cups of coffee and water, reminded her to take her medicine, and scolded her if she overdid it. Things weren't much different from actually being in the hospital herself.

She'd taken to reading aloud to her twin and when she measured the pulse in Anna's fingertips after a story, it was always just a little stronger than before she started. Anna's pulse jumped particularly lively when Amelia read a romance or thriller, so she devoted herself to those genres.

Oh, how she wished for the sound of Anna's voice, the sight of her bright smile, the warmth of her hug.

"Wake up, sister," she would whisper sometimes, over-whelmed with that bone-deep yearning. She'd monitor the fin-gertip pulses and watch Anna's eyes in case they fluttered, but if her twin responded, it was so subtle Amelia couldn't detect it.

Robin would arrive early, a true meadowlark, and send Amelia home to sleep. Kevin made sure to be gone by the time Amelia got to the condo. Without ever speaking a word about it, they successfully managed to avoid being alone with each other a ma-jority of the time and they hadn't once discussed Anna being in a coma because of Amelia.

But she could feel the resentment churning in him.

Not that she blamed him. She couldn't forgive herself.

* * *

ON THE THIRD evening, when Amelia came in to relieve Kevin, she saw him in the waiting room before she got to the ICU.

Her heart leaped at the sight of him. Why wasn't he in Anna's room? Had something happened to her?

She raced over to where he sat playing on his phone. "What is it?" she gasped. "What's wrong with Anna?"

He looked up at her as if she'd lost her mind. "Anna's fine. They're bathing her."

"What?" It took a minute for his answer to register. She'd slept too long and felt groggy. "Oh."

"Have a seat." He nodded at the spot beside him and went back to his cell-phone game.

Caught off guard by his invitation, she slipped her tote bag off her shoulder, and gingerly eased down. Her surgical scars were healing nicely, but she was still a little stiff and achy.

They sat in silence, but it wasn't as awkward as it might have been. His engrossment in the game helped.

Amelia drew in her energy, the way she'd done as a kid, imaging herself growing smaller and smaller until she disappeared.

Without raising his head from his phone, Kevin mumbled, "It hurts to look at you."

She was about to apologize but noticed his gaze was fixed and he wasn't really studying the phone.

Across the waiting room, a man kept staring at her. He was thirtyish, reedy and balding. His clothes were rumpled. He wore a black Metallica T-shirt and shabby sneakers. There were stacks of empty coffee cups on the table around him and a party-size bag of Flamin' Hot Cheetos.

She shifted her gaze from the unsettling man back to her brother-in-law.

"I'm crazy about her, you know," Kevin whispered. "She's the love of my life."

Amelia kept perfectly still, hoping he'd continue talking if she didn't say anything. She was still trying to process her feelings about Anna not waking up from a coma. A dark jumble of feelings. So many feelings that she needed an industrial sieve to strain through them all.

"From the first time I saw her our freshman year of high school, I knew that one day I was going to marry her."

That was so sweet. Amelia put a palm to her heart.

"I've never loved anyone else." He paused and sent her a sideways glance. "I've never *been* with anyone else."

High school sweethearts. Each other's first and last. This was the kind of marriage they wrote love poems about.

"I know that makes me something of a freak in this day and age—to be married to the woman I lost my virginity to." Kevin raised his chin. "But I'm damn proud of it and damn proud of her."

"I have no idea what it feels like to be loved like that." The wistful words were out of her mouth before she even realized it.

"The hell you don't!" Kevin said so loudly that several people in the waiting area turned to stare.

Lowering his voice, he went on, "Anna loves you like that. I can't even begin to understand how that works, but she loved you from the moment you walked in our door."

"She has a huge heart."

He glowered. "I know you didn't feel the same way about Anna."

"You're right," she admitted. "I didn't. Not initially. No one taught me how to love unconditionally. Until Anna, I had no idea such a thing was possible."

She could feel the heat of Kevin's icy stare. Finally, Amelia was able to look him squarely in the eyes. Pain and sorrow were etched into his handsome face.

Empathy washed over her. It was an emotion she fought hard to compartmentalize because it had the power to throw her into such a mental tailspin, she wasn't sure she could recover.

Across the waiting room, the balding man who'd been staring at her looked from his phone to Amelia and back again.

Several times.

What was that about? Feeling self-conscious, Amelia ran a hand through her hair and ducked her head.

Kevin reached down and for the first time, she saw his briefcase on a side table. He opened it up and took out the blue silicone envelope with Amelia's will in it and tapped the corner restlessly against his knee.

Her chest tightened. He had the will. Was that responsible for his thawing?

"I finally read this. Anna couldn't read it. She was afraid it would jinx you in surgery. That if she read the will, you wouldn't make it." He gave a humorless chuckle. "My wife can be a little superstitious, but it looks like she had good reason."

Amelia pressed her knees together. Her back throbbed. The ibuprofen was wearing off, but she could handle physical pain. She stayed quiet, waiting for him to continue.

He moistened his lips with the tip of his tongue, kept tapping the envelope. "You're leaving all your assets to my children?"

Silently, Amelia nodded.

"I don't know what to say." Kevin sounded truly humbled.

One side of his mouth twitched as if he wanted to smile but couldn't summon the effort.

"Anna and Allie and Logan are my only family." She turned her head to meet Kevin's gaze again. "*You're* my only family."

His eyes glistened. He sniffled, blinked. "This sucks so damn much."

"That you're my family?" Now it was her turn for a humorless laugh.

"No." His voice shook. "That we're on the verge of losing Anna just when you two found each other."

"It does indeed suck."

"You're one helluva warrior, Brandt." Respect for her shimmered in his eyes and it meant the world to Amelia and gave her hope.

"You're one helluva warrior, too, Drury."

"Why do you think Anna calls me Viking?" His face softened.

"I thought it was because of the tall, blond, broad-shouldered thing."

"Well, there is that."

A nurse appeared in the doorway of the waiting room. She made eye contact with Kevin and crooked a finger for him to follow her.

"Looks like they're finished with her bath." He stood.

"I'll go sit with her. Take Robin out for a good meal. You both deserve some self-care."

"I want to tell Anna good-bye first." Kevin returned the blue envelope to his briefcase and snapped it closed. "No, no," he amended quickly. "Not good-bye. Good night. I want to tell her good night."

"Yes, tell her good night." Amelia moved to stand but dizziness swirled her head, and she had to grab hold of Kevin's arm to keep from falling over.

"Whoa there." He put a hand to her shoulder. It was the first time he'd ever touched her. The concern on his face was genuine. "Are you okay?"

"Fine. Just got up too soon and lost my balance."

He dropped his arm, rubbed the furrow between his eyebrows. "Maybe you should go home. I could stay the night."

"You need rest. Anna would want you to stay strong and healthy for the children."

That got to him. Fear flared in his eyes and she knew where his mind went because hers plowed there too. If Anna didn't pull out of this, Kevin was the only parent Logan and Allie would have.

Kevin scowled. "Maybe I'll stay a while longer just to make sure your dizziness passes."

That was sweet of him.

"I'm fine," she said. All right, she was having some pain, and her stomach was queasy because of it, but it was nothing to get alarmed about.

They started for the ICU. As they passed the balding man who'd been staring at her, the guy hopped to his feet, blocking their exit.

"Hey," said party-size Flamin' Hot Cheetos. "You're *her*."

Amelia didn't know why, but an icy chill ran through her. Maybe it was the contentious look in the man's eyes or the way he sounded so completely sure of himself.

"You're the chick in the recording." He picked up his phone with orange-stained fingers and hit play on the YouTube video.

On-screen, someone had made a recording of Anna's grand gesture. It showed the buses arriving, the Moonglow Cove marching band—the entire scene that Amelia had watched from her penthouse window unfolded all over again.

It was touching.

It was sweet.

And then a photograph of her playing the cello popped on the screen along with the caption—*Former Chicago Symphony Cellist Is an Evil Twin.*

Jolted, Amelia took a step back.

"What the hell?" Kevin glowered at the man.

"You've gone viral, baby." The man wagged his tongue. "People love a good evil twin story. You blow out your kidneys with heroin, then your sister gives you her kidney and she goes into a coma. Can I interview you? I'm a freelance journalist."

"Who put that recording up?" Kevin demanded, widening his stance and puffing out his chest.

"Are you coma girl's husband?" Flamin' Hot Cheetos asked.

Kevin clenched his jaw. "Shut up."

"You are her old man." The man nodded. "The grieving husband, and yet, here you are playing patty-cakes with the woman who put your wife in a coma. What's that all about? Some kind of twin kink? Or maybe you're just going to take up with this one once the wife croaks?" He jerked a thumb at Amelia.

This seemed more and more like an ambush. As if the creep had just been staked out in the waiting room looking for a chance to confront Amelia. She had no idea how the story had gotten out. Probably because the four school busloads of people holding signs had attracted attention.

Anyone determined to do a little digging could find out what was behind the story. Twins separated at birth finding their way back to each other was newsworthy. Especially when one of those twins was a former Chicago Symphony cellist with a serious heroin habit. Add complications from a kidney transplant with the good twin ending up in a coma and you had a gossip rag trifecta.

Shame overtook Amelia and mixed with her guilt in an ugly cocktail of self-loathing. She was the cause of this. She couldn't blame the sleazy journalist. He was just doing what sleazy journalists did. *She* was the real problem.

"Get out of our way," Kevin said, the tops of his ears turning scarlet. He clenched his hands at his sides. He looked ready to blow his top.

The guy paid no attention to Kevin. Instead, he stared Amelia right in the eyes and said, "One quote. A sound bite. That's all I need. How does it feel to know your twin is dying because of *your* bad choices?"

"Okay. That's it!" Incensed, Kevin cocked back his right fist.

If the guy—who'd clearly honed his dodging skills—hadn't ducked the moment Kevin swung, her brother-in-law would have decked him. It looked like a comic ninja fight scene with

Kevin pummeling air as the guy gracefully sidestepped each intended punch.

"Kevin." Amelia touched his shoulder. "This guy isn't worth it. If you connect, he'll sue you. Please don't make things worse."

That seemed to get through to him.

A crowd had gathered; every person in the waiting room was on their feet and ringing the action. They were pulling out their phones to record the altercation. Life in the twenty-first century was wide open. There were no secrets anymore, at least not for long, and maybe that was a good thing.

To the Cheetos journalist, she said, "You want a quote from me?"

"Yeah." The guy's eyes lit up. "I do."

"Be a better human being."

"Like you?" His upper lip curled in a snarl.

"No," she said. "Like my sister."

"And if you can't take that for answer," Kevin said, "here's a piece of advice. Stay away from my sister-in-law or we'll get a restraining order."

"Ahh, I get it now." The man nodded. "You two *are* hooking up."

Kevin snorted and his ears turned red again, and Amelia just knew he was going to deck the guy, but just then two hospital security guards came trotting off the elevators with their hands on their holstered stun guns.

"It's okay," Amelia whispered to Kevin. "He's not worth losing your temper over. Let's go see Anna."

"What's going on?" one of the security guards asked sternly.

Several people started talking at once, explaining how the

"journalist" had started the trouble. As the security guards escorted the man from the building, Kevin took Amelia's hand and led her into the ICU.

In the oddest of ways, she and her brother-in-law had finally bonded and while the incident hadn't felt good, it certainly felt like a good start.

CHAPTER TWENTY-SEVEN

Anna

The Awakening

Turtles.

Anna dreamed of turtles.

Or rather, she dreamed she *was* a turtle.

Heavy, slow, walled off. Her body left like an anchor, tethered by a hard, dark shell.

When Anna was six, her father had bought her a turtle for her birthday. Anna wanted a dog, but Robin said no because she wasn't old enough to take care of one properly.

The turtle had been a compromise. A bargaining chip. Take good care of the turtle and maybe later when she was older, she could have a dog.

Her parents hadn't counted on Anna's nurturing instincts. Under Anna's care, the turtle had flourished, growing too big for its backyard pen at their cottage on the beach. She'd named the turtle Myrtle—okay, not the most creative name in the world, now she saw where Logan got critter-naming skills— then Myrtle turned out to be a boy, so she'd changed his name to Myron.

Then one day, Myron was gone, escaping his pen and making turtle tracks down to the ocean. She'd been heartbroken but she understood Myron had been unable to resist the call of the wild.

In her place of darkness, she felt the lure of that call herself. The freedom of taking a deep, long dive into the unknown and just letting go and sinking down into the darkness.

How easy it would be to allow life's ebb and flow to whisk her to endless peace—no more struggling, no more fighting, no more trying to please everyone else.

But no more life, either, whispered a voice at the back of her head.

No more hugs and kisses from her children. No more making love to Kevin. No more walks on the beach. No more cakes to bake. No more companionable moments to share with her mother. No more adventures with her twin sister.

At the thought of her family, she shoved against the call of that sweet unknown, suddenly desperate to get back to the surface. To see her family's faces. To hug and kiss them. To tell them just how much she loved them.

She had to return.

Swimming like a turtle, she pushed through the thickness, headed *up*, *up*, *up* out of the sediment at the bottom of consciousness.

Anna became aware of noises, sounds outside the bubble of her mind. Where was she? What was that whooshing noise? She heard a whistle, like a mechanical bird, then realized it was a cell-phone ringtone.

Tweet. Tweet.

That was Kevin's ringtone.

Was Kevin here? Just on the other side of the void?

Her heart lurched. She concentrated, trying to listen more, trying to rouse her other senses. There was a smell in the air. An institutional odor of disinfectant and damage. But underneath it, she smelled something else—her husband's signature scent of beaches, basil, and bergamot—and her heart beat faster. She could feel the power of her pulse bounding throughout her body. In her throat, in her toes, in her fingertips; a hard, hot *tick*, *tick*, *tick*.

Kevin.

He was here.

Although she wasn't quite sure where "here" was. Everything was muddied in her mind. *Open your eyes.*

She tried, but her lids were so heavy it was as if they were anchored closed by metal weights.

Am I dead?

The thought occurred to her, but it brought no distress. At her core she felt peaceful. She didn't want to die, but if she did, she knew she'd be okay. She would see Dad again and her grandparents and she'd get to meet Caroline, the girl whose place she usurped.

That thought led to another and she began to remember things in piecemeal fragments—Amelia, the bus tour of Moonglow Cove citizens, the surgery.

Had the surgery already happened? Was that why pain gnawed at her body?

Pain.

For the first time she was truly aware of the pain. It bit into her harder now that she brought her attention to it, and she let out a soft moan.

A man shouted.

Kevin.

Calling for a nurse.

For a while she was awash in pain, too overcome to notice what was happening outside of her, but she let go and slowly sank back down into the sediment and slept.

* * *

THE NEXT TIME Anna roused, the pain was tolerable, a nagging annoyance more than anything else.

She felt the pressure of someone taking her hand. A familiar hand. Big and masculine. She tried to talk, but there was something in her mouth. She moved her jaw, her tongue coming in contact with hard plastic.

"She's awake! She's awake!" Kevin cried out.

Prying her eyes open, she saw through blurry vision her husband standing at the foot of her hospital bed, waving two nurses dressed in green scrubs into the room.

The nurses examined her and took the tube out of her throat, bustled and clucked, excited she was back. During it all, Kevin stood at the end of the bed, watching them work, his gaze fixed on her.

He wore faded jeans and a simple white T-shirt and a vulnerability so raw it hurt to look at him. Grief and worry had stripped him bare, in that moment he was all of eighteen again. The kid she'd fallen in love with.

Tears brimmed in his eyes, then silently rolled down his cheeks. The only times she'd seen her husband cry had been at the birth of their children. The sight of her beautiful man weeping over her brought tears to Anna's eyes, too.

The nurses finished up with Anna's care and answered her questions about her illness, telling how long she was in the coma and her treatment regime, and then they left the room.

Kevin moved closer, pulling up the chair right next to the bed and reaching for her hand. His palm was warm and strong. Her anchor in the storm.

"Amelia?" she croaked.

"She's fine. She's good. The kidney is working great." Kevin's face flushed with earnestness. "You knocked it out of the park, Bean."

Anna exhaled. *Thank God Amelia was alive and doing well.*

"Is there anything you need?" Kevin leaned over the bed railing to brush a strand of hair from her forehead.

"Ice chips?" Her mouth was so dry, her throat scratchy.

"On it." He disappeared and returned a short time later with a cup of ice and plastic spoon.

"Do you want me to feed you?" he asked.

She nodded—her arms felt so weak—and opened her mouth.

He dropped a spoonful of ice onto her tongue.

The coldness was bracing and the wetness a blessing on her dry tongue.

"More," she said, her voice growing stronger with the moisture in her throat.

Kevin gave her more ice and finally, she shook her head, letting him know she'd had enough.

"We don't have much time alone. I texted your mom and Amelia when I realized you were coming back to us and they're on the way. Before they get here . . ." He drew in a deep breath and blew it out. "We need to talk. There's so much to say."

"I-I—"

"Shh, shh, you rest." He kissed his finger and pressed it to her upper lip. "When I thought I was going to lose you . . ."

"L-lose me?" Just how sick had she been?

"You've been unconscious for eleven days. Remember what the nurses just told you? We didn't know if you were going to wake up or not." He paused to collect himself.

Wow, okay, that was a long time to be in a coma. She tried to smile at him, but it took a while for her mouth to respond.

"Anna, I was so scared." He squeezed her hand.

Finally getting the smile to take, she squeezed back.

"I've never been so terrified. All I could think was that we'd never really resolved the problems between us."

"You mean . . ." She swallowed. Ouch. Talking hurt her throat, but she was determined to get past it. There were things she needed to know. "Amelia?"

"No. Amelia was merely a catalyst, not the cause. Anna, all

I've ever wanted was to take care of you. You're so bright and loving and sweet and open, but you don't fully realize how dark the world can be."

Her husband's hair was mussed, and he ran a hand through it now, mussing it even more. Her heart reeled with love for him. Even in the midst of worry, he looked so big and strong. Her protector. He took that job so seriously, even when she didn't need protecting. He was the troubleshooter in the family, the dragon slayer, and while all that endeared him to her, she wasn't a damsel in need of rescuing.

But maybe he was a knight in need of a mission and because she resisted turning to him for solace, she'd made him feel unimportant in her life. She'd been trying to save everyone else, while he'd been trying to keep her safe while she went about it.

She saw it clearly now, the stumbling block of their marriage. Her need to help and his need to protect had come into conflict. First last year, when they'd lost her father and the whole world had gone through so much upheaval and both their businesses had floundered because of it, fine cracks had appeared in the foundation of their marriage.

The marriage she'd once believed unshakable faltered a bit. Now she knew a certain belief wasn't enough for a marriage to flourish. It needed nurturing from both parties. A commitment to open and honest communication.

Anna had seen Kevin's protective instincts as controlling and resisted them. He'd seen her resistance as rejection. The truth was, often his job kept him on the road for such large chunks of time, she'd learned how to get along without him.

And while it was great to be independent, she'd stopped sharing her day-to-day struggles with him. When had they stopped turning to each other for emotional support? They'd both fallen down on the job.

It had come in increments she supposed. The times when he was on the road and she had to fend for herself. Not that she blamed him for that. She wasn't helpless. But when he came home, it just seemed easier somehow to not share anything troubling that had happened while he was away. How could he know what went wrong when she never told him? Although, to be fair to herself, he never asked, maybe because it was simpler not to as well.

Yes, somewhere along the way things had gotten off track.

"I don't want to fight anymore," Kevin said. "I don't want to be away from you, and I don't want a wall between us. I want us to be like we used to be. Remember those days? When we were a team?"

"I do," she whispered, drawing on every ounce of physical strength she had left in her. *I do.* The same words she'd said on their wedding day.

"I want to go back—no," he interrupted himself. "I want us to go forward from this moment on and build a better life, a better marriage."

"Do you really mean it?" She breathed, scarcely daring to hope they could right the ship of their listing marriage and sail once again into safe harbors.

"Anna, you're the only woman I've ever loved. The only woman I've ever wanted. I've been selfish and self-centered, and

I haven't been there for you the way you deserved. This thing with Amelia—"

"I get it. You don't like her."

"That's not it at all. She's your twin sister. I didn't not like her—I just didn't know her. How can I not like her? She's been sitting by your bed every night since they released her from the hospital."

"She has?"

He nodded. "In her will, she left everything to our kids. Her condo, her sixty-million-dollar trust fund. When I saw that, I understood that Amelia truly does love you. And whenever I think of all the reasons I love *you*, the sacrifice you made for your sister will be at the top of the list."

"You're not angry with her?"

"I doubted Amelia's motives at first and there's nothing wrong with being suspicious of strangers, but even then, that's not really why I had issues with her. I told myself she was a charlatan but that was only because I couldn't face the truth."

"What truth?" Her voice was so soft she could barely hear herself.

"I was *jealous* of Amelia. Plain and simple. I was jealous and I acted like a possessive jerk. You were right to be upset with me."

"Oh, Kevin, there's no need to be jealous. I have enough love to go around."

"That's why people adore you and why I worry. I'm scared as hell you're going to love the wrong person and get your heart broken."

"So, see, you weren't really jealous of Amelia as much as you were protecting me." A little thrill ran through her. It was nice that her man cared about her so much.

"Please forgive me." He interlaced their fingers, kissed her hand. "I'm a clumsy oaf, but I am determined to do better."

The feel of his mouth against her skin sent goose bumps flying up Anna's arms. She moistened her lips, preparing to give a speech despite her sore throat.

"Of course, I forgive you. You're the only man I've ever loved. You're my first, my last, my one, my only, my always." She had to pause a moment before she could continue. "But I'm not blameless. I got my sense of self from rushing around helping other people—"

"That's a good quality!"

"No, it's not. Not always. Because feeling like I have to help others assumes that I know best what they need. I don't. Amelia showed me that."

"She is pretty perceptive," he said. "She certainly had my number and was kind to me anyway."

"She showed me that I was so busy doing for others that I neglected my own husband. I was so sure of your loyalty that I took you for granted."

"We're in the same boat on that one."

She lifted a hand and cupped his cheek with her palm. "I've missed you, Viking, but rather than tell you how much I missed you, I hid my feelings by jam-packing my day with so many people and activities I didn't have time to think about being lonely."

"I've been absent for too long. You've essentially been a single parent."

"In some ways. I know you love the kids and me, but it got too easy to hide my problems from you when you were home. I wanted to keep those times when we were together as stress free as possible."

"How can I blame you for building a life of your own, when I wasn't there when you needed me and when I was there, I wasn't really listening to you half the time. I fell down on my job. I was a poor husband."

"You weren't a poor husband. You were on the road, earning a living. I understood."

"That's the part of the problem, Anna. You shouldn't *have* to understand."

"Meaning?"

"You shouldn't have to be a sometimes-wife. Being on the road isn't working anymore. I want to open my own insurance company. I want to be home with you and the kids. I want a proper schedule."

Anna let out a little gasp and her pulse gave a jump-skip bump against her veins. "Kevin, do you mean it?"

He leaned over and kissed her lightly, a gentle brushing of their lips, so sweet and tender. It was exactly what she needed in the moment, although as soon as she got well, she'd expect much more passionate kisses than this one.

And often!

When he settled back into his chair, he cradled her with his gaze. "I want to recommit to our marriage, Anna. I want another ceremony. I want to go to therapy to help us find our way back to each other. I'll do whatever it takes to show you that I *am* the man of your dreams and I'm going to spend the rest of my days proving it."

Fresh tears brewed in her eyes and she couldn't stop them from sliding down her cheek. Kevin reached for a tissue from the box on the nightstand and dabbed her face dry.

She smiled at him from the misty shine of joy. She hadn't known how badly she needed to hear this from him.

"You're my world," he said.

"And you're mine." Gingerly—her limbs were far stiffer than she imagined—she scooted over and patted the mattress beside her. "Could I have a cuddle?"

"Bean." His nickname for her came out soft and low. He kicked off his sneakers, lowered the bed rail, and stretched out beside her.

Then slowly, tenderly, he positioned himself on his side, and drew her to him until they fit together like two spoons on the narrow bed.

In his arms, she felt whole and, in her happiness, drifted off to sleep and dreamed again.

This time, not of turtles, but of a wide-eyed sixteen-year-old cheerleader, dancing at the prom for the first time with the man who'd one day become the love of her life.

CHAPTER TWENTY-EIGHT

Amelia

The Healing

On August 21, thirty-six years after the twins were born, Amelia and Anna shared their first birthday celebration together.

Five weeks had passed since Anna woke up from her coma, and while her twin still tired easily, she was healing. Upon returning home to Moonglow Cove, she and Kevin had been seeing a marriage counselor. Kevin had also secured a business loan to start his own insurance company, and on the street behind the bakery, he had opened his business in the same building where Mike had his furniture store and Gia had her kite shop. The entire block was a family affair.

Anna had told Amelia things between her and Kevin were better than they'd ever been, and they were planning a trip to Hawaii to renew their marriage vows on their anniversary on the same beach where they'd honeymooned.

Amelia was so happy for her sister.

As for her relationship with Kevin, she and her brother-in-law had formed an easy camaraderie. After he'd stood up for her against that creepy guy in the hospital, she'd understood him much better. Her brother-in-law was a man who got his identity from how well he protected those he loved. He was ever vigilant for incoming threats. Once she knew that about him, it was easy to figure out how to get along with Kevin.

Trust him.

As for Amelia herself, she'd put the condo in Chicago on the market and purchased a modest bungalow right on the beach not far from where Anna lived. She'd joined the Harmonious House-wives and had started giving cello lessons. She was booked three months in advance. She didn't need the money. She taught for the joy of passing along her love of the cello.

Now, on the twins' birthday, their family and friends had overtaken the picnic area of Paradise Pier. The guest list was huge, seventy people, the bulk of them who'd come to Chicago on the school buses.

Kevin, with Robin's help, had organized the whole thing as a surprise party.

In truth, it was chaotic but in such a wonderful way that even introverted Amelia didn't mind all the hubbub, and Anna, who was happiest around lots of people, particularly those she loved, lapped up the attention.

Pete and Veronica were there, along with Kevin's six siblings and their families. There were so many of them, Amelia had to make a list of their names on her phone so she wouldn't forget them. She was living in Moonglow Cove now and eager to embrace the community that had readily accepted her. Robin brought Winnie. Mike and Gia were there. Darla, who'd made the birthday cake, had closed the bakery early, so she could join in the fun.

Everyone was excited to toast their good health.

Caterers stood at the ready to serve the crowd crispy fried chicken, mashed potatoes and gravy with biscuits, fried okra and coleslaw and corn on the cob. For drinks, there was tea, lemonade, bottled water, and canned sodas. Once everyone had eaten, the caterers passed out champagne for the adults who wanted it and sparkling cider for those who didn't, along with disposable plastic champagne flutes.

Kevin stood at the head of the guests-of-honor table and raised his champagne glass.

"A toast," he said and looked at Anna. "To my beautiful wife who has agreed to remarry me."

That brought cheers and congratulations from the audience.

"And to my sister-in-law, Amelia." With his glass still raised, he turned to Amelia, who was sitting directly across from Anna. "The person we never even knew was missing. Thank you so much for coming to Moonglow Cove and making our lives so much richer."

More toasts were made. More champagne and sparkling cider flowed. Laughter and conversation drowned out the noise from the amusement park rides on the pier. Kids chased each other around the park, playing tag. "Happy Birthday" was sung. Darla's scrumptious chocolate cake with white icing was served and drew much praise.

Amelia met her sister's eyes across the table. Anna smiled and mouthed, *I love you.*

Happiness leaked from Amelia's pores. For the first time she felt as if she truly belonged somewhere.

Kevin sat beside Anna, slipping his arm around her back. "Are you having a good time?"

"The best time. This is the most incredible surprise party ever."

"How about you, Amelia?" Kevin asked.

"It's a little noisy," Amelia admitted. "But the party is spectacular, Kevin. Thank you so much for this surprise."

"Daddy," Allie called, from where she was playing on the lawn with the other children. "Could you come show us how to throw a Frisbee to Cujo?"

"Be right there, sweetheart." He leaned in and kissed Anna. "Gotta go. Daddy duty."

"And you love it." Anna grinned at him.

"I do." Kevin went off to play with the children and their dog.

Robin moved from the table she'd been sitting at to take the spot that Kevin had vacated. She leaned over to kiss Anna's cheek. "How are you holding up?"

"Perfect. Everything's perfect. It's the most perfect day. I wish I could bottle this day and come back to drink from it whenever those potholes show up."

"Savoring the moment is an important skill." Robin smiled across the table at Amelia. "How are you, second daughter?"

"Happy," Amelia said, and it was deeply true. She'd never been so happy. "Thank you for your part in it."

"We're so lucky to have you in our lives," Robin said and squeezed Amelia's arm. "So very lucky."

"I feel the same," Amelia said, starting to feel tapped out with all the emoting. She'd found a new, more expansive way of being in the world, but she was still who she was. She'd never be as open, welcoming, and accepting as her twin. But that was all right. The world couldn't handle two Annas. Amelia brought her own strengths to the table.

On the heels of the school bus video that had gone viral on social media, they'd gotten calls from several media outlets wanting an interview. Anna thought it would be healthy to tell their story, plus, she just knew it could help someone else out there who was navigating the scary waters of contacting long-lost relatives.

Who was Amelia to argue with her reasoning? Her twin's motives, like everything about Anna, were pure. She always led with her heart, and Amelia loved her for it.

They'd done an interview last week, traveling to a TV station in Houston. They'd had such an overwhelming response, and sharing what had happened to them turned out to be as cathartic as Anna predicted. Cleansed, they felt no need to do more interviews.

Robin made eye contact with Amelia. "Anna told me you two were thinking about writing a book and that you had interest from a publisher?"

"I thought it might help us work through some stuff, but . . ." Amelia pressed her palms together in her lap.

"But?" Robin raised an eyebrow.

"The one thing holding us back is that we don't have any real proof of what happened that night in the hospital and I don't know that we'll ever have it."

"Can't it just be a mystery?" Robin asked.

"That's what I keep telling her," Anna said. "But Amelia wants all the ducks in a row before diving in."

Robin rested her arm on Anna's shoulder. "I can tell you this. After I got back from Chicago, I went to see Winnie and I told her that I forgave her."

"How did she react?" Anna asked.

"She watched me intently, so I repeated it. I forgave her *everything*. I told her that if it hadn't been for her, I wouldn't have had a daughter at all. That while what she had done was wrong, she'd given me you and I wouldn't ever take that back."

"Wow," Anna whispered.

"What did she say?" Amelia asked.

"She said 'thank you.' I think my forgiveness helped her. Because when I went to pick her up, Myra said she's been sleeping much better since I'd visited her."

"Forgiveness is a powerful thing," Anna said, and Amelia watched her search for her husband and find him giving Logan a piggyback ride as they played Frisbee with Cujo.

"It is indeed," Amelia murmured.

"To tell you the truth," Robin added, sounding a little surprised, "*I'm* sleeping better, too, and I decided to take a break from wine."

"Really, Mom?" Anna sounded overjoyed.

"During the time you were in the hospital, I didn't touch a

drop. I wasn't leaving you alone and I didn't want my thinking clouded. I realized that I'd been using wine to fill up my empty evenings without your father."

"How are you filling your evenings now?" Amelia asked.

Robin's cheeks pinked. "I met a man in church . . ."

"Mom!" Anna exclaimed. "Why didn't you tell me?"

"I think I just did." Robin giggled.

"What's his name?"

"Luther, but don't say anything. It's new. Just shhh." Robin shyly dipped her head.

Anna pantomimed zipping her lips and then silently clapped her palms with her fingers splayed.

Amelia enjoyed the sweet moment.

"Luther!" Winnie sang out in a high clear voice. "Luther Cosgrove. Born 1952 to Annabelle and Thomas Cosgrove. I was in nurse's training and his was the first birth I attended."

The three of them looked down the long picnic table to where Winnie was parked in a wheelchair eating birthday cake. She caught them staring at her and waved as enthusiastically as Logan did when he saw a friend.

In unison, they all waved back and laughed.

Winnie laughed, too. It was an uproarious sound bursting from behind the frosting stuck to her upper lip.

"She's lucid," Robin said, looking gobsmacked. "It *is* Luther Cosgrove. And, yes, he's a younger man. I'm a cougar."

"Mom." Anna teasingly rolled her eyes. "The age difference has to be greater than five years for you to declare yourself a cougar."

"Oh, really? Well, there goes that fantasy." Robin pantomimed crumpling up an invisible piece of paper and tossing it over her shoulder.

Over the past few weeks, Amelia had really come to know and appreciate Robin's sense of humor. She was grateful that her twin had such a wonderful mother. She couldn't begrudge Anna getting to grow up the way she did. At least one of them had had a happy childhood.

Life was indeed ironic.

Just when you were expecting the worst, you could end up with the very best and Amelia, the poor, little rich girl who'd once lost her twin, had been found indeed. The relationships she'd made were priceless.

"Mom," Allie said coming up to her mother. "Can we go build sandcastles on the beach?"

"Honey . . ." Anna pulled her daughter to her. "This was a surprise party, so Mommy didn't bring swimming suits or—"

Allie lifted up her T-shirt to show her mother she had on a swimming suit. "You can just sit on the sand and watch me."

"We don't have any sand pails or towels."

"Maw-Maw's got us covered." Allie beamed at Robin. "Right, Maw-Maw."

"Here's the car key." Robin gave the key fob to Allie. "You know where I keep the beach gear."

Allie grabbed the key and took off, skipping to Robin's Camry parked nearby.

"Don't forget the sunscreen," Robin called after her.

Allie waved a hand over her head.

"Looks like we're going to the beach," Anna said.

"What about Winnie?" Amelia asked.

Everyone else was playing around the park or had walked to the beach or Paradise Pier. It was just them and Winnie and the caterers left at the picnic pavilion.

Winnie waved at them again.

"Wheelchair and sand? Not happening," Anna said.

"I can walk," Winnie said. "I'm only in this chair because this one"—she pointed a thumb at Robin—"insisted in case I got dizzy. Let's go!"

"Guess that's settled." Amelia laughed.

Allie zoomed back with her sand pail and beach towels, and the five of them headed for the ocean.

They all played in the sand with Allie, including Winnie. They dug and mounded and packed and sculpted. Soon they'd built a spectacular sandcastle with turrets and a moat and a fire-breathing dragon—which was actually a misshapen stick—to guard it.

"Can we make me into a mermaid, Mom?" Allie asked.

"Sure." Anna glanced around. "If everyone else is up for it."

"I love making mermaids," Robin said.

Winnie was on her knees with the child-size plastic shovel, grinning as if she'd hit pay dirt.

"Amelia?" Anna looked at her.

"I'm in." Amelia smiled.

It was late afternoon, but the sky was overcast, keeping the temperature balmy, and they all applied fresh sunscreen. They dug a little trench and Allie settled into it, giggling as they covered her with sand and fashioned her a mermaid tail. The sound of the waves, the caw of the seagulls, the chatter of children playing along the water accompanied their task. It was the loveliest of music. Relaxing, and peaceful.

Amelia was mesmerized. It might have been awkward being here like this with her sister and her twin's mother and daughter and the midwife who'd brought them into the world, but it wasn't.

It was sweet and gentle, and their bond touched Amelia to her core.

Probably, they'd never again spend time together like this. The poignancy of the moment washed over Amelia and sudden tears sprang to her eyes. Horrified at her lack of emotional control, she put a hand to her mouth. Tasted gritty sand.

"You're crying!" Anna sounded alarmed. "You hardly ever cry. What is it, Amelia? What's wrong?"

"I think you b-br-broke me," Amelia stammered.

"Broke you?"

"I can't compartmentalize my emotions anymore. I was just thinking how beautiful and special this day is and then I started doing"—she waved a hand at her eyes and sniffled—"this."

"That's so awesome!" Anna wrapped her in a big hug. "You're finally getting in touch with your feelings."

She'd always been in touch with her feelings, she'd just never been able to express them very well. But Anna made letting down her guard so easy.

"It's like I'm learning how to be human," Amelia said. "My past is so riddled with mistakes—"

"Shh," Anna said. "The past is gone. It's a new life now. A new you."

What a lovely thing to say.

"Oh!" Anna exclaimed, fingering her wrist. "My bracelet is missing."

"When did you last notice having it on?" Robin asked.

"It caught the sunlight when we came down to the beach. It's got to be here." Anna gathered her hair in her hand to keep it from falling in her face as she searched the sand.

Amelia understood the sense of panic. She'd felt it when she'd broken her keepsake bracelet. They'd never been able to find all the pieces.

They searched for the bracelet for some time but couldn't find it.

"We'll send Kevin back here with his metal detector," Robin assured her. "We'll find it."

"I can't believe it's gone."

Amelia wrapped her arm around Anna's shoulder. "We don't need bracelets to let us know we belong together."

"You're right."

"Mom," Allie said, still in her mermaid sand prison.

"Yes, sweetheart."

"Frozen."

Anna grinned at her daughter. "Oh, you smart thing. You are so right." Then, as tears streamed down *her* face, she started singing "Let It Go."

Amelia glanced over to see Winnie and Robin were crying too.

They had all lost so much. Suffered so much. There was no

one to punish. No fingers to point. No blame to lay. Blame and recrimination would solve nothing, salve nothing, save nothing. Forgiveness was the only way through this—forgiveness and radical acceptance for what was.

Anna took Amelia's hand and reached for Winnie. Winnie took Robin's hand and Robin took Amelia's. They stood in a circle, the four of them standing over the little mermaid beaming up at them with joy as they sang at the top of their lungs.

The past was gone.

Let it go.

The pain hurt.

Feel it and then let it go.

Their time together was precious.

Fully experience it and then let it, too, go.

For that was the rhythm of the earth. The ebb and flow of tides. All part of the life cycle of birth and death and rebirth. They looked into one another's eyes. A community of women drawn together by circumstances, flourished by love.

In that moment, Amelia was surely born again, and she knew that well and truly, at long last, she'd finally found her way home.

CHAPTER TWENTY-NINE

Robin

The Key, the Safe-Deposit Box, and Everything

After the twins' birthday party, Winnie Newton died during the night. Myra Marts found her the next morning in her bed, clutching Anna's keepsake bracelet to her chest, a soft smile on her face.

Robin cried when she heard the news.

Myra asked nicely if they could come clean out Winnie's room sooner rather than later because they had a waiting list.

Robin, Anna, and Amelia arrived at the memory care facility that afternoon with two big boxes to pack up the sum total of Winnie's life. Myra gave Anna the keepsake bracelet she'd found Winnie holding on to and Anna slipped it into her pocket and then they set to work clearing out her things.

In the hallway, they heard a nurse trying to coax a patient into taking his pills and the squeak of a rolling cart's wheels. A sparrow perched on a branch outside the window and fluffed his feathers. An aerosol plug-in dispensed a citrus-scented spray into the air.

A pang of sadness hit Robin, but she pushed it aside. She was here for her daughters. Yes, somewhere along the line, she'd started thinking of Amelia as her daughter too.

In the closet, Anna found a wooden cigar box. "What do you suppose is in here?"

"It looks like a keepsake box," Amelia said.

Robin bit her bottom lip. "Do you think—"

"That the key to her safe-deposit box is in here?" Anna finished.

"There's only one way to find out," Amelia added.

Anna sat down on the end of the bed that had been stripped of sheets. "Should I open it?"

"Yes," Robin and Amelia said in unison and sat down on either side of her.

"Here goes nothing." Anna blew out her breath.

Robin watched her daughter open the box. The rusty hinges creaked, and the smell of stale tobacco entered the room.

On the top, looking as if it had been fondled many times over the years, Anna found a red heart-shaped envelope. She fingered the paper gone crisply stiff with age. It made a wispy scratching sound against her nails.

Inside was a card of a cute cartoon bunny holding a bouquet of flowers with the caption *Love you bunches.*

In a childish scrawl with blue crayon it said: Happy Valentine's Day Mommy.

Robin's heart wrenched at the sight of Paul's card to his mother, and her chest tightened with so much damn guilt she could hardly breathe. A tear formed at her eye, but she brushed it away, hoping her daughters hadn't noticed.

Anna shuffled through the papers, setting aside first one and then the other. Love letters to Winnie from her husband when he'd been stationed in Korea. Artwork from Paul. Several pictures of Anna and Mike as children, Winnie their proud surrogate grandmother.

At the very bottom of the box, Anna found it. The key that matched the one Robin had found in Heathcliff's desk. The key that opened the mysterious safe-deposit box at Moonglow Cove Central Bank.

The sight of it drummed a sense of dread throughout Robin's entire body.

Now that the key had been found, they had no choice but to open that safe deposit, but what on earth would they find?

* * *

An hour later, the three of them were sitting in a tiny room at the bank, the safe-deposit box in front of them on a long table. The bank attendant had left them alone to sort through the contents.

Robin wished she was by herself. She had no idea what was inside that box and, frankly, the possibilities terrified her.

What secrets were they about to uncover?

Bigger question. Did she honestly want to know?

"Mom." Anna handed Robin the key they'd found in Winnie's cigar box. "Will you do the honors?"

Robin wasn't so sure it was an honor, but she inserted the two keys in the two locks, glanced up at her daughters, who nodded, and simultaneously, she turned them.

The lid to the safe-deposit box popped open.

Anna sat on one side of her, Amelia on the other. They peered over Robin's shoulders and she inhaled their unique scents. Anna with her yeast and cinnamon fragrance and Amelia's more complex scent of ylang-ylang and roses. There was the difference in her daughters right there—homey for people-person Anna and sophisticated for elegant Amelia.

Inside the safe-deposit box, they found a stack of letters, a long white jeweler's box, and a photograph.

Robin recognized the picture right away. It had been taken in the summer of 1968. The same year Martin Luther King and Robert F. Kennedy were assassinated. The year the Beatles released *The White Album*. The riotous year Nixon was elected president.

The year Robin surrendered her virginity to Paul Newton.

In the photograph, she, Paul, and Heathcliff were sitting on the trunk of Paul's 1965 Thunderbird convertible. All three were grinning at the camera, and Paul, who was on the left, had his arms slung companionably around Robin's shoulder, who was in the middle, and Heathcliff was studying Robin from his peripheral vision with hungry eyes.

They looked so impossibly young in their long hair and bell-bottom jeans. The boys both sported scraggly mustaches and Robin wore a maxi dress with a garish yellow, orange, and lime-green geometric design. They were all giving the "peace" sign.

It was a snapshot of a long-ago time that she thought she'd put behind her. The photograph brought all the memories back into sharp focus, and she momentarily forgot to breathe.

Robin took out the photograph and set it aside, determined to power through this without feeling her emotions. Later, she could process them. Right now, she needed to stay strong for her daughters.

Anna picked up the picture and studied it while Robin took out the envelopes. One said: *For Anna.* Another said: *For Robin.* The third was labeled simply: *Heathcliff.* Robin recognized that handwriting. It was Paul's.

"Which one do we open first?" Anna whispered.

"Should we start with the one on top?" Amelia asked.

"That's the one made out to me. Mom?" Anna rested a hand on Robin's forearm. "What do you think?"

"Amelia's right. It was on top. If the letters are supposed to be read in some kind of order, it makes sense to start with the first one." She handed the letter marked *Anna* to her daughter.

A long moment passed with Anna staring down at the envelope. The air inside the room felt stale, motionless.

Finally, Amelia said, "Would you like me to open it for you?"

Anna nodded. Passed the envelope to Amelia.

Amelia broke the envelope's seal and took out several sheets of lined white notebook paper and began reading.

Dear Anna, if you're reading this, Winnie and I are both dead, and you've stumbled across our terrible secret.

Line by line, Heathcliff Straus explained about the hurricane. The loss of electricity. The darkness. The lack of staffing. The chaos. The rich couple from up north who were having twins in the bed beside Robin's. How their baby had died. How he'd stood there in the dimly lighted room holding their lifeless Caroline in his arms.

Everything unfolded perfectly for the switch. If you'd been twin boys, it wouldn't have worked. If there had been enough nurses in the ward, it wouldn't have worked. If the lights hadn't gone out and the supervisor hadn't taken Amelia to the incubator in the hallway it wouldn't have worked. But it all fell into place like falling dominoes. One look in Winnie's encouraging face and I knew what I had to do. It wasn't about right or wrong at that point. It was about saving your mother from the worst pain of her life. All she'd ever wanted was a baby and I hadn't been able to grant her greatest wish until that night.

Robin closed her eyes. The pain cutting through her was almost too much to bear as the memory of that night steamrolled through her consciousness. There was no more hiding. No more denying. No more lying to herself.

"Mom? What do you remember about the night we were born?" Anna draped an arm around Robin's shoulder. "Can you talk about it right now?"

She was the mother. She should be soothing Anna and not the other way around.

"It was so dark we could hardly see anything. The nurses had flashlights, but it was a big ward with nine of us in labor." Robin paused.

The clock on the wall ticked loudly.

"I remember the pain more than anything," Robin murmured. "So much pain, and not just from the contractions. There was a stabbing sensation, like a knife blade, and that seemed so wrong. But the doctor wasn't there, and there were only two nurses and they were attending a mother across the room."

She was back in time, reliving it as she spoke. The flashback she'd spent her adult life struggling to keep at bay.

"It happened in a rush, and you were born in a gush of hot blood, and I was so weak, I could barely lift my head and call to your father."

"It wasn't me. I wasn't your child." Anna reached for her hand and squeezed it.

Robin threw her a grateful look. Anna didn't sound angry at all, just curious. Her daughter's acceptance eased some of her anxiety.

"The baby didn't cry." Robin reached for Anna's other hand and they sat there clasping each other, their gazes fused. "But it was so noisy, the wind from the hurricane, the laboring mothers around us screaming and crying. It was like being in a madhouse and everything was blurred, as if it was a nightmare . . ."

They all sat in silence for a moment, absorbing that.

"I was barely aware that they'd brought in another woman and put her in the bed next to mine. I do remember them saying something about having twins, but I was so busy trying to give birth to you . . . to Caroline," Robin amended.

Anna looked deep into her eyes. "It must've been terrifying."

"Deep inside me, I knew something was wrong with the baby," Robin said. "But I kept drifting in and out of consciousness, and when I asked your father about you . . . er . . . about Caroline . . . he said you were a fine, healthy baby and that he thought you looked exactly like an Anna and maybe we should consider changing your name."

"But you never called him on it?"

"They gave me pain medicine and when I woke up the next day, Heathcliff handed me the beautiful baby bracelet with your name on it . . . I thought, she really does look like an Anna. Your dad said he had gone out to have the bracelet made special, and I believed him." She pressed her lips into a flat line. "Because I *wanted* to believe him. He was a good man and I had no reason to distrust him. We had wanted a baby so badly, had tried for years to have you, that I didn't dare question anything."

"Under the circumstances, I wouldn't have either," Anna said, staring into her eyes.

Robin felt her daughter's love in the deep center of her heart. "Thank you for understanding." Robin turned to make eye contact with Amelia. Held out her hand to her. "I hope you can forgive me, Amelia."

"There's nothing to forgive," Amelia said and then added, "Mom."

That one word, which she knew did not come easily to Amelia, shifted everything and the weight of the world rolled off Robin's chest.

"I'm confused about something," Anna said. "Why did Winnie risk her job, her livelihood, even prison to give you and Daddy someone else's child?"

"Maybe it's in the rest of your dad's letter?" Amelia waved at the additional pages of Heathcliff's handwritten note in front of her.

"I'm feeling strong enough to read it now."

Nodding, Amelia passed the letter back to Anna.

Robin moistened her lips, and her heart was beating so loudly in her ears that she could barely hear anything else.

Clearing her throat, Anna began where Amelia had left off.

My darling daughter, I want you to know one thing, and to never, ever doubt it. Your mother and I love you more than life itself. It's always been that way, and it will always be that way, we wanted you so very badly. Badly enough that I was willing to switch you with our dead baby. It was at once the worst thing and the best thing I've ever done. Your mother does not know about this, she believes you are her natural-born daughter. And I never wanted her to learn the truth while Winnie and I were alive. I did it partially to protect Winnie, but also because I didn't have the guts to face you. I'm a flawed man. But when we lost our baby, and Winnie was there with you in her arms, looking at me, and letting me know that it was okay . . . I succumbed.

To my grief, to the dreams that I did not want to lose, to my love for my wife. To the chance to make things right, fix what nature had destroyed, but the time has come to make things right with you.

The letter went on, to tell Anna about Amelia. Where she was from, the name of Anna's biological parents, everything Heathcliff had found out about her twin.

> Go to Amelia. Find your sister. Reunite with her. I pray this letter doesn't come too late, but for Winnie's sake, I had to stay silent until now.
>
> I'm sorry that I have left this legacy and been too cowardly to tell you the truth while I was still alive, I simply couldn't bear to watch the love drain from your eyes when I told you what I'd done. I hope you can find it in your heart to forgive me. I wouldn't blame you if you can't. Just know that everything I've done has been out of love for you.
>
> —Your devoted father, Heathcliff

Anna was crying so hard she could no longer read the words.

Robin picked up the letter. Her own tears fell onto the old ink and smeared it. The letter was dated 1990 when Anna was only four years old. Heathcliff had been preparing for this for a long time.

"It still doesn't explain about why Winnie did it," Amelia murmured.

"Mom." Anna sniffled. "Maybe it's in your letter."

Here it was. The time for all the secrets to come out. No holding back. Robin opened the envelope addressed to her.

The letter wasn't from Heathcliff. That was the first surprise. It was dated October 25, 2001. The day after Heathcliff had returned home from his volunteer stint at Ground Zero following the destruction of the Twin Towers.

In a tremulous voice, she read.

Dear Robin,

　　Heathcliff has come to see me to tell me about what has happened to him in New York and ask me to write this letter. You won't receive it until we've both passed away, but we couldn't take our secret with us to the grave.

　　If you've read Heathcliff's letter, you're probably wondering why I did what I did. Why I helped him switch out your dead baby for Anna Brandt. I participated because of what Heathcliff did for Paul . . . for me.

A feeling of such dread came over Robin that she wasn't sure she could keep reading. She hauled in a deep breath, rallied, and continued on.

　　Paul's death wasn't due to a hunting accident. He and Heathcliff didn't go hunting that day as he told the police.

Robin fisted her left hand as her right hand held the letter and the air leaked from her lungs and past her teeth in a soft whistle.

　　My son was prone to depression and he'd been struggling emotionally after his father committed suicide on New Year's Eve. I did the best I could for him. Took him to doctors. Had his blood tested. Got him on medication and into counseling. He'd get these horrible black moods.

Oh! How well Robin knew Paul's dark moods. An ancient chill ran through her, an overwhelming sense of doom.

When you broke up with him, my son took it so hard. He was head over heels for you.

"Mom?" Anna whispered. "You used to date Paul?"

Silently, she nodded but was unable to meet her daughter's gaze. She didn't like the way the puzzle pieces were falling together, although somewhere at the back of her mind, she'd known the truth.

"Paul was the guy with the sailboat, wasn't he?" Anna asked. "The one who took you on a 'Magic Carpet Ride.'"

All Robin could do was bob her head. If she spoke right now, she'd completely fall apart. She passed the letter to Anna.

Amelia picked up the photograph, studied it. "You were with Paul when this picture was taken. Not Heathcliff."

Robin covered her eyes with her palm, nodded again. She didn't want Anna to keep reading the letter. She was terrified to hear what came next, even as she suspected what was in the letter.

After you ended things, Paul left the house in blind grief. He didn't come home for an entire day.

In a panic, I called Heathcliff and asked him to go look for Paul. I didn't know at the time that you were with Heathcliff.

"Paul was just a fling for me." Robin pulled her hand down her face. "We were drunk and stoned and it was the sixties . . ." That was no excuse for toying with Paul's affections. She'd known he cared more for her than she did for him.

Exhaling audibly, Anna continued with Winnie's heart-wrenching letter.

Heathcliff found Paul's body in the woods on some public land where they often hunted. Paul had shot himself and left Heathcliff a suicide note. Heathcliff hid the note and altered the scene to make it look like Paul had tripped while hunting, and the gun went off. Then he called the police. They took Heathcliff at his word. Moonglow Cove is a small town and back then, forensics wasn't what it is today, and eventually they ruled Paul's death an accident.

Anna set the letter down. "Oh my gosh, Mom, how horrific for you all. I am so, so sorry."

Heathcliff wanted to spare me the pain of knowing Paul took his own life just as his father had. Because the police ruled his death an accident, Paul's life insurance policy paid out. It was only years later, when I came across Paul's high school journal, that I realized the truth. His writings were those of a young man in emotional turmoil. In retrospect, I suspect he might have been bipolar. I confronted Heathcliff and he admitted it and showed me Paul's suicide note.

All three of them peered into the safe-deposit box at the remaining letter marked with Heathcliff's name in Paul's handwriting. Robin shivered.

"Mom, do you want me to stop?"

"Keep reading, Anna."

I found what really happened. I hated that Heathcliff carried that secret for so long and I was so grateful to him for being such a good friend to my son. When Heathcliff lost his child, and the opportunity presented itself to spare him the pain I'd gone through, I just took it. No parent should ever have to lose a child. I just hope you and God can forgive me.

Robin started crying then, great retching sobs to the bottom of her soul. Amelia leaned over to wrap her arms around her as she cried, as Anna finished reading the letter.

I didn't write this to blame you for Paul's death, Robin. I don't hold you responsible. In fact, I'm so happy I was able to give you the daughter you deserved. I do hope you can forgive me, and I pray someday Anna can be reunited with her twin. I hope this letter will help in some small measure to ease your suffering. —With love, Winnie

After that, they cried for all they'd lost, wiped away their tears, regrouped, and opened the last letter.

Paul's suicide note.

It was simple. To the point.

Heathcliff, this is not your fault. I love you and Robin both and I want you to be happy. Give her the life and love she deserves, my friend. I can't. I'm counting on you to take care of her. —Your friend forever, Paul

Robin's heart caved in. This was simply too much grief for one day, but there was still the long white jeweler's box. There was a label on the box with Anna's and Amelia's names on it.

"Should we open it?" Anna asked.

"Might as well." Robin pressed her lips together and braced herself.

Inside the box they found two bracelets, almost identical to the keepsake bracelets they'd been given as babies. Except this time, the medallion on each was a heart, each engraved with both their names.

Winnie and Heathcliff's parting gift to the twins. They must have had high hopes that Anna and Amelia would find their way back to each other eventually.

As Robin left the bank with her two daughters at her side, wearing their new bracelets, one thought hung in her mind.

Love might not be a straightforward affair, but, boy, is it worth the effort.

CHAPTER THIRTY

Anna

The Resolution

Per Winnie's instructions, she was cremated. For her memorial service the pews were packed with people the midwife had brought into the world, and over three hundred people showed up for the wake at Anna's house; the mourners ended up spilling out into the backyard and throughout the Strauses' two-acre front-yard garden.

But the scattering of her ashes over the Gulf of Mexico was a private affair. Honoring the request that Winnie had left for them in her letter, Anna, Amelia, and Robin performed the sacred task, renting a small motorboat at dusk.

Anna took the helm, but she didn't want to be there. This was good-bye and she wasn't ready to let go yet. Her fingers gripped the steering wheel as she maneuvered the boat toward the dying sunlight. Just when she'd started to understand Winnie, she'd lost the only grandmother she'd ever known.

A text appeared on her phone that she'd balanced on the dash of the boat.

It was from Kevin, texting her from home where he was watching the kids. Thinking of U. No need 2 answer. Just know I'm here 4 U. Always.

Anna smiled, her heart full of heartbreak and at the same time deep gratitude for what she had and where she was in her life and the lessons that she'd learned this summer.

What perfect timing. Kevin's text bolstered her spirits and her courage. He was such a good man, ready to own his mistakes and do something about them. She was so glad they'd found their way back to each other.

"Everything okay?" Amelia asked.

Anna glanced over her shoulder at her sister and smiled softly. Both she and her twin wore their matching double-name medallion bracelets. Her mother was sitting on the seat across from Amelia, holding the box with Winnie's ashes in her lap.

"Everything is just as it should be."

When they were far enough away from shore and other boats, Anna killed the engine just as the sun was starting to set. Without even being asked to do so, Amelia moved to the back of the boat and dropped the anchor.

They gathered at the front of the boat.

"What now?" Amelia asked.

"Should we sing something?" Robin cradled the box close to her chest.

"'Amazing Grace' was her favorite song. I have it on my phone," Anna said. "I used to play it for her when I visited her on Sundays after church."

Quickly, she scrolled through her music until she found it. She got the song playing and as Alan Jackson's lyrical voice rolled out across the water, they solemnly scattered Winnie's ashes over the waves and sang a celebration for the life of the lost soul who'd made their lasting connection possible until long after the sun went down.

EPILOGUE

Two Years Later

On their thirty-eighth birthday, Amelia and Anna held their book signing at the bakery. The Harmonious Housewives provided entertainment and bouquets of yellow roses and Darla supplied the refreshments.

A long line to meet the authors snaked out the door. Curious tourists mostly, since their close friends and family had already gotten autographed books the day their author copies arrived.

But family had shown up to give moral support. Kevin, Mike, Gia, Pete and Veronica, and Robin, of course.

Life had changed so much in two short years.

Ella and Emily, Anna's two-month-old twin daughters, slept in the bassinet hand carved by their uncle Mike. They were such good babies and slept right through the hubbub. The baby girls were developing a deep sisterly bond as strong as the one shared by their mother and her twin sister. And these two sweet infants would never be separated.

Robin was engaged to Luther Cosgrove. He made her smile in a way she hadn't since before Heathcliff had died, and everyone was eager to welcome him into the family. Newly retired, Luther had an RV and he and Robin had already taken a few shorter trips together and were planning an excursion to New England in the fall.

As for Anna, her marriage was stronger than it had ever been. Their new daughters had renewed everything. A fresh start.

And Amelia?

The transplant had been a complete success and she felt better than she had in years. She adored playing with her twin nieces and with them around, she felt no need for children of her own and didn't feel less than because it was safer for her if she didn't have any.

She'd started dating a nice guy. Nick Goodman. Nick was a local doctor who was also an amateur musician. He had a five-year-old son who was Logan's best friend. That was how they'd met, and Amelia could see things getting serious between them. Especially now that the book was finished and out there in the world.

Nick was kind and patient and understanding and, well, just plain *normal*. Amelia loved that about him.

Guests filled the bakery, talking and eating and getting their books signed. It was a special time.

Amelia looked at Anna and Anna smiled, and they held out their bracelets to each other, lining up their wrists. Then laughing, they signed another copy of *The Keepsake Sisters* and knew they would never keep secrets from each other again.